Elizabeth Took Up the Damp Cloth and Carefully Bathed the Wounded Geoffrey's Brow . . .

She carefully slid her hands behind the knight's neck to rest entwined in his hair. This time it was she who pulled him to her and touched his mouth with her own in a sweet, gentle caress. A warm tingling sensation spread through her limbs. His hold tightened and he became the aggressor, his mouth suddenly hard and demanding as he forced his tongue deep into her parted mouth. Alarmed more by her own uninhibited response than by his assault, Elizabeth jerked back from his rapidly weakening hold.

With a soft laugh she whispered, "You burn with fever, my lord, and will remember none of this."

To her consternation, the warrior slowly smiled.

Books by Julie Garwood

The Bride
Honor's Splendour
The Lion's Lady

Published by POCKET BOOKS

Gentle Warrior

Julie Garwood

POCKET BOOKS

New York   London   Toronto   Sydney   Tokyo

An *Original* Publication of POCKET BOOKS

 POCKET BOOKS, a division of Simon & Schuster Inc. 1230 Avenue of the Americas, New York, NY 10020

Copyright © 1985 by Julie Garwood
Cover art copyright © 1985 Scott Gladden

ISBN: 0-671-70143-6

First Tapestry Books printing October 1985

First Pocket Books printing November 1989

10 9 8 7 6 5 4 3 2 1

POCKET and colophon are trademarks of Simon & Schuster Inc.

Printed in the U.S.A.

To Gerry, with love, for all the support and encouragement, but most of all, for never doubting.

Gentle Warrior

Prologue

"Gentle knights were born to fight, and war ennobles all who engage in it without fear or cowardice."

Jean Froissart, French Chronicler

1086, England

IN SILENCE THE KNIGHT PREPARED FOR BATTLE. HE SAT astride a wooden stool, stretched his long muscular legs before him, and bade his servant to pull on the steel-mailed hose. He then stood and allowed another to fasten the heavy hauberk over the quilted cotton undershirt. Finally he raised his sun-bronzed arms so that his sword, a gift prized mightily for it came from William himself, could be attached to his waist by means of a metal loop.

His thoughts were not of his dress nor of his surroundings, but of the coming battle, and he methodically reviewed the strategy he would employ to gain victory. Thunder broke his concentration. With a frown the knight lifted the opening flap of the tent and raised his head to study the heavy cloud formation, unconsciously brushing the dark hair from his collar as he watched the sky.

Behind him the two servants continued their duties. One picked up the oiled cloth and began to give yet another polish to the warrior's shield. The second mounted the stool and waited, holding the open-faced conical for the knight. The servant stood thusly for several long moments before the warrior turned and noticed the helmet outstretched before him. With a negative shake of his head, he disclaimed it, preferring to chance possible injury in return for freedom of movement. The servant frowned at the knight's refusal to wear this added protection, yet wisely chose not to give verbal argument, having noted the scowl upon the warrior's face.

His dress complete, the knight turned and walked with quick long strides until he reached and mounted his powerful steed. Without a backward glance, he rode from the encampment.

The knight sought solitude before battle and rode hard and fast into the nearby forest, oblivious to the scraping both he and his destrier suffered from low-hanging branches. Having reached the top of a small rise, he reined his now-snorting animal to a halt and gave his full attention to the manor below.

Rage filled him anew as he thought about the infidels nestled within the castle below, but he pushed the anger aside. He would have his vengeance after the manor was once again his. Only then would he allow his rage to go unchecked. Only then.

The knight turned his attention to the layout before him, again impressed by the simplicity of the design, noting the wide, uneven walls stretching almost twenty feet into the sky and completely surrounding the multiple structures within. The river banked the walls on three sides and this pleased the knight considerably, for entry from the water would be almost impossible. The main building was constructed primarily of stone with but an occasional piece of sod, and was flanked on both sides by clusters of small huts, all facing the large grassy courtyard. When it was all once again his, he would make it impregnable, he vowed. This could not be allowed to happen again!

Dark angry clouds linked together in an attempt to block the rising sun, resulting in gray streaks arched in protest across the sky. The wind gave sound to the eerie sight. Gusty howls intermingled with low whistled moans that caused the warrior's black mount to prance in agitation, but the knight quickly calmed him, using his heels as his command.

He again looked to the sky, saw that the swollen clouds were now directly overhead, and thought that it was as if night would once again descend. "The weather does nought to quiet my mood," he muttered. Was this a bad omen, he wondered, for he was not entirely without superstition, though he scoffed at those who were ruled by it, ritualistically seeking signs before each and every battle to predict the outcome.

The knight once again reviewed his bid for victory, looking for possible flaws in his battle plans, and could find none, yet still he could not feel content. In frustration, he picked up the reins and turned the charger, intent on returning to camp before total darkness was full upon him. And it was then that the sky exploded in a silver flash of light, and he saw her.

She stood slightly above him on the next rise, and seemed to gaze directly down at him. But she was not looking at him, he realized; no, her gaze was directed beyond him to the castle below.

She sat erect upon a flecked mount and was flanked by two enormous creatures vaguely resembling dogs, but of what breed he knew not, since their stance suggested more wolf than dog. He drank fully of the picture before him, noting she was slight of stature with long pale hair free about her shoulders, and even from that distance he could make out well-rounded breasts cupped tightly against the white material of her gown by the force of the persistent wind.

His mind could make little order out of what he saw but that she was indeed more beautiful than any he had ever known. The light receded but was replaced within seconds by another more powerful burst, and the knight's initial surprise gave way to stunned disbelief, for now he sighted the hawk flying low toward the girl. She seemed unafraid of the beast circling overhead and in fact raised her hand as if to salute an old friend.

The knight closed his eyes but for a moment, and when he reopened them she was gone. With a start, he goaded his steed into motion and raced toward the vision. Horse and rider rounded each tree expertly and with great speed, yet when they reached their destination she was nowhere to be found.

After a time the knight gave up the search. His mind accepted that what he had seen was real, but his heart insisted she was but a vision, an omen.

His mood was greatly improved when he rode full gallop into camp. He saw that his men were mounted and ready. Nodding his approval, he gestured for his lance and his shield bearing his coat of arms.

Two servants hurried toward the waiting knight, holding the kite-shaped shield between them in order to share its weight, and when they reached his side, they waited in silence for the warrior to lift it. To their confusion, the knight hesitated, a small smile lifting the corners of his mouth, and stared for long seconds at the shield below him. His next action further bewildered not only his servants but his watching followers as well, for he leaned down and with his index finger slowly traced the outline of the hawk embedded upon the shield.

He then threw back his head and relented to a deep resounding laugh before effortlessly lifting first his shield with his left hand and the lance with his right. Raising both high into the air, he gave the cry for battle.

Chapter One

LONG THIN FINGERS OF LIGHT SLOWLY BEGAN THEIR ritualistic climb into the darkness, uninhibited by clusters of pale and empty clouds, in their unchallenged bid to bring forth the dawn. Elizabeth leaned against the splintered frame of the hut's open doorway and watched the progress of the sun for several long minutes before she straightened and walked outside.

A massive hawk, gliding effortlessly in wide circles high above the trees, saw the slender figure emerge from the hut and increased his speed, descending to a large mud-splattered boulder adjacent to the girl. His screech and vigorous flapping of brown and gray wings announced his arrival.

"There you are, my proud one," Elizabeth greeted. "You are early today. Could you not find sleep either?" she questioned in a soft voice. She regarded her pet with a tender smile and then slowly raised her right arm until it was stretched taut just slightly above her slender waist. "Come," she commanded in a gentle voice.

The hawk tilted his head from side to side, his piercing gaze never leaving her face, and began to emit a gargled sound from deep within his throat. His eyes were the color of marigold, and though there was a wildness about them, she was unafraid. Indeed, she met his stare with complete trust and again bid him come to her. Within a whisper of a second, the hawk had landed on her bare arm, but she did not flinch from either his weight or his touch. His jagged claws were blade sharp, yet she wore no glove. Her smooth and unblemished arm gave testimony to the hawk's gentleness with his mistress.

"What am I to do with you?" Elizabeth asked. Her blue eyes sparkled with laughter as she studied her pet. "You grow fat and lazy, my friend, and though I have given you your freedom, you refuse to accept it. Oh, my faithful pet, if only men were as loyal as you." The laughter was gone from her eyes, replaced by overwhelming sadness.

The sound of approaching horse and rider startled Elizabeth. "Go," she commanded the hawk, and he immediately took to the sky. Panic edged her voice as she called to her two wolfhounds and ran for the safety of the surrounding forest. The two dogs were at her side by the time she had flattened herself against the thick bark of the nearest tree, and she gave them the hand signal to be still. Her heart was racing wildly as she waited, silently cursing herself for leaving the dagger in the hut.

Marauders, entire gangs of displaced, unclaimed destitutes, roamed the countryside, and all those outside the protection of the walls were easy prey for their violence and depravity.

"My lady?" The sound of her faithful servant's voice penetrated the terror gripping Elizabeth, bringing relief immediately. Elizabeth slumped forward, her head bent, while she recovered her breath. "My lady? It is Joseph. Are you there?"

The rising alarm in his voice forced Elizabeth from her hiding place. She quietly rounded the tree and slipped up behind Joseph, gently tapping his stooped shoulder with one trembling hand.

With a startled yelp the old man jumped back and whirled around, very nearly knocking down his mistress in the process. "You gave me quite a start," he chided, but at the look of distress on Elizabeth's face, he forced a smile, showing an absence of several teeth in the process. "Even though you frown, your lovely face still has the power to humble me."

"You flatter me as always, Joseph," Elizabeth responded with a grin, and her servant was again bewitched by the husky yet musical lilt in her voice. He watched her as she turned and walked to the door of the hut and was mildly surprised that her beauty still had the power to startle him each time he would gaze upon her, for he had seen her raised since infancy.

"Come and share a cool drink with me and tell me what brings you here this day," Elizabeth said. Her proud bearing faltered then, confusion clouding her eyes. "I have not forgotten the day, have I? This isn't your usual day to bring me food, is it? Or have I truly lost all sense of time?"

Joseph noted the despair in her voice and wanted to take her into his arms and offer comfort. It was an impossible ambition, he realized, for she was his mistress and he her humble servant.

"It has been nearly a month since my family—"

"Do not speak of it, my lady, and do not fret," Joseph soothed. "You do not go daft, for I was here just two days past. Today I bring important news and have a plan I wish you to consider."

"Joseph, if you again suggest that I go to my grandfather, then you have wasted a trip. My answer will be the same today. Never! I will stay close to my home until I can bring vengeance to my family's murderers. This I have vowed!" She stood glaring at him as she spoke, her stubbornness outlined by the defiant tilt of her chin, and Joseph found that he was forced to gaze at his boots in order to escape the chill from her eyes.

Elizabeth folded her arms and waited. "What say you?" she demanded. When her servant did not immediately reply, Elizabeth sighed with exasperation and continued in a softer voice. "Be content, Joseph. I have sent little Thomas to safety. That must be enough."

His reply was not what she expected. Elizabeth watched his shoulders slump even further than was their natural inclination. The servant rubbed his bald head and cleared his voice. "The evil ones have gone."

"Gone? What do you mean, gone? How can this be? Where have they gone?" Her voice increased in volume with each question, and she was unaware that she had grabbed the loyal servant by his cloak and was vigorously shaking him.

Joseph raised his hands and gently pulled free from her grip. "Please, my lady, calm yourself. Let us go inside," he suggested, "and I will tell you all I know."

Elizabeth agreed with a quick nod and hurried inside. She tried to compose herself as was befitting her position, but her mind rebelled at the task, concentrating on the number of unanswered questions and conflicting emotions instead.

The one-room hut was sparsely furnished. Elizabeth sat on the edge of one of the two wooden stools, her hands folded in her lap, her back straight, while she waited for Joseph to light the fire in the hearth. Though it was late spring, the hut was damp and chill.

It seemed an eternity before Joseph was seated across from her. " 'Twas shortly after I left here last, my lady. The day of the storm," he qualified, "I had

9

just reached the second rise above the manor when I first saw them approach as a cloud of dust on the winding road below. Though there were only two hundred or so of them, they still looked to be a deadly fighting force. Why, the ground fairly trembled beneath me so awesome was the sight. I saw their leader, for he rode well ahead of his men and was the only one without benefit of a helmet.

"Once they had battered down and entered the gates, for it was obvious to me that they cared not for the element of surprise, I rode closer, my curiosity pushing aside all caution. By the time I found a better vantage point, their leader had drawn up his force into a half-circle, and behind a wall of shields, they advanced. It was a sight to see, little one. I watched their leader take his stand, a gigantic figure, I must admit, for he carried a great sword I wager two lesser men could scarcely lift. I watched as his sword swung countless times and lay low as many. 'Twas then that the storm broke—"

"Were they from Lord Geoffrey?" It was a bare whisper, but Joseph heard.

"Aye, they were Lord Geoffrey's men. You knew that he would send forces."

"Of course I realized this, Joseph," she sighed. "My father was vassal to Geoffrey, and his lord would reclaim what is his. Still, we did not send word to him. How did he arrive so soon?"

"I do not know," Joseph confessed.

"Belwain!" The name was a shout of despair. Elizabeth jumped up and began to pace.

"Your uncle?" Joseph asked. "Why would he—"

"Of course," Elizabeth interrupted. "We both know that my uncle was behind the massacre of my family. *He* went to Geoffrey. My God, he betrayed his own men to win Geoffrey's favor. What lies he must have told."

Joseph shook his head. "I always knew he was an evil man, but even I did not think he would go to such extremes."

"Our cause is lost, Joseph," Elizabeth replied in an agonized whisper. "Lord Geoffrey will listen to my uncle's lies. Thomas and I will be placed in Belwain's hands, and Thomas will be murdered, for only when my little brother is dead can Belwain become master of my home. Only then."

"Perhaps Lord Geoffrey will see through Belwain's plan," Joseph answered.

"I have never met Lord Geoffrey," Elizabeth said, "but I know he is said to possess a fierce temper and is most disagreeable at times. No, I do not think he would listen."

"My lady," Joseph implored, "perhaps—"

"Joseph, if I had only myself to consider, I would go to Lord Geoffrey and beg him to listen to my words, for Belwain's perfidy should be told to all who would listen. But I must protect Thomas. Belwain thinks both my brother and I are dead."

Elizabeth continued to pace back and forth in front of the hearth. "I have made up my mind, Joseph. Tomorrow we leave for London and the safety of my grandfather's home."

"And Belwain?" Joseph asked with hesitancy. A dread of what her answer was going to be made Joseph brace himself. He knew his mistress well. She would not allow Belwain acquittal for his evildoing.

"I will kill him."

A log sizzled and a loud *pop* sounded in the silence that followed Elizabeth's statement. A chill settled in the old servant's bones. He had no doubt that his mistress would do as she said. Still, he had not explained all of his news, and bracing his leathery palms against his trembling knees, he rushed to finish the task. "Geoffrey's men have Thomas."

Elizabeth's pacing abruptly stopped. "How can this be? He is with grandfather by now. You saw him leave with Roland. Surely you are mistaken."

"Nay, my lady. I saw him at the castle with my own eyes. Thomas was asleep by the fire, but it was *him*. I had a clear view. Upon inquiry I learned that he is considered mute." Joseph raised his hand when he saw his mistress was about to interrupt, and hastily continued the tale. "How he came to be with them I do not know. Geoffrey's men will tell me nothing, but one thing is certain: they do not yet realize who the boy is, and he is being well cared for. Why, the one near death is the very one who saved his life, it is said."

"Joseph, you talk in riddles. Who is near death?" In her frustration, Elizabeth pulled at a stray lock of golden hair blocking her vision and swiftly brushed it back over her shoulder. Joseph in turn let out a long sigh and scratched his heavy beard before he continued.

"Their leader took a blow to his head during the battle. They say he is dying."

"Why did you risk going to the manor, Joseph?"

"Maynard the stable master sent word to me that Thomas was there. I had to see for myself," Joseph explained. "When I heard that the leader of Geoffrey's men was dying, I sought out the next in command. I thought of a rash plan and . . ." Joseph again cleared his throat before continuing. "I told them I knew of one well-versed in the art of healing and that I would bring this healer to tend their master on the condition that once he was well, the healer could safely leave. The lord's vassal argued mightily over this, saying that he need make no promises, but I could not be budged, and in the end he agreed."

Elizabeth had listened intently to Joseph's plan, and with angry words demanded, "And what if he does not mend, Joseph? What, then?"

"It was all I could think of to get you near Thomas.

12

Perhaps you can find a way to free him once you are inside. Do not frown so," the servant pleaded. "Your mother tended the sick and many times I saw you accompany her. Surely you have some of her ways."

Elizabeth considered what Joseph said. Her stomach seemed to twist into knots as she worried over what course of action to take. Getting Thomas to safety was the most important issue. If Lord Geoffrey's men learned of her brother's identity, they would take him to their leader. According to the law, Thomas would be next in line to rule the manor, but he would be placed under her uncle's care until he was of age. As Thomas's guardian, Belwain would make sure his only obstacle to his position of power was removed. The law was the law.

No, there wasn't really any choice. "It is a good plan, Joseph. God be willing, their leader will mend. If not, we will have done all we can." Elizabeth slowly made the sign of the cross, and Joseph quickly followed suit.

"God willing," Joseph repeated as a prayer. "God willing."

"I would prepare myself for the journey while you saddle my mare, Joseph." A smile softened the command. Joseph immediately retreated, shutting the door firmly behind him. He rounded the hut and hastily readied the animal for his mistress. A few minutes later he was back and saw that Elizabeth had changed into a blue gown, simple in design yet rich in texture, and of the exact color of her eyes.

He accepted the bundle of herbs his mistress handed him and helped her into the saddle. He was having second thoughts about his rash plan, and his worry was not missed by his mistress. Elizabeth leaned down and gently patted his wrinkled hand. "Do not worry, Joseph. It is long past the time for action. All will be well."

As if to ensure that his mistress's words would hold true, Joseph again crossed himself. He then mounted the gelding he had borrowed from Herman the Bald, the assistant stable master, and led the way through the forest, his dagger drawn and ready in case of mischief along the way.

In less than an hour's time Elizabeth and Joseph reached the battle-damaged gates to the manor at the top of the winding road. Two burly guards stood back to allow them entrance, standing clear of the menacing wolfhounds that flanked Elizabeth's horse. Surprise registered on their faces but they kept their silence, only grinning with raised eyebrows at each other when the group had safely passed.

When the pair reached the inner bailey, Joseph was first to dismount and he quickly rushed to assist his mistress. He felt her tremble when she placed her hand in his, and knew that she was afraid. A surge of pride fairly overwhelmed him when he gazed into her eyes, for her outward appearance showed only a calm and composed exterior. "You do your father proud, my lady," he whispered as he lifted her from the saddle. Aye, she had inherited her bravery from her father, Joseph knew, and he only wished that Thomas could see her now. For in truth, it was Joseph who was terrified of what was to come, and his gentle mistress was his calming tonic.

The sounds of men at work had been loud and furious when they first entered the manor, but now an ominous silence descended, chilling in its intensity. A sea of foreign faces stared at her intently. Elizabeth stood next to her horse for a moment and then summoned all of her courage and, head held high, started to walk into the throng of watching men.

Hadn't Joseph said that there were barely two hundred of them? she wondered. Well, he was mistaken, she decided, for there were at least two times that number. And all of them were gaping! Their crude behavior didn't intimidate Elizabeth. Pride straightened her shoulders, giving her a regal appearance. The wind caught her hood and snatched it from her head, and the heavy mass of sun-lightened curls quickly accepted their freedom, falling in disarray about her shoulders.

Elizabeth continued to walk with quiet dignity into the great hall, pausing only long enough to remove her cloak and hand it to the hovering Joseph. She noticed that he clutched her bundle of medicines in a tight grip, for the veins in his hands seemed to bulge from the pressure, and she gave him a quick smile in an effort to relieve some of his anxiety.

Outwardly oblivious to the men's frank appraisals, and flanked by her loyal wolfhounds, Elizabeth turned and made her way to the great hearth at the far end of the hall. All were silent as she warmed her hands before the roaring fire. She wasn't really cold, but used the time to compose herself before confronting her audience. When she could delay no longer, she turned and met the gazes staring at her. The dogs sat, one on either side of her.

Slowly she scanned the room. Home was gone; the banner and tapestry hanging in shreds against the damp stone walls, a reminder that death had entered Mont-wright; no echoed laughter remained in Elizabeth's memory, only screams and torment filled her soul. This was just a bare room now; she could not even picture her mother sitting next to her father at the long oaken table . . . no, only see again and again the raised sword swinging toward her mother's neck . . .

A cough stopped her thoughts. The heavy silence was broken. Elizabeth willed herself to turn her gaze from the torn and charred banner and focus on her audience. A bold red-haired soldier with a ready smile jumped up from his position at the great table and rushed over to stand directly in front of Elizabeth, blocking her view of the rest of the men. She judged him to be a squire, for he was too old to be a page, yet too young to have been knighted. His silly grin almost made Elizabeth smile but she was careful to keep her expression neutral.

The squire gazed into Elizabeth's blue eyes and said in a loud voice, "You are a beauty. How will you care for our lord?"

When she did not respond to his gibe, for, in truth, she wasn't sure just how to answer his question, he called to another, saying, "She has hair born from the sun. I wager it feels like the finest of silks." He raised his hand to touch the curls then, but her voice, though soft, cut through his action like a knife.

"Do you not value your life?"

The squire stopped in midstride, his smile vanishing, for he had not missed the sound of the low growling from the dogs. He glanced at each animal and saw that the hair on the backs of their necks was raised and that their teeth, gleaming with dagger edges, were bared for attack.

When the young man looked again at Elizabeth, his face had paled, and he wore an angry frown. "I would do you no harm, for you are under the protection of the Hawk," he whispered. "You need have no fear from me."

"Then have no fear of me," Elizabeth whispered for his ears only. She smiled then, and the squire's anger evaporated. He knew that though the soldiers watched, they were unable to hear the exchange. She had saved his pride, and he was thankful. He smiled again. Elizabeth signaled the dogs and both relaxed against her sides, tails thumping against the rushes.

"Where is your leader?" she asked.

"If you will follow me, I will take you to him," the squire suggested, his voice eager.

Elizabeth nodded her agreement and followed the boy. Joseph waited at the bottom of the steps and she gave him another smile as she accepted the bundle of herbs. She then hurried up the winding flight of steps. It was a difficult task but Elizabeth forced herself to remove all memories of times past when she had raced up the steps with her sisters and her little brother. The time for weeping would be later. Thomas's future depended upon her now.

At the top of the first landing, another, older knight appeared. A scowl marred his sharp features and Elizabeth braced herself for another confrontation. "You are a woman! If this be some trick . . ."

" 'Tis no trick," Elizabeth responded. "I am versed in remedies that could help your leader and I will do all that I can to save him."

"Why would you give your help?" he demanded.

"I offer no explanation," Elizabeth answered. Irritation and weariness flowed through her but she was careful to hide these emotions. "Do you wish my help or not?"

The knight continued to glare at her for a moment longer. It was obvious to Elizabeth that he was suspicious of her motives, but she refused to calm his fears, remaining stubbornly silent while she matched him stare for stare.

"Leave the dogs here and follow me." The order was clipped and fairly shouted.

"Nay," Elizabeth promptly replied. "They go with me. They will cause no mischief unless someone tries to harm me."

To her surprise he did not argue over this, though she noticed that he ran long fingers through his brown-and-gray-speckled hair in a gesture she was sure was pure exasperation.

He did not lead her to the triangle of doors housing the larger bedrooms to the left, but turned to the right and, lifting the burning torch from its lodging against the stone wall, hurried down the narrow corridor to stand before her very own bedroom. Two sentries guarded the door and both looked up in surprise when they glimpsed Elizabeth.

With marked trepidation Elizabeth followed the

knight through the entrance. Quickly she scanned the room and was frankly amazed, for it was exactly as she had left it. Her chamber was smaller than the others, but it had been her favorite of all the bedrooms, both for its isolation from the others and for the breathtaking view it allowed from the small window that overlooked the forest beyond.

The hearth took up most of the far wall, and was flanked by two wooden chairs with royal-blue cushions her sister Margaret had sewn for her.

Her gaze moved to the banner hanging above the hearth, its blue color matching the cushions with pale yellow threads interwoven in the design of her two wolfhounds. The banner's only other coloring was that of a deep burgundy, near the top of the tapestry, outlining the design of her pet hawk. Her heart ached as memories of the many times she and her mother had worked on the banner assaulted her.

No! her mind cried. 'Tis not the time. Elizabeth shook her head and this action was not missed by the watching knight. He, too, studied the banner and then turned back to Elizabeth. He recognized the fleeting torment she tried to hide. Speculation and curiosity appeared in his eyes but Elizabeth gave him little attention. She had turned to look upon the bed, and with the blue and yellow draping tied back on each side, she had a clear view of the leader. She was immediately struck by the largeness of the man, thinking he was even taller than her grandfather.

His hair was the color of the raven, and almost touched the drape at the head of the bed while his feet nearly hung over the other end. For some unexplainable reason, even in his weakened condition, he frightened her, and she stood transfixed while she studied the harshness of his features. He was a handsome knight, she admitted, handsome and . . . hard.

The warrior began to thrash about from side to side,

moaning in a weakened yet deep voice, and his movement prompted her into action. She quickly placed her
hand upon his damp, bronzed forehead, gently brushing the wet hair out of her way as she felt his skin. Her
milky white hand was in stark contrast to his deeply
tanned and weathered skin, and her touch stilled his
motion.

"He burns with fever," Elizabeth remarked. "How
long has he been like this?" Even as she spoke, she
noticed the swelling above his right temple and gently
probed around it. The warrior's companion watched
her from his position at the foot of the bed, a frown
upon his face.

"I saw him take the blow. He fell to the ground and
has been like this ever since."

Elizabeth frowned in concentration. She wasn't sure
what she should do next. "This makes little sense," she
countered, "for a blow does not bring the fever." She
straightened then and with determination in her voice
commanded, "Help me strip him."

Elizabeth did not give the companion time to question her motives, for she immediately began to unfasten
the lacings at the warrior's back. The knight hesitated
for a brief minute and then helped by pulling the
chausses from the lower half of the now-sleeping form.

Though she tried mightily, Elizabeth was unable to
pull the quilted hauberk, made of thick cotton, and
soaked with the fever's sweat, over the massive shoulders, and she finally admitted defeat. She instinctively
reached for the dagger she carried at her waist, thinking
she would have to cut the material in order to sponge
the heat from the warrior's chest.

The companion saw the glint of metal and, not
understanding her reasoning, knocked the knife to the
floor with the back of his hand.

The dogs began to growl but Elizabeth quickly
silenced them and turned to face the knight. Her voice

was gentle and devoid of all anger. "Though you have no reason to trust me, you need have no fear. I was merely going to cut his shirt."

"What is the need?" the knight demanded with frustration.

Elizabeth ignored the question and bent to retrieve her dagger. She split the shirt at the neck and tore the garment wide with her hands. Without looking at the angry companion, she commanded that he bring her cool water so that she could bathe the sweat and heat from his lord.

While the knight relayed her orders to the sentries outside the door, Elizabeth scanned her patient's arms and neck, looking for possible injuries. She willed her eyes to travel lower and felt her cheeks grow warm. Knowing that she blushed at the sight of his nakedness made her angry with herself, though in truth she had never seen a naked man before. Although it was the custom for the daughters to assist in the bathing of the visiting gentry, her father held too much distrust with the appetites of his friends and decreed that the servants would do the assisting, not his daughters.

Curiosity overcame embarrassment and Elizabeth quickly looked at the lower half of his body. She was mildly surprised that he did not display the fiercesome weapon she had heard that all men possess, and wondered if the female servants she had overheard had exaggerated, or if all men were built like this one. Perhaps he was defective.

Elizabeth concentrated on the task at hand and crossed to her chest. She removed clean linen and tore the material into long strips. When the water arrived, she began to sponge the warrior's face.

He is as still as death, she thought, and his ragged breathing is much too shallow. He carried an angry red scar that began at the edge of his left eye and curved, as a half-moon, ending somewhere behind his ear, well hidden by the black, slightly curling hair. With the wet cloth she gently traced its jagged outline, thinking that the scar did little to detract from the leader's appearance.

She washed his neck and chest, noting still more scars. "He has too many marks to suit me," she voiced aloud.

Elizabeth stopped sponging when she reached his waist. "Help me turn him," she said to the companion.

The companion's patience was at an end, his frustration evident with his bellow, "By all the saints, woman, he needs not a bath but a cure."

"I would know that the blow to his head is all he carries," Elizabeth replied just as loudly. "You have not even taken the time to remove his battle clothes."

The companion's response was to fold his arms against his chest, a fierce glare upon his face, and Elizabeth concluded that she would get no assistance. She gave him what she hoped was a scathing look, and then turned back to the warrior. She reached across the bed and grabbed the unresisting hand with both of hers. Though she pulled with all of her strength, the warrior did not budge. She continued to pull, unconsciously biting her lower lip in her effort, and thought she was making progress when the hand she held jerked back to its former position. Elizabeth went with it, and ended up draped across the lord's massive chest. She frantically tried to pry her hands free, but the knight now had a firm grip and seemed, even in sleep, disinclined to cooperate.

The vassal watched Elizabeth's puny attempt to free herself, shaking his head all the while, and then yelled, "Out of the way, woman." He released the hold and roughly hauled her to her feet. With one sure movement, he flipped her unresisting patient over onto his stomach. Irritation turned to horror when the vassal saw the blood-covered undershirt stuck to the warrior's back, and he stepped back in shock.

Elizabeth was most relieved when she saw the injury,

for this was something she could handle. She sat on the side of the bed and gently pried the material from its festering imprisonment. When the companion could clearly view the extent of the diagonal gash, he raised a hand to his brow. Unashamed that tears filled his eyes, he whispered in an anguished voice, "I never thought to check . . ."

"Do not berate yourself," Elizabeth replied. She gave him a sympathetic smile before continuing, "Now I understand what is causing the fever. We will need more water, but this time it must be hot, just to boiling, please."

The vassal nodded and hurried out of the room. Within minutes a steaming kettle was placed on the floor next to Elizabeth. In truth, Elizabeth dreaded what she must do, had seen her mother do countless times in the past for those with similar injuries. Repeating a prayer for guidance, she dipped a clean strip of cloth into the kettle and grimaced from the discomfort it caused her hands. She ignored the pain and rung the cloth of excess water. She was now ready, and yet she hesitated. "You will need to hold him down, I fear," she whispered, "for this will pain him considerably . . . but it needs be done." She lifted blue eyes to meet the vassal's anxious frown and waited.

The companion nodded his understanding and placed both of his hands on the broad shoulders of his leader.

Still she hesitated. "I must draw the poison out or he will surely die." Elizabeth wasn't sure if she was convincing the vassal or herself that the pain she was about to cause was necessary.

"Aye," was the companion's only response. If Elizabeth had listened closely, she would have heard the gentle understanding in his voice, but she was too distraught over the agony she would soon inflict.

Taking a deep breath, she placed the steaming cloth full upon the open wound. The leader's reaction was swift and furious. He tried to lift the branding cloth from his back with a fierce jerk, but the vassal's hold was great and he was unable to shed his torment. The agonized cry from the leader tore at Elizabeth's heart and she closed her eyes in distress.

The door to the bedroom burst open and the two guards rushed inside, swords drawn. Fear and confusion showed in their expressions. The vassal shook his head and told them to put their weapons away.

"It must be done." The words from Elizabeth calmed the guards and they retreated to their posts outside the door.

"He would never cry out if he was awake," the vassal said to Elizabeth. "He does not know what he is doing," he explained.

"Are you thinking it makes him less a man to vent his agony?" Elizabeth asked while she placed a second cloth over the wound.

"He is a fearless warrior," the vassal replied.

"The fever rules his actions now," Elizabeth answered.

The companion's nod made Elizabeth want to smile. She turned back to her patient and lifted both strips from the wound, bringing yellow and red residue with them. She repeated the procedure countless times, until only bright red blood oozed from the deep opening. By the time she was finished, her hands were as red as the wound, and blistered. She rubbed them together in an effort to ease the sting, and then reached for her bundle. Speaking more to herself than to the vassal, she said, "I do not think there is need to seal the wound with a hot knife, for it bleeds clean and true and not overmuch."

The leader was unconscious, and for that Elizabeth was thankful for she knew that the medicine she must pack the wound with was not soothing. She applied a liberal amount of the foul-smelling salve and then bandaged his entire back. Once this was done, the companion turned the leader for her and she forced water containing crushed sage, mallows, and night-shade roots down his throat.

There was nothing more to do. Elizabeth's muscles ached from the strain and she stood and walked to the window. She lifted the fur blocking the wind and was surprised to find that darkness had descended. She leaned wearily against the stone and let the cool air revive her. Finally she turned back to the companion, noting for the first time how tired and haggard he appeared. "Go and find some rest. I will watch over your leader."

"Nay," he replied. "I can sleep only when the Hawk has recovered. Not before." He placed another log in the fire while he spoke.

"By what name are you called?" Elizabeth questioned.

"Roger."

"Roger, why do you call your leader the Hawk?"

The vassal looked at her from his bent position in front of the fire and then gruffly answered, "All those who fight in battle with him call him thus. It is the way of things."

His noncommittal reply made little sense to Elizabeth but she didn't want to irritate him by questioning him further on the matter. She would get to the heart of the need now. " 'Tis said there is a boy here who does not speak and that the Hawk saved his life. Is this true?"

"Aye." Suspicion was back in the vassal's expression and Elizabeth knew she would have to tread softly.

"If he be the one I am thinking of, I know of his family and would be willing to take him with me when I leave."

The companion eyed her thoughtfully. His lack of reply was maddening but Elizabeth forced herself to remain calm. "What say you, Roger?"

"I will see what I can do, though only the Baron can make that decision."

"But Baron Geoffrey never travels here! It would take a month of masses before word returned that I might take the boy. Surely he would want the child reunited with his parents. Can you not act in his stead? I am sure he would be pleased not to be bothered, for Montwright is but a small, insignificant holding compared to his others." Elizabeth almost added that she had heard her father say so on countless occasions. And she knew it to be true, for Baron Geoffrey had never paid her father a visit. No, Lord Thomas always traveled to the Baron's main holding when business needed to be conducted.

The companion was surprised by her vehement outburst. "A month? You have only to wait until the fever leaves and he awakens to ask him," he argued. "And you are mistaken, lass. There is no such thing as a holding too insignificant for Geoffrey's inspection. He protects all who pledge fealty, from the highest to the lowest."

"Are you telling me that the Hawk can give me permission? He can act in the Baron's stead?" Elizabeth asked, her voice hopeful. "Then of course he shall," she rushed to answer herself, "for I have taken care of him. He can do no less." She smiled with relief and clasped her hands together.

"Do you not know who you have just tended?" Roger asked, a smile tugging at the corners of his mouth.

Elizabeth frowned at him and waited.

"The Hawk *is* Lord Geoffrey, overlord of Montwright." Roger sat down in one of the chairs and propped his feet up on the other, waiting her reaction.

"*He* is Baron Geoffrey?" Astonishment sounded in her tone.

"Aye," Roger acknowledged. He crossed his ankles

and smiled. "Why are you so surprised? All know of the Hawk," he said with arrogance. "His reputation is well known."

"Yes, but I thought him to be old . . . older than . . ." She motioned to the sleeping warrior and studied him a long minute, her mind racing with this turn of events. Her father had never mentioned that his overlord was so young. Elizabeth had just assumed that he was an old man, like the lesser barons she had met. She leaned back against the cold stone and looked back at Roger. He seemed amused by her ignorance.

"He is the youngest and the most powerful under William," Roger answered. Pride underlined his words.

"*If* the lord mends, then he will be under my obligation, will he not?" Elizabeth asked. She said a quick prayer that it would be true, that Geoffrey was an honorable man, for then perhaps he would listen to her. She could convince him of her uncle's evilness. She must convince him! If he mended . . .

A loud rap on the door interrupted Elizabeth's thoughts. Roger motioned her to stay and went to open the door. He spoke in whispered words to the sentries and then turned back to Elizabeth. "Your servant wishes to speak with you."

Elizabeth nodded and followed one sentry to the end of the corridor where Joseph stood waiting. She could tell by his expression that he was upset. "Joseph, it is the Baron himself who I am caring for."

"Aye," Joseph said. He waited until the sentry was well out of earshot and back at his post before continuing, "Will he heal?"

"There is a chance," Elizabeth said. "We must pray now. It is Thomas's only hope," she added.

Joseph was frowning more ferociously and Elizabeth shook her head. "This is good news, Joseph. Can you not see that the lord will be under my obligation whether I be a woman or not. He will have to listen to me. . . . "

"But the one in charge," he said, motioning toward her bedroom, "the vassal . . ."

"His name is Roger," Elizabeth informed her servant.

"He has sent for Belwain."

"What is this?" Elizabeth demanded. She lowered her voice and said, "Why? How do you know this?"

"Herman the Bald overheard his orders. The messengers left an hour ago. It is true," he said when Elizabeth began to shake her head, "Belwain will be here in a week or more."

"Dear God," Elizabeth whispered. "He must not arrive before I talk with Geoffrey." She clutched at the servant's sleeve, panic in her voice, and rushed on, "We must hide Thomas. We have to get him away from here until I can be sure of Geoffrey. Belwain must *not* know we still live."

"It isn't possible, my lady. Belwain will know as soon as he is within the walls. Too many have seen you return. He will know. And it is only a matter of time before this Roger learns the truth."

"I must think," Elizabeth whispered. She realized she was pulling on the servant's tunic and dropped her hand. "Talk with Herman. He is faithful and will keep his silence. And he is a freeman, Joseph. The two of you, you must take Thomas, hide him. There are many places. Can you do this?"

"Aye," Joseph answered, straightening his shoulders, "I'll not fail you. I will find a place."

Elizabeth nodded, placing her trust in the humble servant. He would not fail her. "It will only be for a short time, until Geoffrey awakens," she said.

"But what of you? If the lord does not awake, if the sleeping spirits continue to hold him and Belwain gets here . . . and if the lord dies . . ."

"I will have to leave," Elizabeth said, more to herself, than to Joseph. "I'll not be here when Belwain arrives. If the lord awakens soon, perhaps I can speak with him before Belwain has a chance to weave his lies." She shuddered and then said, "If not, and he dies, then you must bring Thomas to me. Somehow we will make it to my mother's father. He will know what to do."

"Will you return to the waterfall?" Joseph asked, fear in his voice. He would not be able to ride with her now that he was given the duty of taking Thomas, and his worry for his mistress was tremendous.

"I will not stay here," she whispered in a harsh voice. "Belwain has violated these walls. I'll not be here to see him return. I'll not."

"Aye, my lady, calm yourself. Surely the warrior will awaken before you must leave, before Belwain arrives, and he will listen to you," he said, his voice soothing, as if he were speaking to an injured child.

He waited while his mistress calmed her breathing. The change that came over her whenever her uncle's name was mentioned frightened the old man. He knew that she had witnessed the slaughter, understood the anguish and torment pulling at her soul, and believed, as she did, that Belwain was behind it all. Still, he wished she could speak of it, tell to let some of the pain out. . . . She was so very different from her two half sisters, Margaret and Catherine. Perhaps it was because she was half-Saxon.

When Master Thomas had arrived at Montwright with his two little daughters, he was a hard, unhappy man. But all that had changed within six months, for he had met and married a fair-haired Saxon beauty. His Saxon wife was a hellion, to be sure, but Thomas had a way with her, and soon all could see the couple were coming to terms with each other. A year later, little Elizabeth was born. Thomas decided he was not destined to have a son and poured his love into the little blue-eyed babe. Those two held a special bond between them, and when, ten years later, little Thomas was born, the bond still remained.

While Elizabeth did not copy her father's masculine traits, she did imitate his reserved manner, his way of masking his feelings. Both Catherine and Margaret would wear their emotions on their faces, for all the world to see, but not Elizabeth. Joseph believed that Elizabeth was the thread that held the family together. She was so fiercely loyal, and family was the most important thing to her. She was the peacemaker and the rebel-rouser, her father's pride when she rode beside him on the hunt, her mother's frustration when she tried her hand at sewing. Aye, it had been a happy, contented family, until now. . . .

"Did I tell you that Herman has sent three men to Belwain's holding? Mayhap they can gather the proof we need, for if they talk with Belwain's servants . . ."

"Herman is a good man," Elizabeth interrupted. Her voice was relaxed now, and the servant let out a little sigh of relief. "But I do not think Belwain's servants will speak the truth. They fear him too greatly. Joseph, tell Herman I thank him for his effort," Elizabeth whispered.

"He loved your family too, my lady. It was Thomas who freed him. You were just a babe and probably do not remember, but Herman will not forget the debt to the Montwrights."

"Yes," Elizabeth returned, "I have heard the tale." She smiled and added, "I could not understand why everyone referred to Herman as the Bald, for his head was thickly covered with hair, and my father would grow quite embarrassed whenever I asked him the reason."

Joseph assumed that she still did not know the reason, and blushed. He hoped she would not ask him to explain. It was a silly men's joke and he certainly would not damage his mistress's delicate ears with the truth.

The happy memory with her father helped to lift Elizabeth's spirits. She whispered, "We will get through this, Joseph. Now I must get back to the Baron. Pray, Joseph. Pray Geoffrey heals. Pray that he will listen to me. Listen and believe."

She patted the servant on his stooped shoulder and slowly made her way back to the bedroom. Her stomach was churning again and she fought the urge to throw up. The thought of Belwain returning to Montwright was overwhelming. Had there been no little brother to consider, then Elizabeth would have welcomed the news. She would have planned her trap, and met Belwain with an eager embrace, her dagger at the ready.

She would bide her time. Revenge would be hers. Her resolve kept her upright, her steps sure. It kept her sane, in this insane time, this insane situation. Revenge and her duty to her little brother. Only when her brother's life was protected and his lands secure and only when Belwain paid with his life for his mortal sins could Elizabeth allow the abyss of desolation yawning before her to make its claim. Only then.

When Elizabeth opened the door to the bedroom, she found her two animals had taken up vigilance on either side of the lord's bed. They had taken to the warrior, Elizabeth surmised from their watchful attendance. She resumed her seat on the wooden stool next to the bed and once again sponged the lord's forehead.

For two more days and nights Elizabeth continued her vigil beside the lord. She changed his dressing countless times, saying the Paternoster twelve times each and every time she sprinkled marrow and sage upon the healing wound, just as her mother had taught her.

She took her meals in the room and only left the leader's side when absolutely necessary. On one such occasion, as she made her way down the steps, she spotted Thomas in the great hall. He looked up and gave her a glance, and in that fleeting second, Elizabeth recognized that he did not know who she was. She did not let that disturb her, for there would be time in the future to help him mend. And perhaps it was for the good that little Thomas did not remember. He too had seen his family murdered, and if God was indeed a good and compassionate God, then mayhap little Thomas would never remember any of what took place.

Elizabeth turned her attention to Joseph, standing next to her little brother. The servant looked pointedly at the boy and then nodded to Elizabeth. With a little nod of her own, Elizabeth acknowledged that he would do what was necessary, and continued on her way.

She had made up her mind that she could wait only one more day. Then she would leave. And tonight, while the soldiers slept, Thomas would be taken by Joseph. If only the Baron would cooperate! If he would just wake up and listen to her! With these thoughts Elizabeth returned to her patient.

Roger had taken control of the dogs, seeing to their food and exercise, a task he disliked immensely if his grumblings were any indication. The reason was the dogs' strange behavior whenever Roger approached the sleeping knight. "They act as if *I* would harm my lord," he muttered with disgust.

"They protect him," Elizabeth said, smiling. She too was surprised by the animals' obvious loyalty to the warrior and could not explain it.

Several times during the second day Roger left her alone with his lord and Elizabeth acknowledged that she had finally gained his trust.

It was the middle of the second night when Elizabeth, sitting beside the sleeping form, again took up the damp cloth and bathed his brow.

The warrior now lay in a deep, seemingly untroubled

sleep, his breathing no longer shallow. Elizabeth was pleased with his progress but thought that the fever still held him prisoner.

"What manner of man are you," she whispered, "that so many are so loyal?" She closed her eyes then, for the quiet was soothing, but when she reopened them, she was shocked to find the warrior's deep brown eyes intently watching her. Elizabeth's reaction was instinctive; she reached out to touch his forehead. His left hand intercepted hers and slowly, effortlessly, he pulled her toward him. When her breasts were pressed tightly against his bare chest, and their lips were but inches from each other, he spoke. "Protect me well, nymph."

Elizabeth smiled at his words, sure that he spoke with delirium.

They continued to stare at each other for an eternity of seconds and then the lord's other hand moved to the back of her neck. With gentle pressure he forced their lips to meet. His mouth was warm and soft and the feeling was not unpleasant, Elizabeth decided. As soon as it began, the chaste kiss ended, and again they studied each other.

Elizabeth could not seem to draw her gaze away, for his eyes, rich and velvet and as dark as his hair, seemed to hypnotize her with their intensity.

Like a child who knows he will not be caught, Elizabeth grew bold and gave in to her innocent curiosity, carefully sliding her hands behind the knight's neck to rest entwined in his hair. The softness against the hard muscles surprised her and she slowly began to massage his neck. Still they watched each other. If Elizabeth had been more astute, she would have noticed that his eyes were no longer glazed over with fever.

She made her decision. This time it was she who pulled him to her and touched his mouth with her own in a sweet, gentle caress. She did not really know how to proceed, for she was totally unskilled in the art of making love and was much like a struggling toddler taking his first cautious steps as she experimented against his lips. A warm tingling sensation began to spread through her limbs and she enjoyed this novel feeling.

Her curiosity satisfied, she tried to pull back but the lord was no longer passive in her embrace. His hold tightened and he became the aggressor, his mouth suddenly hard and demanding as he forced his tongue deep into her parted mouth, bruising her tender lips in his assault. Elizabeth's body reacted swiftly to his sensual attack, tentatively touching his tongue with her own in the beginning of the duel as old as time. It was an amazing moment. Feelings Elizabeth had never known she possessed fought for recognition, urging her onward in this new unsatiable quest. Alarmed more by her uninhibited response than by his assault, Elizabeth jerked back from his rapidly weakening hold. She fought to control the trembling of her body, rubbing her swollen lips with her fingers, looking everywhere but at his face, for she knew her cheeks were flushed with embarrassment.

Finally she willed her gaze to return to his face and sighed with relief. The warrior was falling asleep. Within seconds his eyes were closed.

With a soft laugh she whispered, "You burn with fever, my lord, and will remember none of this."

To her consternation, the warrior slowly smiled.

Chapter Two

ON THE SIXTH DAY THE LORD AWAKENED.

The mist from the drug-induced sleep was slow to recede and in its wake, confusion and momentary disorientation clouded the warrior's mind. He opened his eyes to bright sunlight and stared at the area visible to him from his position on his side while he struggled to remember where he was. It looked so familiar and yet so strange and new. A frown marred his rugged features as scenes of the battle flashed before his eyes, interfering with his need to know what had followed.

With a muttered oath of frustration, the knight rolled onto his back. A stab of pain, not unlike the initial thrust from the enemy's sword, shot up his shoulder blades and he inhaled deeply in an effort to stop the tremors coursing through his body. The brief flicker of pain in his eyes was his only acknowledgment of the injury, for pain was an accepted constant in his life. To give it voice was to weaken. Strength, invincible and absolute, was Lord Geoffrey's power, and weakness, the hated antithesis, belonged only to lesser men.

"Welcome back to the living, my lord." The gruff voice of his faithful vassal, Roger, removed the scowl of concentration from the knight's face. Now he would have some answers. He nodded, noting his vassal's haggard appearance. The proof of his companion's vigil during his illness was obvious. His loyalty pleased the lord.

"What day is this?" Geoffrey asked, his voice rough from sleep.

"It has been six days since you were felled," Roger answered.

The lord frowned over this information, glancing around the room once again while he formulated questions in his mind. The sight of the banner hanging above the hearth halted his wondering gaze. For a long silent moment, Lord Geoffrey studied the design. Suddenly the memory of his "vision" blocked all thought, all movement. She was alive, she was real, and the scenes of what had transpired within this room were as clear and fresh as the new day.

"Where is she?"

"You remember?" Surprise sounded in the vassal's voice.

"Yes," Geoffrey answered in a soft voice. "Bring her to me." The terseness of the command after the gentle acknowledgment jarred Roger.

"She has gone."

Lord Geoffrey's bellow of outrage could be heard in the courtyard below, and was both intimidating and somewhat heartening. It clearly stated his displeasure over some matter, but also indicated that he was well on the mend. Roger took the verbal blows with practiced ease, knowing full well that the tirade would soon end and that he would then be allowed the opportunity to explain all. Lord Geoffrey possessed a fierce temper that was quick to ignite, but he was a fair man. One only had to wait until the anger eased, provided one was courageous enough, Roger mused, and then state his case.

The command finally came. "From the beginning, Roger. Tell me."

Roger's narrative was swift and without interruption. Only when the telling was complete did he pause for breath, for though he had served his lord nearly five summers, it was a fact that his leader still had the power to undermine his ability to think clearly when he was as upset as he now appeared.

"My lord, I would have bargained with the devil, and met his terms willingly, to save your life." It was said as a fervent vow, and Geoffrey could find little fault with his friend. His loyalty was absolute. "Still, I did try to find out where she lived. Yet everyone I questioned seemed not to know her."

"Do they speak the truth?"

"I do not think so. I think they try to protect her, but I do not understand why."

"The boy she asked about . . . bring him to me," Geoffrey commanded. He forced himself to control his frustration and alarm. She was gone! Outside the walls, unprotected . . .

Roger hurried to the door and gave the order to one of the sentries. He then returned to the chair before the hearth and sat down. "The boy almost got away," he began, shaking his head. "One of the guards intercepted the girl's servant stealing away with the lad. I have questioned the servant but he will tell me nothing. I thought I would wait for you to make sense of all of this."

"The boy will tell me all I need to know," Geoffrey said.

"He still does not speak, my lord. How——"

"Do not question me," Geoffrey interrupted, his tone sharp. "I must be certain."

Within short minutes, the child stood before the lord. He showed neither fear nor timidity, meeting the leader's probing stare with a wide grin. Geoffrey was amused by the lad's fearlessness, for it was true that grown men were known to quake in their boots when Geoffrey turned his attention to them, yet this wisp of a boy acted as if he was about to break into a fit of giggles. He was dressed in peasant garb and in need of a bath.

The child wasn't afraid. Thrilled was a far better description, for the man who had saved his life, the warrior who destroyed the band of men waylaying his protectors on the isolated route to London, was finally awake. The child's memory began with Lord Geoffrey, and although the leader could have no knowledge of this fact, he was impressed with the innocent acceptance and trust in the lad's eyes.

"You will not die now?" the child asked. Both Roger and Geoffrey showed surprise that the boy could speak, but before either of them could remark on the matter, the little one continued, "Everyone heard you yelling and they smiled."

The child sounded so relieved and so sure of himself that Lord Geoffrey found himself smiling.

"Tell me your name," he commanded in a gruff voice.

The child opened his mouth, frowned, and then shrugged his shoulders. His voice held surprise when he replied, "I do not know my name."

"Do you know where you came from, how you came to be here?" Roger asked the question and the boy turned to stare at him.

"He saved me," the child said, pointing at Geoffrey. "That is how I came to be here," he explained. "I am to be a knight." The boy's shoulders straightened with pride. He had figured that out all by himself.

Lord Geoffrey exchanged a look with Roger and turned back to the boy. "Who do you belong to?" he asked, although he already held the answer.

"To you?" The child no longer looked so sure of himself. He clutched his hands together while he waited for an answer.

The nervous action was not missed by the warrior. He had rarely dealt with one so young, but the instinct to protect, to guard, pulled at him. "Aye," he answered, inwardly wincing at the harshness in his tone. "Now leave me. We will talk again, later."

The child looked relieved. The lord watched him run to the door, wishing the boy to smile instead of frown and wondering why he felt this way. The fever must have left him weak in spirit as well as body, he decided.

"My lord?" the boy asked from the doorway, his back facing the leader so that his expression was hidden.

"Yes?" the lord answered impatiently.

"Are you my father?" He turned then, and Geoffrey had a clear view of the torment and confusion on the boy's face.

"No."

His answer brought tears to the youngster's eyes. Lord Geoffrey glanced at Roger with an expression that clearly stated, "Now what?" Roger cleared his throat and muttered to the boy, "He is not your father, lad. He is your lord. Your father was his vassal."

"My father is dead?"

"Aye," Geoffrey answered. "And you are in my care now."

"To train to be a knight?" the boy asked with a frown.

"Yes, to train to be a knight."

"You are not my father, but you are my lord," the boy stated very matter-of-factly. "'Tis almost the same thing," he announced, challenging Lord Geoffrey with an unwavering stare. "Is it not?"

"Yes," the warrior answered with exasperation. "'Tis the same."

Neither the lord nor Roger said another word until the door was closed behind the child. They could hear him boasting to the guards posted at the door, and Roger was the first to smile. "Thomas surely had his hands full with that one," he chuckled. "And he was not a young man when the boy came along, if my mind serves me well."

"How could I have forgotten?" the leader asked. "Thomas had several children, all female, and fully grown before his wife gave him a son. His pride reached London," Geoffrey added.

"And the girl?" Roger asked.

"She is his sister. You have only to look at the boy's eyes, Roger, to see the truth. They are replicas of hers." Geoffrey swung his legs over the side of the bed and stood. His legs felt weak but he braced them against the side of the bed and took a deep breath, willing himself strength. "She hides from me, Roger, and I will know the reason."

"We were told that the entire family was killed," Roger said. "And the boy was dressed as a peasant . . ."

"Obviously for his protection, for he is heir to Montwright. . . . "

"The servant who tried to take the lad, perhaps he can tell you the answers to this riddle," Roger advised.

"Yes. I am sure he knows where his mistress hides," Geoffrey agreed. "He will tell me why she is afraid."

"Afraid?" Roger laughed. "I doubt she is afraid of anyone or anything. Why, she had all of us doing her bidding. Horace tells all who will listen how the golden one walked into the great hall and enchanted all who were present. All but me," Roger added.

"You were not enchanted?" the leader inquired with one raised eyebrow.

"Humbled," Roger admitted with a sheepish grin. "I am too old to be enchanted."

Geoffrey chuckled and walked over to look out the window. He stared out at the forest while he listened to Roger.

"When I first saw her, I was filled with anger. I did not expect a slip of a girl to tend you and I was convinced that you were dying. But she knew what she was about. Her lack of fear intrigued me. She was a contradiction," Roger admitted, "but I noticed the vulnerability in her when she asked me about the boy. I was too exhausted at the time to put two and two together. I see the connection now."

"Why did she leave, knowing that her home was once again secure? To chance the outside when she could be well protected here . . ." Geoffrey turned from the window and added, "I *will* find her."

"And when you do?" Roger asked.

"I will make her mine," the warrior answered in a hard, determined voice. "She will be mine."

The vow was made.

It took less than an hour to conduct the necessary business of righting Montwright. Roger had been most efficient, and the men were all hard at work reinforcing the walls. Lord Geoffrey dressed—all in black, as was his mood—and waited impatiently in the great hall for the servant to be brought before him.

He was becoming wild with anger, frustration, and worry. Finding the girl before harm befell her was becoming an obsession. He admitted as much but could not explain it. He only knew that seeing her in the forest before the battle to regain Montwright Manor was indeed an omen, and the omen had become reality, had it not, when he awakened to find her caring for him? His reasoning reeked of superstition, yet he was powerless to control it, and for the first time in his twenty-seven years, he found himself ruled by emotion. It was a chilling admission. Emotion had no place in his

life. It clouded reason. Discipline and logic, as cold
and sharp as the blade he swung for power's sake,
ruled his every action. And it would be so again, he
pledged, just as soon as the girl was found. Found and
claimed.

"Here he is, my lord," Roger said from the doorway.
He shoved the trembling servant to the floor in front of
the lord.

Lord Geoffrey turned from his position in front of
the hearth and gave the servant a hard look. "Your
name?"

"I am called Joseph, my lord. Loyal servant to
Thomas," he added. The servant knelt and bowed his
head, showing his respect.

"You have a strange way of proving your loyalty to
Thomas," Geoffrey said in a hard voice. "Trying to
take his heir to the outside could well cost you your
life."

"I meant him no harm, my lord," Joseph whispered.
"I was trying to protect him."

"Protect him from me?" Geoffrey's bellow fairly
unnerved the servant.

He shook his head and tried to find his voice. "Nay,
my lord! We only thought to keep little Thomas safe
until you were recovered."

"And you thought him unsafe here?" Geoffrey
asked.

"It was overheard that Belwain, uncle to little Thomas, had been sent for. My mistress believes that Belwain was behind the murders of her family. She did not
want Thomas here when her uncle arrived."

"And that is why she has left?" Geoffrey asked,
rubbing his chin in a thoughtful gesture.

"Aye, my lord." Joseph sagged his shoulders and
chanced a look at the fiercesome man before him.

"And are you loyal to me?" Geoffrey asked.

"Aye, my lord," Joseph answered, placing a hand on
his chest where his heart beat a wild pace.

"Stand and prove your loyalty," Geoffrey demanded in a harsh voice.

Joseph immediately obeyed. He stood with his head slightly bowed and waited for the next order. It was not long in coming.

"Tell me where your mistress hides."

"Near the waterfall, about an hour's ride from here, my lord," Joseph answered without hesitation. "When she learns that you are awake, she will return to talk with you," he predicted.

"Her name?" Geoffrey demanded, though his tone was not as forceful now that he knew the servant would cooperate.

"She is Elizabeth, and she is youngest daughter to Thomas," Joseph answered. His hands began to ache, and he only then realized he was gripping them. Taking a deep, shuddering breath, he tried to calm himself.

"Was she here when the attack began?"

"Yes, my lord," Joseph replied, shivering with the memory. "All but Lady Elizabeth and her little brother were killed. I was able to help them escape but not before they both witnessed their mother—"

"I know," Geoffrey interrupted. "I was given the body count . . . and the way of their deaths was recounted to me." His mouth settled into a grim line at the memory of Roger's recent description of the mutilated bodies. "And you say she witnessed this?"

"Both she and the boy. The little lad has not spoken a word since, until today," he amended. "And he seems to have no memory of the event."

"Do you know who was behind the attack?" he asked the servant.

"I did not recognize any of them, for several wore black hoods, but my mistress believes Belwain responsible. With your permission, my lord, I will bring her to you."

"No," Geoffrey answered. "*I* will bring her back."

Roger's voice interrupted the discussion. "My lord? The priest has arrived."

Geoffrey nodded, inwardly sighing with relief. Though the dead had been buried, they had not been blessed. "See to his comforts, Roger. He is to stay here until I return."

"May I show you the way to the waterfall, my lord?" Joseph's timid voice turned Lord Geoffrey's attention back to him.

"No," Geoffrey answered. "I go alone. Her father was a loyal vassal. It is my duty. You have done your mistress a disservice by keeping silent, but I will not fault you, for I have heard of her stubborn inclination. And you did save her life. I will not forget that! Still, the responsibility for her well-being now rests with me. Your job is done."

Joseph felt as if a weight had been lifted from his shoulders. He watched Lord Geoffrey as he strode out of the hall, thinking that Elizabeth would indeed be well protected. Lord Geoffrey appeared to be a man of steel, Joseph gauged, and his strength would be Elizabeth's shield against all who would try to harm her. One question remained, nagging Joseph from the recesses of his mind: who would protect Lady Elizabeth from Lord Geoffrey?

Not a cloud marred the horizon as Geoffrey made his way through the forest in search of the waterfall. He had ridden hard for over an hour when the sound of rushing water, echoing through the lush green foliage, drew his attention. He quickly dismounted and secured the reins to the nearest tree branch and then began to make his way through the denseness. The mist from the cascading water mixed with the heat from the afternoon sun and formed a blanket of steam that covered his boots.

He knew from Joseph's description that the hut was

well hidden within a cluster of trees just beyond the gathering pool. He was headed in that direction when a splash, followed by a faint cough, stopped his advance. Geoffrey automatically drew his sword and turned, waiting for another sound that would give him advantage over his enemy, when he caught a glimmer of gold reflected through the branches. He moved slightly to get a better look. His breath caught in his throat at the sight before him. His vision—the golden one, as his men had so aptly named her—rose out of the water like the goddess Aphrodite. He watched, hypnotized, as she moved to the shallow end of the pool and stood. Her legs were braced apart and she stretched her arms high over her head in a lazy, unhurried motion. Streamers of sunlight poured through the canopy of branches and bathed his goddess in gold.

With a slow, graceful motion, Elizabeth brushed the hair back from her forehead. She sighed, content for the moment, enjoying the feel of the sun's warmth upon her shoulders and the contrasting cold of the clear water slapping against her legs. She forced herself to block all thoughts, all worries. In her heart she knew that her trusted servant would move heaven and earth to hide Thomas from Belwain's eyes, until Geoffrey could be made to listen. But the waiting . . . it was becoming unbearable. Perhaps the fever had returned, and the warrior was dead. Perhaps Belwain had arrived at Montwright and convinced everyone that he had nothing to do with the murders. Stop, she demanded. There is nothing to be done but wait, she told herself. Wait and pray. A woman's lot in life, Elizabeth decided with despair.

Scooping water into her cupped hands, she poured the liquid down her neck. Geoffrey was close enough to see her shiver, to watch the drops of water slip down between her full breasts, past the narrow waist he was sure he could span with but one hand, and farther down, into the blond, curly triangle at the junction of her legs. Her nipples grew hard from the chill but it was Geoffrey who shivered in reaction. Innocent sensuality radiated with her every motion and Geoffrey was hard-pressed to control his emotions, to suppress the primitive desire raging inside of him.

The gentle sway of her hips as she walked from the pool and gathered her clothes nearly made him wild with need. He took a deep breath, gaining control. He was Baron Geoffrey, overlord of all William had bequeathed! He would not take her now, though he thought he would go mad if he didn't taste her soon. Yes, he would have her. Of that there wasn't any question. She would belong to him. It was a simple fact of life. The law. What the lord wanted, he took.

The dogs Geoffrey remembered suddenly appeared at their mistress's side, hovering while she completed her dress. The animals were huge creatures, but from the way they both nudged her as she turned and disappeared into the forest, Geoffrey knew they would protect her well.

He was about to replace his sword and follow Elizabeth to the hut when an abrupt scream penetrated the stillness. It was a woman's scream. Geoffrey raced toward the sound, his sword at the ready. He could hear the dogs' ferocious growls, screams and shouts from men . . . at least three, judging from the different guttural sounds. Geoffrey crashed into the clearing in front of the hut and took in the tableau in one second's breath of time. There were three of them. Two were struggling with the dogs while the third half-carried, half-dragged the resisting girl toward the hut. The sight of such filth holding such beauty, his beauty, completed the transformation. The fair and noble ruler of the manor was gone, replaced by the Herculean warrior intent on a single action: to kill. There would be no hearing, no fairness, no understanding. The enemy had dared to touch what was his, and whether they realized that fact or not bore no significance. The price for their lust, for their stupidity, would be death.

The warrior's bellow of outrage stilled Elizabeth's attacker. Terror washed the lust from his eyes as he flung Elizabeth from his arms and turned to face the challenge. The look of fury on the warrior's face changed the attacker's mind. He turned to look for a means of escape from the intent he read in those cold black eyes. His hesitation was his death sentence. Geoffrey's blade whistled as it sliced through the air, guided by the warrior's strong arm, until it plunged down through the man's shoulder, cutting bone and muscle as easily as if they were sheep's fur, in its quest to find and pierce the heart. With one additional jerk of his wrist, Geoffrey completed the kill, removed the sword, and turned to deal with the two men behind him. "Call your animals," he ordered over his shoulder, and Elizabeth, stumbling to her feet, obeyed without question.

Geoffrey allowed both men time to stagger to their feet and reclaim their weapons before he moved forward. Then he stood, his legs braced apart, his sword at his side, waiting. The two men crouched and began to circle the warrior, and their puny attempts to kill him brought a smile to the warrior's face. A smile that didn't quite reach his eyes. Before either man could issue a scream, Geoffrey killed them with two swift slaps from his blade.

Stunned, unable to comprehend how the lord came to be there, defending her, Elizabeth could only watch in a daze. When Geoffrey finished the deed and turned his attention to her, Elizabeth felt her knees buckle from the power, the raw force that radiated from him.

"Come to me." The harshness of his voice startled her. There was a different kind of terror pulling at her now, and Elizabeth couldn't understand what was happening. Shouldn't she feel relief? This man had saved her life, killed for her. Perhaps it was because he was so much larger than she remembered, or perhaps it was because he had killed so easily, so effortlessly . . . so unemotionally. She was too confused, only knew that the danger was still there, clinging to the air, mingling with the scent of death and sweat. Tension enveloped both of them as they stared at each other. Elizabeth stood rigid and straight, facing the force that poured from him. Power. It was there in his stance, in his muscled legs braced apart in sureness and victory, in the tightly fisted hands resting on his hips, but most of all in his face. And the power drew her to him.

Elizabeth met his stare and slowly walked over to him. She stopped directly in front of him and waited. For what, she knew not.

Geoffrey's body relaxed. Elizabeth could see the tension, the violence, evaporate. He took a deep breath and his eyes warmed a little. And the fear left her.

"I have just killed for you." His tone was arrogant and challenging.

Elizabeth watched as Geoffrey cleaned his blade and then replaced it before she replied, "Yes, you have saved my life. I am in your debt," she acknowledged, her voice soft.

"That is so."

"But I have also saved your life," Elizabeth added, "for I was the one who tended your wounds."

"I remember," Geoffrey answered.

"And therefore, you are in my debt, are you not?"

"I am your lord." What was Elizabeth leading to? Geoffrey wondered. What was her plan? *"You* belong to *me."*

Elizabeth didn't answer, waiting for him to continue. A long moment passed and the lord frowned his displeasure. It would do her cause no good if she alienated him, for her fate was in his hands. In truth she did belong to him. Was that all he wanted? Her acknowledgment that he was now her lord?

"You belong to me," he repeated.

Elizabeth was about to agree when his hand moved as lightning to the back of her neck, his fingers locking forcefully in her hair. "It is I who decide your future," Geoffrey stated.

Elizabeth frowned with frustration. He was supposed to be in her debt. He should be grateful, but instead, he was demanding that she acknowledge her position to him.

Geoffrey was not pleased; he twisted her hair until she cried out in pain. Still he did not relent, but pulled her closer until her chest was flat against the cold steel links of metal covering his. Elizabeth shut her eyes against the pain and the look in his eyes, her mouth tightly closed so that she would not cry out again. She was trembling inside but vowed he would not know of her apprehension.

Geoffrey stared down at Elizabeth's face, smiling at the way she tried to mask her fear. There was a streak of rebellion in her eyes. He had not missed that, and it pleased him. He judged she would not intimidate easily. She was spirited and courageous, Geoffrey guessed, for she had lived outside the walls with only her animals for protection. 'Twas unheard of for a gently bred lady to do such a thing, yet she had done it. Stubborn too, Geoffrey knew, with perhaps a bit of wildness in her nature. He would tame the wildness without breaking the spirit. And the taming would begin now. His mouth descended to hers in a kiss that was meant to conquer. He would have her submission! He felt her jerk with the initial touch of his mouth, but he ignored her efforts for freedom, forcing her by merely tightening his hold in her hair until she opened her mouth to protest. And then his tongue invaded, tasting, probing, taking. His assault was not gentle, for in truth he knew little of wooing the weaker sex; still, he made an effort not to overwhelm her. She was gentle-bred, he reminded himself, and while he thought to drug her with his sexual prowess, he soon found that it was he who was fast losing control. She tasted so sweet, so fresh, and when she finally began to respond, when her tongue timidly touched his, he felt a wave of hot fire race through him.

The effect on his captive was just as startling. Did she struggle? Elizabeth thought that she did, but when the kiss ended, she found that her arms were wrapped around his neck. Had he placed them there? No, she answered herself, she had done that herself. Her face rested against the mail covering his chest. Shame tried to claim her attention, but Elizabeth fought it. She had not forced his embrace but only submitted because of his superior strength.

She felt Geoffrey's hand tighten and only then realized that his arms were around her waist. He smelled of leather and sweat. It wasn't unpleasant to be held by him, Elizabeth admitted.

"Your kissing has improved, Elizabeth," Geoffrey said against her forehead. A deep contentment he had not known before enveloped him; the feel of her against him was right, he felt it was right in his heart. He inhaled the fragrance of wildflowers scenting her hair and almost sighed aloud, his pleasure was so great. He knew he should let go of her and take a firm, intimidating stand so that she would well understand their relationship from the beginning, for he was her lord and she his subject, but he couldn't seem to drop his hands, to erase the smile. He would have to guard against letting her know the power she held over him. It would most likely be his downfall if he showed her his weakness for her. He knew from past experience that the fairer sex could easily manipulate any man, regardless of their physical strength, if the man allowed it. No woman would lead him around by the crook of her finger; no, he would do the leading, and she would be most thankful to follow.

"I was but curious," Elizabeth stated, referring to the kiss she had stolen when she was caring for him. "I have not kissed much," she added as she pushed against him to break the hold.

"I have no doubt that you are pure," Geoffrey remarked, and Elizabeth noted that the arrogance was back in his voice. His smile warmed her, and Elizabeth returned the gesture. She would have to watch herself with this one, she decided. He had a way about him that pulled at her, beckoned her. But he was too powerful, too overwhelming for her likes, she reminded herself; he would be like the stone walls of her fortress, unbending, and it would do her no good to become involved with such a man. No, she could never allow such an attraction to nurture. She had no wish to be swallowed up by his strength, only to be spit out as a former shell of herself when he turned his attention elsewhere. She turned her back on him and tried to remember what they were talking about. Pure, he thought her pure, he had said. "How could you know?" she found herself asking, "that I am pure," she qualified. She turned back to him and waited for his reply. Although she thought he had made the remark to ease her worry that he might have judged her wanton, she found herself irritated. Instead of being relieved that he did not think her a camp follower, she found herself somewhat insulted. Were her kisses so lacking?

"It was obvious, Elizabeth," the lord answered. "Though to take advantage of a man in a weakened condition tells me much about your character." He was teasing her, the laughter was there in his eyes. It surprised her, for she didn't think he was a man who laughed much. She returned his smile.

She could see that the kiss had lightened his mood, and sought to take advantage of the moment. "You are feeling well now?"

"Aye," Geoffrey replied.

"You have called me by my name, my lord. How did you learn—"

"It was easy to solve part of the riddle," Geoffrey answered. "Still, I would like more answers. When we return to the manor . . ."

"I would . . . if it pleases you lord, I would like to talk with you now, before we return to Montwright."

Geoffrey frowned over this request and then nodded. He walked over to the mud-splattered boulder adjacent to the hut and leaned against the edge, his long legs outstretched before him. He wasn't aware that he stroked the dogs leaning against his sides as he watched Elizabeth. "Begin by telling me why you did not stay inside the walls. Why did you come back here?"

"I could not stay there with Belwain coming, I could not." Elizabeth calmed her voice and walked over to stand between Geoffrey's legs. She folded her hands as if she was preparing for her morning prayers and said, "It is a long story, my lord. Will you listen to me?"

"Aye," Geoffrey replied. He was eager to hear her tale, to understand what had transpired at Montwright.

"My parents, my sisters, one of their husbands . . . all killed," she whispered. "And Belwain, my father's younger brother . . . he is to blame. He must be punished."

"From the beginning, Elizabeth," Geoffrey encouraged in a gentle tone. "Tell me what you saw, what you heard."

Elizabeth nodded and took a deep breath. "I did not see them arrive. Little Thomas and I were out riding when it began. The family had gathered to celebrate my little brother's birthday. It was a tradition," she explained.

Geoffrey nodded and then realized that she was looking right through him, didn't seem to notice his encouraging gesture at all. Memory had control of her mind now, and from the torment etching her features,

Geoffrey knew a chilling account was about to be told. He wanted to gather her in his arms, to hold her and offer comfort, but he sensed she would not accept his compassion from the way she held herself erect. Memory was taking her to hell's nightmares, and all he could do was listen.

"My eldest sister, Catherine, and her husband, Bernard, came all the way from his holding near Granbury, but Rupert, ailing from liver upset, could not attend. He allowed Margaret to come, though . . . Oh, God, but if he had not been so agreeable! She would still be alive." Elizabeth took a deep breath, a calmness settling over her features. She told the rest in a flat, emotionless voice. "Thomas and I came in through the side entrance, intent on changing our clothes before our mother caught sight of us, for we were covered with mud. There is a stairwell, well hidden from the great hall, with a tapestry hung over the door on the second landing. As I neared the top I could hear screams and shouts. I knew then something was wrong. I made Thomas stay on the steps and opened the door. No one saw me, but I could see everything from my position. There were bodies, dead, mutilated bodies, strewn about the floor like so many soiled rushes. Those doing the killing were dressed as peasants but they wielded their swords like trained soldiers. Several of the men wore black hoods to conceal their faces. I tried to find the one in charge when I caught sight of my sister Margaret. I saw her stab one of the men in his shoulder, and then run toward our mother. The man she injured followed her and plunged his knife into her back, and Margaret went down. I felt little Thomas against my side then, and turned to shield him from the view and to find safety for him. One of the attackers, his voice was somehow familiar to me even then, called the order to find the boy. 'Find the boy or we fail,' that is what he screamed, and I knew they meant to kill little Thomas. I had to protect him. He was now heir . . . I couldn't help my mother, but I couldn't seem to move either. It was as if I was frozen in place. I just kept watching her. They were tearing at her clothes. My mother's clothes! She broke away and raked her nails against the face of one of her captors. He screamed with pain and then the one who had killed Margaret . . . he came up to my mother with an ax in his hand. He raised it high into the air and the blade came down, down and across her neck, and her head, her head was torn from her body!"

She had never said the words until now. She wanted to crumble to the earth and die. The pain was so intense, the screams of her family so agonizing, so deafening, that she involuntarily placed her hands over her ears.

Geoffrey did not say a word. He gently reached out and pulled her hands from her face and held them.

His action helped Elizabeth gain control. She looked at him then, really looked at him, and saw the compassion in his eyes. "I don't remember much after that. I took Thomas back down the stairway and we stayed there until Joseph found us and took us to the outside. We sent word to Bernard's relatives and to Rupert."

Geoffrey pulled Elizabeth toward him, wrapping his strong arms around her. He wanted to erase the horror but knew that wasn't possible. "Did you recognize any of the men?" he asked.

"No, but the man Margaret stabbed . . . his voice was familiar to me," Elizabeth suddenly remembered. "Blood covered his garb."

"What of the other men? Did you know any of them?"

"No," Elizabeth replied, her shoulders sagging.

"Your servant told me that you sent your brother to London. Why?" he asked after a time.

"I did not know what else to do," Elizabeth said. "The law would give Belwain guardianship and I thought you old and senile. And I had no proof that it was Belwain behind the deed. My mother's father lives in London and I thought to keep my brother safe with him until I could find the proof . . . or kill Belwain myself," she said.

"Tell me your reasons for believing Belwain is responsible," Geoffrey said.

"He is the only one to gain," Elizabeth began. "He was my father's younger brother and lusted after Montwright. Father gave him a portion of the land for his own but Belwain was not content. Still, my mother told me Belwain used to be a merry man until little Thomas was born, then the relationship changed with my father. I do not know if that is so, for I was too young to pay much notice. I do know that last time my uncle visited my father they had a terrible argument and Belwain said he would never return to Montwright land. He threatened my father and I remember being frightened by his words, but my father seemed unaffected. I heard him tell my mother that Belwain's temper would calm and he would become content once again."

Elizabeth pulled her hands free of Geoffrey's hold and said, "Belwain would inherit the Montwright lands if we were all dead, wouldn't he?"

"Aye," Geoffrey acknowledged. "But you are not all dead," he reminded her.

"This same law gives Belwain guardianship of little Thomas, does it not?"

"That is so," Geoffrey replied.

"And if you give my brother over to his care, he will kill him," she predicted. "And me also," she added, almost as an afterthought.

"You will not be given into his care," Geoffrey stated.

"Then you believe me?" Elizabeth asked, her voice hopeful. "You will kill Belwain?"

"I believe that you think Belwain responsible," Geoffrey hedged, "and he has the greatest to gain, but I need proof before I challenge him."

"Proof! There is no proof," Elizabeth all but screamed. She pushed away from Geoffrey and added, "Belwain will not go free. He must pay for what he has done. I will kill him."

"If Belwain is responsible, I will kill him," Geoffrey said. "When he arrives at Montwright, I will question him."

"And you think he will admit his sins?" Elizabeth asked in a desperate voice. "He will lie."

"Lies can trap," Geoffrey returned. "I will find who is behind the deed and I will determine the punishment. It is my responsibility."

"Will you give me your word that Belwain will not become guardian to Thomas?" Elizabeth asked.

"If Belwain is innocent of your charges, I could not break the law," Geoffrey stated. "Thomas would be placed under his guardianship. *If* he is innocent."

Elizabeth took a step back, shaking her head. "You are overlord to Montwright lands, and now that my father is dead, little Thomas is your vassal. It is your duty to protect him!"

"Do not tell me my responsibilities," Geoffrey barked. He stood up and unconsciously put his hands on his hips. "I know them well enough. Until I know the truth in this matter your brother will stay with me." His voice gentled as he added, "Trust me, Elizabeth. I will not let any harm come to the lad."

Elizabeth wanted to believe him. While he had not promised to charge her uncle immediately, he did state that he would keep her brother safe for the time being. It would have to be enough. At least Geoffrey had listened to her and had not pushed her accusations aside. If he decided Belwain innocent, then Elizabeth would take matters into her own hands.

"Come, Elizabeth. The hour grows late. We will talk of this when we are within the manor."

"I need not be there when you question Belwain," Elizabeth argued. "And I have no wish to look upon his evil face. No," she continued, ignoring the anger she read on his face, "I will stay here until Belwain has been—"

The roar interrupted Elizabeth's sentence. In one swift action the lord lifted her high up into his arms. The dogs began to growl but the warrior ignored them as he turned and started back toward the waterfall.

God, but she was a stubborn bit of goods, Geoffrey thought with irritation. She seemed to have absolutely no fear whatsoever of her master, and that both amused and angered the knight. He wasn't used to such brashness. And yet, he reasoned, he did not wish her to cower in his presence. She confused him, he admitted, confused . . . and delighted him. Still, he would have to do something about her disposition, her inclination to argue. She would have to learn her place, her lot. He couldn't very well present her to William until she learned to curb her tongue. While William's opinion did not rule Geoffrey's life, he admitted that he did not wish his king to think Geoffrey's wife was but a shrew! Wife! Aye, he told himself, she would be his wife. There could be no other way to keep her with him. It would be a grave insult to the late vassal, Elizabeth's father, if he took Elizabeth as mistress. Thomas was a loyal and honest man; Geoffrey could not shame his memory by soiling his daughter and then casting her aside.

I do this for Thomas, Geoffrey found himself thinking. He did not think that he loved Elizabeth, for he did not think he could love any woman. Past betrayal had sealed his heart against such vulnerability. Yet the fates had decreed, from the moment he sighted her on the rise above the manor before the battle, that they be together. He did not understand why he wanted her at his side, why she had come to mean such a great deal to him in such a short time, but he would follow his inclinations. Perhaps it was all superstition on his part and she was his talisman. He did not know and did not care.

Besides, it was time, he almost said aloud. Time for the begetting of sons.

"Put me down, my lord," Elizabeth ordered for the third time. She saw that the scar on the side of his cheek had grown quite red and decided that she had over-stepped her position. "Please," she amended in a soft voice. "I have my horse and my possessions to gather."

"Tomorrow your servant can fetch your things."

What a stubborn, unbending man Lord Geoffrey was, Elizabeth thought. Odd, but she found she wasn't upset any longer. A deep faith that he would right the wrongs to her family made her content for the moment.

They did not speak again until they were well on their way back to the manor. Elizabeth sat in front of the lord on his powerful charger and could not help but lean against him as they rode through the forest at a neck-breaking pace.

"Do you know what you will do with me? Where you will send me?" Elizabeth asked, thinking that she would like to stay near her brother.

"Aye," Geoffrey replied in a rough voice. He was trying to concentrate on getting them to safety, his senses alert, but Elizabeth's nearness was unsettling. From the moment he had lifted her into his arms, a sense of well-being, of calmness, invaded the warrior. It was as if he could breathe again, and she was the fresh air he needed to survive. He tightened his hold, pleased when she did not protest. The top of her head was nestled just under his chin, and the knight found it a hard task not to rub his cheek against the softness of her golden hair.

Elizabeth waited for what seemed an eternity for Lord Geoffrey to continue, but the lord seemed disinclined.

"My father had signed a marriage contract when I

57

was just a babe," Elizabeth finally said, "but Hugh, the man I was to marry, died two years past. I do not know if another was arranged," she added. Perhaps Geoffrey could tell her, for Thomas would have to gain his permission for any marriage contract to be valid. It was the law.

"There will be no marriage contract," Geoffrey stated with finality.

"I will not be married?" Elizabeth asked with surprise.

"Yes, you shall be married," Geoffrey said. "To me."

Had not Geoffrey been holding her secure, Elizabeth would have fallen off the horse. She twisted around until she could look him directly in the face, and blurted the first thing that came to her confused mind. "Why?"

The lord did not answer, and from the hard line of his jaw Elizabeth surmised he would not tell her any more.

She turned back and stared straight ahead. Montwright came into view as they rounded the water's bend, and fear twisted her stomach into knots. She found herself clutching Geoffrey's hands but could not let go. Belwain and his men might well be waiting inside.

Elizabeth closed her eyes and said a quick prayer. Nothing can ever be as it was, she lamented. Her parents and sisters were dead, and now she was solely responsible for keeping little Thomas safe. She had no one to turn to, no one to champion her cause, save this stubborn, battle-scarred lord. Would he be strong enough, cunning enough to keep them safe?

Chapter Three

THE WEDDING WOULD BE TODAY!

Elizabeth could not understand the reason for the hurry, yet she was powerless to stop the proceedings. The lord's mind was made up. And her demands for an explanation were completely ignored. It was as if Geoffrey was in a race against time, and he must be married by nightfall. It made absolutely no sense to Elizabeth.

Geoffrey lifted her off the horse and carried her into the castle, like so much baggage, up the curving staircase and into her bedroom before she could catch her breath.

"I wish to see my brother," she demanded against his neck, but the warrior refused with a shake of his head. God but he was stubborn!

"After the wedding," he finally told her as he dumped her on the bed. "I shall have a bath prepared for you," he added. And with that, he left.

For the first time since finding Elizabeth, the lord was pleased to see that she was fairly speechless. The look of confusion on her face when he announced that they would be wed this very day would be remembered, and savored, for many a night. Good, Geoffrey thought. He would keep her confused.

In truth, he did not understand the hurry for the marriage, only knew that he could not go another night without her beside him. And since the priest had arrived to see to the blessing of the dead, Geoffrey saw no need to wait. It would not be a traditional wedding with the participants proclaiming their vows on the steps to the manor's church, for the church had been burned to the ground. The ceremony would have to take place in the great hall, but it would still be a valid marriage. And once she was his, in name and body, then Geoffrey could find peace. Only then could he get back to the business of being a baron.

Elizabeth tried to understand her lord's reasoning for marrying her, and finally decided that he did it to protect her, and to honor her father. "He thinks he's failed my father," Elizabeth said aloud, for her father had placed his loyalty in Geoffrey's hands for his protection. It was the way of the times. Still, it was Thomas's duty to protect his own home, not Geoffrey's.

Elizabeth paced the confines of the room, her mood growing quite ugly by the time two men entered the chamber with a large wooden tub. They returned with buckets of steaming water, again and again, until the tub was near to overflowing with hot water. No one spoke a word during the entire procedure, although Elizabeth did a lot of scowling, and the two men a bit of grinning.

A warm bath, instead of the frigid water from the waterfall, beckoned. Elizabeth found the rose-scented chips of soap her mother had given her on her last birthday, still wrapped in the strip of white linen at the bottom of her chest. She quickly removed her tunic and climbed into the tub. Taking her anger out on her hair, she scrubbed until her scalp began to sting in protest. She had thought the bath would be soothing and help her straighten out her thoughts, but found she could not relax. Belwain had not yet arrived, and Elizabeth found herself praying that some terrible mischief befell him on his route to Montwright. No, she decided, that was a wicked prayer, and more important, an inappropriate way to meet his death. Vengeance would not be cheated.

A fire was blazing in the hearth, and Elizabeth, wrapped in the bed cover, knelt before its warmth and began to dry her hair. There was too much to consider, too much to deal with, and Elizabeth felt overwhelming fatigue.

Lord Geoffrey found her in such an unguarded position. His eyes were tender as he leaned against the door and watched her. Elizabeth heard the door open but refused to acknowledge the intrusion. She adjusted the cover more securely against her bosom and continued to dry her hair. Had she turned, she would have glimpsed the gentleness in his gaze, the smile that came upon him when he watched her struggle with the cover. He thought she was the most beguiling, the most enchanting nymph, all soft and silky and smooth. The light from the fire cast a glow on her uncovered shoulders, giving her a golden look, but by her stiffly held frame he knew she was upset. The hint of defiance warmed him as much as her appearance. He considered that her anger, fully unleashed, could scorch a lesser man.

Elizabeth couldn't stand the silence any longer. "Are

you going to stand there all night?" she asked. She turned and he saw that her face was flushed from the heat of the fire, her eyes a blazing blue.

"You are not eager for this marriage?" His voice was soft, his expression mocking to Elizabeth's ears.

A lioness, Geoffrey decided, from the mane of rioting curls to the wild, wary expression in her eyes. He fought the urge to grab her, touch her.

"I have no feelings one way or the other," Elizabeth lied. She stood then, thinking that kneeling in his presence would give him the idea that she was of the submissive sort. Whether he be her lord or not, she would never cower before him.

Geoffrey acknowledged her comment with a nod and walked over to the window. He lifted the heavy piece of fur blocking the wind and gazed out. It was as if he had dismissed her, Elizabeth thought, wondering what she was supposed to do.

"You need not marry me, my lord. Your protection is enough," Elizabeth pointed out. "And you are in a position to marry anyone . . . to marry even for love."

He acted as if he hadn't heard a word she said, and Elizabeth continued to wait.

"Foolish men marry for love. I am not foolish." He hadn't bothered to turn to her but continued to look out the window as he spoke. Odd, but his voice, though forceful, was lacking any emotion.

Foolish, she repeated to herself. He thought love foolish. She didn't disagree with him. She could be as realistic as he. And he was right. It was unheard of to marry for love. It wasn't practical. And yet . . . there was a romantic corner of her mind that wished Geoffrey did love her and that she did love him. Aye, foolish indeed. Wasn't it enough that she was drawn to him? Found him physically pleasing? No, she admitted, physical beauty should have no importance in a lasting relationship. Her mother had taught her that. It was what was buried beneath the surface that determined a good match. Besides, Elizabeth was a little frightened by Geoffrey, and that wouldn't do at all! She hated being frightened. She had already glimpsed a stubborn inclination in his nature, larger than her own. No doubt the marriage would be a stormy arrangement, and after all the turmoil she had recently been through, the prospect of more was as welcome to her as a sore tooth.

Elizabeth realized that Lord Geoffrey knew very little about her, had no idea just what he was getting for his wife. What would he think when he learned that she was far better versed in hunting and skinning a rabbit than needlepoint and homemaking? How often had her father blamed her Saxon heritage for her wild ways? Blamed her mother's full Saxon father for encouraging her unorthodox behavior? It was the grandfather who gifted Elizabeth with the hawk and then the wolf-hounds on his annual visits to the manor, all to irritate his daughter's husband. The two protagonists played goading games with each other. And it was Elizabeth who benefited from the friction between the two men. Grandfather boasted that his granddaughter was a throwback to their Viking ancestors, and he only had to point to her blond hair, her blue eyes, and her proud carriage to prove his statement.

But if the grandfather was to blame for Elizabeth's independence, so was her father. Had he not treated her as a son for many years?

How would her grandfather get on with Geoffrey, Elizabeth wondered, should they ever meet? Would the gentle giant play the same antagonizing games with Geoffrey that he had with her father? The thought of the chaos he could cause made Elizabeth smile. Geoffrey turned from the window in time to catch her smile. He wondered at its cause, frowning.

Elizabeth met his gaze and waited. She noticed then that he too had bathed, for his hair was wet and slightly curling around his collar. He had changed too, into a tunic as black as midnight, with the design of his crest, in gold threads, upon his right breast. The fabric was tight against his powerful chest, and each and every time she saw him, his largeness appeared greater than before. She did not like feeling intimidated by him, but couldn't continue to match his stare, for his hot gaze was so lustful that she feared he would soon see the terror she was trying so hard to hide.

"The priest is waiting," he suddenly announced, his tone surprisingly gentle.

"Then you have not changed your mind?" Elizabeth asked, her voice no more than a whisper.

"Aye, I have not changed my mind. We will be married," Geoffrey said. "Get dressed. The guards will escort you when you are ready. Do not keep me waiting," he warned. He did not wait for her response but turned and left the room, slamming the door behind him with such force that the logs in the fireplace shifted from the wind that stirred them.

Elizabeth found herself hurrying to do his bidding. She would have the marriage over and done with! She dressed in a plain white gown, winding a gold chain around her waist as her only decoration. Her hair was damp and it was difficult to get order achieved, but she finally managed to secure it to the back of her head with a gossamer-thin strip of ribbon.

Her hands trembled as she opened the door and followed the guards down the corridor, toward her fate.

Geoffrey stood at the bottom of the stairway, his hand extended. Elizabeth placed her hand in his and walked with him into the great hall.

She was startled to see that all the men in the room were kneeling, their heads bowed. It was awesome to see so many show such respect.

The priest's benediction turned her thoughts back to the vows she was about to exchange. He was asking her to pledge herself, body and soul, into the keeping of the man kneeling beside her.

It was all happening so fast. Elizabeth could not even remember kneeling. How had her hand gotten into his? Where had the ring come from? "To love and to honor, to cherish . . ." The priest's monotone voice insisted, quietly demanded. I do not know if I love him, Elizabeth found herself thinking, even as she repeated the words, "I, Elizabeth Catherine Montwright, do hereby . . ." Her voice was a thread of a whisper, but the priest seemed content, merely leaning forward with a benevolent smile upon his leathered face as he listened to her replies.

"I, Geoffrey William Berkley . . ." His voice, proclaiming his many titles, was forceful and clear. And then it was over, and Geoffrey was lifting her to her feet. He gave her a firm kiss and then turned her, presenting both of them to his men. She heard his deep sigh just seconds before the hall was filled with a resounding cheer.

The noise and the shouts escalated in volume and intensity. Elizabeth saw her brother, standing next to the lord's companion. She instinctively started to go to him, only to be stopped by her husband's hand. "Wait," he instructed, placing his hand on her arm.

He nodded to Roger and a path was cleared. Roger pulled Thomas to stand before the couple. The little boy only had eyes for Geoffrey, the worship there for all to see. He hadn't given his sister so much as a glance. "I do not think he remembers you," her husband said. "But that will change," Geoffrey added when he noticed her distress, "for his voice has returned and he now talks constantly."

Elizabeth nodded and smiled and then knelt before her brother so that they were at eye level. He ignored her as she softly called his name.

"Thomas, I am your sister," she insisted for the second time. The little one finally turned when Roger nudged the back of his head.

"I am to be a knight," he boasted. Then, remembering his manners, he knelt down and bowed his head. "I will guard you, my lady, from this day forth." He peeked up at Geoffrey to see if he had pleased his lord.

Geoffrey nodded and helped Elizabeth to her feet. She turned to take her brother's hand but found that he was already halfway across the hall, following Roger.

Elizabeth turned back to her husband and allowed him to lead her toward the table and the wedding feast. "Where are Thor and Garth?" she asked as she sat down.

"Who?" her husband asked.

"My dogs," Elizabeth explained. "They are called Thor and Garth. My grandfather named them," she added with a small smile. "I was wondering if perhaps little Thomas remembered them."

"The dogs are locked in the quarters below," Geoffrey answered. "Your brother is afraid of them."

"But that cannot be true!" Elizabeth exclaimed. She had reached her limit for surprises in one day. "He saw them raised from pups."

"I do not lie." Geoffrey's voice was quiet but firm. Elizabeth studied him while he settled himself at the table beside her, but could tell nothing from his expression. It was as if he wore a mask to keep his emotions carefully concealed from her. Yet, even so, she decided that she might have offended him.

"I believe you," she replied. "I was not suggesting that you lie," she qualified, "it was just a surprise."

Her explanation pleased her husband and he favored her with a smile that showed beautiful white teeth. The smile was almost boyish but the scar that marked his cheek canceled any suggestion that he was a playful youth. That, and the way he looked at her, Elizabeth thought with a shiver of nervousness. His eyes held a sensual promise of things to come.

"The boy hides behind Roger whenever the dogs are about. The animals obviously remember your brother," he said, "and are constantly trying to nudge him into play. The future heir of Montwright lands wailed until Roger could not stand the sound another second. If his fighting arm is as strong as his lungs, your brother will be a mighty warrior when he grows up."

It was Elizabeth who now felt like wailing. Tears filled her eyes and she squeezed her hand into a fist, only then realizing that Geoffrey was holding it. She promptly relaxed her grip, lest he think she was being overly emotional. "He never used to be afraid of anything or anyone," Elizabeth said. "Father worried that he would never develop any common sense." Sadness underlined her explanation.

Geoffrey seemed unaffected by her distress. "He has seen much to change him." He handed her a cup filled with sweet red wine before adding, "In time your brother will mend. It is the way of things."

And will I mend? Elizabeth asked herself. Will time make the memory of my mother's screams fade into insignificance? Will time make the murders less an atrocity? And if healing includes forgetting, then perhaps the wounds should stay raw and bleeding. I cannot put the hate aside, Elizabeth thought, not until Belwain is dead.

"Congratulations, my lady." The softly spoken words and the familiar voice shocked Elizabeth. Her head jerked up and she met the stare of her mother's elderly servant, Sara.

"Sara," she exclaimed with a smile. "I thought you dead." Elizabeth turned, the smile still in place, and said to her husband, "My lord, may I present my mother's most loyal servant, Sara. Sara," she said, turning her gaze back to the white-haired woman, "my father's overlord, Baron Geoffrey William Berkley."

"Nay, Elizabeth," her husband contradicted against her ear, "no longer your father's overlord but your husband."

Elizabeth blushed slightly and nodded at the gentle reprimand. She would correct her error now. "My husband, Sara . . ." she began. Her attention was distracted by the number of familiar-looking servants carrying platters of food into the hall. "Where . . . how . . ."

"They have all returned, now that you are here," Sara said, folding her hands in front of her. She was looking at Elizabeth but sensed the Baron's frown and quickly amended her sentence. "When word was told that your husband had rid our home of the defilers, then we returned."

The servant glanced at the lord and then lowered her eyes with respect. "With your permission, my lord, I would help my lady prepare for bed this evening. Her serving girl was slain during the raid."

Geoffrey nodded his consent. The servant smiled, reached out her hand as if to pat Elizabeth, and then thought better of it. Elizabeth caught the action and it was she who patted the servant. "Thank you, Sara, and praise God that you are well," she said.

When the servant had returned to her duties, Elizabeth turned back to her husband. There were tears in her eyes.

Geoffrey was amazed at her composure. There was a fragile strength about her. She was not like other women he had known, but he had recognized that fact from the beginning. A quiet dignity radiated from her. Her temper was quick to flare, Geoffrey knew, but the tears were closely guarded.

He wished to see her smile again. "And do you wail as loud as your brother?" he asked her.

Elizabeth could not tell if he was teasing or not. "I never wail," she said, shaking her head. She thought then that her boast sounded terribly prim.

Her husband grinned with delight. "And do you never smile at your husband?" he inquired against her ear.

The sweet, warm breath against her earlobe felt like a gentle stroke and Elizabeth found she had to pull away before she could answer. "'Tis too soon to tell," she tried to tease, though her voice sounded like a husky whisper to her ears, "I've only been married a few short minutes, my lord." She lifted her gaze to his then, her eyes sparkling with mischief, and Geoffrey was struck speechless by their intense color. She continued to become more magnificent, more desirable, and he wondered how that was possible.

"And are you pleased to be married?" he asked when he could find his voice.

"It will be a most difficult adjustment," Elizabeth said, her voice serious. She continued to meet his stare and added, "My husband is not well known by me and the stories about him are terrible indeed."

Geoffrey was taken aback. He thought she might be jesting, the sparkle in her eyes told him that, but her expression was neutral and her voice most serious. He found he didn't know how to reply. No one had ever spoken to him in this manner. "I am your husband," Geoffrey said, frowning. "What stories have you heard about me?" he demanded.

"Too many to count," Elizabeth replied, trying not to laugh.

"I will hear them all!" His voice increased in volume, keeping pace with his escalating temper. As soon as he snapped the order, he wished he had not. He did not wish to frighten his bride on this their wedding night, but he obviously had. Elizabeth had turned her head away from him, shielding her face from his view. Now, as awkward as it might be, Geoffrey would try to soothe her. The problem, of course, was that he wasn't quite sure how to go about it.

He slammed his goblet down on the table to vent his frustration and then turned Elizabeth's chin toward him with the tip of his finger. He decided that he would simply smile at her and then she would know that she was still in his good stead.

He was totally unprepared for the smile that formed

her expression, the soft lilting laughter that reached his ears. "I was teasing, husband. Please do not frown. I did not wish to upset you," Elizabeth said, trying to control her smile.

"You are not afraid?" He found himself asking the absurd question and had to shake his head.

"You do not like to be teased?" Elizabeth answered his question with one of her own.

"I do not know if I like this teasing or not," Geoffrey said, trying to sound stern and failing miserably. Her smile was like the sun entering the damp, candle-casted room, warming him. "Unless *I* am the one to tease," he admitted with a grin.

Elizabeth laughed again and said, "Then this marriage—"

"A toast!" The command came from Roger, in a loud, forceful voice. Elizabeth glanced up and saw that the vassal held a goblet high above his head. Balanced somewhat precariously on one shoulder was little Thomas, giggling while he held on to the knight's head of hair with both hands.

Geoffrey found himself irritated with the interruption. He had enjoyed the easy banter with his wife and wondered what she was about to say. He forced himself back to the festivities but first whispered to Elizabeth, "Later, wife, you shall tell me these terrible stories about my character later."

Keeping her stare directed on Roger and her brother, Elizabeth answered in a soft voice, "Perhaps, my lord. Perhaps."

A sense of rightness settled over Elizabeth with each sip of the warming wine. In fact, she felt warm all over, inside and out. "Where have you found this wine, my lord? We are unaccustomed to such quality," she said.

"Even when you celebrate?" Geoffrey asked with surprise.

"We drank ale on every occasion," Elizabeth replied. "And shared from each other's trenchers," she added, referring to the wooden plates the servants were placing on the table.

"Your father was a wealthy man," Geoffrey stated.

"Aye, but frugal," Elizabeth said. She laughed then and leaned toward her husband, her hand casually resting over his. "My grandfather used to tease my father something fierce over his tight purse," she confessed in a conspiratorial voice.

"You have a fondness for your grandfather, don't you?" Geoffrey asked, smiling at her behavior.

"Yes, we are very alike," she acknowledged. She took another sip of her wine and smiled at her husband over the rim of her goblet.

"Enough," Geoffrey decreed, removing her goblet. "I want you awake on our wedding night."

His indelicate reminder of what was to come removed Elizabeth's warmth. The smile faded and she lowered her gaze to her plate. She had eaten but a fraction of the quail pie and none of the swan or the wildberry tarts prepared for the celebration.

She watched as more and more delicacies were placed on the table. There were appreciative ohs and ahs when the cooked peacock, redressed in its skin and feathers, was placed before her. Geoffrey served her after he had washed his hands with the wet cloth his squire provided him. A page assisted Elizabeth.

The priest and several of Geoffrey's thegns joined the couple at the table. Little Thomas was not allowed to sit with them, due to his age and his position, but each time Elizabeth saw him, she noticed that his cheeks were as swollen as a chipmunk's with food. His manners were equal to her dogs, she thought, but soon he would become one of Geoffrey's pages and learn the correct way of things.

Several of the men broke out into verses of a popular and somewhat risqué ballad. And then the red-haired squire, flushed with drink, began to sing in a deep baritone voice. The hall quieted and all listened to his song.

His ballad was about the hero Roland and his faithful sword, Joyosa, and how the brave man led the ancient troops to victory. According to the verse, Roland rode well ahead of the invaders, singing in a clear voice while he tossed his sword countless times into the air like a juggler. He was the first to die and offered no resistance. And now he was legend.

To Elizabeth, Roland was foolish indeed. She decided she was not of a romantic nature. Dead was dead, whether one became legend or not. She wondered if Geoffrey would agree with her observation.

"It is time," Geoffrey announced when the song ended and the cheers to Roland's memory subsided. He took her elbow, nodded to her servant, and stood. "Go. I will join you shortly."

Elizabeth wanted to leave, all right, but her destination was the great doors leading to the outside, and not her bedroom. She almost smiled at her childish thoughts of escape. Almost.

She lifted the hem of her gown and followed Sara, keeping within the light of the torch the servant carried, stopping only once on her way up the curving staircase. She found her husband in the middle of a group of men, watching her. He seemed ignorant of the soldiers' talk, staring intently at his bride. Elizabeth's heart raced at the sensuous caress, the promise his dark eyes held.

"Mistress?" Sara's voice pulled at her, but Elizabeth couldn't break the force that held her gaze locked with her husband's.

"Yes," she whispered, and then, "I'm coming," but it wasn't until the servant tugged at her elbow that she was able to turn back to the kind woman.

Sara kept up a steady chatter of village news until she had Elizabeth stripped of her garments and a new fire blazing in the hearth. Elizabeth's hair remained twisted in the ribbon atop her head with several wisps falling and framing the sides of her face. She brushed a loose tendril aside and slipped into the robe the maid held open for her.

Having Sara there, helping her, did much to calm Elizabeth. The day had been quite overwhelming. Elizabeth felt both exhausted and keyed up.

"Your hands are trembling," the old woman remarked. "Is it from joy or fear?"

"Neither," Elizabeth lied. "I am just overly tired. 'Tis been a long day."

"Mistress? Did your mother ever talk to you about the duties of a wife?" Sara asked with a bluntness that made Elizabeth's cheeks grow warm.

"No," she answered, avoiding Sara's gaze, "but I have overheard stories my sisters exchanged. Besides, a woman doesn't have to do anything, does she?" Her voice held a note of panic, an echo of her inner turmoil.

The servant nodded. "When a man becomes excited, he wishes his mate to respond," she said very matter-of-factly. "I worry that you will make him angry if you—"

"I do not care if he becomes angry or not," Elizabeth replied, straightening her shoulders. "I just hope that he will be quickly done."

"There are ways you can make the deed quick," the servant hinted. She folded back the covers on the bed and turned back to Elizabeth. "But it will take courage . . . and boldness, my lady."

Elizabeth found herself intrigued with the conversation. Sara wasn't acting the least bit embarrassed by their delicate topic but stood there with a tranquil expression on her face and spoke as if they were discussing new ways of stuffing quail. Sara, Elizabeth reminded herself, was at least three times her own age, and maybe that was why her attitude was so blasé.

"What must I do?" Elizabeth asked, determined to do anything to get the night over and done with.

"Entice him," Sara announced, nodding her head at Elizabeth's puzzled expression. "He is eager to bed you," she said. "I saw the look in his eyes. Every man has only so much control, mistress. You must—"

The door to the bedroom suddenly opened and Geoffrey filled the entry. Elizabeth was standing in front of the fireplace, unaware that the light from the fire outlined the slender shape of her body through the thin robe. Her stomach knotted at the look in her husband's eyes as he slowly took his fill of her, from the top of her head to the tip of her toes, which peeked out beneath the robe, but she matched his stare and his appraisal and prayed that her trembling would soon stop.

Sara left the room and she was alone with her husband. His gaze was intimidating, and when she could stand it no longer, she turned her back to him, pretending to warm her hands before the fire. Her mind raced for an ending to the discussion she was having with Sara. Entice him? Play the whore? Is that what the servant suggested? No, she decided, she could never do that. And why would enticing speed the deed?

Realizing that she probably looked like she was hiding, Elizabeth slowly turned back to her husband. He was sitting on the edge of the bed, removing his boots and staring at her.

If only he would smile, Elizabeth thought, instead of looking so serious, so intent. She felt like he was trying to see inside her, know her thoughts and feelings, find her soul. And capture it. He looked capable of the task, and Elizabeth almost made the sign of the cross but caught herself in time.

Without saying a word, Geoffrey stood and began to remove the rest of his clothing, surprised to find that his hands were fumbling with the simple buckles. Had he not known better, he would have thought his hands shaking. He continued to look at his wife, willing her to show him some of the fear she kept so well hidden. He knew it was there, locked behind the rigid stance. Yet he was not displeased when she did not. She was his wife, his property. And he had chosen well.

Elizabeth watched him try again and again to undo the latchings. She wanted to suggest that he give some attention to his task instead of staring at her but did not think he would understand that she was teasing. Instead, she slowly walked over to him, a smile lifting the corners of her mouth, and unlatched the three buckles.

Geoffrey watched her, inhaled the sweet clean scent of her.

"I should change your bandage," Elizabeth said, taking a step back, "and apply more salve."

"It has been attended to," Geoffrey answered, his voice husky. He was removing the rest of his clothing as he talked. Elizabeth tried to remind herself that she had seen him naked before, but that was when he was unconscious and raging with fever. His desire now had changed his physique considerably, and the transformation terrified her.

"Do not be afraid." The softly spoken command confused Elizabeth. Geoffrey placed his hands on her shoulders. He did not draw her to him but seemed content to lazily study her eyes, her nose, and most especially, her mouth.

"I am *not* afraid," Elizabeth contradicted, her voice clear and strong. "I have seen you without your clothes on." At Geoffrey's puzzled look, Elizabeth explained, "When I took care of you, it was necessary—"

"I remember," Geoffrey said, smiling inside at the way his wife's face colored with her admission. His hands began to gently massage her shoulders, stroking the knots of tension he knew he caused. "And I have also seen you without your clothes," he said.

His words startled Elizabeth and she was only vaguely aware that his hands had moved to her waist, to the knot that held her robe secure.

"When was this?" she asked, frowning.

"At the waterfall," Geoffrey answered. "You were bathing."

"And you watched me?" she asked, both embarrassed and somewhat indignant.

"I had already decided to wed you, Elizabeth. It was my right."

Elizabeth pushed his hands away and took another step back. She felt the bed behind her knees and knew she could go no farther.

"When did you decide," she asked, her voice a whisper, "that you would wed me?"

Geoffrey did not answer her but stood there and waited.

He wasn't making this moment less awkward, and the uncertainty of what was to come was agonizing. I must get the deed done, Elizabeth decided. Slowly she untied the belt to her robe. Before her courage could desert her, she removed the covering and let it drop to the floor. "And do you still want me?" she asked, her voice husky and, she hoped, enticing.

From the surprised look on her husband's face, Elizabeth decided that maybe enticing was easy work. His stare was so hot that she felt the heat, like an embrace, wrapping around her. She felt like she was being caressed. "Aye, wife, I want you," Geoffrey answered, his voice hypnotic. "Come to me, Elizabeth. Let me make you mine."

It would not take much more to push his control over the edge, Elizabeth naïvely decided. Then, in her mind's view, he would most probably throw her upon the bed and take her. It would be painful, she knew, but quickly over.

An overwhelming need to have him hold her first, to stroke and comfort her, made Elizabeth's head spin. She took the first step and was but a breath away from touching him when she stopped and lifted her hands to her hair. She pulled the ribbon free, and the tight crown of curls quickly unwound, falling down below her shoulders. And still her husband did not move. He did not seem overly crazed with excitement or lust either, and Elizabeth realized that she would have to play a far better temptress than she first thought, if she was going to cause him to lose all control.

She raised herself on tiptoes and placed her hands around his neck, moving forward until her breasts were touching the warm mat of hair covering his chest. The contact of her skin against his was surprising; her eyes widened in reaction. Geoffrey smiled then, as if he was pleased with her aggression.

He picked her up and gently placed her on the bed. Before she could move over to allow him room, Geoffrey came down full upon her, all sinewy strength and power touching silky smoothness from neck to toes. His frame seemed to swallow hers. He braced himself on his elbows to share some of his weight, and watched his wife's reaction to his intimate touch.

Elizabeth closed her eyes against the rioting feelings tugging at her senses. His skin was like warm steel; his maleness, the very scent that was Geoffrey, intoxicated her. She felt herself tremble and bravely tried to move her legs apart, knowing, in her heart, that the power of him would most probably tear her apart. I will not scream, she repeated again and again to herself, squeezing her eyes tighter still as if that single action might help lessen the pain of what was to come. "I am ready," she whispered in a ragged voice.

Geoffrey felt her brace herself against him and smiled. "Well, I am not," he whispered in return, and widened his smile when her eyes flew open with obvious distress and confusion. His eyes were full of tenderness and golden chips that showed his amusement. 'Tis not funny, Elizabeth felt like screaming. Instead she whispered in a voice that sounded very much like a plea, "Be done with it, husband." She tried to move her legs farther apart but Geoffrey blocked their movement with his own. Elizabeth looked into his eyes and waited. She wet her lips with the tip of her tongue, an unconscious gesture, and forced her body to relax.

And then Geoffrey slowly leaned down and kissed her, a deep, draining kiss that played havoc with Elizabeth's emotions. Her mouth opened under his tender assault, and she accepted his invading tongue with a sigh, pulling him closer. For long moments he continued to taste the sweetness she offered. He demanded, and he gave, and she did not want the drugging kisses to end. When he pulled his mouth free and moved to her throat, Elizabeth tried to force him back. Geoffrey took hold of her hands and held them secure with one of his, yet she did not feel the prisoner, for his thumb gently stroked the palms of each, sending little shivers that reached the tip of her toes. She felt like she stood on the edge of a storm and that streamers of lightning were shooting through her limbs. Geoffrey moved to her side, keeping one muscular leg securely anchored on top of hers. And all the while his mouth continued to taste, moving with deliberate thoroughness to her straining breasts. The torment was becoming unbearable and she could not keep the moan from echoing throughout the room when his mouth finally touched her breast. His tongue teased her nipple erect, flicking and circling with excruciating thoroughness that pushed Elizabeth further and further into the eye of the storm. Finally he took the aroused bud into his mouth, sucking it until tremors of pleasure shook Elizabeth.

She was unaware that her hips had begun to move in an erotic motion, back and forth. Heat of such intense need was building deep within and Elizabeth could remain passive no longer. She pulled her hands free and began to touch and stroke her husband. His muscles felt like knotted iron, the hair on his chest crisp and warm. Elizabeth marveled at the difference in their bodies, wanting to know all of him. Her hand slid lower but suddenly stopped at Geoffrey's indrawn breath.

She hesitated another second and then continued her exploration. When she reached the heat of his desire, Geoffrey's hand stopped her. His voice was harsh when he said, "No, wife. I do not have that much patience."

"It is wrong?" Elizabeth asked, horrified that she might have done something terrible. She pulled her hand back with a forceful jerk but Geoffrey caught it.

"No," he answered, stroking her cheek with his other hand. *"Nothing* is wrong between husband and wife." He placed her hand around his neck and looked deep into her eyes.

"Then why—"

Geoffrey's mouth stopped her question. His movements then became more forceful, more concentrated. His knee forced her legs apart and his hand slid into the soft curls protecting the core of her need. Elizabeth tried to push his hand away but Geoffrey ignored her. With each touch, each stroke against the velvet softness, Elizabeth felt her control slip further away. She clung to him, kissing his neck, his shoulder, rubbing her tongue against his hot skin, tasting the oalty film, inhaling the musky scent that was her husband.

The sensations she was experiencing were too raw, too new. She became frightened by the power he was yielding and again tried to push his hand away.

Geoffrey held her still by locking his hands against her hips. "You are so beautiful, Elizabeth. I would know all of you." His voice was a growl against her skin. He lowered his head to her waist and began to circle her navel with his warm wet tongue. Elizabeth groaned and automatically sucked in her breath. She tried to find her voice to protest, to tell him no, what he was doing was wrong, he must not . . . but his mouth was moving lower, and lower still, and all the words, all the thoughts parted with her trembling legs, exploding into fragments of white-hot pleasure so intense that she thought she would die with the sweet agony when his tongue began to stroke her there. The intimate sparing of his tongue against the most intimate, the most guarded part of her very being, the rough caress of his unshaven face against the ultrasensitive skin on her inner thighs, drove Elizabeth to the brink. She begged him with her moans to cease this tender torture while her hands held him there, against her.

"You taste so good . . . so sweet," she heard him say in a ragged whisper.

He was slowly driving her crazy. "Please, Geoffrey," she moaned as she arched against him. "Please . . ." She didn't know what she asked for, only wanted the agony to end.

"Easy, my love," Geoffrey whispered, but Elizabeth was beyond understanding what he was saying. His voice was soothing, his touch wild; she arched her hips more forcefully and raked her nails through his hair.

Her frenzied movements made Geoffrey wild with need. His body trembled and Elizabeth could feel the raw hunger take over. Instead of frightening her, she became more excited, pulling him up toward her face.

Geoffrey's control snapped. He covered her mouth with his, hungrily taking her with his tongue. Elizabeth matched his passion, kissing him again and again with desperate urgency. She found herself becoming the aggressor, wanton with her need, and Geoffrey tried to let her have her way a while longer, until her nails, digging into his shoulder blades, became painfully insistent.

"I want you as I have never wanted another woman," he told her in a ragged whisper. He knelt between her legs, his hands holding her hips. Elizabeth reached up and locked her hands behind his neck, trying to pull him back down to her. She felt him hesitate at the threshold and instinctively arched at the same instant that he plunged. Pain ripped through the sensual haze and she cried out. She tried to pull away but Geoffrey held her tightly against him, and only when he was deep inside her did he stop, giving her time to adjust to him.

He soothed her sobs with honeyed words, promising again and again that the pain was over.

"We are done?" Elizabeth managed to ask, her voice trembling.

"Only just begun," her husband answered. He sounded as if he had just run a great distance, and Elizabeth knew the control he was maintaining for her sake. His consideration for her made her want to please him. He was breathing hard against her cheek. Elizabeth turned her head and found his lips, kissing him passionately.

Geoffrey returned her kiss, cupping her face with the palms of his hands. Then, slowly at first, he began to move. And the pain was forgotten.

Her legs slipped up around her husband's hips. She heard him tell her to hold him, and she tightened her arms around his neck. And then she heard nothing more. She could only feel. Escalating pleasure had taken control. She was racing with the wild beat of her heart into the center of the storm and her husband was guiding her, pushing her.

"Now, Elizabeth," came his ragged whisper, "come with me." And she was there with him; she felt the separation of body and soul, felt the explosion as bolts of lightning ignited and burst into flame inside her with the forceful thrust from her husband. It was terrifying, and it was magnificent.

She called his name and heard him say her own.

It was some time before Elizabeth returned to reality. The gentle descent back to the present was made warm and safe by her husband's body covering her own. She opened her eyes to find Geoffrey smiling down at her. "I never knew . . ." she whispered. The sense of wonder and amazement at what they had just shared was impossible for her to put into words, but Geoffrey knew from her expression. He tenderly pushed a wet strand of hair away from her temple and kissed her there. She felt the wetness on her cheeks and realized that she had been crying.

He smiled again—a pleased and arrogant smile, Elizabeth decided—and she wondered just who had enticed whom.

She closed her eyes and smiled. Geoffrey rolled onto his back with a loud, contented sigh and Elizabeth immediately felt the cold sweep of air chill her glistening skin. Sleep demanded her attention, sleep and the warmth of her husband's body. She pulled the covers up and over both of them and rolled into his arms, nudging him until he turned to his side and wrapped his arms around her.

She was just about to drift off to sleep when she heard her husband's voice. "You are mine." It was a quiet statement of fact.

"Yes, husband, I am yours," Elizabeth acknowledged into the darkness. "And you are mine." Her tone challenged him to deny it.

Elizabeth waited for what seemed to her impatient nature an eternity. Geoffrey did not answer. His deep, even breathing told her that he had fallen asleep. Her irritation turned to exasperation when he began to snore.

Elizabeth refused to give up. He had demanded her pledge, and now she would have his! She shoved him as hard as she could and fairly yelled into his ear, "And you are mine, Geoffrey."

Geoffrey still did not reply, but he did give her a quick squeeze and a hint of a smile. To Elizabeth, it was an acknowledgment of her claim. It was enough. The pledge was given.

Content, husband and wife slept.

Chapter Four

ELIZABETH WAS AWAKENED BY THE SOUNDS OF MEN AT work in the courtyard below. In that instant before memory cleared, she thought she heard her father's deep voice yelling instructions to his soldiers. She pictured him strutting around the training men with his hands locked behind his back. No doubt his pride and joy, little Thomas, was just two steps behind, his hands also locked behind his back, imitating his father's every move.

Roger's bellow jarred Elizabeth. She opened her eyes and took a deep breath. Nothing can ever be as it was, she realized, and the past could not be undone.

Yet in the morning light, the future did not look as bleak, as forbidding. Until yesterday Elizabeth had no thoughts or cares for the future; her only concern was

Belwain and planning her revenge. Now it appeared that she would have both: a future and justice.

Elizabeth rolled over onto the spot where her husband had slept. The linen was cold beneath her and she knew her husband had been gone for some time.

She was glad for the solitude. So much had happened so fast that Elizabeth hadn't had time to do more than react. Now perhaps she could sort out her feelings. She stretched and felt the soreness caused by her husband. Her husband! She was now married, and Baron Geoffrey was *hers*. In the light of day, the events lasting deep into the night before made Elizabeth blush. What a contradiction this man was turning out to be! He was such a gentle lover, sensitive to her wants and needs, wants and needs she hadn't been aware she possessed. Elizabeth would never have guessed that such sensitivity lurked behind her husband's shield of strength. Tender and gentle . . . her gentle warrior. Aye, it was a contradiction. What other surprises were in store for her? she wondered.

Perhaps it will be an easy arrangement, being married to Geoffrey. By the standards of nobility, it was an excellent match from her position. Her parents would have been pleased.

More significant, her brother's future was now secure. Elizabeth believed that Geoffrey would indeed protect little Thomas. "We are no longer alone, little brother," she whispered. Hope, newfound and fragile, eased Elizabeth's worry.

Kicking off the covers, she slipped out of bed and knelt down, automatically making the sign of the cross before her knees touched the cold stone floor. In the habit of rushing through her morning prayers, all recited aloud in Latin as her mother had taught her, Elizabeth finished the ritual in bare minutes. She added an additional Paternoster for the repose of her family's souls, and ended the prayer with the same vow she had made each and every morning since the massacre. She

GENTLE WARRIOR

promised to see Belwain punished, and would give her life, if need be. The fact that she was praying for vengeance, an act in great contradiction to all the Church taught, did not deter Elizabeth. In this instance she would follow her grandfather's beliefs. It would be an eye for an eye. The oldest law would prevail.

The ritual completed, Elizabeth hurried to dress. She wished to look her best when she joined her husband. Never having given her appearance more than a necessary glance in the past, Elizabeth was a little surprised at herself. Being pledged to Hugh for so many years removed the need for primping for the opposite sex, for Hugh had always been far more interested in the number of new horses purchased and by how many coins whenever he visited Montwright Manor. He never remarked upon her appearance. Father had called Hugh frugal, which by her father's tight standards was quite a compliment. Elizabeth had come to think of her future husband as . . . predictable. Predictable and boring.

Her wardrobe was sadly lacking in choices. Long ago, her father had dictated that too many clothes made one give undue attention to one's appearance, and such attention more than hinted of vanity. And vanity was a sin.

Elizabeth decided on a beige gown with blue borders. It fit rather snugly across her breasts and was high-necked, with long flowing sleeves. She tied a blue rope around her waist and slipped her dagger into its leather sheath and onto the loop of the belt.

It took her another ten minutes to find the mate to her beige leather shoes, lodged behind the drape at the head of the bed, and when both shoes were found and slipped into, she turned her attention to her hair. She brushed it until it crackled and then tied it with a ribbon at the base of her neck.

There, she was done. Pinching her cheeks to give them additional glow, and wishing she could find her

85

tiny mirror to check her appearance, she straightened her shoulders and went in search of her husband.

She found Sara in the great hall, and saw the disorder. The castle must be made as spotless as it used to be, Elizabeth decided, in honor of her mother. Elizabeth deterred her search for Geoffrey and organized the servants, placing Sara in charge to supervise the sweeping and scrubbing.

"Throw out these reeds," she said, referring to the soiled rushes. "And replace them with new. Perhaps we should sprinkle some rosemary about to get rid of the staleness that lingers. What say you, Sara?" Elizabeth asked the servant.

"Aye, my lady. And Dame Winslow will bring us fresh wildflowers just like she used to do for your mother. We will have the place as right as new in no time."

Elizabeth nodded. Her gaze turned to the shredded banner hanging by sheer willpower of its own on the far wall. "Sara, have someone remove the banner," she ordered in a whisper. "I do not need to look upon it to remember what was done here. I'll not forget."

The servant impulsively grabbed Elizabeth's hand and squeezed it. "I'll see to it, my lady. None of us will be forgetting."

"Thank you, Sara," Elizabeth replied. She gave the banner one last look and then turned to leave the room.

The servant used the hem of her sleeve to wipe the gathering tears from her eyes as she watched her new mistress. Oh, if only she had the power to lift some of the weight and heartache burdening one so young! "'Tis so unfair," she grumbled to herself.

"Pardon me, Sara?" Elizabeth turned from the doorway and smiled. "I did not hear you."

"I was just asking myself if you and the Baron will be leaving soon," Sara improvised. She knew it wasn't her place to ask such a question, but she had no wish to talk of the killings again.

Elizabeth was surprised by the question. She had not even considered the possibility of leaving Montwright. It was her home. Yet leaving, and soon, was more than likely. Geoffrey had many holdings superior to Montwright lands and he had his own domain. "In truth, I do not know," Elizabeth told the servant. "Where is my husband, Sara? Have you seen him about? I must discuss this issue with him."

"I have not seen him this morn," Sara replied. "Perhaps he is in the courtyard, or in the soldiers' keep below. I could send Hammond to check," she added, for while Elizabeth could freely roam about the estate, it was strictly forbidden for a woman to enter the soldiers' quarters located one flight below the great hall.

"I will find him," Elizabeth said.

It was easier said than done. Elizabeth strolled around the courtyard but did not interrupt any of the men to ask of her husband's whereabouts. She stopped and watched several knights struggle with a large vat of sand, wondering what their plan was. The redheaded squire, called Gerald, was glad to give her an explanation. "Vats of sand will be placed at intervals along the ledge circling the top of the wall, my lady."

"For what purpose?" Elizabeth asked, frowning.

"See the one that is in place already, over there?" Gerald asked, pointing to the west. His voice fairly screamed the question into Elizabeth's ear.

"Aye, I see it," Elizabeth answered.

"And see how it perches on those stones?"

Elizabeth nodded, inwardly smiling at the squire's loud enthusiasm.

"The fire to heat the sand will be contained within the circle of stones."

"But for what purpose?" Elizabeth asked.

"To heat the sand," Gerald restated, "until the sand is so hot it is almost liquid sun."

"And when it is almost liquid sun?" Elizabeth asked.

"Then it is propelled by the metal discs over the wall and will do much damage to anyone trying to gain entrance . . . if there be another attack."

From the look on the squire's face, he was a bit disappointed that she wasn't showing much enthusiasm. "I had not heard of such a thing, such a weapon," she said. "It is truly effective?"

"Aye, my lady. The sand can burn the body something fierce. Why, if it lands right, it can blind—"

"Enough," Elizabeth hastened to interrupt, for he was painting a gruesome picture for her and she had the feeling he was just beginning to warm to his topic. "You have convinced me," she added.

The squire nodded and grinned. Elizabeth thanked him for his time and explanation, and thought that he reminded her of her pet hawk the way he puffed up with her praise.

She continued to look for her husband but did not find him in any of the small huts clustered in semicircles around the courtyard. She was pleased to see that all the huts were being reinforced with fresh-smelling straw and wattle, long thin wooden rods that gave additional support. The huts were the real foundation of the castle, and though they were built on a small scale by others' standards, they housed trained craftsmen who were highly skilled and most efficient in seeing to all the needs of the manor. The leatherworker resided in one hut; the baker with two cooking pits and one clay oven in another; the falcons and their trainer with his variety of cages and perches in yet another. In another cluster the carpenter resided, next to the candlemaker. The last and, by her father's standards, the most important was the oversized hut set to one side of the castle, all alone, and nearest to the barn. It contained the toolsmith and his supply of iron and steel. The weapons were made there.

In the bailey beyond the walls, the slaughter of the animals was seen to and the making of honey-fermented ale watched over. There had been plans to add a winepress, but that reality had not come to pass before her father's death.

Elizabeth wondered when the craftsmen had last been paid. Was that now her responsibility? She considered. In the past her father had paid the freemen in coin and food. Deductions were taken from their pay for protection and a place to live, and for the number of candles used and recorded by Dame Winslow. The candlemaker's wife could not write, but her method of keeping track was just as efficient. She used small pebbles. Each time a candle was handed out, Dame Winslow placed a pebble in that freeman's cup. When payday arrived, the cups were placed before Elizabeth's father and it was he who would calculate amounts. Who would see to this duty now? she asked herself. Another question to put to her husband, Elizabeth realized. But Geoffrey was nowhere to be found. Elizabeth went into the barn and found her mare in one of the stalls and made a mental note to thank Joseph for bringing her animal back for her. She saw that Geoffrey's huge stallion was gone. A knot of fear grabbed at her when she realized he had ridden into the forest, for there was danger out there, and then the absurdity of her reaction made her laugh. Had she not survived with but her dogs on the outside for weeks? And was not her husband capable of taking care of himself?

The thought that perhaps Geoffrey was touring the outer bailey, seeing what damage was done to the peasants' huts residing at the base of the winding road below Montwright, made Elizabeth head in that direction. She reached the gates to the outside but found her way blocked by two guards.

"Please open the gates," Elizabeth asked.

"We cannot, my lady," one of the men said.

"You cannot?" Elizabeth frowned and looked from one soldier to another.

"Our orders," the second explained. "From the Hawk."

"What order did my husband issue?" Elizabeth asked. She kept her tone pleasant and neutral.

"That you remain inside the walls," one of the guards answered in a hesitant voice. He did not like the frown that came upon his mistress's face and hoped that she wouldn't press him. He had no wish to upset her, though he would obey the Hawk's orders no matter what.

"So I am . . ." Elizabeth started to comment that she was a prisoner in her own home and caught herself in time. She would discuss this with her husband. It would be unseemly for her to make any comment, good or bad, to his guards. They were doing their duty for their lord. "Then you must follow your orders," she said, smiling.

Turning, she started back, wondering why such an order had been given. Did it apply to everyone or just her? Was her husband worried that she might try to leave? Return to the forest? Elizabeth could understand his unsureness of her up until yesterday evening. But last night she had given him her pledge. She had admitted that she belonged to him. She was his wife. Didn't he realize that her pledge was the same as a sacred vow to her? Shaking her head, Elizabeth decided not. Trust. It must be earned. And in time, she was sure she would gain his trust, his confidence.

And how sure of him am I? Elizabeth asked herself. Do I trust him? She thought that she did, knew that he was an honest man. He had dealt well with her father, she remembered. And her father had called him a fair man. High praise from one who was as frugal with his praise as he was with his coins.

Elizabeth admitted that her knowledge of her husband was quite limited. She knew nothing of how he dealt with women, how he would treat a wife.

A blur in the sky caught her attention. Elizabeth

glanced up and saw her hawk circling, and without so much as a second thought for her audience, she extended her arm and waited. She was so intent on watching her pet descend that she didn't notice the hush that came over the group, or see the startled, disbelieving expressions.

The hawk landed on Elizabeth's arm and met her stare with a loud gargle of greeting. Elizabeth noticed that her pet was full-breasted from a recent meal and whispered words of praise for his hunting ability.

The hawk increased his gargling and then suddenly began to flap his wings with distress. "I hear him too," Elizabeth whispered, for the sound of approaching horse and rider was growing closer. Her voice soothed the hawk and the flapping ceased. Elizabeth looked up and saw her husband, sitting on his horse, watching her. Her dogs flanked the stallion's sides, their breathing labored from their run. Knowing how nervous the hawk became whenever the dogs were about, Elizabeth took mercy on her pet and commanded, "Go." The hawk immediately left its soft perch and took to the air.

Elizabeth lifted the hem of her gown and started toward her husband, intent on asking him to spare her a few minutes. She focused on the hard line of his mouth, remembering his lovemaking, and wondered what he was thinking. She could feel the soldiers staring at her and realized from their gaping expressions that she had made a spectacle of herself with her pet hawk. She felt embarrassed that she had drawn so much attention. Keeping her eyes firmly on her husband's features, she continued her slow, dignified pace.

The cheer caught her by surprise. Startled, she turned to see what the commotion was all about. They were still staring at her. And they were yelling. Had they all gone daft? She looked back to her husband for an answer, but his face was a mask as he watched her.

It was Roger who gave her an explanation. He came up behind her and placed his hand on her shoulder, saw her husband's scowl, and quickly removed it. "They honor the Hawk . . . your husband," he said, "and cheer the Hawk's mistress. You are worthy, my lady."

"But they do not realize. The hawk is my pet," she said, looking to the sky. "I have raised it from—"

"It does not matter," Roger interrupted, smiling. "The hawk has his freedom and still he returns. It is because you are worthy."

It is because they are all silly, superstitious men, Elizabeth thought. And of what am I worthy? Being wife to Baron Geoffrey, she supposed. Out of the corner of her eye she saw her husband dismount and start toward her. So he was finally going to acknowledge her, Elizabeth thought with irritation. She suppressed the feeling and turned from Roger to smile at her husband. He must have a considerable amount on his mind, and she needed to burden him further with matters concerning her brother and herself. There wasn't any place for irritation. Besides, Elizabeth admitted, it was a childish reaction. And she was no longer a child, but a woman, a wife.

She was the first to speak. "Good morning, my lord." She gave a small curtsy as she spoke and then started forward, about to lean up and place a chaste kiss on his cheek as her mother had done whenever she greeted Elizabeth's father, but his frown canceled her intent. It was as if he had read her aim and did not wish the contact.

Elizabeth felt her cheeks grow warm from the subtle rejection. She also felt awkward. She took her gaze from his, embarrassed, and noticed the dogs. Instinctively she patted her side with one hand, a silent command she used to bring her dogs to her sides. The dogs ignored her and continued to hover next to her husband, nudging him for attention. Their switch in allegiance was the last straw. She felt like screaming. And what would her husband think of that? she asked herself. To make such a scene in front of his knights . . .

why, she doubted that he would ever live it down. Not that she would ever cause such a scene; she had far too much pride and dignity. Still, it was an amusing fantasy, and it did help to lighten her humiliation.

Geoffrey was speaking to Roger. Elizabeth waited as patiently as possible for him to finish his orders and give his attention to her. She noticed that the longer her husband spoke, the harder Roger scowled. What was causing his change in mood? She moved forward again so that she could hear her husband's conversation.

"How many ride with him?" Roger asked her husband.

"No more than fifty, according to Riles," Geoffrey answered.

They both looked so intent, and then Geoffrey turned his gaze to her, and in that instant, she knew. Even as the realization hit, the sounds of thunder in the distance, thunder from the hooves of hard-ridden horses, came to her ears. Belwain was coming!

All color drained from her face. Instinctively her hand went to her waist, to the sheath containing her dagger. She pulled the weapon free, holding it so firmly that the handle felt like it was a part of her hand. The wildness in her eyes mirrored her thoughts. I must find Thomas. I have to hide him. Where is he?

Geoffrey watched the transformation in his wife with a heavy heart. He longed to take her into his arms and offer comfort, to soothe the wildness in her gaze, to heal the injury. But he could not. And she would have more torment before the day was out.

Elizabeth turned, her destination unknown, her only thought to find her brother. Find and protect. She seemed to forget the dagger in her hand and that her husband was even present.

Geoffrey placed his hands on her shoulders and gave her a gentle shake. "Do not do this," he said in a soft voice.

Elizabeth stepped back and broke the hold. She tried

to walk around her husband but he moved and blocked her path.

"I must find Thomas," she explained in a hard voice. "Do not stop me."

"Go to our bedroom and wait," Geoffrey ordered. Elizabeth began shaking her head but Geoffrey ignored her refusal. "I will send your brother to you."

"Now? You will send him to me now? Before Belwain sees him?" she asked. The desperation in her voice washed over Geoffrey like liquid sun, like the sand from the vats, scorching him with her grief and terror.

"Roger," Geoffrey said, never taking his gaze from his wife, "the boy is in the tanner's hut. Take him to Elizabeth's room."

"Aye, my lord," Roger replied. He turned and headed toward the hut at a fast pace.

Elizabeth stared after Roger until she felt Geoffrey's hand on hers. Looking down, she watched almost as a third person, as her husband pried her fingers loose, one by one, from the dagger. Only when he had possession of it did she react. "I must have my dagger. . . ."

"You will not need it. You will stay in our room." His order was hard. He pulled her to him, held her secure with one arm, and lifted her chin with his other. "I will have your word on this, Elizabeth."

"And you would believe my word?" Elizabeth asked. She was trembling and knew her husband could feel it.

"I have no reason to doubt you," Geoffrey countered, looking deep into her eyes.

"I do not know if I can give it," Elizabeth answered. "First you must tell me what you will do with Belwain."

Geoffrey was not angered by her order as he could well understand her hesitancy. "I need not explain my actions to you, wife. Remember that." He softened his tone and added, "Trust me."

"And if I do not?" Elizabeth asked.

"Then I will post guards and lock you in our room," Geoffrey answered. "Until I talk with your uncle, hear his side—"

"He has no side, only lies," Elizabeth said.

"Enough! I will have your word."

"Aye, husband. I will give you my word. I will wait until you have spoken with Belwain." She relaxed in his hold but her gaze continued to be defiant. "But hear me well, husband. I will trust you in this matter. And if you do not deal with Belwain, then I will."

"Elizabeth!" Geoffrey raised his voice and felt like shaking her into understanding his position. "Do not threaten me. Your uncle will have a fair hearing. It is William's law I follow. To hear all sides of an issue before rendering judgment. And *you* will abide by my decision."

Elizabeth could not answer him. She knew in her heart that she would be unable to accept any decision other than total guilt for her uncle. Yet she did not voice this admission because she believed that Geoffrey would find in her favor. He believed her, had said as much when they talked at the waterfall and she told him what had happened.

"I will go to my room now," Elizabeth said, hoping to end the conversation.

Geoffrey decided not to press her. The approaching soldiers would be at the gates in bare minutes. Still, he did not wish to end the discussion in such a harsh manner. "I have promised to protect you and your brother. Remember that."

"Aye, husband," Elizabeth said. She kept her expression neutral and started toward the doors. When she reached the top step, she turned back to her husband, found that he watched her, and nodded. "I trust you, my lord." To herself, she added, Do not fail me.

Chapter Five

As soon as Elizabeth was safely inside the castle, Geoffrey turned his attention to the waiting men. "Harold, double the number on the walls," he said to one knight. To another he announced, "Only Belwain will be allowed entrance this day." Roger caught his glance and he stopped his orders while he watched the older knight carry little Thomas, like a sack of grain under his arm, toward the castle doors. Without turning back to his soldiers he said, "Send Belwain to me when he arrives. I will be waiting inside."

Geoffrey started toward the great hall when he was intercepted by his loyal squire, Gerald. He ignored him until he reached the handle to the heavy doors. Roger, finished with his duty of delivering the boy to his sister, almost collided with the eager squire, who had lunged ahead of his lord to open the door.

"Stay outside with the men," Geoffrey told the squire.

"I would stay near you, my lord," the squire argued, a worried frown on his freckled face.

"For what purpose?" Geoffrey asked.

"I would protect your back," the squire stated.

"That is *my* duty," Roger all but barked at the lad.

The reprimand had the desired effect on the squire. He seemed to shrink considerably before his lord's eyes. "You two believe that my back needs protecting?" Geoffrey asked.

"From what is being said, my lord," the squire answered before Roger could open his mouth.

"Then Roger will see to the task," Geoffrey announced. "Today you will protect my walls," he added. "Your duty is to watch and listen. And learn."

The disappointment of not being in on the interview with his new mistress's uncle showed on the squire's face but Geoffrey was in no mood to appease. He had too much on his mind. "Follow my orders without question, Gerald. There are no second chances if you are to become a knight. Is that understood?"

The squire placed a hand over his heart and bowed his head. "Aye, my lord. I will follow your orders." He glanced up, saw the nod from his leader, and quickly turned to leave.

"He needs to learn to hold his tongue, that one does," Roger told Geoffrey as they walked side by side into the great hall.

"Aye, and to cover his emotions. But he is still young—only fifteen, if I remember. There is still time to mold him properly." Geoffrey smiled at Roger and then added, "He is quite skilled on the battlefield, always there to hand me whatever weapon I desire, seemingly fearless of injury to himself."

"But that is his duty," Roger protested.

"True, but he does it well, does he not?" he asked his companion.

"Aye, he does, and he is loyal," Roger admitted.

"Perhaps I will assign him to you, Roger," Geoffrey decided. "You could teach him much."

"No more than you, my lord," Roger stated. He sat down on the bench and leaned his elbows on the wooden table. The linen cloth had been removed and the scratches in the wood were visible. "Besides, the lad would drive me to the brink with his eagerness. I'm too old to waste what patience I have left."

Geoffrey chuckled. "You are not that much older than I, Roger. Do not give me such paltry excuses."

"If you order it, I will see to the boy's training," Roger conceded.

"I will not order it, my friend. The choice is yours. Think on it and advise me later."

"Think you Belwain responsible for the murders?" Roger asked, changing the subject.

Geoffrey's face lost its smile. He leaned against the table's edge and rubbed his chin in a thoughtful gesture. "I do not know," he said after a minute. "My wife believes him guilty."

"And so do the servants I spoke with," Roger added. "They all remember the argument the two brothers had and how Belwain made many loud threats."

"That is not enough to condemn a man," Geoffrey answered. "Foolish men say many things in anger that they later regret, and an angry tongue does not mean one is guilty. I will hear what he has to say before I decide."

"It would seem to me that he is the only one to gain from his brother's death."

"Not the only one," Geoffrey contradicted in a quiet voice. "There is another."

His scowl stopped Roger from asking more. He would have to be content to wait and see what happened. He had no doubt that his lord would get to the bottom of the riddle, find the one responsible. Having been in Geoffrey's service for so long, Roger had come to understand how his lord thought, how he reasoned. The Hawk was a careful man, given to logical inclinations, and did not make rash judgments. He believed in fairness and rarely based his decisions on hearsay. In truth, Roger acknowledged with pride, his lord was a fair and reasonable ruler.

Would his lord's reasoning be affected or influenced by his new wife? Roger considered. Geoffrey certainly was taken with her, Roger knew, though he tried mightily to act quite indifferent when she was about. But then Roger was also taken with her. No, whether it be his wife's family or not, Roger felt sure his lord would proceed as he always had in the past. He would not kill without just cause.

The door to the castle opened and both men turned. Two guards appeared at the entrance, a stranger between them. Belwain had arrived.

Geoffrey motioned to the guards and they quickly departed. Belwain, small in stature and elegantly dressed in peacock green and yellow, but with a wide girth, hesitated at the entrance to the hall. "I am Belwain Montwright," he finally announced in a nasal whine. He dabbed at his nose with a lacy white handkerchief while he waited for a response.

Geoffrey stared at the man before him for a full minute before answering. "I am your baron," he said in a forceful voice. "You may enter."

The lord leaned against the wooden table again and watched his wife's uncle as he hurried into the room. The man was walking as though he was being hindered by an imaginary rope tied to both ankles. Geoffrey found Belwain's voice as offensive as his motions. It was high-pitched with a scratch attached to it.

There was absolutely no resemblance to Thomas Montwright, Geoffrey thought. He remembered Thomas as a tall, vibrant man. The younger brother, now kneeling before him, appeared to be an old woman in men's garb.

"I pledge you my fealty, my lord," Belwain said, one hand over his heart.

"Do not give me your pledge, for I will not accept it until I know what is in your mind. Stand!" The harshly ordered words had the appropriate effect. Belwain was suitably intimidated, Geoffrey decided. His eyes, glazed with terror, told Geoffrey that.

When Belwain was standing before him, Geoffrey said, "Many blame you for what happened here. You will now tell me what you know of this matter."

The uncle took several gulping breaths before answering. "I knew nothing of the attack, my lord. I heard of it only after the fact. As God is my witness, I had nothing to do with this. Nothing. Thomas was my brother. I *loved* him!"

"You have a strange way of mourning your brother," Geoffrey said. At Belwain's confused expression, Geoffrey continued, "It is proper to wear black, and you do not."

"I wore the best that I owned, to show honor for my dead brother," Belwain answered. "He liked colorful tunics," Belwain added, stroking the sleeve of one arm as he spoke.

Disgust welled up in Geoffrey's throat like burning bile. This was no man standing before him but a weakling. The lord kept his expression neutral, but found it a difficult task. To gain additional control, he turned and walked over to the hearth.

Turning back to Belwain, he said, "The last time you saw your brother there was an argument?" Geoffrey's voice was almost pleasant now, as if he was greeting an old friend.

Belwain didn't immediately answer. His eyes, like a cornered rat, darted from his lord to the knight sitting at the table, and then back to Geoffrey again. He seemed to be considering his options. "It is true, my lord," he answered. "And I shall carry the burden of saying harsh words to my brother for the rest of my days. We parted last in anger, of that I am guilty."

"What was the argument about?" Geoffrey inquired, totally unmoved by Belwain's tear-filled admission. Compassion was the last thing in Geoffrey's mind.

Belwain watched the lord, saw that he seemed unmoved by his impassioned speech, and continued in a less dramatic voice. "My brother promised me additional land for planting. Yet each year he would further the date for handing over the land, always with some insignificant reason. My brother was a good man but not given to generosity. And the last time I saw him, I was sure I would get the land. I was sure! He had used up his reasons," Belwain added, "but again he dangled the carrot before me and then at the last minute withdrew it."

Belwain's face had turned a blotched red as he spoke, and his voice lost some of the whine. "I had reached my limit and was tired of his games," he said. "I told him as much and we began to yell at one another. He threatened me then, my lord. Yes, he did! He threatened his only brother. I had to leave. Thomas had a terrible temper and many enemies, you know," he added. "Many enemies."

"And you believe one of his 'many enemies' killed him and his family?"

"Yes, I do." Belwain nodded vigorously. "I tell you again, I had nothing to do with it. And I have proof that I was nowhere about. There are those who will tell you if you will allow me to bring them inside."

"I have no doubt that you have friends who will state you were with them while your brother and his family were slaughtered. No doubt at all," Geoffrey said. His voice was mild, but his eyes were chilling.

"Yes," Belwain said, standing taller. "I am not guilty and I can prove I am not."

"I have not said you are guilty," Geoffrey replied.

He tried to keep his voice neutral, for he had no wish to let Belwain know what he was feeling inside. Belwain, he hoped, would be lulled into a false sense of security, and perhaps become more easily trapped. "I have only just begun to look into this matter, you understand."

"Aye, my lord. But I am sure that in the end I will be a freeman. Perhaps the new lord of Montwright lands, eh?" Belwain stopped himself just in time. He almost rubbed his hands with delight. It was easier than he had anticipated. The overlord, though quite intimidating in appearance, was most simple in his reasoning, Belwain hastily judged.

"Thomas's son is heir to Montwright," Geoffrey answered.

"Yes, that is most true, my lord," Belwain hurried to correct himself. "But as only uncle, I assumed that, once proven innocent of this terrible deed, that I . . . that is, that you would place the boy under my guardianship. It is the law," he added with emphasis.

"The boy's sister does not trust you, Belwain. She believes you guilty." Geoffrey watched Belwain's reaction to his statement and felt a rage begin to boil inside. Belwain was sneering.

"She knows nothing! And she will change her tune when I am in charge," he scoffed. "Too much freedom that one has had." There was genuine dislike in his voice, and he almost lost his life in that moment it took for Geoffrey to gain control.

He is a stupid man, Geoffrey thought. Stupid and weak. A dangerous combination.

"You speak of my wife, Belwain."

His statement had the desired effect. Belwain lost all color and almost collapsed to his knees. "Your wife! I beg your forgiveness, my lord. I did not mean, that is—"

"Enough!" Geoffrey barked. "Return to your men and wait until I send for you again."

"I am not to stay here?" Belwain asked, the whine back in his voice.

"Leave me," Geoffrey bellowed. "And be content that you still have your life, Belwain. I have not ruled out your guilt in this matter."

Belwain opened his mouth to protest, thought better of it, and snapped it shut. He turned and hurried from the room.

"God! Can he be brother to Thomas?" Roger said when the doors were closed. He all but shuddered with revulsion.

"He is afraid and yet brazen at the same time," Geoffrey answered.

"What think you, Hawk? Is he the one? Did he do it, plan it?"

"What do you think, Roger?" Geoffrey asked.

"Guilty," Roger stated.

"Based on?"

"Based on . . . disgust," Roger admitted after a time. "Nothing more. I would like for him to be guilty."

"That is not enough."

"Then you do not think him guilty, my lord?"

"I did not say that. It is too soon to tell. Belwain is a stupid man. He thought of lying about the argument with his brother but decided against it. I could read the indecision in his eyes. And he is weak, Roger. I think too weak to plan such a bold thing. He appears to be a follower, not a leader."

"Aye, I had not thought of it that way," Roger admitted.

"I do not think he is completely innocent, but he did not do the planning. Of that I'm sure. No," Geoffrey said, shaking his head, "someone else is behind the deed."

"What will you do now?"

"Draw the guilty out," Geoffrey stated. "And I will use Belwain as my tool."

"I do not understand."

"I must think over my plan," Geoffrey said. "Perhaps I will take Belwain into my confidence. Make false promises to him. Suggest that the boy will be given into his care. Then we will see."

"What is your reasoning, my lord?"

"Whoever planned this wanted *my* lands. They attacked Montwright and they therefore attacked me. You operate on the premise that it was only Montwright the guilty was after. I do not limit my thoughts in just one direction, Roger. I must look at all the possibilities."

"Sometimes the most simple conclusion is also the most correct," Roger answered.

"Know this, Roger. Nothing is ever as it appears. You fool only yourself if you believe what is easiest to believe."

"A good lesson, my lord," Roger said.

"One I learned early in life, Roger," Geoffrey admitted. "Come," he suddenly said, "there is much to do today. Set up the table outside and I will see to the disputes among the freemen and pay them for their work."

"I will see to it," Roger said, hurrying to stand. He knocked over the bench in his haste but didn't bother to right it. His lord was already at the doorway, waiting. "Roger, I again place the boy Thomas in your care. I will go up and talk with my wife and send the lad to you. Wait here."

Roger nodded his ascent, silently wondering what his lord would say to his wife. He knew that Lady Elizabeth expected immediate death for her uncle. How would she react to her husband's decision to wait for justice? The Hawk was about to ask a great deal from a mere woman, Roger thought. But then, from his contact with the Baroness, she was far more than a mere woman.

"My lord?" Roger suddenly asked.

Geoffrey turned from the stairway, one raised eyebrow his question.

"What of Lady Elizabeth? Would you wish me to look after her today?"

"No, that is my duty," Geoffrey answered. "As unseemly as it is for a woman to stay at my side, it will be done today. I would know where she is every minute that Belwain and his men are about."

"You would protect her from Belwain," Roger said, nodding.

"And Belwain from her," Geoffrey said, with a hint of a smile. "She would try to kill him, you know. And there is a thought in my mind that she just might be capable of the deed."

Roger nodded again and tried not to smile.

It took Elizabeth some time to get control of herself. She alternated between grabbing the squirming little boy and holding him against her to trying to explain to him why she was in such a state.

Little Thomas remembered nothing. Not even how to play checkers, a game the two of them had played countless times in the past. It was just as well, Elizabeth decided, for her mind was too preoccupied for games.

When Geoffrey opened the door to their room, he found Elizabeth standing by the window, clutching her brother's hand. The little boy looked bewildered.

"Go to Roger, lad. He waits for you at the foot of the steps." Geoffrey's order lightened the expression on Thomas's face. He pulled free of Elizabeth's hold and ran for the door. It was Geoffrey's hand that stayed him. "Listen to me, Thomas. You do not leave Roger's side. Do you understand me?" His voice was firm.

The boy felt the seriousness of the order. "I will not leave his side," he said, frowning.

Geoffrey nodded and the boy hurried out the door. Slowly, while he gathered his thoughts and considered how much to tell his wife, Geoffrey shut the door. He turned to deal with Elizabeth and was surprised to find her bare inches from him. Her face and posture appeared relaxed, but her eyes told the truth. There was torment etched there, torment and pain.

Unused to comforting, Geoffrey awkwardly placed his hands on her shoulders. In a soft voice, he said, "I will have your word, Elizabeth, that you will hear what I am going to say. Hear and abide by my decision."

Elizabeth frowned. He was asking the impossible. "I cannot give you my word, my lord. I cannot! Do not ask this of me." She tried to control the anguish in her voice but found it impossible.

"Will you listen to me, then?" Geoffrey asked.

"You have found Belwain innocent." Geoffrey could feel Elizabeth's shoulders sag beneath his hands.

"I have not said that," Geoffrey answered.

"Then he is guilty in your eyes?"

"I have not said that either," Geoffrey snapped, growing irritated.

"But—"

"Stop this! I have asked you to listen to me," Geoffrey stated again. "And I do not want your interruptions until I am done. Will you give me that much, wife?"

Elizabeth could tell her husband was irritated with her and knew that he was finding it difficult to keep his patience. She was puzzled also by his manner. "I will not interrupt." The promise was made, and she would keep it.

"To begin," Geoffrey said, lightening his tone, "I do not have to tell you anything. You understand this?"

Elizabeth nodded, wishing him to go on. "You are my wife. I need tell you nothing. In future I most likely will not. It is not your place to know what I am thinking, what I am doing. Do you also understand this?"

In truth, Elizabeth did not. Her father had shared all his joys and worries with her mother. And that was as it should be. Why didn't her husband understand this? Were his parents so very different from her own? she wondered. She made a mental note to question him on this later. For now, she would agree. She nodded again and folded her hands.

Geoffrey let go of her shoulders and turned from her. He walked over to the two chairs, adjusted his sword, and sat. Propping his feet up on the edge of the bed, he looked over at his wife.

"Your uncle is nothing like your father," he began. "I find it hard to believe that they are indeed brothers." He stopped then, looking past Elizabeth.

"It is too simple, this solution," he said, more to himself than his puzzled wife. Elizabeth longed to interrupt, to ask him what he meant, but she kept her silence.

"I do not think Belwain is the one behind the massacre." There it was said. Geoffrey watched his wife react.

Elizabeth met his stare and waited. She sensed he was testing her somehow, but didn't understand his reasons. Didn't he know the agony she was going through?

Her composure pleased the warrior. "Answer me this, Elizabeth. Do you consider your uncle to be intelligent? Tell me what you know of his character."

Elizabeth sensed her answer would be important to her husband, though she did not know why. "I believe him to be self-centered and interested only in his pleasures."

"Your reasons?" Geoffrey asked.

"Whenever he came to visit, he never took time with my sisters or my brother, or me for that matter. The family didn't interest him. And as soon as my father came home, Belwain would begin with his wants, his needs. He was always asking for more, but never giving." Elizabeth walked over to the bed and sat down before she continued. "There was no love inside of Belwain, that is why I think him more than capable of doing the killings. He was totally lacking in loyalty too. I cannot give you an example of this but I know it in my heart. And to me, there is nothing more unholy than lack of loyalty. As to intelligence, no, I do not think Belwain uses his mind overly. Otherwise he would have learned long ago how to deal with my father. He would have used a different approach to get what he wanted."

"He is weak. Don't you agree?" Geoffrey asked.

"Yes, he is weak," Elizabeth agreed. "But full of evil too."

"I do not disagree or agree with you," Geoffrey said. "His manners do not please me," he admitted.

"My mother told my father that Belwain suffers from the king's complaint," she whispered. "I heard her."

"The king's complaint?" Geoffrey had never heard the expression.

Elizabeth's cheeks colored but she answered her husband's question. "To prefer men to women . . ."

Geoffrey acted like a bolt of lightning had been shot through his body. He came out of the chair in one giant bound. "William would cut out your tongue if he heard your blasphemy," he bellowed.

"Then it is not true?" Elizabeth asked, outwardly oblivious to her husband's anger.

"No, it is not true," Geoffrey barked. "Never utter those words again, wife. It is paramount to treason."

"Yes, husband," Elizabeth agreed. "I am glad it is not true."

"William is married," Geoffrey snapped. "And it is not proper to discuss—"

"But you can be married, can you not, and still prefer the company of other men?"

"Stop this, I say!" God, but she was exasperating! To speak of such a subject as though she was discussing family trivia both infuriated and amused him. She had much to learn.

"Yes, my lord." Elizabeth's voice sounded repentant, but Geoffrey wondered how sincere she really was. "I am sorry, husband. I have led you away from our topic."

"Uhmmm," Geoffrey grumbled deep in his throat. He sat back down and shook his head, in an action meant to clear his thoughts.

"I will tell you what I have thus far concluded, wife. Your uncle is a weak man. Weak and stupid."

"May I question you, husband?" Elizabeth asked, her tone mild.

"You may," Geoffrey stated.

"Will you kill him or must I?" Her softly spoken question jarred Geoffrey.

"For now, neither will. We have need for Belwain, Elizabeth. Now you will ask no more questions until I am done," he hurried to add.

Elizabeth nodded, frowning.

"I do not think he is the one behind the plan, though I feel he somehow participated. He is a follower, and too stupid to plan such a feat."

Elizabeth knew her husband spoke the truth. It was a difficult admission for her to make. Yet even from the beginning, while she concentrated all her hate on Belwain, there was a nagging uncertainty that he was not alone in the deed. Guilty, yes! But others involved? It was a possibility she had refused to consider until now.

"Belwain will be the bait, wife. I believe he will lead us to the one in hiding. I have a plan," he added, "and you will give me your word that you will cooperate."

"But who else stands to gain, husband?" Elizabeth asked, unable to keep her silence a moment longer.

"There is another," Geoffrey said. "Though I will not speak his name to you yet. I could be wrong. You will have to trust me in this, Elizabeth."

Elizabeth didn't respond but continued to look at her husband and wait.

"I now ask a most difficult thing from you," he said. "It will require courage."

"And what is that?" Elizabeth asked.

"You saw what happened, and you remember what those who didn't wear masks looked like," Geoffrey said. "Tonight the troops of Belwain will be allowed inside."

Elizabeth's eyes widened but Geoffrey continued on. "Do not worry, we far outnumber his soldiers. There will be no danger. I will have you beside me at dinner, and you will have a chance to see if any of his men were part of the attack."

"Belwain will sit with us?" Elizabeth asked.

"He will sit with us," Geoffrey acknowledged. "I want him to think he is innocent in my eyes, Elizabeth. If he feels secure, he will slip."

"You ask a great deal," Elizabeth whispered. "I do not know if—"

"Can you be content with Belwain's death and live with the thought that there is another just as guilty?" Geoffrey argued.

Elizabeth took a long time to answer. "No, I could not be content. I would know all of the truth."

"Can you do what I ask?"

"Aye," Elizabeth answered, wondering inside if she really could or not. She honestly didn't know. "But could we not ride to their camp outside the walls instead of allowing them entrance?"

"No," Geoffrey announced. "It is safer for you here."

Elizabeth squared her shoulders and stood. "There is much to be done before tonight. I will instruct the cook," she said. Her hands were trembling. There was so much to think over. Elizabeth felt overwhelmed with confusion.

"Come here, Elizabeth," Geoffrey ordered, his tone gentle.

Elizabeth nodded and slowly walked over to stand at her husband's side. Before she could so much as blink, Geoffrey pulled her onto his lap and kissed her soundly on the lips. His breath was warm and mint-tasting. Elizabeth began to respond when Geoffrey ended the kiss. "I did not hurt you last night?" he asked in a quiet voice, smiling at the becoming blush his question spurred.

"Not overly much," Elizabeth answered, turning her gaze to his chin. She felt him chuckle and glanced back up to look into his eyes. There was tenderness there now. "I did not hurt you, my lord?" she asked innocently.

"Not overly," Geoffrey answered when the surprise of her question receded. He found he liked it when she teased him, liked to see the hint of a sparkle come into her eyes. God, but if he could end her torment over her family's deaths as soon as possible, he would. He wished to see only joy in her expression, hear her laughter.

He lifted her off his lap and stood up. "This is not the time for loving, wife. It is daylight," he explained.

"We may only show affection during the night?" Elizabeth asked. She had meant her question as another jest, but her husband was vigorously nodding his head in agreement. "You are serious?" she asked, all but laughing.

"Of course I am serious! Do not mock me, Elizabeth," Geoffrey said in a firm voice. "It is unseemly to show affection in front of my men. You would do well to learn that," he admonished. "Know your place, woman!" His tone did not sound angry to Elizabeth but reminded her of an elder instructing a younger one in the ways of the court. She found herself furious over his attitude.

"And where is my place, husband?" Elizabeth let her anger show. She placed her hands on her hips while she waited for an answer.

Geoffrey walked to the door and opened it before turning back to his wife.

"I asked you, where is my place, husband? Where do I stand?"

Geoffrey found himself confused by the obvious anger in his wife's voice. She acted much like his stallion when a burr was caught under his saddle.

"Where do you stand?" he repeated, frowning. "What is your meaning?"

"Aye, where do I stand?" Elizabeth all but shouted. "Do I stand beside you or behind you, husband? Answer me that."

"Why, behind me, of course. It is the way of things." From his wife's expression, Geoffrey gauged his answer had not pleased her. He slammed the door before she could reply, shaking his head. Aye, she had much to learn, this new wife of his. Much indeed!

You are wrong, husband mine, Elizabeth thought as soon as the door slammed. I'll not be hovering behind you, she vowed. Like my mother, I will stand beside you in this marriage. Oh, he had much to learn, this new husband of hers. Much indeed!

Chapter Six

GUYTON, THE BAILIFF IN CHARGE OF THE ENTIRE MANOR, had been slain during the attack, as had Angus, the reeve, a first tenant in charge of cultivation of the lord's land. And there were others missing, unaccounted for, Elizabeth knew. New appointments had to be made, and soon, for Elizabeth could all but feel the chaos and confusion in the atmosphere.

Although her husband was in charge of all that transpired, Elizabeth knew it was also her responsibility to help in any way she could. Her mother had ruled with her father, at his side, and often remarked that it was her lot in life to ease the burden of leadership. Elizabeth could do no less.

The first thing she would do was what she had promised her husband. She searched out and found

Sara and placed her in charge of the arrangements for dinner. She felt confident that she could trust Sara to see that her orders were carried out, and when the servant had repeated each instruction back to her mistress, Elizabeth was content that all would go as planned.

"The fare will be meager by Belwain's standards, Sara. There would be sufficient quantities of shoulder of wild boar with pheasant pasties and pigeon pie, but no delicacies such as roasted peacocks or swans, nor poultry either. "Make sure that there is more than enough sweetmeats for dessert, and have the servants include cloves and ginger after that."

"We'll need plenty of ale, my lady, for the sweet-meats and the spices will make the men ravenously thirsty."

"That is the plan, Sara. Tell the servants that no cup is to be left unfilled. Enough ale will muddle their minds and loosen their tongues."

Sara nodded vigorously. "I see your plan, mistress, and I tell you I am greatly relieved. At first I could not understand how that . . . man could be allowed to sit at your father's table. Why, I thought it was sacrilege you encouraged," she added in a whisper.

"There is reason." Elizabeth found herself comforting the old woman. "You must continue to have faith in me, Sara. Do not doubt my motives. Trust me." Familiar words, Elizabeth thought. Easily asked but quite difficult to give.

Elizabeth patted the woman on the arm and left the room. Her destination was the courtyard, where her husband was holding court. The villeins, those who worked for her father but had some rights of their own to the land, and the cotters, those who usually had no rights to any property but served the lord faithfully, had all been informed that Geoffrey would hear their disputes and offer decisions. Elizabeth was anxious to observe her husband, to see how he questioned, to have some insight on how he reached his decisions.

Geoffrey's back was to Elizabeth when she started down the steps. A long wooden table had been placed a little distance in front of the steps, and her husband sat in the same high-back chair that her father had used. Roger stood behind Geoffrey, his hand resting almost absentmindedly on the hilt of his sword at his side. There was a crowd gathered, all men, split into two sides in front of the table, with a cleared space in the middle. A lone man, Elizabeth recognized him as one of the leatherworkers, stood in the center, his head bowed.

The squire gestured to Elizabeth and pointed to a stool next to him. Elizabeth walked over to where the lad stood. "You are to sit here," the squire informed Elizabeth.

"My husband's orders?" Elizabeth asked in a whisper so as not to interrupt the proceedings.

The squire nodded, pleased that his mistress understood.

Elizabeth turned and stared at the back of her husband's head, willing him to look over his shoulder at her. So I also sit behind you, husband? Stand behind you, sit behind you, is that your way of thinking? she asked herself. Well, *I* think not, Baron Geoffrey. You have much to learn, husband mine, and the lessons will begin now.

Elizabeth smiled, more to herself than the grinning squire, and then lifted the wooden stool. The squire could do no more than gape as his mistress carried the stool to the table. Roger was watching her, Elizabeth realized, and she glanced up to see his expression. He gave her a small shake of his head, hoping she would understand that what she was about was not acceptable, but Elizabeth only increased her smile, nodding that she understood well enough. Roger's expression turned from a frown to a bland, almost bored expression it must have taken years to perfect, but his new mistress wasn't the least bit fooled. She could see the laughter in his eyes.

Oh, but she hoped Geoffrey wouldn't make a scene! Why, she didn't even know if he was inclined to beat his wife. And though she had heard that he had a fierce temper, she had yet to see it.

Well, it was too late for second thoughts now. She took a calming breath and placed the stool next to her husband. Smoothing her gown, she sat down and folded her hands demurely in her lap. Though she wished more than anything to chance a glimpse at her husband's expression, she did not. With total concentration she kept her gaze straight ahead and waited.

Geoffrey was in the middle of a sentence when his wife appeared at his side. He lost his train of thought as he watched her out of the corner of his eye take her place next to him. Her audacity stunned him into temporary speechlessness.

Elizabeth felt his anger blow over her like a hot wind and she braced herself for the explosion. Had she misjudged him so completely? she asked herself. She thought he would never make a scene in front of his men. Never mind, she told herself, what will be cannot be stopped. But if he does rant and rave, and if I am cast out and back inside, I will return to his side, again and again, until he must tie me in chains to keep me behind him.

Geoffrey refused to acknowledge his wife sitting beside him. He had no wish to cause a commotion, to give those watching the impression that his wife did not fear him, that she was disobedient. Later, he thought with a scowl, later he would see to her punishment.

Elizabeth felt the threat of immediate danger pass. The wind cooled the goosebumps on her skin. Odd, she thought, but she hadn't realized how nervous she had become. Why, she was almost frightened! Almost, she reminded herself.

It was hard not to smile, but Elizabeth did her best. It was not so very difficult training a new husband, not too difficult at all.

You have much to learn, Elizabeth, Geoffrey thought with irritation. He judged it would not be a difficult task, once his new wife understood his rules, his way of thinking. Not too difficult at all.

Geoffrey cleared his throat and tried to remember what he had been saying when the interruption occurred. "Where was I?" he muttered over his shoulder to Roger. The vassal bent down and said a few words into his lord's ear but stopped when Geoffrey nodded.

"The charge against you is grave indeed. Did you understand that it is forbidden to hunt in your lord's forest?"

"I understood the rules, Baron," the leatherworker replied. "I have been a loyal freeman to Thomas Montwright for many years."

Several men in the crowd nodded their agreement. Elizabeth knew the man standing before her husband and wondered what charge had been brought against him. He was called Mendel, she recalled, and he possessed a gentle nature. She could not imagine Mendel guilty of any crime, grave or small. Elizabeth fought the urge to ask her husband who had brought what charges against the man, but decided to wait. Being throttled in front of a crowd did not appeal to her.

"The charge is hunting within the lord's forest," Geoffrey restated, "and while it is my understanding that Lord Thomas, rest his soul, allowed the hunting of some animals, the deer was off limits to all but himself. Yet you were seen dragging the dead carcass."

"I do not deny it," Mendel answered. "I did kill the animal, but there was good reason."

117

Elizabeth almost nodded her encouragement but caught herself in time. It was extremely difficult to stay an impartial witness to the proceedings, and she only then realized the weight her husband carried. Justice was a heavy burden.

"State your reason," Geoffrey ordered.

"The deer was injured and in pain," Mendel replied. "The front right leg was broken. I do not know how it happened, but when I came upon it, I could see the agony. I made a clean kill to stop the pain and was bringing the carcass when I was intercepted by your soldiers. That is the truth as I know it," Mendel said.

"Is there one here who can give testimony to this man's good faith?"

"Aye, my lord," called out a voice. The crowd parted, and Maynard, the stable master, walked to the center.

"State your case," Geoffrey said.

"I have known Mendel many years, my lord, and have always found him to be honest and truthful."

"Roger? Did you check the animal as I instructed?" Geoffrey asked.

"Aye, Baron. The bone was broken," he said.

"Tell me this, Mendel. Why were you in the forest? To hunt rabbits, perchance?" he asked, his tone mild.

"Nay, my lord. I have paid a pence and one-half for the privilege of keeping two pigs within the area, and I was but checking on them."

"Uhmmm," Geoffrey grumbled. He stared at the man before him for a long minute while the crowd shuffled from foot to foot.

"I find you innocent, Mendel."

The crowd was pleased. A cheer rolled through the crowd and Elizabeth smiled her pleasure.

Elizabeth found herself content to sit beside her husband for the next two hours and listen as one after another came before their lord to state their grievances.

By the time court was done, Elizabeth had a better understanding of how her husband's mind worked. His questions were always direct and to the point; yet when two men told opposite stories, Geoffrey was quick to find the truth. Seeing him as judge made her feel more confident that he would be able to find and punish *all* those responsible for her family's deaths.

The crowd began to disperse, and Elizabeth thought it wise to excuse herself before her husband turned his attention to her. She had no wish to push him too far with this first lesson in just where her place was.

She was, unfortunately, not quite quick enough. Her husband's hand rested on her arm like the weight of three trebuchets. "Because Belwain and his men are about, I have today allowed your bold behavior." He squeezed her arm and added, "I have made an exception, wife. Do you understand?"

"I hear you, my lord, though I do not know why you are so displeased. My mother always sat beside my father. It is the way of things," she said, looking at him with innocence.

"It is *not* the way of things," her husband answered. His voice had risen in volume and the scar on his cheek grew a starker white against his tanned skin, a dead giveaway, Elizabeth had learned quickly, that he was indeed angry. He applied more pressure on her arm, willing her to lose her calm expression.

"It is not?" Elizabeth asked with as much innocent surprise as she could muster. She placed her hand gently on top of his. "I have only my parents' example to follow, my lord."

Geoffrey released the hold on her arm and pulled his hand free. "It is *not* proper to touch as this in public, wife." He sighed when she did not agree with him, knew she did not from the look on her face. Why, she seemed fairly amazed with his statement. "This is not the time for a discussion, Elizabeth," he decided aloud.

"Tonight I will take the time to instruct you in your duties and your place."

"I look forward to the lesson," Elizabeth replied, trying hard to keep the irritation out of her voice. And tonight I will instruct you, my lord, she thought.

Geoffrey considered his wife, glimpsed her anger, and was surprised by it. Didn't she realize how patient he was being with her? He guessed she did not, and felt great frustration. She had been through a great deal and he knew her emotions were strained to the limit of her endurance. For that reason he would continue to be patient.

Where had he received his ideas? Elizabeth asked herself. Not to touch in public? To show no affection except at night, in the privacy of their bedroom? Ridiculous, she scoffed to herself. There was nothing wrong with husband greeting wife with a kiss, or wife placing a chaste kiss upon her husband's cheek when first they met during the day. Who had raised him? A pack of wolves perhaps? She knew his parents were now dead, Roger had told her that, but what were they like with each other when her husband was a little boy? Did they never show any affection for each other? Perhaps there was no love between them, she decided. But then, there is no love between Geoffrey and myself, yet. It was too soon for love, wasn't it? And wasn't the touching, the showing of consideration for each other, a necessary beginning for true and lasting love to grow? Oh, what a confusion! Elizabeth's head felt like it was spinning with all the rules her husband kept hinting at. Am I the one so amiss in my thinking? she asked herself. Is it wrong to wish for laughter and shared secrets, an occasional embrace to show a specialness for one's spouse? A longing for these very things brought loneliness and sadness. Without another word to her husband, Elizabeth stood up and took her leave, walking slowly back into the hall. Sara immediately intercepted her, and Elizabeth thankfully put her confusing thoughts concerning her husband and his behavior aside. There was work to be done.

An hour later, Elizabeth felt very much like a limp rag. It appeared to her that no order could be undertaken until Elizabeth herself said the words, sometimes again and again until the servants understood just what she wanted. Most of the servants were untrained in the tasks she requested, and Elizabeth kept her patience. They were doing the best that they could.

"If Gerty breaks another cup we will not have enough for the drinks, Sara," Elizabeth muttered when she heard a third crash.

Sara might have answered but Elizabeth couldn't hear her over the wail coming from outside. She recognized the voice and knew little Thomas was terribly upset about something. Just as she was about to see what the problem was, the doors burst open and the little boy came flying into the great room. Roger was right on his heels, trying to grab the wolfhounds, who were busy nudging the youngster in his shoulder blades, propelling him along.

"They think you are playing, Thomas." Elizabeth found she had to yell over his screams to be heard. She grabbed Thor, the bigger of the two animals, by the fur on the nape of his neck, while she watched Roger lunge for and miss the other, falling to the floor with a loud clatter. She almost fell down herself when her brother tackled the back of her knees and clung to her skirts.

"Stop that screaming," Elizabeth yelled, "or I will give you something to yell about."

"Amen to that," Roger muttered, struggling to stand up. It was a difficult task, for Garth, a most affectionate dog, was standing with front paws on the knight's chest to give him better advantage while he licked at the scowl on Roger's face.

"What is happening here?" Elizabeth and Roger both looked up and saw Geoffrey standing in the doorway. Even little Thomas peeked out from behind

Elizabeth's back to look at the lord. Elizabeth decided that her husband, legs braced apart and hands on hips, looked quite exasperated. But then, so was she. Another crash resounded in the background, and Elizabeth felt like grinding her teeth in reaction.

"Come here, Thomas," Geoffrey commanded. His voice was harsh, and Elizabeth immediately wanted to shield her small brother from her husband's anger. She did not think that Geoffrey would harm the lad, but she worried that his hard words would upset her sensitive brother immensely.

Geoffrey pulled the dog off the knight with one sure motion. "Sit," he told the animal, and praise be, the dog decided to obey. "I am waiting, boy," Geoffrey told her brother, folding his arms across his chest.

Couldn't he use a little gentleness in his tone when addressing such a small child? Elizabeth asked herself. She frowned at her husband, hoping he would see her displeasure and soften his commands.

Little Thomas saw that both dogs had quieted, and making a wide circle around the dog his sister held, he ran to Geoffrey.

"Was that you I heard all the way from the walls, bellowing like an infant?" he asked the boy.

His reference to a baby had the desired effect. Little Thomas quit crying and wiped his tears away with the sleeve of his tunic. "I do not like them," he stammered. "They want to bite my arms off."

Elizabeth could not keep silent any longer. "That is nonsense, Thomas," she snapped. "See how their tails wag? They only do that when they are happy."

"I will keep the dogs chained a while longer, Thomas," Geoffrey said. "But from now on, it will be your duty to take them their food and see that they have enough water. And if I hear that you have not done this duty, you will be punished. Do you understand me?"

"I will do it, my lord," Thomas answered. "And I

won't be afraid. If the dogs are tied, they cannot bite me."

Geoffrey let out a sigh and nodded. "No, they cannot bite you, and after you have seen to their food, they will grow to rely on you."

"Mistress?" Sara called from behind. "The new vat of ale has been spilled. It was an accident."

Elizabeth closed her eyes against Sara's excuse for yet another accident. "See that it is cleaned up, Sara," was her only reply.

"I will chain the dogs," Roger interrupted. "Lad, you come with me."

The call that someone was approaching the gates stopped the knight's action. He looked at Geoffrey and then grabbed Thomas, slinging him up and over his shoulder.

"We have company," Geoffrey announced. He was looking at his wife as he spoke. "Your grandfather."

His calmly stated news lifted the fatigue and frustration from Elizabeth. Joy welled up and she all but hugged her husband. "He is truly here?" she asked in a breathless voice, smoothing her hair in an unconscious gesture.

Geoffrey watched the excitement in his wife with a hint of a smile. He was pleased that she was happy with his news, and decided that he liked it considerably when she smiled. Soon, he thought to himself, she will realize her good fortune, and she will smile like that at me. Not that it truly mattered, if she smiled or not. Still, it would make for an easier arrangement. He did not ask himself why that was so, why he liked to see her content, for he considered it insignificant. Happy or not, she belonged to him. That was the way of things. "You are pleased?" he found himself asking Elizabeth.

"Aye, my lord, most pleased," Elizabeth answered, clasping her hands. She started to hurry past him then, intent on greeting her grandfather, but Geoffrey's hand stayed her.

"We will greet him together," he announced.

Elizabeth realized that that was the proper way and nodded her agreement. Geoffrey let go of her arm and walked beside her to the top of the steps leading to the courtyard.

The gates opened with her husband's order, and her grandfather, riding a white charger Elizabeth had not seen before, came galloping into the courtyard. He was dressed, as he always was, in gray tunic and hose, with the fur of some wild animal's skin draped as a cape over his shoulders and around his feet. Another band of fur covered most of his white-blond hair, tilting over one blue eye like a patch. He stood proud and tall, this radical grandfather of hers.

If Geoffrey was amazed by the figure dismounting before him, he hid his feelings well. Elizabeth glanced up at him, a smile on her face.

Her grandfather was an extremely tall man with a gait as enormous as his build. As bold as ever, he smacked the back of his horse and sent him flying away and then turned to walk toward Elizabeth.

"I came as soon as your word reached me," her grandfather began in his powerful voice. "You are the baron here?" he asked.

"I am," Geoffrey acknowledged.

The giant nodded while he studied the man standing next to his granddaughter. When he was through with his appraisal, he nodded again and turned his attention to Elizabeth. "You have no greeting for your grandfather?" he asked in a soft voice.

He was watching her closely, saw the fatigue in her eyes, the lines of worry.

Elizabeth needed no further urging. Nor did she turn to her husband for approval. She ran down the steps and threw herself into her grandfather's open arms, clasping her hands behind his neck. "Thank God you have come," she whispered into his ear as he lifted her high into the air.

"We will talk later, child," her grandfather whispered back. In a louder voice he said, "You are well, little Viking?" using his pet name for her.

"I am no longer little Viking, Grandfather, but a Baroness. Put me down and I will introduce you to my husband," she said. She glanced over at Geoffrey, read his scowl, and added, for his benefit and his pride, "My husband is a most patient man when my behavior becomes improper."

Although he knew the man holding his wife was her grandfather, he still found himself irritated that another touched her.

The grandfather placed Elizabeth back on the ground, gave her another enthusiastic hug, and then turned to Geoffrey.

Looking at the warrior, he said, "Granddaughter, was the marriage forced?" There was a hint of a threat in his voice, but Geoffrey remained composed. He too turned to his wife and waited her response. Her words would determine his action.

"No, Grandfather, it was not forced." She was looking at her husband as she spoke, her expression serious. "I am most content."

Geoffrey's shoulders seemed to relax a bit to Elizabeth's way of thinking, though he still did not smile. But then he rarely smiled, Elizabeth reminded herself. Why, coaxing a bit of lightheartedness into his expression was as difficult as trying to force the sun to shine during a rainstorm. It was simply beyond her power.

Her grandfather's voice interrupted her wonderings. "Then, why the hurry, I'm asking. I would have liked to see you wed," he said.

"There was so much chaos that my husband thought it best to hurry the vows. And it would not have been proper to celebrate the event after what took place here, Grandfather."

"Still another reason to wait," her grandfather argued. He still hadn't taken his gaze from the tall warrior, and Elizabeth noted that the friendliness was gone from his tone. He antagonizes, Elizabeth realized as she watched him fold his arms across his chest and continue to stare at her husband. What was his game, his purpose? she asked herself, growing worried.

"It was *my* decision," Geoffrey answered. His tone matched her grandfather's and Elizabeth thought the two resembled hostile opponents now. "Do not dare to question it."

Geoffrey well knew he was being tested, though he did not understand the reasoning. Regardless of the motive, it was time he showed this new challenger who was in charge.

"You do not kneel before me," Geoffrey said. "You have failed to give me your pledge, though you know I am baron here." His hand settled on the hilt of his sword, a silent message that he was prepared to battle if necessary.

"I am an outcast," her grandfather answered. "You would consider my pledge honorable? Binding?"

Geoffrey nodded. "I would."

The scowl left her grandfather's face as he considered his next move. "Know you all the facts, my lord? I am Saxon, full blood, and once a noble. Still you ask my fealty? I have no lands to protect."

"I would have your loyalty or your life. The decision is yours."

Elizabeth could not understand what was happening between the two men. Fear swept over her as she watched the mental battle going on between her husband and her grandfather. His life? He had demanded his fealty or his life? No, she wanted to scream, do not ask this. He is his own man, loyal to no one but his family. Family! Aye, she realized, that was the key to this frightening game the two played. Was Geoffrey demanding acceptance by asking the pledge? And if so, why?

Geoffrey witnessed his wife's distress and hoped that

she would not interfere. It was imperative that he have her grandfather's trust and loyalty, and though he had not voiced his reasons to his wife, he expected her to keep her silence.

"Go to your husband." The quiet instruction was heard by Geoffrey.

Elizabeth felt torn in half between the two. She wanted the time to explain her grandfather to her husband, and to explain her husband to her grandfather, but there was no time. She let go of her grandfather's embrace and walked to stand on the step, beside her husband.

Silence filled the area as the two giants considered each other. It was a most difficult moment for Elizabeth. She did not know what she would do if her grandfather refused to bend to her husband's will, did not know if her husband would truly carry out his threat to do battle . . .

The game ended. With absolute ease, her grandfather flipped off his cap and knelt on one knee before her husband. He placed his right hand over his heart and said in a clear and forceful voice, "I, Elslow Kent Hampton, give you my loyalty and vow on this day nare to betray you."

It was an emotional moment for Elizabeth. She had never seen her grandfather so intent. His word was his bond, and all he had to give. It was his honor, his soul. Did her husband sense this about her grandfather? she wondered. No, he could not, for he barely knew him, she reminded herself. He could have no idea that her grandfather was as fiercely loyal as she was.

"Stand," Geoffrey said. All harshness was gone from his voice and Elizabeth could tell he was pleased. Her husband walked down the steps and placed a hand on his new relative's shoulder. "There is much I would discuss with you, and before night arrives, now that I have your loyalty."

Geoffrey was not prepared for the mighty whack he

received on his shoulder, nor the deep bellow of laughter that filled his ears, making them ring. "You will have my time, my lord, for time is all I have to give. And there is much on my mind also . . . much I would like to ask you."

"So be it," Geoffrey responded.

"You would have fought for my pledge?" the grandfather asked, chuckling.

"Aye, and won too," Geoffrey replied, smiling.

"Do not be too sure of yourself. I've still strength left in these old bones. I'm thinking I'd have the advantage of the wisdom age gives." His eyes sparkled at Geoffrey's reaction.

The lord began to laugh. "Not a chance," he replied. "I have the strength of younger bones, old man, and would have cut you down in one quick blow."

"Ha! We will never know for sure, now, will we?" her grandfather teased. He threw his arm around Geoffrey just as if they had been boyhood friends and changed the subject before her husband could answer. "Know you the treasure you have in your new wife?" he asked. And then, before Geoffrey could speak, he said, "I have a terrible thirst for a cool drink, Baron. Share a toast with me to your marriage."

Geoffrey was chuckling as the two men walked up the steps and disappeared behind the doors. Her grandfather was saying something in a low voice and then her husband's deep laughter reached her ears. He was actually laughing! Elizabeth looked to the sky and saw that the sun was shining. Amazing, she thought. There wasn't a single rain cloud in sight!

It was nearly the dinner hour, and still Geoffrey continued in deep conversation with Elizabeth's grandfather. They sat at the long table, across from each other, with cups of ale before them. Twice she tried to join them in their discussion but both times the talk would stop and both men would simply stare at her. They made it very obvious that they did not wish her present.

She knew the talk concerned Belwain and the "other" that Geoffrey had hinted at and decided that they were planning their course of action. God, give me the strength to see this charade through, to look at Belwain and not plunge my knife into his heart.

Elizabeth grew increasingly restless. She sought solitude and went for a walk, and although she could not bring herself to visit the graves, she headed in that direction. The sun was setting, casting an orange glow to the horizon. In the distance, on the knoll, she could see the wooden crosses anointing the freshly turned earth, marking the area where her family was buried.

"Granddaughter?" Her grandfather's voice intruded and she turned and watched him make his way to her.

"I was this very minute wishing you were by my side," she said, smiling. "Grandfather, I am so very glad you are here." She grabbed his hand with both of hers and held it in a tight grip.

"You were going to the graves?" her grandfather asked.

"No," Elizabeth admitted. "I cannot say good-bye yet."

"And have you wept for your parents, your sisters?" he asked, his voice soft.

"No. Perhaps when it is done, when Belwain is punished—"

"Do not wait," her grandfather said, "cry for them now, before it becomes too bottled up inside you. It will tear at your insides then and make you a bitter woman. Your mother would not have wanted that."

Elizabeth considered his advice and nodded. "I will try, if it will please you, Grandfather."

"You always please me, Granddaughter. Don't you know that?"

Elizabeth smiled. What he said was true. He gave her his love without restrictions, without rules. And most important, he accepted her for what she was.

"You have a new life now, Elizabeth. Are you truly content with Geoffrey?" he asked.

"It is too soon to know that," Elizabeth replied. She let go of his hand and the two began to walk, side by side. "I try to follow my mother's example in playing the wife, but find it a most arduous task. Geoffrey is nothing like father. He is so hard . . . like steel. And he covers his emotions so that I am never quite sure what he is thinking. I do not think he is content with me but that too is too soon to tell."

"What makes you think him discontent?" her grandfather asked. "You have only been married one day," he said, trying not to smile.

"Almost two, Grandfather, but you are right, it is too soon to make such a judgment. Still there are his rules . . ." Elizabeth paused, gathering her thoughts. Was it disloyal to discuss her husband with her grandfather? she considered.

"Rules?" her grandfather asked, nudging her into a decision.

"Yes," Elizabeth answered. "Rules of how I should act, what I should do. I think he considers me ill-prepared to be his wife, and in truth, he is right. It is but a role I play and I do not know how long I can wear the mask of deceit."

"I do not understand," her grandfather said.

"I have not shown my temper once since meeting Geoffrey and have tried to act with great humility." She saw that her grandfather was about to laugh and frowned up at him. "I have been a gentle, obedient wife these past two days."

"The strain must be terrible," her grandfather said, chuckling. His tone grew serious but the twinkle remained in his eyes when he added, "I do see your problem. You wish to be meek but find it not in your character."

"Exactly." Elizabeth was pleased that her grandfather understood. "It is most difficult indeed. To keep my thoughts inside."

"Is it that you wish to be master here?" he teased.

"No, of course not!" Elizabeth was surprised by his question. "Please do not jest with me. I am most serious."

"Then what is it you wish?"

Elizabeth stopped walking and turned to her grandfather. "To be a good wife, to rule with my husband, to stand at his side."

"And you do not think this will come to pass?" her grandfather asked.

"Nay, I do not," Elizabeth answered, shaking her head for emphasis. "He would have me locked inside the walls, without a comment of my own, I fear. And when he discovers I have no talent with the needle, or with the household affairs, he will undoubtedly despair. Oh, but I wish I had spent more time with my mother. It will mean nothing to Geoffrey that I can hunt with the best of his men and bring down as many kills. Worse, when he sees me without my mask, I fear he will—"

"Why do you think he married you?"

"Because of my father, and his failure to help him in his time of need," Elizabeth responded. That was such an obvious conclusion she couldn't understand why her grandfather hadn't realized it.

"Think you he marries each time there is a situation like this?"

"Well, of course not, but this is the first time he has been called on to—"

"Elizabeth, you confuse yourself with your thoughts and conclusions. Your husband was not at fault for what happened here. The safety within these walls fell to your father. A trap was laid for him, and there wasn't any way that Geoffrey could have prevented what occurred." Her grandfather sounded a little exasperated and Elizabeth grew irritated.

"Then why do you think he married me?" she asked.

"I do not think that Geoffrey does anything he does not want to do. I think he *wanted* you for a wife."

"Because I was his responsibility," Elizabeth added. "He felt it was his duty." Elizabeth sighed and added, "Honor is the reason, he is an honorable man."

"I agree that he does not know you in full yet, but I believe he will be most pleased when you remove your 'mask' and be yourself. Do not try to imitate your mother. In time you will learn the duties of being a good wife, just as Geoffrey will learn how to be a good husband."

"Do you like him, Grandfather?" Elizabeth asked. His answer was important, as she valued his opinion. He was an astute judge of character, and not easily fooled. She hoped his reply would be favorable to Geoffrey, admitted that she wished him to admire her husband. Why, she couldn't explain.

"Yes, I do like him. He seems an honest man. He is much younger than the other barons of his stature, from what I was able to learn. And much favored by the king himself."

Elizabeth swelled with pride, as if it was she who was receiving the compliments. She nodded and said, "Roger hinted that he saved the king's life."

"I would believe it," her grandfather agreed. "He seems to possess many good qualities, Granddaughter."

"But there are faults too," Elizabeth said to counter the praise. She did not wish her grandfather to become overly impressed, to place her husband upon a pedestal. He was, after all, only a man. And pedestals could crumble. "He is very stubborn."

"And you are not?"

"No! I am a most agreeable person."

"Then you will have no problem adapting to your baron's rules?" her grandfather teased.

"I did not say that," Elizabeth replied, laughing at the way her words had been twisted. "Perhaps it will be easier if I ignore the rules completely. What say you to that?"

"He will not be so easily led, Elizabeth," her grandfather warned. "But there will be joy in the battle, I believe."

"Have you seen your grandson?" she asked, changing the subject.

"Aye, he was brought to me," her grandfather answered. "He did not recognize me and I felt like weeping like a woman when he did not."

Elizabeth could not imagine her grandfather weeping and shook her head. "You carry your grief inside you too, Grandfather. Why, in all these years, the only time I have seen you cry was when you bested my father and laughed so hard that tears rolled down your cheeks."

"I will miss them all," he said in a quiet tone.

"Even my father?" Elizabeth asked.

"Especially your father. I'll miss our battle with words, the jests we played on each other. He was a worthy opponent and a good husband to my daughter. She was happy."

"Yes, they were happy." Elizabeth nodded, feeling the sadness in her shadow.

"I have a heavy heart that little Thomas does not remember them. Heavy, indeed."

"But, Grandfather, he saw it happen. And it was too much for him," Elizabeth replied. "Geoffrey says in time he will remember, when his mind stops protecting him from the horror."

"We will find the ones who did this," her grandfather muttered. "They will all die."

"Did Geoffrey tell you his thoughts? I believe Belwain is the one responsible but he considers my uncle only a follower. He hints of another who would have equal gain."

"Aye, we talked and he shared his thoughts. He believes we must not rule out all the possibilities."

"And what do you think, Grandfather?"

"I am an old man and need time to think on this," her grandfather stalled.

"You only remember your age when it is convenient," Elizabeth replied.

"And you know me well," her grandfather answered. "Tell me this. Do you remember the stories about Hereward the Wake?"

"Only that when the battle for control of England was waged, it was Hereward who fought the longest."

"He was a powerful Saxon noble and held out the longest against the invading Normans. He fought near the fens around Ely."

"I have heard ballads sung in his praise," Elizabeth whispered, "though I do not think our king would be pleased if he heard them. The songs glorify his enemy. Why do you bring this up?" she asked, frowning. "What has Hereward the Wake to do with Montwright? There is a connection?"

"Perhaps," her grandfather said. "Hereward is long dead, but there are still his faithful followers. And more have recently joined their ranks, those who wish William removed from power and the return to the old ways. Geoffrey knows of this band of men and must consider that Montwright was attacked to cause havoc."

Elizabeth's eyes widened while she considered what her grandfather said. "How do you know of this group of rebels?" she asked after a time.

"I was asked to join with them," her grandfather admitted. He watched Elizabeth closely, judging her reaction.

She was horrified. "It is treason you speak," she whispered. "Oh, but you would not—"

Her grandfather smiled and said, "No, I would not. It is not honorable, for I had already accepted William."

"Did you tell Geoffrey that you—"

"No, I did not mention that I was approached by one of their leaders, child. But I did tell him that they were a threat, to be careful. I feel caught in the middle of this struggle, Elizabeth. Some of the leaders are old men now, displaced and full of hatred for all they had to give up. I do not feel loyalty to them but I am not inclined to name them either."

Elizabeth took hold of her grandfather's hand again and squeezed it.

"Why do these rebels persist, Grandfather? William has been our king for many years now. Can they not accept him?"

"There have been several uprisings over the years, many in the first two years of William's rule, but nothing I fear on the scale that is soon to come. Greed is the motivation, I think. These men do not wish for a better way of life for all, only themselves. They make rash and foolish promises to all who will listen, even promising that when William has been dethroned, the danegeld will be done away with."

"But wasn't there a tax levied in the time before William?" Elizabeth asked. "Called by another name perhaps, but—"

"It is not significant, child. What matters is that they are all fools, these rebels, but with a deadly purpose."

"I am frightened for you, Grandfather. Will there be penalty for not joining with this band?" Elizabeth found herself wringing her hands and stopped herself.

"I do not know," he whispered. "Perhaps it is no coincidence that my only daughter and most of her family were murdered just days after I refused. I do not know," her grandfather said, "but as God is my witness, I will find the truth."

Both Elizabeth and her grandfather could hear the footsteps on the path behind him. They turned as one and saw that Roger was approaching.

"Roger comes," Elizabeth said. "Have you spoken with my husband's vassal yet? He is usually by my husband's side."

"I have met him," her grandfather answered. He said no more until Roger stood before them.

"The Baron wishes to speak to you," Roger said, addressing Elizabeth.

Elizabeth nodded and started down the path. Her grandfather did not follow and she turned, waiting for him. "Grandfather?"

"You go on, Elizabeth. I will visit the graves first. I would say good-bye to my daughter."

Elizabeth nodded, knew that he needed to be alone for a few minutes. She motioned Roger to her side and walked beside him back to the hall.

"Is it true that my husband saved the king's life?" she asked.

"Aye, and he was only a boy at the time," Roger said.

"Tell me, please," Elizabeth asked.

"There was poison in the wine that Geoffrey carried to William," he said. "Geoffrey knew this as he had seen the deed done by one of the nobles. As he approached William's place, he tripped and the wine spilled to the floor. William was angry over the clumsiness and was about to punish the lad when one of the dogs began licking the wine from the floor. Within seconds the dog went into fits and died. It was obvious to William that the wine was the reason. He made everyone save Geoffrey leave the hall and then questioned the boy. The plot was uncovered and the guilty punished."

"Why did he not just yell out what he had seen?" Elizabeth asked.

"He had only been a page in William's court a short time, but already knew not to speak unless asked. It was a rule he would not disobey."

"Aye, my husband seems to place great import on rules," Elizabeth said, smiling to herself.

"It is the way of things," Roger announced, borrowing his lord's phrase. "Without rules there would be chaos."

"But being rigid at all times," Elizabeth began, "seems most predictable. Surprises are sometimes a nice change from the daily hardships. Don't you think?"

Roger glanced over at his mistress and shook his head. "Surprises imply that one is not prepared. Geoffrey is always prepared."

"Therefore nothing can surprise him?" Elizabeth asked.

"Nothing."

"You make my husband sound most predictable, Roger."

"It is a compliment I give him."

Elizabeth did not agree that describing her husband as predictable and rigid was a compliment. Rigidity left little room for spontaneity. No, it was no compliment, she decided. In truth, it sounded quite dreary.

"And do all follow his rules, Roger?" she found herself asking.

Roger looked surprised by her question. "Of course," he said. "He would have it no other way. Nor would we! He is our lord, our leader."

"Do not frown so, Roger. I was not discrediting my husband or your loyalty. I merely wish to learn as much about my husband as I can."

Her explanation placated the knight and he relaxed his scowl.

She decided to change the subject and said, "Roger, I wish to thank you for your guard over my brother. I know you do this because my husband ordered it, but it must be a hardship and I—"

Roger coughed and Elizabeth guessed it was with embarrassment. "I do my duty," he muttered, "and would give my life to protect the boy."

Elizabeth smiled and knew that what he said was true. "My worry is lessened because you are in charge of him," she admitted. "Tonight—"

"He will be well guarded," Roger interrupted. "Have no fear concerning him."

"With you about, I have no fear. Thank you, Roger."

He was about to say that he did only what his lord ordered, but recognized the lie. He would protect the boy whether he was ordered to or not. Had not his new mistress helped him in his hour of need? When his lord lay near death and he had no notion as to what to do? And now he had an opportunity to lessen her fear. He could not refuse, nor did he wish to. She had captured his loyalty.

He nodded, indicating that he had heard the remark. Compliments make him feel awkward, Elizabeth decided. For that reason she did not smile or make a jest about his discomfort but changed the subject once again. "I fear my parents' room will be overrun with rats." She sighed and continued, "It must be made ready for my grandfather, and I am sure he has no liking for their company." Her chattering ceased when the only reply she could get from Roger was a recognizable grunt, telling her that he was not interested in mundane household matters, she surmised.

They reached the doors and Roger escorted her into the hall where her husband waited. There were several of Geoffrey's men in the room, all wearing serious expressions. There was tension in the air and Elizabeth knew the talk was concerned with grave matters.

Later she would excuse her behavior on her nerves, the tension that was building up inside her over the coming encounter with Belwain, but that was only half the truth, she admitted. He just looked so forceful standing there, so rigid. And those hands, those velvet hands he held in such iron fists upon his hips, as if he was just about to let go with some great wrath. Oh, he was predictable, this new husband of hers, she thought as she stood at the entrance and waited for his attention. Predictable indeed. And that, she later told herself, that was the other half of the reason. He was so sure of everyone's reactions, and yes, their behavior too. He was *too* sure!

She was through waiting. She knew he saw her out of the corner of his eye as he listened to what one of the knights was saying. She tried to listen too, but the distance was too great and the knight's voice too low.

When Geoffrey nodded to his vassal, Elizabeth took that as his dismissal and started across the hall. He turned to watch her, his expression well hidden, as usual. Could he read the determination in her eyes? She hoped not, and suddenly increased her pace until she was almost running. She threw herself into his arms. Geoffrey's reaction was instinctive; he placed his hands on her waist to steady her, a most surprised look on his face. She saw it and was immensely pleased. I am *not* so predictable, she wanted to shout, not so easily molded, husband.

She was not done. Before he could mask his reaction and stand her away from him, she clasped her hands behind his neck and stretched up on her tiptoes to place a kiss on his cheek. "Good evening to you, my lord," she whispered. She let go when she felt his intake of breath but continued to smile. Taking a step back, she tried to assume what she hoped was a subservient and obedient stance, though she had no previous practice in the art of docility, and said, "You wished to speak with me?"

The lilt in her voice, the sparkle in her eyes . . . Geoffrey felt as if the sun had just penetrated the walls, amazed at the joy she brought into the room. He glanced around and saw the soldiers watching and smiling.

He could not allow it, of course, should not, this independent streak in her, this need to disobey his most explicit order to behave in public with absolute decorum. Why, she was openly defying him! Aye, that was the truth, he decided. She wished to irritate him, but for what purpose? What was her game?

Her manner told him she awaited his reaction. He was about to chastise her with hinted threats he would carry out later, to give her what she expected. The teasing challenge in her eyes stopped him. It is what she expects, he realized.

His expression had turned back to the mask and so Elizabeth was quite unprepared for what happened next. Without saying a word, Geoffrey placed his hands on her shoulders and pulled her to him. Her reaction pleased him, and he favored her with a smile of his intent seconds before his mouth settled on hers. It was no gentle kiss, not from start to finish. His mouth opened on hers, demanding a response. She felt overwhelmed and quite embarrassed, felt his hands holding her hips against his in a most intimate way. She tried to pull away but could not. He was too strong.

How dare he? she demanded as she tried to push his tongue away with her own, how dare he maul her like this?

Her anger kept her from responding for a time, but then that too dissipated, and the warmness of remembrance, last night's passion, filled her. She found herself responding in spite of her intentions. And that was more humiliating than being kissed so passionately in front of an audience.

Geoffrey found her resistance fade and relaxed his hold. He continued to take his fill but stopped when he found himself more affected than he wished. The taste of her was intoxicating, he decided.

He kissed her once on the forehead after releasing her lips and chuckled out loud at the dazed expression on her face.

"You forget yourself," she whispered in a furious voice, pushing at his hands, which still lingered on her hips.

"I never forget myself," Geoffrey answered, grinning. "You have indicated by your embrace that you have a desire to be treated as a—"

It was as far as he got. Elizabeth's foot came down on his with a gasp of outrage. "Whore?" she interrupted. "You were going to say whore? Well, you are very mistaken, Baron. I wish for affection and you give me a mauling."

He continued to smile and her temper exploded. "Fine, lord and master! I have learned this lesson. In future there will be no display of affection. *None!* I will give you the cold indifference you seem to wish."

It was a wonderful exit line, Elizabeth thought, but found that her husband disagreed. He wouldn't let go of her.

"I have heard of your temper, mistress," he said. His voice was gentle and soothing, the exact opposite of the anger she had thought her words would have caused. "Perhaps later we might find time to discuss this unladylike bellowing of yours. You are lucky that you find yourself married to such a mild-tempered husband."

She could only listen to his words with an open mouth, could not think of a single retort to his ridiculous analysis of his temperament.

And then he was gone, exited from the room, and only the echo of his deep laughter remained.

Elizabeth shook her head with despair. So much for predictable, she thought. Aye, she repeated. Predictable indeed!

Chapter Seven

WHEN ELIZABETH HAD FINISHED HER DUTIES HELPING TO clear the varmint and the clutter from her parents' room, she went to her own bedroom. More dust had settled on her than the dustbin. She washed and changed into a gown of pale green, with an overtunic a shade darker and decorated with silver threads circling the top. Sara helped her fix her hair into a coronet atop her head, saying it looked quite lovely, even with the wisps of curls that kept slipping out.

Elizabeth waited until Sara had left the room before tying a second knife to a piece of ribbon and securing it under her gown around her thigh. She then clipped the silver chain that went with her overtunic, her bliaut, around her waist, letting it ride low, just above her hips, and slipped the other dagger in place there. She would use it to cut the meat, as it was the only utensil used and each carried his own, and no one would consider it unusual for her to carry it. But I could also use it to kill Belwain, she considered, if there be a need.

Little Thomas and Geoffrey's main squire, Gerald, were waiting in the hall when she opened the door. Behind them stood three soldiers, all holding drawn swords. "With your permission, we are to wait in your room until the visitors have left," the squire announced. "I am to keep your brother company and they," he said, motioning to the guards with a tilt of his head, "they will watch the door."

Elizabeth took a step back and allowed the two to pass by. She patted her brother on the top of his head and said to Gerald, "There is a chess game and checkers too, in the chest next to the fireplace."

"I am quite good at both games," the squire boasted.

"I do not know how to play," her brother answered.

"Of course you do, Thomas," Elizabeth replied. "You have just forgotten. In time you will remember."

She shut the door behind her and slowly walked to the landing. From the sounds coming from below, she knew Belwain and his men had arrived. She hesitated at the top step, felt her courage try to desert her, and admitted that she honestly did not know if she would be able to see the evening through without trying to kill her uncle.

She touched the dagger at her side, patted it as if it had life, and whispered, "Our time will come."

"Who are you talking to?" her grandfather asked from behind.

Elizabeth turned and tried to smile. She was relieved to see him, knew that he would help her get through this evening. "My dagger," she said. "I console my weapon. You do not think me crazed?"

"I do not," he answered, shaking his head. "And does your dagger have a name?"

"You tease me," Elizabeth said. The smile was more natural now for her grandfather.

"I do not tease," her grandfather answered. "It is most common to name your sword or your dagger."

"I thought only kings named their swords."

"They also, child. Do you remember the tales of the mighty king Charlemagne?" With her nod, he said, "There are songs about his love for his sword, named Joyosa. Truly."

"Roland's name for the sword at his belt was Durindana, and there are songs about it," she volunteered.

"So you are not so daft to talk to your dagger, Elizabeth," her grandfather said. "I wager your husband talks to his," he added.

Elizabeth doubted that but said, "I know he places great pleasure on his weapon but I do not think he talks to it." She found herself chuckling over their ridiculous conversation. "Knights are filled with superstition, I think. To name their weapons, to—"

"It is most serious, this work of killing or being killed. The knight knows that without his weapons he is powerless. That is why he honors his equipment. Every item in his stock has its significance."

"You are making fun of me," Elizabeth said. "I do not believe you."

"Your education is lacking, Granddaughter," her grandfather answered. He took hold of her hand and started down the steps. "Take the knight's spear," he said. "Now, that is a most useful weapon, is it not?"

"Aye."

"The straightness of the spear symbolizes truth to the knight's way of thinking and its iron head suggests strength."

"So a curved spear would never do," Elizabeth said, smiling at her absurd remark.

"Of course not," her grandfather answered, "and it would be most ineffective."

"What about the other 'stock'?"

"The helmet indicates modesty, and the spurs diligence."

"My husband does not always wear his helmet so he is not modest?" she asked in a teasing tone.

"Do not bait me when I try to teach you something." Her grandfather's voice was full of laughter.

They had reached the bottom of the steps and started into the great hall. He felt his granddaughter increase her pressure on his arm and knew her stress. Still, his voice continued in the same light tone as he said, "Now, the shield is almost as important to the knight as his sword, though he does not have it buried with him, of course."

"And what does the shield remind the knight of?"

"That by using it he has saved his body and therefore remembers to use his body to protect his lord. In your husband's case, his lord is King William."

"What about the bow and arrows that you made for me? What do they represent?"

"You know that the soldiers do not use the small bow," her grandfather chided her. "They are fitting for a knight's use."

"My father thought my new weapon—"

"Ineffective?"

"Actually, he called it stupid, useless."

"Enough! You wound me, for I carved the arrows myself, and well you know it!" He laughed then and added in a whisper, "Why do you think I gave you such a bizarre present?"

"To irritate my father, of course," Elizabeth answered, smiling. She was looking into her grandfather's sparkling eyes and hardly noticed that they stood in the center of the room, surrounded by Geoffrey's men and Belwain's soldiers.

"I admit it," he answered, chuckling.

"And that is why you gifted me with the dogs. They

were so small when I first began to care for them, but you knew, didn't you? You knew how huge they would become."

"I did, indeed," her grandfather immediately answered. "Though I did not share the information with your father."

"I am surprised he did not challenge you." Geoffrey's statement turned her grandfather's attention to him. He stood to Elizabeth's side, a smile of greeting on his face.

"It was all a game we played," her grandfather explained. He took Elizabeth's hand, resting on his arm, and placed it on Geoffrey's. "Thomas not only looked forward to my visits, but he demanded them." Elizabeth showed her surprise and her grandfather nodded. "It is true. He would send for me. Did you think I just appeared when the fancy took me?"

She nodded and he continued, "Thomas would send word to me that I was being remiss in my duty as father to his wife. I would then travel to Montwright and he would act as surprised as everyone else when I arrived."

Her grandfather winked at her and turned back to Geoffrey. "I have gotten her down the steps, my lord. I leave the duty of removing her dagger to you."

Geoffrey nodded and pulled Elizabeth close to his side. "You have no wish to offer me a greeting this evening?" he asked in a soft voice.

"I do not," Elizabeth replied. "And I will keep my dagger at my side."

"Only if I allow it," her husband said in a mild tone. "I do not like your hair twisted like that on top of your head. Wear it down when we are together."

Elizabeth's hand automatically went to her hair. Then she realized his aim. "You are as bad as my grandfather, my lord. You confuse me with nonsense when more serious matters need be discussed. You truly do not like my hair this way?" she couldn't help but ask, and almost bit down on her lower lip for her foolishness.

"I do not," Geoffrey answered. "And your garments do not please me much either," he added. He saw his wife's back arch in protest and did his best not to smile. "Tomorrow we will see about having new chainses and new bliauts fashioned for you."

"Is there anything you do like about me?" Elizabeth asked. She let her irritation show by jerking her hand from his arm.

"Perhaps," Geoffrey answered. "I will have to think on it and advise you later."

His strategy was working. He was forcing his wife to think of other matters and hoped, when she came face to face with Belwain, she would not have had time to build her rage. She was like a small fire now, and as long as he and her grandfather continued to throw bits of water in her direction, she could not grow in intensity, becoming an inferno of emotion, out of control.

Elizabeth looked around the room and saw that Geoffrey's men were being friendly with the new soldiers. Everyone held cups of ale and already a free atmosphere prevailed.

"Where is he?" There was no inflection in her voice when she asked the question.

"Outside," her husband informed her. "He is seeing what repairs and changes have been made."

"Perhaps it would be best if I went outside to greet him," Elizabeth suggested in a flat voice.

"I think not," Geoffrey replied. At her questioning look, he continued, "I have your word that you will not try to harm him, and I know you will keep it."

"Then why—"

"Come with me to the table," he said, dismissing the subject. "You are not to leave my side this eve."

Elizabeth nodded and once again took hold of Geoffrey's arm. The crowd parted as they made their way to the long table and sat down. Geoffrey leaned toward his wife and whispered, "Look about you, wife. Do you recognize any of the men?"

"Not yet," she answered, turning her face so that she was just inches from her husband's. She felt very safe sitting so close to him, and that gave her the courage to look around the room, to study each newcomer. "So many wore hoods," she reminded her husband in a whisper.

When Geoffrey took hold of her hand and casually wrapped his arm around her waist, she knew that Belwain had entered the hall. She felt her husband's hand rest on the hilt of her dagger.

Elizabeth straightened her shoulders and gently removed her husband's hand from her waist. "You will trust me as I trust you in this matter?" she asked.

Geoffrey looked down at his wife and nodded.

She turned away from him then and watched her uncle walk toward her. Roger was at his side, wearing a look of disgust.

Her gaze was as cold as winter's sleet, her eyes unblinking, as she studied her uncle. He was dressed as a rooster, in bright reds, except for the brown stain in the middle of his bulging stomach, and Elizabeth thought that he strutted like a rooster too.

Belwain glanced at her and found her stare unnerving. He faltered in his steps and turned to look at her husband.

"Good evening, Baron," he said when he reached the table. He had to turn to his niece and acknowledge her, though he dreaded the task. "You are looking well, niece."

Elizabeth did not answer him, only continued to stare. Belwain cleared his throat and sat down opposite the pair. "My heart aches for your loss, Elizabeth. I, too, feel a great sadness," he added in a hurry.

A goblet of ale was placed before him and he grabbed at it, almost overturning it in his haste and nervousness. He downed the contents in two huge gulps and tried to cover the belch as he wiped his face with the edge of his sleeve.

"Where is the boy?" he asked then.

"You will not see him." Elizabeth's voice was hard.

"It is past his bedtime," Geoffrey stated, his tone almost pleasant.

I cannot do this, Elizabeth decided as she watched the man sitting so calmly across from her. I cannot share a meal with this vile creature. She turned to look at her husband, willed him to understand, and then started to stand. Geoffrey would not allow it. He placed his hand on her shoulder and held her down, though to Belwain, who was watching the couple closely, it looked like an awkward show of affection on the lord's part. Belwain's eyes darted from one to the other and back again, his mind racing with his thoughts. Thank God I did not speak my true feelings concerning Elizabeth to her husband, he thought with a shiver. For some reason, the Baron has found favor with the bitch and would probably be outraged if he knew what I thought of her.

Belwain looked at Elizabeth and smiled. What a shame she did not die with the others, he thought. Such a disobedient, outspoken child, always so unimpressed with his attempts to win her favor. She seemed able to look through his exterior, and know his hatred. He didn't like her, aye, he did hate her . . . all of them, he thought. They were all trying to do him out of what should have been his. And when I am in charge here, she will be gone with the Baron. That, too, was a shame, he decided. He would have liked the chance to make her as miserable as she was now making him. To finally get even with her. He would wipe that expression of cold disdain off her face, skin and all, and then marry her off to one of his friends. Their sadistic ways with women would teach her a lesson she would go to hell with. His smile increased at his fantasy and he almost chuckled out loud. He caught himself in time and coughed.

"Have you given consideration to my rightful request?" Belwain asked Geoffrey, being sure to stress the word "rightful."

What request? Elizabeth asked herself. She turned to her husband and awaited his answer.

"This evening is not the time to discuss the law and your request," Geoffrey answered. He motioned to his servants and pointed to Belwain's empty cup.

Belwain knew better than to press his issue. He nodded his agreement. He could wait. And he would win, no doubt about that, he thought. The law was on his side.

He looked at Elizabeth again and had to quickly pull his gaze away. She knows, he thought, but she can do nothing! His eyes became slits and his shoulders began to tremble with suppressed laughter. He felt himself grow hard with his thoughts and slid his hand between his legs hidden beneath the table linen. There is nothing she can do, he repeated as he stroked himself, nothing. You have no proof, slut, his mind screamed with glee.

Oh, that he could tell her! Yes, he would say, I helped with all of the planning and more! It was I who gave the design and the flaws of your fortress, and my only remorse is that I could not be here when they were all killed. Still it gave me great pleasure just to hear the telling . . . such pleasure that it took all three of his male companions to catch his orgasms, one after the other. It was the greatest day of his life, he decided.

He chanced a look at the Baron and his smile vanished. She has gotten to him, the whore! She has turned his head with false stories about me, that is why he looks upon me with such disgust.

But no matter, he consoled himself. The law be the law, Baron. There is nothing you can do either; you are too honorable, he thought, and almost snorted aloud. You would have proof before you challenge or deny.

Elizabeth found that she could not look at her uncle a second longer. She kept her gaze downcast and did not say another word until the meal was done. She refused to touch the food. It was tainted, with Belwain sitting at the table. She had no stomach for it but noticed that Belwain ate as if it was his last meal on this earth. And well it might, she thought just to ease her torment. Perhaps Geoffrey would change his mind, see that Belwain was the only one behind the murders. She knew she fooled herself, knew Belwain wasn't the only one involved. Her husband's reasoning made sense. Belwain was stupid, too stupid . . . but God's truth, the waiting was becoming unbearable.

When the meal was over and the table cleared, Belwain stood and strutted around the room. He grows more cocky with each drink, Elizabeth saw, and dresses the fool.

She closed her eyes against the sight of him and wished it was possible to close her ears as well. The noise from too much drink was becoming deafening.

And then she heard it. The laugh. It was more like a screech, unusual in sound, but one she had heard before, the day of the massacre. Her eyes flew open with the recognition and she tried to find the one making the sound. There were too many blocking her view. She would find him, she would, she told herself. She stood, jarring her husband with the force, but her eyes were not on him. She continued to search the room, watching and waiting.

The sound issued again, and she found him. He stood near the archway, laughing, with a group of men. She memorized his face and sat back down. Outwardly calm, she turned to her husband and said, "By the door. He was there."

Geoffrey had turned when his wife jumped to her

feet. He saw the paleness in her face, the tension in her posture. He felt like drawing his sword and standing in front of her, to protect her, but he could not. Not if they were to find proof. And so he continued to sit, keeping his expression almost bored if Belwain or any of the others should chance to notice his wife's strange behavior.

He was visually relieved when she spotted one of the attackers. He did not ask her if she was certain, for he knew she was. "Did I not tell you that your uncle was a stupid man?" he asked.

Elizabeth could not answer. She kept her eyes centered on the soldier.

"A fool would bring the very ones back into the nest," he muttered.

"He wore a mask," Elizabeth said, turning back to her husband. "But his laugh was high-pitched and unusual . . . and I remembered it. What will you do now?"

"I will see to it," Geoffrey answered. His tone was grim, but his words told her nothing.

"You do not answer me," Elizabeth returned. She found that tears were clouding her vision and knew that she had reached her limit of endurance. She had to dab at the corners of her eyes with the back of her hand to stop them from touching her cheeks.

Geoffrey brushed her cheek with his hand and caught one of the tears. "Do not let him see you cry. It would give him pleasure and he would smile. And then I would have to kill him, and our plans to find the other would be at an end."

Elizabeth was overwhelmed by his tender words, his gentle touch. She looked deep into his eyes, read the tenderness there, and in that instant she glimpsed the inner man, usually so well hidden behind the tough exterior.

She was about to say, "You would do this for me?" but did not, for she knew that he would. Instead she whispered, "You forget yourself, my lord. I have told you that I never cry."

She gave him the gift of her smile then, and Geoffrey felt it was the finest of all gifts he had ever received. He had to stop himself from touching her. Lately, he realized, he found himself touching her, patting her, even kissing her in front of an audience. He knew better, but when she was about, he did not seem to care. She will have me acting like a pup following her about if I do not watch myself, and my men will no longer follow me. He cleared his throat to shake his thoughts free and said, "And you forget yourself, wife. I have told you to trust me."

"I do trust you," Elizabeth said in protest, "and I honor your decisions. If I did not, Belwain would be dead by now."

Geoffrey had to smile. Her thoughts concerning her capabilities pleased him. He stood up and took hold of her elbow. "You have shown considerable courage tonight, Elizabeth, though I expected no less, you understand. Still, I would tell you I am pleased."

"So you have found something about me that pleases you?" Elizabeth remarked, agreeing to his lightened mood.

When Geoffrey admitted that what she said was true, she said, "Then perhaps, since you are so well pleased, you will tell me what you are about to do with—"

"I will tell you soon," Geoffrey interrupted. "I must see to the necessary preparations first. Now I think it is time for you to retire. The songs grow raw and your presence dampens the men's moods."

"Dampens their moods! You think I care that—"

"The ale has loosened their tongues," Geoffrey interrupted in a low voice. "And once you have gone, their talk will become more free, less guarded."

He was right, she admitted. "I will wait until you are done here," she said. "No matter how late, I will wait up for you. And then you will tell me your plans?"

"We shall see," Geoffrey stalled. He walked by her side all the way to their bedroom. She did not try to kiss him when they reached the door, and he found himself disappointed. He had grown used to her inappropriate displays, and that puzzled him. But there wasn't time to understand it. He had much to do, and before the night was done.

Elizabeth found little Thomas curled up in a ball and sound asleep in the middle of her bed.

"He calls out in his nightmares," the squire named Gerald told Elizabeth.

"Thank you for your assistance this evening, Gerald," Elizabeth said. "I did not worry knowing that you watched over my brother."

The squire blushed with her praise. He offered to carry the child to his quarters but Elizabeth told him that her grandfather or Roger would take the boy to his room.

When she was alone, she found that her hands shook. She took off her shoes and sat down on the bed to unwind her hair. Where had her grandfather disappeared to? she wondered. She had meant to ask Geoffrey if there was a reason for his absence during the dinner, but never got the chance. It was just as well that he had taken his leave, Elizabeth decided, and it was most probably his own idea. She couldn't imagine him keeping his temper around her uncle.

Her brother's sleep became fitful. Elizabeth stretched out beside him and patted his back whenever he would cry out. Her voice seemed to soothe him and his breathing became more regular. Within minutes Elizabeth too was sound asleep.

Geoffrey did not return to their room until the early hours of the morning. He found his wife asleep, fully clothed, on top of the covers, with her brother cuddled up to her side. He saw that she was barefoot and smiled. She seemed more vulnerable without her shoes on, he thought as he lifted the little boy and carried him to the door, where Roger stood, waiting. "Take him to his grandfather and let him sleep with him," he ordered in a soft tone.

He shut the door and turned back to his wife. She looked so peaceful, so very innocent in her sleep. He found it difficult to undress, preferred instead to look at her and dropped his sword in his clumsiness. It clattered against the stone floor, making a sound Geoffrey thought was loud enough to wake the dead. His wife's only reaction to the jarring noise was to roll over onto her stomach.

He finished stripping and began to undress Elizabeth. The small clasp on the back of her gown defied his awkward fingers but he persisted until he had it opened. Geoffrey paused in his chore to touch her soft, flawless skin, noticed that goosebumps appeared wherever he touched her, and most especially on the base of her spine. Elizabeth began to shiver and Geoffrey hurried to finish the task. He pulled the undergarments from her body and then had to pause once again. He grinned when he caught sight of the knife secured to her thigh, shaking his head at her precaution. She places great store in her own ability to defend herself, he thought, and wondered if she ever considered the possibility that the knife could easily be taken from her and used against her. Probably not, he decided. It pleased him that she thought herself so capable, but it made his work all the more difficult too. Weren't women prone, by their nature, to swoon at the sight of battle, and cling, with gratitude, to their protectors? Wasn't it a fact that they were weak and found their strength in their knights? Well, he decided, somewhere along the way, his Elizabeth had failed to learn this most important information concerning her nature. No one had instructed her, told her that she was weak and in need of constant direction. Odd, but that forgotten lesson pleased the lord. It was enough that he knew she needed him . . . even if she did not!

After talking with her grandfather, Geoffrey had a clear idea of just where his wife had formed her radical opinion of herself. Aye, Elslow was quite a character, in both his dress and his mannerisms, but filled with loyalty and other redeeming qualities too. It is good that I do not judge a man by his appearance, Geoffrey thought, praising himself and knowing it.

Geoffrey yawned for the third time. He was thankful that his wife slept, and had no wish to wake her. She would want her questions answered then most probably, and he was too fatigued to give her the long explanations needed. Under ordinary circumstances, he would not discuss such matters with his wife, but in this instance, it was her right, her family buried at the south end of the courtyard.

Elizabeth shivered again. Lifting her, Geoffrey pulled the cover back and placed her beneath the spread. He found he had to discipline himself against the urges filling his mind and body when he touched her. She needs her sleep, he told himself even as he trailed his fingers down her thigh. With a sigh of acceptance, he turned back to his fallen sword. He picked it up and stationed it by the other side of the bed and then joined his wife.

His back itched where the wound healed and he stretched back and forth several times before he got settled. He was about to pull his wife into his arms and let her sleep aginst him, but Elizabeth had the same idea and was quicker. She turned and snuggled up against him, throwing her leg over his thighs too quickly for him to dodge or protect himself. The result was a loud groan, as her aim was most accurate.

Elizabeth tried to stop the giggle but found it impossible.

"You are awake, wife?" The surprise in his voice made her laugh all the more.

"How could I not be?" she asked him.

"For how long?" he asked, pushing her onto her back so that he could look into her face.

"From the moment you opened the door, my lord," Elizabeth admitted. She grinned and tried to roll back into his arms but Geoffrey pinned her to the bed with his hands, a look of exasperation in his eyes.

"And yet you let me undress you when you should have undressed me?" he asked, his voice gruff.

"Is that another rule, husband?" Elizabeth teased.

"It is," Geoffrey announced. "And you have broken it." His eyes teased, as did his chest, rubbing against her breasts in slow motion.

"And the penalty, husband?" Elizabeth whispered, finding it difficult to continue with the teasing tone. His nearness was making her warm all over, and she found she wanted him to kiss her.

Geoffrey read the desire in her gaze and smiled. "I will let you decide the punishment, wife," he said in a husky voice.

"I shall have to kiss you, my lord," Elizabeth said with a mock sigh.

"And that is a punishment?" Geoffrey inquired with a raised eyebrow. His voice was gruff, his eyes full of golden chips.

Elizabeth did not answer, only continued to look at her husband with a look that made the fire in his loins explode into passion. Slow down, he told himself, go easy for her benefit. He took a shuddering breath and rolled onto his back. "Then give me a kiss, Elizabeth. But first, first you must call me Geoffrey."

"Why?" Elizabeth asked. She leaned up on one elbow and considered her husband.

"I like the sound coming from you, and you do not say it enough."

"As you wish, Geoffrey," Elizabeth whispered into his ear. She pulled back, saw that he smiled, and was pleased. "And now I shall kiss you," she told him. "Do I have your permission, Geoffrey?" she teased.

"You have it, Elizabeth," Geoffrey replied.

"Then come here, my lord," Elizabeth said, waiting. Geoffrey did not move. Elizabeth began to drum her fingers on his chest, but that didn't get much of a reaction either.

"I am too weary," Geoffrey announced. "You will have to come here."

"Too tired to turn to me?" she asked, trying to sound irritated.

"Aye, that is the truth," Geoffrey said. "Besides, you are to come to me. Always, Elizabeth." His voice grew intense and Elizabeth puzzled over what he was trying to tell her.

Elizabeth sat up in bed and pushed her hair over her shoulders. Geoffrey had to stop himself from reaching out to touch her. He wanted her to be the aggressor but could not explain his reasoning, only that he wished her to take from him. He placed his hands behind his head and smiled at her.

The anticipation of touching him excited her. Still, it was best not to appear overly eager, she cautioned herself, for if he knew his effect on her, he would have another weapon to use against her. No, that would never do, she concluded. First, before she showed her emotions, she would make him want her as much. Perhaps, she thought with newfound confidence, even more.

She placed her hands on either side of his chest and slowly leaned down toward his mouth. But when she was just a breath away from touching him, she changed her course and kissed him on his chin. He was in need of a shave and his new growth of whiskers tickled her lips. She smiled to herself and kissed him again, on his chest, allowing her breasts to caress as her hands could not. Geoffrey did not say a word but his breathing became more rapid and Elizabeth knew he was not impervious to her. Her mouth moved lower, to the nipples hidden beneath the thick mat of hair on his chest, and her tongue circled each in a motion that caused her husband to flinch. But still he kept his silence, and Elizabeth let out a low, throaty laugh. She felt like a temptress and a nymph too, full of absolute power over the man responding to her. It was an exhilarating feeling.

Geoffrey's hands touched the sides of her face and he gently pulled her up. "I am still waiting for my kiss," he said, his voice deep and velvet.

"Here?" she asked with innocence, pointing to his lips. "Or here?" she suggested, touching the tip of his nose. "Or perhaps," she whispered, sliding her hand below his waist, "here?"

Geoffrey's gaze told Elizabeth he could not remain passive much longer. She was pushing his control away, touch by touch. He knew her game and was amazed by her uninhibited display; his mind would have allowed her to continue, to see just how far she would go, but his body was demanding with his need, becoming more painfully insistent with each passing second. "You will kiss me now," he ordered, caressing her shoulders to soften the harshness in his voice.

"As you wish, Geoffrey," Elizabeth whispered. She was no longer smiling as she reached up the length of him and touched his mouth with her own. The kiss ended the game for both of them. Her mouth opened for his tongue, her hands cupping his face to hold him still. And then the embers of passion ignited and Elizabeth too lost her control. She couldn't seem to get enough of him, tugging at the hair on the back of his head to keep him prisoner.

Geoffrey rolled her onto her back and covered her with his body while he continued to kiss her. The taste of her, sweetened by the ale, made him thirsty for more. His hands stroked and touched, rough in hurry, and when his hand slid between her thighs and he felt the wetness there, he knew her passion matched his own.

He could wait no longer. Nor could Elizabeth. She parted her legs and arched against him, eager to have him inside her. Geoffrey was breathing so heavily that he could not speak, could not form the words to tell her how very much she pleased him, could only groan with his need. He thrust deep, shuddering for control, and heard her cry out. Her nails scraped his shoulders as she tried to push him away.

"You hurt me, Geoffrey," she sobbed into his ear as she continued to struggle against him.

He heard her and immediately stopped all motion. Lifting himself on his elbows, he looked into her eyes, saw the tears streaming down her face. "Shhh," he comforted, "it will not last long, Elizabeth. The pain will be gone." He leaned down to kiss her but she turned her face away.

"I am too sore," she whispered, "you must stop." She was crying now, both from the pain and from the need so conflicting inside her. "But I don't want you to stop either, Geoffrey."

He could not stop, wanted to tell her he could not, and knew she would not understand. She was too innocent of men to understand. Sighing, he rolled with her to his side, willing himself to keep his patience, keeping inside of her by holding her firmly by her hips, whispering all the while words he hoped would soothe her.

Geoffrey pulled her leg up and rested it on his hip. "It will be better now," he said, and when the sobbing stopped, he knew he was right. He kissed her then, a long, intense kiss meant to melt away her resistance and rekindle her passion, and after a time, Elizabeth began to respond. Her hands quit pushing against his

160

chest and began stroking again. And the soreness was gone, or unnoticed, with her renewed passion.

"It is better?" he asked, thinking that he could not remain still inside of her much longer.

Elizabeth moaned a reply and her hips began to move against him. It was all the urging that Geoffrey needed. His mouth covered hers, capturing her moans while his hands pulled her hips closer. He meant to move slowly but could not, thrusting again and again, deeper and deeper still. He heard her cry out again and thought that he caused her more pain, but still he could not stop until the explosion rocked him from the mountaintop he had just climbed. He felt her shudder beneath him and only then realized that he had rolled her onto her back and that her legs were clenching him with the force of her reaction.

When his breathing calmed and he felt her relax beneath him, Geoffrey said, "You are all right?"

She nodded against his shoulder and Geoffrey relaxed. He rolled to his side and pulled her next to him, glancing down into her eyes. They were still glazed with passion, causing Geoffrey to think that she remained unfulfilled. "I have not satisfied you?" he asked, concern in his voice. Elizabeth adjusted herself to his side and settled her head on his shoulder. "I am most satisfied, Geoffrey," she whispered. Her voice was full of wonder and sleepy pleasure. He worries that he does not please me, she realized, and felt a glow of contentment warm her. Soon, she thought, he will realize how much he is beginning to care for me. And one day, she considered, one day he will say the words.

"And have I satisfied you?" she asked, though she knew in her heart that she had. She had heard him cry her name and felt his strength explode into fragments just seconds before her own explosion. Aye, she had remembered calling his name too.

Elizabeth was sound asleep before Geoffrey voiced a reply. He chuckled to himself and closed his eyes. Contentment was here, in this room. It was there, whenever Elizabeth was by his side. He admitted it without argument and fell asleep with a smile on his face.

Chapter Eight

ELIZABETH OPENED HER EYES THE FOLLOWING MORNING with a thousand questions floating through her mind. Geoffrey was still sound asleep, one arm holding her prisoner against him.

She decided to let him sleep a while longer and took great pains not to disturb him as she slipped out of bed. Clothes were spewn about the floor, and once Elizabeth was wrapped in her robe, she quietly saw to cleaning up. She would have to tell him that he snored, she thought, smiling to herself. He won't like hearing that, she knew, and that pleasured her all the more. Ah, but she loved to tease her husband! Too much of her grandfather's character in her, she supposed with a shrug. And he was the master of the game. Geoffrey was such an easy victim, with such a serious disposition and an inclination to scowl most of the day. Why, his very personality made it most appealing to try to goad him, she admitted without guilt.

Elizabeth walked over to the window and lifted the piece of fur. Looking out, she saw that it was a grand day indeed, if the warmth of the air and the brightness of the sun were any indication. It felt as hot as summer, the gentle breeze upon her face.

Grand, she thought again, for today she would find some answers. Her gaze turned to the forest's edge, to where her uncle and his men camped. Today he would receive justice, she thought as she scanned the area. Something was wrong but her mind could not grasp what it was. She shook her head and cleared her thoughts. The men were gone! No, that cannot be, she argued with herself. She ripped the fur from the wall and leaned out for a better look. The facts did not change. Belwain and his men were gone, fled during the night.

Enraged, she turned to her husband. God but he would be furious, she predicted. Why didn't the warning sound when Belwain broke camp? Why wasn't her husband informed? "Geoffrey! They are gone!" she yelled the news. "All of them gone."

Her husband's reaction did not please her. He opened one eye, scowled, and rolled over onto his side, away from her.

He does not understand, Elizabeth thought. She raced over and knelt on the bed, poking him in the shoulder, and repeated, "They are gone, Geoffrey. Wake up and clear your head. You must get up now. You must . . . do something."

Geoffrey groaned, making a sound like an angry beast, and rolled onto his back. "Quit bellowing," he yelled.

"You do not listen. Belwain has gone, fled," Elizabeth said again, and still did not lower her voice. "You must get dressed. We have to go after him. We—"

"I know he has gone," Geoffrey said. At her look of

astonishment, he sighed and got out of bed. "I sent him back to his home."

She could not believe what she was hearing. He had let Belwain leave? "And the soldier I pointed out to you last evening?" she asked in a subdued voice. "You let him leave also?"

"I did," Geoffrey answered, yawning. He walked over to the chest and bent to splash cold water on his face from the basin placed there the night before.

Elizabeth watched him. She tried to keep calm, thinking that Geoffrey must have had good reason. A rage was building inside her but she kept control.

"Will you tell me why you allowed this?" she finally asked. She was still kneeling on the bed but now her head fell forward with undisguised despair, the long strands of golden hair shielding her torment from Geoffrey's gaze.

Geoffrey heard the threat of anger in her voice, and never at his most pleasant early in the morning, he found himself yelling an answer. "Always you question me, woman! I know the import to you, and for that reason I will tell you what plans are being carried out." He came back to the bed and lifted her chin with his hand. "But you will calm yourself and let me wake up first? Do you understand this, wife?"

Elizabeth listened to the clipped speech, so cold and hard, and could only nod. She was too incensed to answer him. Well, the gentle warrior has turned into the angry beast again, she thought. So be it, she decided, and I will match him word for word, shout for shout, if his answers and his explanations do not appease me. There has been enough blind obedience and trust he so easily demands. Yes, he orders me to trust, yet he gives me no reason to do so. No more! I will conform to his will no longer. "I have given you my trust, husband, and I would know *now* if it was a mistake." Her voice was as hard and as cold as his.

Geoffrey ignored her outburst and continued dressing. She knew that he had heard her, he would have had to be dead not to have heard her, but his face was turned from her and she could not see his reaction to her demand. Well, she would have his reaction, his attention. She got off the bed and went to stand in front of the door, blocking it, and stood there with her arms folded in front of her. Let him see my defiance, let him taste my rebellion. I will have my answers!

When his sword was securely anchored at his side, Geoffrey walked over to his wife and gave her his total concentration. His expression hid nothing, for he wanted her to know just how furious her words had made him. Acting much like the hawk he was named for, Geoffrey's arms flashed out and grabbed her by the shoulders before she knew what he was about. He literally hauled her off her feet so that her eyes were just inches from his. "Never," he said in a harsh whisper that chilled her to the bone, "never demand." He shook her once and she could feel his hands trembling against her skin. He looked ready to explode, Elizabeth thought, noticing that the golden chips in his dark eyes now resembled chips of ice; yet she refused to use caution. She opened her mouth to protest, to tell him that it was her right to know what he intended, but Geoffrey shook her again. "Do not say a word to me unless it is an apology."

Elizabeth promptly shut her mouth. There would be *no* apology, save one he should rightfully give her, she decided.

"So be it," Geoffrey muttered. He knew from the look on her face and the angry glaze darkening her eyes that he would get no apology. He had never laid a hand in anger on any woman, but God's truth, this brazen wife made the thought less repugnant. He shook his head again, disgusted with his own thoughts. "You have the stubbornness of a mule," he muttered. He placed her back on the floor, out of the door's path. One final glare, and he was gone.

"So be it," he muttered on his way down the steps. The stubborn wench! Oh, but she could infuriate him like no other. He made the vow that she would pay the price for her stubbornness, her disobedience. He would keep her waiting all through the day before he spoke to her again. By nightfall, he predicted she would apologize.

He slammed out of the great doors and called for his horse. A hard ride through the forest would clear his mind and rid him of his anger. It was either that, or go back to the bedroom and throttle his wife. He smiled at that ridiculous thought, knew he could never harm her, and felt some of his frustration evaporate with the sun's rays. Ah, wife, he thought as he slowed his pace to the stable, there is much for you to learn about humility.

As soon as the door slammed shut, Elizabeth began to jerk her robe off. She muttered and swore—in Latin, should anyone chance to overhear her—all the while that she dressed. A dark blue tunic fit her mood, as somber in its cut and design as her thoughts. She was so angry she found it difficult to know what to do. She needed to get outdoors, feel the sun on her face and the wind lift her hair, feel the freedom she could only find riding hard and fast on her mare. The exercise would calm her, bring her reasoning ability back.

She didn't do more than brush her hair before she headed for the stable, pausing only long enough to gather her small bow and arrows. The bow she slipped over her shoulder, the arrows she secured in the pouch her grandfather had fashioned for her. She clipped the leather pouch to a thin, knotted rope and then slipped it over her head and under one arm.

Geoffrey was just leaving the stable when Elizabeth arrived. He did not acknowledge her, though he was immensely pleased that she had come in search of him. Already she seeks me out to give me her apology, he thought with satisfaction.

Her husband rode past her without a word, and that

suited Elizabeth just fine. She didn't even give him more than a passing glare as she ordered her mare saddled for her.

Geoffrey was gone before she commanded the stable master to saddle her horse. The stable master incorrectly assumed that the lord had given his permission and hurried to do Elizabeth's bidding. No doubt the master was waiting outside for his wife.

The doors to the walls were being pushed shut when Elizabeth galloped full speed through the narrow opening.

She would not ride far, she reasoned as she raced down the winding road, knew even in her anger and frustration how foolish it would be to take such a chance. No, she would only make a half-circle of the area, stay within sight of the walls for protection, where the outlaws would never dare to venture.

Geoffrey paused in his ride, heard the sound of horse and rider approach, and turned back. The sight of his wife riding at a neck-breaking pace down the winding road almost unsaddled him. A yell of fury escaped him before he remembered he was ignoring her, and he found he had to shake his head again at his own behavior. He goaded his stallion and took out after his wife, hoping to intercept her before she reached the narrow path only wide enough for one horse.

Elizabeth saw Geoffrey approach and braced herself for another confrontation. She pulled her mare to a stop, gasping for breath, and waited.

"You defy me again, wife," Geoffrey bellowed when he was within earshot.

"I do not," Elizabeth yelled back. "You never—"

"Silence!" It was a roar she could not dismiss. She nodded agreement, finding herself quite afraid suddenly. The outlaws now seemed preferable to her husband, she thought a little desperately. Would he beat her? she wondered. The look in his eyes when he reached her side told her he was capable of it. Still, she did not think he would. It was a common enough practice for husbands to batter their wives into obedience, but Geoffrey was no common husband.

"You will not hit me." Her calm statement was like a slap at Geoffrey's pride. Of course he would not, he almost yelled. He took a deep breath and grabbed the reins she clutched in her hands.

"I would not," he admitted in a low voice. "I am a reasonable man, Elizabeth, and reasonable men do not beat their wives. They may *wish* to, but they do not."

He waited for her to absorb what he had just said and then continued, "Now tell this *reasonable* man why you ride unescorted. Were you thinking to catch up with me?"

She dared not smile. Odd, but she wanted to, and realized her anger was gone. She saw the control he was seeking to maintain and decided that meekness was called for. The problem, of course, was that she wasn't sure if she knew how to show meekness. "My answer, if I tell you the truth, will probably anger you," she said with eyes downcast.

"Impossible," Geoffrey contradicted. "I cannot become any more angry. And you must always tell me the truth, Elizabeth."

"Very well," Elizabeth said with a sigh. "I was not trying to catch you, Geoffrey. I just needed to ride, to feel free from my worries and my burdens for a time," she admitted with a rush of honesty and an open gaze. "I do not like yelling at you . . . or you yelling at me. It is most distressing for a new marriage."

The intensity of her speech astonished him, pushing all residues of his anger aside.

"It is important that we try to keep our silence when we think harsh words. I learned that from my mother, Geoffrey. Elsewise this marriage will be most unpleasant. You would say things that you would later regret but then it would be *too* late. The hurt would have already been inflicted." She graced him with a small smile then and added, "Of course your words could not hurt *me* as I, I mean, we do not share a deep love like my parents. But if that is to happen, I mean . . . Oh, I make a mess with my explanation." She busied herself with arranging her hair behind her shoulders, embarrassed that she had spoken such thoughts. It was too soon to tell him such things.

"It is your wish that we love each other?" He seemed amused at his question and Elizabeth thought that his eyes fairly sparked with arrogance.

"I did not mean that," Elizabeth stammered. "I only wish to get along with you, and not as your servant, Geoffrey. I am your wife and should stand beside you . . . not hovering somewhere in the background. I think your ideas about marriage most unusual."

"This is my opinion of your views, wife. It is your ideas that are most unusual," he argued in his defense. "And it is because you are so very difficult to deal with that I find myself losing my patience. Think this will change when you are settled in my home?"

Elizabeth shrugged a reply. "It would seem that you are the one with the problem, my lord, for you have just admitted that you have trouble keeping your patience." She smiled at her logic and the expression on his face. "I will be happy to help you overcome this problem," she added, "if you will allow it."

"*I* am not the one with a problem," Geoffrey responded. He smiled and said, "You try to make me yell again, don't you? What is your aim?"

Elizabeth did not immediately answer. She lifted her shoulders and turned her gaze away from him.

"You bite the lion and chance being swallowed by him," he said, rubbing his chin.

"And you are the lion, my lord?" Elizabeth asked, thinking to set another trap.

"I am," Geoffrey acknowledged, seeing the sparkle in her eyes and wondering at the cause.

"Then that makes me your lioness, does it not?" she inquired with a soft voice.

"I had not considered it, but yes, it would make you my lioness," he said with a chuckle.

"Interesting," Elizabeth told her husband. "Did you know that the lioness is the one who hunts and brings the food to her husband?"

"Only because he allows it," Geoffrey stated with conviction.

"And will you allow it for this one day?" she asked.

Geoffrey frowned. "What is it you ask of me?"

"To ride with me into the forest. I will hunt for you and fix your meal and then *we* will return to our duties." And perhaps, she thought, you will tell me your plans for Belwain when we are alone and you are not distracted.

Geoffrey threw back his head and laughed, causing his mount to prance in agitation. "You think you are so capable?"

Elizabeth nodded and he laughed all the more.

There was much work to be done, orders to be given, Geoffrey knew, weighing his responsibilities against the pleasure his wife was offering. Ah, but it was too good an opportunity to let pass by, Geoffrey decided with extreme smugness, this chance to show Elizabeth her limits as a woman.

"Lead the way, lioness," he said, throwing the reins back to her. "Your lion is hungry."

Elizabeth laughed with delight, feeling very much like a child about to play a new game. All the problems would still be there when the game was ended, but the respite was welcome. For this one day, Elizabeth decided, she would rest from her burden. And show this arrogant husband a thing or two in the process.

She spurred her horse into motion, anticipation taking hold. Geoffrey stayed right behind her, letting her set the pace, as she rode into the forest, her golden hair flying with the wind behind her. He caught her laughter and found himself laughing too. Her enthusiasm was catching, he thought to himself, feeling a lightness of spirit he hadn't known he possessed.

Elizabeth finally grew tired of the race and pulled to a stop. She slid from her horse before her husband could reach her side. It was she who grabbed his hand and led him to a sturdy-looking tree and commanded him to sit and rest while she saw to their food.

He could not allow that and said as much. "I will not interfere with your hunting but I must stay by your side. That is the way of it," he added when he saw she was about to protest.

"Then do not make a sound or you will have no dinner," she warned.

Geoffrey watched her take an arrow and position it against the string of the puny bow, and he could not contain himself. He started to laugh again. "You intend to use that . . . toy to catch our game?" he asked.

"I do," Elizabeth snapped.

"Then I will surely go hungry," Geoffrey predicted, though he admitted he didn't mind.

Elizabeth ignored his barb. She walked a short distance from the horses and then stood, as still as the tree beside her, waiting. The arrow was ready . . . If only the rabbit would cooperate!

So intense, Geoffrey thought as he watched his wife. He stood a short distance behind her, listening to the sounds of the forest, his hand in position above his sword. When would she give up this pretense? he asked himself. Admit that she was ill-prepared and needed his assistance? It would be a while longer, he predicted, for she was most stubborn. He sighed and shifted his weight, prepared to outwait her. Elizabeth turned then and glared at him and he ceased his noise.

She didn't miss the smug look on his face, but wished she had. So smug, so sure of himself and his ability only. He waits for me to fail so that he can gloat, she thought. He prepares his laugh and his barbs.

If she had to stand there all day and into the night, she vowed she would. Failure could not be allowed, not if she was to keep any of her pride.

Her prayers for victory were finally answered. A fat, though nimble rabbit raced across the small clearing; Elizabeth took aim and sent the arrow whistling through the air, and if Geoffrey had so much as blinked, he would have missed the kill. The rabbit collapsed to the ground, nailed to the earth by her arrow.

His mouth opened before he had a thought as to what he would say. Truth was, he admitted with a bit of sheepish astonishment, he was fairly speechless.

Oh, how she longed to look back over her shoulder and see her husband's reaction! She did not, of course, as she wished to act most blasé about her accuracy, and she knew that if she looked at him, he would read the gloating victory in her eyes. She pulled another arrow from her pouch and positioned it against the tensed string of the bow, keeping her smile to a minimum.

Elizabeth waited until her arms began to ache and then she changed her strategy. Ever so slowly she began to walk into the denseness, hoping to startle game into motion. Her aim worked, and Elizabeth felled another rabbit.

When she had gathered both rabbits, she turned to her husband and smiled. "I am most fortunate that the rabbits do not know I use a toy, my lord. Don't you agree?"

Geoffrey laughed and said, "They are most stupid animals, wife, but even so, I must tell you, well done."

Elizabeth made a formal bow and replied, "I thank you for the compliment, Geoffrey. I do believe it is your first. You have my appreciation for your kind words." Elizabeth's eyes sparkled with merriment. She felt like throwing her head back and laughing, just for the sheer joy of it.

"I would rather have your kiss," Geoffrey said, and

only then realized how very much he wanted to touch her.

Elizabeth almost asked him if he had forgotten that it was daylight and that he had informed her that kissing was only for the privacy of their bedroom. He was breaking one of his rules, and that fact pleased her. "Then you shall have it, husband," she answered. She dropped the rabbits and walked over to him, swinging her hips in what she hoped was a provocative manner. Placing her hands on his shoulders, she concentrated on her task, wetting her lower lip with the tip of her tongue before she pulled his head down to hers. Their lips met in a long, searching kiss that left them both unsatisfied. And so they kissed again. The playfulness was suddenly gone and Geoffrey became demanding, wrapping his arms around her and pulled her up against his chest. Her reaction to his forcefulness was an uninhibited enthusiasm; her arms clung to him while her tongue circled and entwined with his in this sensuous battle for fulfillment. He turned her and braced her against he bark of a tree, never breaking his hold on her lips. Stroking her breasts through the material did not appease his appetite, nor did her motion with her hips, rubbing so seductively against his own, give him respite.

He growled low in his throat and Elizabeth whimpered an answer. The need to touch her satin skin drove all thoughts aside. He lifted the hem of her skirt with both hands until the material was caught at her waist and then caressed the smoothness that was Elizabeth, pleasured beyond belief when he felt her tremble beneath his hands. He leaned one arm above her head against the bark, trying to ease the growing ache in his loins. He pulled his mouth free and rested his head against the side of her face, breathing heavily into her ear. "This is foolish, wife. We must stop. It is not safe here." His voice, harsh with frustration and need, sounded as if it came from a great distance.

Elizabeth kissed the side of his cheek, her tongue stroking the line of his scar. "It is safe," she whispered. "It is always safe when I am with you." She caught his mouth then and kissed him hungrily. "Please, Geoffrey," she moaned when he tried to pull away from her.

"There are other ways to ease your torment," Geoffrey whispered in a rough voice. He captured her mouth in a devastating kiss that promised fulfillment and slipped his hand beneath her undergarments. When he touched and began to stroke the dewy softness between her legs, she cried out in ecstasy. Geoffrey's tongue began to slowly move in and out of her mouth while his fingers imitated the motion below. And then Elizabeth's hips began to arch more forcefully against his hand; she buried her head in the cup of his shoulder, trembling against the need and desire coursing through her body. Release came in such a rush, shaking Elizabeth with such force that she collapsed against Geoffrey.

Geoffrey thought that he could withstand the sweet torment of holding Elizabeth so near and giving her the pleasure he wished her to have, but found that it was not enough. He held her tightly against him until her breathing slowed and the trembling had stopped, and then stood back from her. Without a word, he began to take his clothes off, willing her with his gaze to do the same.

She was quicker than he, standing proud though shy before him, her clothes at her feet.

Geoffrey took his time looking at her, his passion warm and full of promise. Elizabeth's breasts were heavy with need, the nipples erect and waiting, straining for his touch.

His control amazed her. She watched him place his tunic upon the ground and turn back to her, and was almost overwhelmed by the sheer beauty of his body. He seemed the Viking god her grandfather had told her stories of, she thought, for he was surely as magnificent

in build. And he belongs to me, she thought with
wonder, just as I belong to him.

Geoffrey's hand reached out for her and Elizabeth
rushed into his embrace. He seemed content to hold
her against him, rubbing his hands down her back with
a sigh of pleasure, as he inhaled the sweet scent.

He knelt down beside his tunic and pulled her down
beside him, resting her on her back before stretching
out beside her. His movements were slow and almost
lazy now as he trailed the tip of his finger over one
breast and then the other.

Elizabeth pulled his head down and kissed him
passionately on the lips, willing him to lose his control.

"God's truth, Elizabeth, you make my blood boil
with my need for you," Geoffrey whispered.

"It is the same for me, Geoffrey," Elizabeth admitted, blushing. "I fear you think me wanton," she
added. She parted her legs and tried to pull him on top
of her, but Geoffrey held back.

"Not yet," he whispered as his mouth traveled to her
breasts. His tongue began to stroke first one and then
the other, always close to the nipples but never touching. He was driving her crazy with his tender torture
and she found herself pulling at his hair to stop him.
She heard his soft laughter and then his mouth gave her
what she wanted, what she silently begged for, as he
touched the nipple with his tongue and then took it into
his mouth.

Elizabeth sighed her pleasure, let the exotic feeling
surge through her body, content.

Her limbs felt blissfully lethargic. Geoffrey leaned up
and stared into her eyes, knew that he pleasured her
and determined, before he took his fill, to show her
more of this new sexual world he had introduced her to.

The need to taste her drove him on. His mouth
trailed light, feathery kisses in a circle, around her
navel and then slowly moved downward. He found the
heat, the wetness he had caused, hidden by the triangle

of blond curls, and began to make love to her with his mouth, his searching tongue.

Elizabeth was shocked by the initial touch, did not know that man and woman worshiped each other in such a way, and began to protest. The words died in her throat, washed away by the waves of pleasure her husband caused. She clutched at his shoulders, straining against him as she fought the tension she felt building inside. "Geoffrey!" It was a demand, softened by her gasp.

Her husband knew what she wanted, what she needed to find her release, but held back, keeping her on the brink of the summit until he was sure she was completely out of control. Her throaty moans and the motion of her hips against him told him that it was time. He lifted his head and looked into her passion-glazed eyes as he thrust his fingers inside the velvet heat just once. Elizabeth's entire body arched in splendor. She shook with the force of her climax and then felt herself floating in a sea of colors, all exploding and blending and finally fading.

She opened her eyes to see her husband smiling with arrogant satisfaction.

"You think me terrible?" she whispered with embarrassment.

"I think you beautiful," Geoffrey answered. His voice shook and Elizabeth felt a rush of gratitude for the control he had exercised.

And now it was his turn, she decided. She wasn't sure what she was to do but continued to look directly into his dark gaze as she said, "And does the wife touch her husband in the same way?"

"Aye," Geoffrey replied in a low growl.

"Like this?" Elizabeth asked, taking hold of his hand. She slowly touched one of his fingers with the tip of her tongue and then slipped the whole of it into her mouth and began to suckle it.

Geoffrey's control snapped. His growl of pleasure

was her only warning before he covered her with his body and thrust into her. His mouth captured her moans as he continued to plunder her body and her soul, pushing harder and harder.

Elizabeth wrapped her legs around his powerful thighs and rode with him on the journey toward fulfillment yet again. He was the warrior now, intent on his victory, but Elizabeth was there with him, sharing in his intimate conquest.

"My gentle warrior," she whispered when the storm was ended and the sun was again allowed to shine.

Geoffrey heard her and smiled. He rolled to his side with a contented sigh and said, "You are wrong, wife. I think perhaps you are *my* gentle warrior, with your dagger at your side and another hidden beneath your skirts; aye, you would be a warrior if you could, but you have set yourself an impossible task, for you will never be able to shed your gentleness."

He kissed her temple after his speech, saw that his words had affected her, for her eyes were filled with tears, and felt most content. He was finding it easier and easier to tell her what was inside him, and admitted that he felt no foolishness with his confessions.

"This lion grows hungry," he yelled with mock fierceness, slapping her soundly on her hip.

"This lion is always hungry," Elizabeth laughed, rubbing her hip. She stood when he did and only had to hug him twice while they dressed.

"It is most difficult for you to keep your hands off me," Geoffrey said with extreme smugness in his voice. "Do not pretend such outrage," he added with a chuckle when she tried to glare at him. "I will have to get used to this clinging nature of yours, I imagine," he added with a feigned sigh.

"And is that so terrible, husband?" Elizabeth asked. She picked up the rabbits and turned away from him, looking for a spot to set the fire.

"No, only foreign, that is all," Geoffrey answered. "I will skin the game while you gather twigs for the fire," he announced.

Elizabeth nodded and threw the rabbits to him.

"Why is it so foreign?" she asked. She made a basket out of the hem of her skirt and began to fill it with bits of branches as she talked.

"What?" Geoffrey asked. He was squatting on the ground, a small hunting knife in his hand, and glanced up to look at her. He smiled when he saw that she was barefoot still and thought that she looked like an enchanting wood nymph.

"This showing of affection, Geoffrey . . . there was none between your parents?"

Geoffrey was surprised by her question, but lost his train of thought as he appreciated the enticing curve of her ankles. "Put your shoes on before you hurt yourself."

"After you answer my question," she replied in a saucy voice. She saw that he continued to stare at her legs and smiled. "I like to go barefoot."

"They died before I had much memory of them," Geoffrey answered. "Now put your shoes on or I will do it for you."

Elizabeth dropped the hem of her dress and the twigs fell beside Geoffrey. She spotted one shoe by the base of the tree but couldn't locate the other. "Then who saw you raised?" she asked as she knelt and burrowed under a thorny bush. The tip of her dark boot was visible and she had to flatten herself on the ground to wiggle close enough to reach it. It wasn't a very dignified position, but necessary. And Geoffrey observed the whole scene.

"You were overly zealous in removing your clothes," he remarked with a chuckle. "Always in such a hurry," he chided. The sparkle in his eyes matched his voice and Elizabeth found herself agreeing.

"I hate to wait for anything," she answered with complete honesty. She sat on the ground and shook her boots free of any surprises before slipping her feet into them. "And I especially hate having the subject changed all the time. Now answer me, please."

"Answer what?" Geoffrey asked.

"Who raised you?" She couldn't keep the exasperation out of her voice.

"The king himself," Geoffrey answered. "Throw me your dagger," he ordered, "mine is too large for this task." He was still squatting in the middle of the small clearing, looking at the arrows he had just removed from the game, studying how they were fashioned. "Did your grandfather design these?" he asked when he saw that she was watching him.

Elizabeth stood up and began to brush the dirt from her skirt. "I made those," she boasted, "once my grandfather showed me the way. They are most effective, are they not?"

"That they are, though too puny for a knight to carry," Geoffrey said.

Elizabeth handed Geoffrey her dagger and then knelt down beside him. She began to arrange the twigs in a circular stack and then asked, "How old were you when you went to the king? Did you become his page?"

"One of many," Geoffrey answered. "I was six, maybe seven years old."

"Six! But that is too young. You must be at least eight years old to become a page, is that not so?" She sat back on her heels and frowned.

"Aye, that is usually the way," Geoffrey acknowledged, "though some leave their homes by the age of seven. In my case, there was no one else, save the king, and he was a close friend of my father's."

"Tell me about your parents. Do you remember what they looked like?" she asked.

"No, I do not remember," Geoffrey answered in a

gruff voice. He seemed irritated by her question and Elizabeth wondered at his reasoning. "Now quit your chatter and see to my food," he ordered.

They did not say another word until the meat was cooked and eaten. Geoffrey ate most of the game and Elizabeth was content to nibble on one of the roasted legs.

Geoffrey removed a small sheep's skin from his saddle and offered Elizabeth a drink. Thinking it filled with water, Elizabeth took a large swallow and promptly choked. Geoffrey grabbed her by the shoulders and began to whack her on her shoulders and she didn't know which was worse, to die from lack of clean air, or from being beaten to death.

"Always in a hurry," Geoffrey snapped when she had stopped coughing and could hear him. "It is amazing that you have lasted this long." He shook his head and then decided to shake her too.

"I thought it was water," Elizabeth said in her defense. "And I was thirsty. And you have probably made my shoulders black and blue with your help."

"Your face is still bright red," Geoffrey said, ignoring her sarcasm. Why, he had barely tapped her between her shoulder blades, but then he had come to realize that his wife tended to exaggerate. It was a fault he would have to tolerate. "Come and sit down," he said, hauling her up into his arms.

He lifted her high into the air and then pretended that he was about to drop her to the ground, but his wife was not amused by his play, only glared at him and held on tighter.

He sat down and leaned against the tree, holding her in his arms. Elizabeth rested her head against his shoulder with a sigh. For long minutes they were content to keep their silence, each thinking his own thoughts.

Now is the time for me to bring up the subject of

Belwain, Elizabeth thought. His mood is light and perhaps he will be more receptive to telling me his plans.

"Your brother will go to the king to be his page. I have not decided on the time yet. Perhaps in the fall."

His statement jarred Elizabeth and she spoke before thinking, "You would not! He is still a baby. And I have heard terrible stories about the king. I will not allow it." She knew as soon as she said the rash words that her husband was not pleased. She felt him tense beneath her. His arms tightened around her.

Before he could answer her, Elizabeth said, "I know I cannot allow or disallow, but I cannot believe that you would do such a cruel thing. Surely you jest?" Her voice was soft and hopefully sincere. She lifted her head and looked at him, tracing a finger along the wrinkle on his brow his frown caused. "Being his guardian now, I feel this responsibility, and since he is so much younger than I—"

"Elizabeth," Geoffrey said her name as a sigh, "*I* am the boy's guardian now that I am your husband, and I am also his overlord in future. Now what nonsense is this about the king? You should be proud that your brother will join his court. Don't you know the honor I bestow upon him?" He removed her hand from his brow and held it against his chest. Her touch had an unsettling effect on his senses and he needed to be clearheaded when dealing with his argumentative wife.

Elizabeth nodded while her mind sought a way to make him understand her position.

"What stories have you heard about William?" he asked with mild interest. He pulled her back against him and began to rub the goosebumps from her arms.

"He has a terrible temper and is not of a forgiving nature," Elizabeth said. "I do not want my little brother placed in such harsh conditions. He has been through too much already."

"There are those who say I have a terrible temper,

Elizabeth, and yet you do not seem afraid." He chuckled with his statement, secretly pleased that she had never shown fear of him.

"But they do not know you as I do," Elizabeth stammered, "and you are reasonable. You said so yourself. But King William—"

"Yes?" Geoffrey encouraged when she did not finish her sentence. "King William what?"

"Have you not heard of the town of Alençon?" Elizabeth whispered. She closed her eyes and waited for his answer.

"Ah, Alençon. But that was a long time ago, when William was young and rash and intent on gaining his rightful title," Geoffrey explained.

"Then it is true? He actually became crazed when some fool called him bastard and truly cut off the feet and the hands of sixty men? It is really true?"

"No, it is not true," Geoffrey corrected, and Elizabeth felt a wave of relief. "There were but thirty-two of them, not sixty."

"What! He really did such a terrible thing?" She was so aghast that she almost fell off his lap, as much from the knowledge that the story was indeed true as from the blasé way her husband confirmed it. Why, he acted as if they were discussing chickens or rabbits instead of men.

"It was a long time ago," Geoffrey replied with a shrug. "He holds his temper better now."

"God be praised," Elizabeth muttered. "And you would send little Thomas into his care?"

"Do not upset yourself. We will wait until the boy is older and then I will decide what is to be done. How old is he now?"

"Four." Elizabeth blurted out the lie, thinking he might believe her, as her little brother was on the short side.

"More like seven," Geoffrey stated. "Do not lie to me. Ever."

"I did not lie, only exaggerated," Elizabeth replied. She leaned back against him, the top of her head just under his chin, and had a sudden thought. "He could live with us. There is so much you could teach him, Geoffrey," she said, hoping to stroke his ego into seeing her reasoning. "That would be an honor for him to become your page, as you are a—"

"Enough," Geoffrey groaned. "Your praise has a purpose, wife. I am not so simpleminded that I do not see what you are about. I have promised to wait to make my decision. That will have to satisfy you for the moment."

"As you wish," Elizabeth answered in a demure voice. He couldn't see her face, so he missed the smile of victory. Oh, how easy it was to deal with him, she concluded. He really is a reasonable man. "And now perhaps you feel inclined to talk with me about Belwain?" she asked in a soft voice.

"I do not wish to ruin our pleasant morning," Geoffrey said with a sigh.

"But you promised to tell me what you planned, and I gave you my trust. I did not try to kill my uncle. I held my word," Elizabeth reminded her husband.

"Still, having you so docile and affectionate . . . Very well, I will tell you and you will become angry. It is your right to know—"

"You are stalling, Geoffrey," Elizabeth said. She turned in his arms and placed her hands against the sides of his face. "I will continue to be affectionate, for I can be no other way with you. And I will always have faith in you," she whispered. It was true, she admitted with a nod, she did have faith in her husband. He *was* a righteous man.

Geoffrey read the trust in her eyes and made a gruff sound in his throat. He pulled her hands away, hoping his action would stop the heat building between them. "There were three possibilities I could act on," he said.

"The first was, of course, the most simple and perhaps the one you would approve of: I could kill Belwain and be done with it. But," he said in a louder voice when he saw she was about to interrupt, "then I would not know if he acted alone. We both agree he does not have the intelligence to plan such a well-designed attack and therefore know that there is at least one other just as responsible. Therefore, I ruled out the first possibility."

"Why didn't you just force Belwain to tell you what you wanted to know?" Elizabeth asked.

"If you knew that admitting to a crime would mean your death, would you not keep your silence?" Geoffrey asked. He didn't wait for her answer but continued in a patient voice, "He knows my reputation. No, he would never have admitted his part, even if tortured."

"And the second possibility?" Elizabeth asked, frowning.

"To place the matter before William, challenge Belwain for the truth in court."

Elizabeth was already shaking her head before Geoffrey could explain. He stopped her with his hands and said, "I did not choose that possibility for two reasons. One, I do not wish to bring my petty problems to my overlord. It is my duty to deal with my vassals. William has much on his mind these days," he said, "trying to keep peace in his kingdom and his household too. It is a melancholy time for him," he added. "And two," he continued, "there is the chance that Belwain and his friends, his witnesses, just might convince the king that he had nothing to do with the murders of your family. Then the boy would have to go into his guardianship. It is a risk I do not wish to take."

"But the king would listen to you," Elizabeth argued. "Though I admire your decision not to place the problem before him," she hurried to add, in case she irritated him. He was being most informative and she

185

did not wish to stop his train of thought. "Belwain deserves death, but not at the king's hands," she couldn't help but add.

"Elizabeth," Geoffrey said her name with a weary sigh. "You have but a single purpose and do not know what you are talking about. It is not the king's way to kill anyone these days."

"I do not understand, I admit it," Elizabeth answered, frowning. "What does he do when one is found guilty of some terrible crime if he does not kill them?" she asked with simple logic.

"He does not believe in such harsh action and has not put a man to death since Earl Waltheof."

"Then what does he do?" Elizabeth asked. "Pat them on the back and send them on their way to do more harm?"

"Hardly that," Geoffrey answered. "His methods are just as harsh as death, to my way of thinking. It is the usual custom to cut off their limbs or put their eyes out. Sometimes the punishment kills the guilty, other times not, but I imagine they wish themselves dead."

Elizabeth trembled. She guided the talk back to what she wanted to know. "And the third choice?"

"To wait. I have decided to do nothing for the moment." He took hold of her hands in anticipation of her reaction.

Elizabeth frowned but did not otherwise react. Surely he would continue with his explanation, she thought.

Geoffrey waited for the explosion, surprised and somewhat relieved when it did not come. He had no wish to argue with her. He smiled at her and placed a kiss on her forehead. "I see you are learning patience, wife. That pleases me," he praised. "And now I will tell you the rest of my plan."

Elizabeth kept her somber expression but nodded, urging him with her intense gaze to get on with the telling. She wanted to understand and to agree with him, to find peace and have vengeance too; she found that placing the burden of punishment in his hands was not so very difficult.

"The soldier that you pointed out last night?" he began with a question and continued before she could respond. "He too has been allowed to leave. One of my men, his forty days of work for me completed, has joined Belwain's group. He let it be known his duty to me was ended and that he was in need of extra coin. He will watch and listen and then report his findings to me."

"Why didn't you just force the soldier to tell you the truth?" Elizabeth asked.

"You suggest that I torture him, sweet wife?" he asked, smiling.

"Do not smile at me, Geoffrey. I am not normally such a vengeful person. But you were not there, you did not see them, what they did. I do not mean for you to torture the man, only make him tell you—"

"You are right. It is no smiling matter, this." He pulled her back into his arms and squeezed her. It was the closest he had ever come to saying he was sorry, and he decided that she would have to be content. He could give her no more.

"I accept your apology," Elizabeth said. Her expression was still serious. Geoffrey started to tell her that he had not actually apologized but decided against it. She certainly could twist his words, he thought with some admiration.

She was looking directly into his eyes and Geoffrey read the innocent acceptance there. She has given me her loyalty, without question or much argument. And God help me, I will not fail her. In such a short time she has turned my world upside down and sideways too with her very existence; he would accept the responsibility she trusted him with, just as he had already accepted her as his wife. He refused to ponder the reasons for his feelings, knowing that if he did, he would have to admit to feelings and emotions he thought long ago dead.

"But what is your plan for Belwain?" she asked.

"I have told it," Geoffrey said. "I am going to wait."

"Geoffrey, I am trying to see your reason," Elizabeth said with irritation. "But getting you to explain to my satisfaction is the same as trying to pull a tooth, I swear it."

Geoffrey felt he had told her enough. As far as Belwain was concerned, it was his plan to let him be for the time. She did not need to know that he was setting a trap for the other, and when the trap was closed, Belwain would be named as accomplice. It was too soon to tell her. She would have to wait.

"Have patience a while longer," Geoffrey tried to soothe. "Proof will—"

"Will what?" Elizabeth said, struggling out of his arms. "Pop up in front of you like the flowers of spring?" She stood and turned her back on him. "It could be years before such proof is found unless you look for it. You put all your hopes in one man, this soldier you sent off with Belwain's men. And that is not enough. I made a promise, aye," she yelled, "a vow, to avenge my family and I will see it through."

"You will do nothing," Geoffrey commanded. He came to his feet in one bound and grabbed her by her shoulders. "I will have your word. Leave this business to me." He was yelling again, infuriated for the second time in the space of one morning's time. It was more than any man should tolerate, he decided. She would know her place in this matter.

"I will not give it." Her defiance was like a piece of dry wood thrown on top of his sparks of fury, and an explosion was the only possible outcome.

"You will," he bellowed, "and you will not see food or water until you realize that fact." The way she stood, facing him with her defiance, her small hands balled into tight fists and resting on her hips, both amazed and incensed him. The top of her head barely reached his shoulders, yet she thought she could glare him into her way of thinking.

He pulled her roughly into his arms and all but threw her on top of her mare.

Elizabeth struggled to right herself, and when she was done, she stared straight ahead. "Then you will soon be a widower, my lord," she yelled. Her voice trembled with conviction. "I will starve to death before I give a promise I cannot keep. *My* word is my honor."

"You have the audacity to imply that mine is not?" Geoffrey demanded in another roar that made her mare prance with fright.

He will soon go hoarse if he continues to scream and yell at me, she thought, and then decided that that was not so very terrible at all. It would do him good to lose his voice as penance, and give her ringing ears some quiet.

"I would challenge a man for such foolish words."

"Then challenge me," Elizabeth snapped.

"Enough! Do not speak to me," he said. "And do not raise your voice to me *ever* again!"

Do not do this, do not do that . . . always he orders, and I am truly sick of it. He has no understanding, no sympathy for my feelings. No, she thought with despair, he cannot see my torment, else he would not demand that I wait.

Geoffrey slapped the back of her horse and then followed behind her. Elizabeth never looked back during the ride to the manor. There must be something I can do, she thought, trying to think of a plan. Something . . . someone I can turn to . . .

Chapter Nine

EVERYONE TRIED TO INTERFERE. EVEN THE SERVANTS, Geoffrey thought with exasperation. He should have been angry over their disregard for his orders, but found that he was not.

Two grim weeks had passed, and Geoffrey was ready to call a truce—yes, he admitted without shame, even to concede defeat. He would welcome it just to glimpse one small smile from his wife.

His every thought concerned her, he realized as he walked into the great hall. There were several servants busy cleaning the area, and two of his loyal knights sat, drinking from cups at the table. He walked over and sat in the chair he had used when he assumed the role of judge, placed next to the hearth, and waited. He was conditioned to what was happening around him, and sat there without expression until one and all had fled the room on missions they just then remembered. Aye, even my knights desert me, Geoffrey thought. But he was smiling; he knew the reason for their vanishing act. They feared him. It was true, and it did not displease him overly. It was a fact that he had been known to blow his temper on occasion . . . but what man, pushed to his limit of endurance, would not? he asked himself.

It did not matter, he told himself. He was used to being alone. It was his way . . . as a child raised among the battle-hardened warriors and now as his own ruler—save William as his overlord, of course.

Yet he was not alone, not even now, in the emptiness of the silent hall. She was always with him. She haunts me, Geoffrey muttered with disgust.

He could not understand it, this hold she locked him within. As a small boy he had learned to harden himself against the need for food or water; as a squire he had braved the frigid winter nights, all for short periods but long enough to learn the discipline of body. But how to discipline himself against Elizabeth? he found himself asking. What form of exercise could he call upon to accomplish that?

He braced his hand against his brow and closed his eyes. He was weary of the fighting with his wife, though they had barely exchanged a word since their argument in the forest. Except at night, when their bodies came together, only then did they speak. He remembered that first night after their argument with both arrogant pride and a little shame. He had not forced her, knew that he could never force her, yet he was not gentle with her either.

The sight of her had inflamed him when he had finally sought his bed. He had indulged in perhaps one too many cups of ale, but his head was still clear. She had thought him drunk, and he did not tell her otherwise.

She was standing in the center of the room, but once

she read the intent in his eyes, she began to slowly back up, until she could not take another step. "You stalk me like a panther," she had whispered, "and I do not like it."

"So now I am compared to a panther, when only this morning I was your lion," Geoffrey had drawled as he began to strip his clothes from his body. "You have a fixation for animals, wife," he said. His gaze never left her mouth, for, God's truth, he was fascinated by the pouting lips, remembered the magic of their touch.

Elizabeth wet her lower lip with the tip of her tongue. She was nervous, clutching her robe together like a shield against his raking gaze.

"I do not want you to touch me," she said, trying to sound forceful and knowing she failed miserably. Every pore in her body was beginning to tingle with anticipation of his touch, but there was no way that he could know, was there? "I do not—"

"I do not care what you want," Geoffrey muttered. He stood just inches from her, completely nude, his hands resting on his hips. "Take your clothes off, wife, or I will tear them from your body. *I* want you."

Elizabeth thought about refusing him, but from the intent look in his eyes, she knew it would be futile. She was his wife, she reminded herself as she began to remove the robe. It was her duty. Duty, yes, she thought, but there will be little pleasure in the deed, she promised him.

She let the robe fall to the floor and matched his stance, her hands on her hips, her head tilted back defiantly. "You are an arrogant, unreasonable brute, but you are my husband and I will not deny you. Be warned, Geoffrey, you will get little pleasure from the marriage act this night, for I absolutely refuse to respond to your touch. Is that understood?" she asked. Her breasts were heaving from her nervous speech and his grim expression.

He surprised her by throwing his head back and laughing until tears filled his eyes. He was surely drunk, she thought with disgust. How could she teach him a lesson if he was too drunk to care? "I believe you are right, wife. There will be little pleasure, indeed. When I touch you, 'little' is the last word I would use to define both of our reactions." He did not give her time to react to his words, but hauled her up against him, felt her gasp at the intimate contact, and laughed again. "So you will not respond to me this eve?" he asked with a challenge in his voice.

"I will not," Elizabeth whispered in a shaky voice as her husband trailed wet kisses down the side of her neck. She found she had to clutch his arms, thick with sinewy strength, to stay on her feet. His tongue, stroking against the sensitive area at the base of her neck, was already forcing moans from her throat. She was able to continue to stand quite rigid in his embrace, until his hands slid down her back and began to massage her bottom. When she began to melt like butter against him, he pulled her roughly up against his hard desire, kneading her softness against his body.

"You will beg me to take you," he whispered, jerking her head up for his kiss. His mouth silenced her protests, his tongue invading and seeking hers.

Elizabeth instinctively began to suck and pull on his tongue, and was pleased when she heard him groan.

He lifted her high in his arms and carried her to the bed, where he forced her on her stomach, coming down on top of her. She thought she would suffocate before he lifted himself and began to kiss her, all the way down her back. By the time he reached the base of her spine, Elizabeth was clutching the covers with both of her hands and moaning her need. Geoffrey slipped one hand between her legs and began to stroke the fire building inside Elizabeth.

"Tell me you want me," he demanded. His fingers

were relentless and Elizabeth would have told him anything to stop the sweet torment he caused.

"Yes, Geoffrey," she gasped when his fingers invaded her warmth, "I want you." She groaned. She tried to roll over, to take him into her arms and body, but Geoffrey stayed her actions. He knelt between her legs and lifted her hips.

"Say it again," he demanded, his voice harsh.

"I want you," Elizabeth cried. "Please, Geoffrey," she begged, beyond caring that she was indeed begging him.

Geoffrey growled his satisfaction and entered her swiftly, filling her completely. Elizabeth began to sob with pleasure, her eyes closed in building rapture. She was reaching the peak when Geoffrey stopped, turned her, and pulled her up into his arms. He kissed her deeply, hungrily before falling to the bed with her in his arms. He stretched out on his back and pulled her on top of him. Elizabeth clung to his mouth, moaning against him when he once again entered her. She leaned back, moving slowly at first and then increasing her speed until the explosion of mind and senses caused her to sob his name. He answered her call, arching against her with a force that penetrated her soul. He held her securely against him with his hands on her hips while the tremors of release enveloped both of them. Their gazes found and locked with each other's, and there was no victory in Geoffrey's expression, no submission in Elizabeth's; no, there was only shared wonder by both.

Elizabeth slowly closed her eyes and collapsed against his chest, rose and fell with his labored breathing, and tried to gather her wits. It was a difficult task she set for herself. Everything continued to be heightened. Her senses were still finely tuned, yet flooded with stimuli. The musky scent of their lovemaking permeated her body, making it difficult to do more than sigh with acceptance. Even the candle, casting a golden glow on their glistening bodies, seemed an erotic happening.

Please, Geoffrey, do not gloat or laugh at me, she silently begged. She realized she was stroking the hairs on his chest and stopped. "Each time is like the first," she whispered against his skin, and then wished she had kept her thoughts to herself. His breathing had slowed and there was the possibility that he would soon fall asleep. Perhaps he would not remind her of his challenge and his obvious victory.

"No, love, each time is always better," he said in a husky voice. His hand began to leisurely stroke and caress her thigh. "Look at me, Elizabeth," he commanded, "I would know if I hurt you."

Elizabeth propped her head up on her hands and gazed into his eyes. She fought the urge to lean forward and kiss him once again. "You did not hurt me," she said in a soft voice.

His hands smoothed her hair away from her face before cupping the sides of her cheeks with such excruciating tenderness that tears filled Elizabeth's eyes. He leaned forward and placed a warm, gentle kiss on her parted lips. "What we have . . . this thing between us, it would be blasphemy to use it as a weapon to hurt the other. Never will you try to hold back what is mine," he said. His voice held no anger, only a sweet caress as he continued, "And never will I hold back what belongs to you."

"But, Geoffrey," Elizabeth whispered in return, "how can—"

"The battle between us stops at the bedroom door, wife."

"And resumes in the light of each new day?" she asked, unable to keep the sadness out of her voice.

"If you wish it," Geoffrey acknowledged.

Elizabeth did not have an answer for him. She closed her eyes and leaned her cheek against his chest. His words confused her. Perhaps, she thought with a yawn, perhaps in the light of day she would be able to sort it all out.

Geoffrey had been so sure that the following morning, after he had demanded that neither hold back from the other in the privacy of their bedroom, that his docile wife would give him the apology he had demanded. Docile! Ha, Geoffrey snorted aloud, that was certainly not the word to describe his new wife. Why she had had the temerity to ignore his request for an apology. He shook his head as he remembered how she had boldly walked over to the window and pointed to the sun. Oh, how she angered him! And at first that anger kept him unaffected. He locked Elizabeth in their room and commanded that she was to receive neither food nor water . . . nor visitors. And everyone seemed inclined to let him have his way, he thought, smiling to himself, most probably reasoning that the spat between husband and wife would be settled by nightfall.

But it was not, of course, and the interference began the next day, subtle at first, and then more obvious to the most ignorant of men. Geoffrey would go to the bedroom and find the door unlocked. Food would mysteriously appear in their room on trays no one remembered carrying. But his wife did not take a bite or a sip. By the third day, it was Geoffrey himself trying to entice her. And by the end of the fourth day, he commanded it. "I will not have you dead at my feet," he remembered telling her. And when she had raised one eyebrow in question, he had muttered something about becoming fond of her grandfather and her little brother and not wishing to distress either of them.

It was then that he devised another plan to pull her back in line, and had actually thought it would work. And with other women, it might have, he told himself. But not Elizabeth. She was like no other! The bolts of fine material went unnoticed and the seamstress had to ask him to command her into being fitted for new gowns. He, of course, had done it, more furious with himself than with her. Know your opponent! How often had that statement been drummed into his head. The problem here, Geoffrey admitted, was that he did not know Elizabeth's mind as well as he might; and in truth, he did not want her to be his opponent.

"With your permission, Geoffrey, I would have a few words with you." The interruption brought Geoffrey back to the present. He looked up and saw that Elizabeth's grandfather, Elslow, stood before him.

"You walk with the silence of a hunter," Geoffrey complimented. "I did not hear you."

"Your mind was elsewhere?" Elslow asked, smiling with knowledge.

"Aye, it was," Geoffrey admitted.

"On my granddaughter, no doubt." Elslow stated it as a fact, and waved his hand in dismissal when Geoffrey started to protest. "Enough of this, Geoffrey. You behave like a child in this matter."

Geoffrey was so flabbergasted by his new friend's statement that he could only shake his head. "You risk much with your errant words, Elslow," he said in irritation.

Elslow was unaffected by the implied threat. "Nonsense, Geoffrey. I risk nothing. It is you who risks it all." He pulled up a stool—without permission, Geoffrey noticed—and sat down facing the lord. He took a long time adjusting his long legs in front of him and only when he was comfortably settled did he look again at the Baron. "She gets her stubbornness from her father's side of the family, you know," he said, grinning.

Geoffrey found himself laughing. "She is that," he acknowledged. "I cannot give her what she wants, Elslow, not yet. And because of it she has no faith in me."

"She thinks you do not care," Elslow said. It was the first time in the two weeks that Geoffrey had spoken about his wife, and Elslow was very pleased. He sensed his grandson-in-law wanted to make peace.

"How can she think I do not care! Why, I actually called her 'love' one evening. Granted, it was in the heat of passion, but still, it was an . . . endearment. She is the only woman I have—"

Elslow was trying hard not to laugh. "Talk with her and use more honeyed words. Explain your position," he urged.

"I will not." The quiet refusal was devoid of anger. "It is not my place to explain," he argued. "She must learn patience. That is the way of it."

"And did you get your stubbornness from your mother or your father?" Elslow asked, grinning.

Geoffrey looked surprised by the question. "Neither," he said. "I do not remember my parents."

"That explains your confusion over her feelings," Elslow said very matter-of-factly. "But I tell you this, Geoffrey: I have learned over the years that we dislike in others what we find in ourselves."

Geoffrey stood up and almost tripped over Elslow's feet. "Walk with me and explain your riddle."

Elslow nodded his agreement and followed Geoffrey outside. He did not speak until they were out in the courtyard and headed toward the south end of the area.

"You are both stubborn and that is fact," Elslow said. He imitated Geoffrey's pace, also clasping his hands behind his back as they both charged up the slight incline. "Geoffrey, you are older and stronger in both spirit and body, and therefore you should make amends. Teach her what you expect with a gentle hand and a sweet tongue, else you will lose her."

"And did I ever have her?" Geoffrey found himself asking.

"Oh, yes, son," Elslow said. He smiled to himself and thought, They do not yet know that they love each other and that is their problem. Each guards against the other. "From the moment she said the vows, she became yours."

Geoffrey shook his head and hurried the pace. "You are mistaken," he muttered. When Elslow did not answer, Geoffrey glanced over at him and continued, "Always she talks about the great love between her mother and her father. I have never seen such a love, not even between William and Matilda, God rest her soul." He gave Elslow another long look and then said, "At times I thought Elizabeth made her stories up. No two people would let themselves become so attached to each other . . . so vulnerable. It is foolish."

"They did not have a choice," Elslow stated. "But it did not happen overnight as my granddaughter would have you believe. Your king married my daughter to Thomas to gain Montwright, and I can give testimony to the fact that the two newlyweds fought like lions and tigers in the beginning. Twice my daughter ran away from him," he said, laughing. "She even took his two daughters with her!"

"Tell me this tale," Geoffrey asked. He found himself grinning as he thought about what Elslow was telling him, wondering if Elizabeth knew these details of her parents' lives.

"Thomas had two pitiful-looking little girls," he began. "They looked like orphans, though dressed in finery, with a sadness in their eyes that tore at the hardest of hearts. They were little more than babes when their mother died and then they were taken from all they knew and placed in the cold home at Montwright. It only took my daughter a month to right the situation. The first time she ran away from her husband, she came to me, in London, and the transformation that had taken place with the little girls was amazing. She loved them and the children blossomed under her care."

"But what did Thomas do?" Geoffrey asked.

"Why, he came after her, of course," Elslow replied. "Used his daughters as his excuse for not beating her. He loved her from the start but was too stubborn to admit it."

Geoffrey stopped in midstride and turned to Elslow. "I do not understand why you did not hate him. He took what was yours and cast you out."

"My mind was set against him, I'll admit that," Elslow replied. "But then I saw my daughter with his two little girls. She had become their champion. I saw too how Thomas looked at her and read the caring in his eyes. I told him I would kill him if he harmed her, and instead of becoming angry with my threat, he agreed that I should do just that. He gave me his word to honor and protect her, and he held it to his dying day."

Geoffrey tried to picture Thomas in his mind but the image was vague. "He was a humble man, as I recall, and on the quiet side."

"He was content."

"Like I used to be," Geoffrey snapped. "Until your granddaughter came into my life. I will have this chaos end, Elslow, and things returned to normal."

Elslow knew he had said enough. He nodded and took his leave. He would give Geoffrey time to absorb what they had discussed, and then he would again prod him. The role of peacemaker was new to Elslow and he found himself quite thirsty from his effort. He quickened his pace in his quest for a cool goblet of ale. Maybe he could challenge Roger into another game of chess, he considered, smiling with anticipation.

Geoffrey stood where he was, his mind considering what Elslow had said. He straightened his shoulders and took a different direction, his hands once again clasped behind his back, as he circled the side of the fortress.

Little Thomas called out a greeting, and Geoffrey paused in his walk. He watched the little boy run toward him, holding a small spear in his arms. Elslow had fashioned the toy spear just the evening before.

"And what are you about?" he asked in what he considered his pleasant voice.

"I am going to learn the quintain," the child yelled.

"And who is going to teach you this exercise?" Geoffrey asked, smiling.

"Gerald," Thomas said, pointing to the squire, who was now coming around the side of the fort with his horse trailing behind. "See what he made?"

Geoffrey looked to where Thomas pointed. There, pounded into the ground, stood a five-foot post. Across the top was another piece of board, placed crosswise. Hanging from one end was a straw figure of a knight, and from the other end hung a bag of sand. The object of the exercise was to thrust the lance at the pretend knight, but with sureness and quickness, else the bag of sand would swing around in time to knock the rider from his saddle. The quintain was an exercise that the older squires preferred, and too dangerous for one as small as the child standing in front of him. "Today," he said, "you will just watch. And perhaps tomorrow you can sit in front of Gerald while he practices this most difficult exercise," Geoffrey stated.

Gerald swung up into the saddle of his horse then and showed Thomas how the exercise was done. The child was so impressed that he dropped his spear and clapped his hands with approval. "Again," he shouted, running closer to the squire, "do it again."

Gerald, seeing that he had his lord's undivided attention, was eager to comply. He was anxious to show his lord how nimble and quick he was. He turned the horse and raced him toward the target and swung his lance like an ax. His aim was for the area of the chest, but he misjudged in his enthusiasm, and the lance severed the clump of straw just below the helmet, causing the body of straw to fall in a heap while the head swung in its decapitated state.

Gerald was mortified. To show such clumsiness in front of his baron was humiliating. He started to call an apology for his aim when he caught sight of the child's face. What he saw there stopped him cold. He could only stare. And then the scream erupted from the lad, piercing the air like the release of a tormented soul from hell, the sound so devastating that Gerald had to cover his ears to keep the torment from reaching his soul.

Geoffrey was the first to react. He raced over to the child, turned him to look into his face. The anguish he saw there caused an ache to lodge in his heart. Again and again the child screamed, and all Geoffrey could do was hold him fast against him. It was little comfort, he knew, as the boy did not seem to recognize that he was being held.

Roger, with Elslow trailing behind, raced toward them. Geoffrey motioned to them that it was all right, and then lifted the child into his arms. The screams lessened then and the boy began to sob. He was soon exhausted from his shock and rested his head on Geoffrey's shoulder, clinging to him with his hands while he confronted his memory. "My mama," he sobbed.

"You are safe now, Thomas. Safe," Geoffrey chanted while he patted the boy on his back. His words calmed the child and the heart-wrenching sobs subsided.

Both Roger and Elslow stepped out of his path as Geoffrey walked by, still holding the child in his arms. His intent was to take the boy to his sister.

And then Elizabeth appeared. She came running toward them with a look on her face that saddened Geoffrey as much as the child's distress. She stopped when she saw they were coming toward her, though she continued to look terrified.

Geoffrey could tell by the way she was staring at her

brother's back that she thought him injured, and he shook his head and said in a gentle whisper, "He remembers."

Elizabeth understood. Tears filled her eyes and she nodded, reaching one trembling hand out to touch her brother. Geoffrey took hold of it and pulled her into his other side. With his arm circling her shoulders, he began to walk again.

She found herself leaning against him. The terror that her brother was horribly injured was over. She felt the safety and the peace of Geoffrey's hold and, for the moment, called a truce. They were united for this short time, both offering their comfort and their strength to the little one in need. Without exchanging a word, the three of them walked into their home.

"Thomas, do not hang out that ledge," Elizabeth ordered. "You will fall two stories down and lose your brains." The boy ignored Elizabeth's command and continued to lean out the window of her bedroom, spitting down at his unsuspecting victims between giggles of absolute seven-year-old delight.

Geoffrey opened the door to their room in time to hear his wife's next words. "If you do not climb down from there this very instant, I will tell your lord and he will be most angry," Elizabeth threatened. "And if I ask it, he will give you a sound thrashing."

The promise worked, and her little brother hurried to the floor, knocking over the stool he had climbed as a ladder. "Maybe he will not listen to you," Thomas said with another giggle. He liked to see his sister lose her patience on occasion, especially when he was bored with confinement.

"He will listen." The quiet assurance nearly knocked the child over. Thomas turned wide blue eyes to his lord and turned a scarlet red.

Geoffrey frowned at the boy and then turned to his

wife. Holding his mask of indifference for the child's benefit, he said in a serious tone, "Do you wish me to thrash him or not?"

Elizabeth knew that he was teasing from the glint of warm gold lighting his eyes. She almost laughed and then saw that her brother was watching her.

"I must think this over, husband," she said, pretending to consider the idea. "Since yesterday this impetuous brother of mine has caused much havoc. He placed honey in Gerald's helmet—"

"I thought he would think it funny," Thomas interrupted with obvious distress. He did not like having his sins paraded before his new lord.

"Gerald did not think it the least bit funny," Elizabeth snapped, keeping her expression firm, "and today Roger has confined him to our room because he tries to ride on the backs of my dogs. And now," she ended, "he disregards my orders and tries to spit on your soldiers. What think you of this behavior, my lord?"

Geoffrey shook his head and considered the child bowing his head before him. It had been five short days since the little one had regained his memory and in that time Geoffrey saw a complete transformation overtake the boy. He was wild and totally without caution, and had been saved from certain death at least twice a day by someone or other.

"What say you in your defense?" he asked the child. Laughter was building inside of him but he dared not show it. The child needed to know that there were limits and that he must stay within them, else he would never see his own knighthood. Besides, Geoffrey reasoned, if he so much as showed a grin, his wife would most probably thrash him.

Thomas knelt down and put his hand over his heart. He peeked up to see if his dramatic action had pleased the warrior and found the huge man frowning still. Closing his eyes tightly, he said, "I am sorry and I won't do it again. I promise," he said in a hopeful voice.

"You are totally without discipline and I wonder how you will ever become a knight," Geoffrey stated. "Now stand and follow me. I will put you to work so that you cannot get into further mischief."

"Husband? May I have a moment with you?" Elizabeth's softly spoken question felt like a tender stroke against his heart.

"Go and wait for me at the bottom of the steps," he told the child.

As soon as the door shut behind the child, Geoffrey began to chuckle.

"It really isn't funny," Elizabeth said with exasperation. "Father let him run like a wild cub. He has absolutely no manners."

"He is not so very bad," Geoffrey answered, "and in time he will learn what is expected of him."

"Sara told me that you ordered the packing begun," Elizabeth said, changing the subject. "What—"

"I was going to tell you tonight, when we were alone," Geoffrey said. He was still cautious when he visited with his new wife, for he enjoyed the temporary settlement between them and did not wish it to end. "We will leave for my home in a fortnight. I must see to a matter away from here first," he said, deliberately not telling her his destination or intent, "but it will not take overly long, and when I return I wish you ready."

"And Thomas?" Elizabeth asked, finding herself dreading his answer. She clasped her hands together behind her back so that he would not see her trembling.

"He will stay here with your grandfather as his temporary guardian for a time," Geoffrey said. "I do not wish to pull him from what is so familiar to him yet. He has been through enough changes for a time." He smiled at his wife when he saw her surprised reaction to his words. "You think me such a monster that I would not consider the boy's feelings?"

"I do not," Elizabeth whispered, returning his smile. "I think you most reasonable."

"Next summer Thomas will come to live with us. That should give me ample time to nail down my possessions so that he cannot destroy them."

His jest concerning her brother's wildness and clumsiness widened her smile. She nodded her agreement and said, "I will help you, husband." She walked over to him, shy but determined, and put her arms around his waist. "Then you will not send my brother to the king?" she asked. "You have changed your mind?"

"I have," Geoffrey admitted, liking the feel of her against him. He stroked her hair and added, "I find that lately I have changed my mind about many issues."

"Such as?" Elizabeth inquired, smiling up at him.

He started to answer but Elizabeth reached up and kissed him before he could utter a word. He returned the light touch with another and then another. "Such as liking your affection for me," he said finally. "I have become most accustomed to your blatant displays, wife, understanding, of course, how you cannot help yourself."

Elizabeth laughed and a sparkle entered her eyes. Geoffrey had come to know that certain look and waited for the jest or trap she was about to set. Aye, he thought to himself, he was beginning to understand her well.

"Think you so irresistible?" she asked.

"In truth, I did not, until you came into my life," he answered. "The scar bothers many," he said when she began to place soft kisses, one after another along the length of it, "but you . . ." He could not remember what he was saying as his wife's mouth had reached the lobe of his ear and her warm breath was making him warm with desire. "Stop this foolishness, wife," Geoffrey demanded. "It is daylight and there is much I must see to." He tried to keep his voice strong and determined but knew he failed miserably.

Elizabeth pulled back and gave him a long, sultry

look. "Aye, husband," she agreed in a whisper that felt like a stroke against his groin, "there is much to be done."

Geoffrey pulled her back into his arms and kissed her hungrily. "You are without discipline, wife," he told her with a sigh.

It had begun as a game for her, this intent to show him that he found her irresistible too, but Elizabeth forgot her aim. The game was ended with his ravishing kisses, his exciting promises whispered against her ear.

She did not remember later who undressed whom, or how, only knew the explosion to her senses when she was back in his arms and skin was touching, caressing skin.

"So hot, Geoffrey," he heard her moan against his mouth, "you make me so—"

His tongue stopped her words, thrusting inside with velvet insistence.

Elizabeth let her wild need take over. She dug her nails into his shoulders when he turned her and braced her against the wall and entered her. He wasn't gentle with her, nor she with him. He held her against his hips and tried to concentrate on slowing the pace, wanting her to find fulfillment before he, but her frenzied movement against him made that thought leave his mind. He drove into her again and again, as wild now as she, and barely heard her throaty cries against his shoulder.

"I love you, Geoffrey." The words, the verbal commitment, tumbled out with her physical release. She could no more stop their flow than she could stop the tremors racking her body. "I do, I do," she whispered as a litany when she felt her husband shudder against her.

Elizabeth rested her head on his shoulder, traced a circle with the tip of her tongue, tasting the salty perspiration she had caused, inhaled the rich, sensual scent that was Geoffrey, and glorified in pleasured contentment. He was holding her so tightly against him that she had trouble catching her breath, but she didn't mind or make protest. She closed her eyes in blissful peace and relaxed her grip on him.

Geoffrey's breathing slowed, but he continued to hold her against him, unwilling yet to let the moment pass. "You intoxicate me," he whispered in a husky voice.

"Just as you intoxicate me," Elizabeth answered. Her voice sounded lazy and as soft and light as her mood. She smiled and knew that she was smiling inside as well.

Geoffrey straightened his shoulders and let Elizabeth slide to the floor. He was looking intently into her eyes, as if he was searching for something there, Elizabeth thought.

Her lips were swollen from his kisses, her eyes wide with innocent trust, and Geoffrey thought she was the most beguiling, most enchanting woman in the world.

"I have not pleased you?" Elizabeth asked in confusion. She did not understand why he continued to look at her so intently.

Geoffrey placed his hands on the sides of her face and answered, "You have said that you love me, Elizabeth. Was it spoken in passion only or did you mean it?" He frowned then, waiting for her answer, his heart suspended above the abyss of uncertainty.

"I love you." She admitted the truth again in a shy voice and wished that he would let her go so that she could shield herself from his stare. She was opening herself to him, giving him the vulnerability she usually kept well hidden and protected. "I did not know it until I said it," she whispered then.

Geoffrey smiled, his eyes full of tenderness. He rubbed the side of her cheek with his thumb before leaning down and kissing her gently on her lips. "You please me, wife," he whispered. "I do not know about love as you do. My years of training did not expose me to such feelings." Geoffrey let go of her then and began to pick up his clothes. Elizabeth stood still, willing him to continue his speech.

Geoffrey knew that she waited and found himself irritated that she wanted more from him. He ignored her while he dressed and then turned back to her. "I am most pleased that you love me," Geoffrey said. "And mayhap when I am an old man I will tell you the same." His arrogant voice stunned Elizabeth and she folded her arms in front of her, ready to do battle. She realized then that she was quite naked, and hurried over to the foot of the bed to reach her robe. When she was covered and the belt secured, she turned back to him and said, "I have not asked for your love, Geoffrey, and God's truth, I do not know why I love you."

"You do not understand, wife," Geoffrey placated. "There is no place for love in a warrior's life. Only foolish men allow this feeling to guide them. When I am old and have many sons, then I can allow myself to become—"

"Foolish?" Elizabeth asked. She found her anger gone and suddenly felt like laughing. Poor Geoffrey, she thought with exasperation. He had so much to learn yet! You will love me, husband, else I will throttle you.

"Do not dare to laugh at me when I tell you my feelings." Geoffrey shook his head at how easily she could make him angry.

"I was not laughing," Elizabeth said, trying to sound contrite. "Only smiling."

"Do not correct me," Geoffrey muttered.

A loud knock sounded at the door, and Geoffrey found himself thankful for the interruption. "What is it?" he yelled louder than he had intended.

"Both messengers have returned, my lord," a soldier called to her husband.

Elizabeth frowned, wondering where the messengers came from, but decided, from her husband's sour expression, not to ask him. There were easier, less noisy ways to find out, she thought.

"Geoffrey?" Elizabeth's voice called him back as he started out the door.

"What is it?" he snapped. His mood was fast becoming furious, and all because she tried to make him reach into his soul and give her words he was not ready to release. In truth, he did not know if they were there, these words of declaration she prodded for. There was a chance that he did not possess them, and that, Geoffrey admitted only to himself, frightened him more than the vulnerability she wanted him to give her. He had never been frightened before. There was much to think over, and the sooner Geoffrey left her presence, the sooner he could confront his confused feelings. He did not like the chaos she paced him through, would not have it. "Our subject is ended, wife, until *I* decide to speak of it again." He turned again and was out the door before Elizabeth could move.

"Geoffrey!" She yelled his name at the top of her voice, and then covered her mouth with her hands, so that her laughter would not reach him.

Her husband appeared at the doorway, his hands on his hips and a scowl on his face. "What is it?" he roared in a voice that would have knocked a grown man to his knees.

She was totally unintimidated. Well, by God, he would remove that smile from her face and show her fear or . . .

"You have forgotten your boots, my lord."

Elizabeth laughed the whole time she dressed, stopping several times to wipe the tears from her cheeks. Aye, she loved him, she thought when she regained her control. There was freedom with her new knowledge, and a lightness of spirit. She pictured the expression on

his face when he realized he was barefoot, and promptly went into another fit of giggles.

And then she remembered the messengers and decided to find out what they were reporting, where they
had come from. She hurried with her hair, brushing it
back and free, and smoothed the hem of her new
lavender tunic.

As quietly as possible she hurried down the steps but
paused at the entrance to the hall when she heard her
husband say in an angry voice, "He ignores *my* summons, does he?"

Elizabeth moved to the wall, else her husband spot
her and lower his voice, for her curiosity was great.
Who had ignored his command and why? she wondered. Curiosity removed any guilt of the sin of eaves-
dropping. After all, her husband was yelling loud
enough to wake the dead, as was his usual custom,
Elizabeth thought.

"I did not speak to him directly, my lord," the
messenger said. "One of his men told me that he had
locked himself in his room and was mad with grief over
the loss of his wife. He also told me that he has refused
food and is trying to starve himself to death."

Geoffrey leaned against the hearth, rubbing his chin
in thought, but glanced up in time to see a flash of
lavender by the edge of the doorway. He waited a
moment and, when the spot of material did not move,
knew his wife was listening. He smiled and determined
to give her something to hear that would irritate her as
much as she irritated him by listening to his conversation. Aye, he thought, he was beginning to like these
games the two of them played. He cleared his throat
and said, "Mad with grief?" His voice was full of
disbelief. "No man becomes mad with grief over the
loss of a wife. No man! Why, they are too easily
replaceable. Now a horse, this is another matter," he
added in a loud voice.

Elizabeth reacted to his barbs with a gasp of outrage.

Now it was she who stood at the doorway with her hands on her hips and a scowl on her face. "A *horse?*" she yelled at him across the room. "You would better me with a horse? You dare to—to—"

"Why, Elizabeth, did you chance to overhear?" he asked. His eyes laughed at her discomfort, though his voice was quiet and full of mock surprise. He grinned then, and Elizabeth knew she had been tricked.

"Do you see through walls, husband?" she asked with exasperation. She walked into the hall and came to his side, waiting for his answer.

"It would be well for you to think so," Geoffrey answered. He winked at her, right in front of the messenger, Elizabeth realized, and she found herself blushing at his small show of affection.

"I apologize for the interruption," she said, smiling up at him.

"And?" her husband demanded with one raised eyebrow.

"And for overhearing," she muttered. "Though I will most probably do it again."

"It is undignified," Geoffrey retorted.

"It is that," Elizabeth admitted, "but it is also the only way I can find out what goes on, too," she reasoned. "Where is this messenger from," she asked, "and did I miss the other?"

"You missed the other," Geoffrey advised her, thankful that she did not know he came from Belwain, "and I was now listening to a report concerning your 'crazed' brother-in-law, Rupert." He could not keep the irritation out of his voice.

"Rupert!" Her voice was a whisper of anguish. Oh, poor Rupert. Elizabeth found herself overwhelmed with guilt and shame. She had not given her sister's husband a thought since the tragedy. No, she decided, she had been too wrapped up in her own grief to think of the torment he must be going through. Dear God! How would she feel if she had lost Geoffrey as Rupert had lost his love, his wife! Elizabeth bowed her head and said a silent prayer for her thoughtlessness.

". . . and that is all I have to report." The messenger's last words brought her attention back to what was being discussed.

"You have done well," Geoffrey said. "Go and find food and drink now."

The messenger genuflected before Geoffrey and then left the room.

Geoffrey immediately turned to his wife and said, "Elizabeth, tell me what you know of this Rupert."

"I am so ashamed, Geoffrey. I should have gone to him to offer him my comfort. He was my sister's husband and I knew that Margaret and he dealt well with each other, from the way they behaved when they visited us. They were a well-matched couple, my mother used to say."

"But what of Rupert himself?" Geoffrey asked. "What can you tell me about him? Can he really be 'mad with grief,'" he asked. "Is he so weak that he cannot leave his room to see his wife's grave?" There was ridicule in Geoffrey's voice and Elizabeth shook her head, saddened by his questions, his tone.

"You do not understand," she whispered. And now I fully know the difficulty in your nature, she thought. You do not love me, else you would comprehend. A weight, like a stone, lodged against her heart, and Elizabeth turned away from her husband so that he could not see the sorrow in her eyes.

Geoffrey misunderstood his wife's obvious withdrawal, incorrectly assuming that discussion of her relatives opened the wound she was trying so hard to cover. He placed his hand on her shoulder and slowly turned her to face him once again. "Tell me the story of what took place here once again, Elizabeth. I know that it is painful for you and I am sorry, but I have need to hear it all again. To make sure," he said.

Elizabeth puzzled over his last words and wished he

had not asked her. "Will my telling you help you understand something?" she asked. Geoffrey nodded, and Elizabeth added, "Then I will tell you." She took a calming breath and closed her eyes and repeated her story. Geoffrey did not interrupt once and she was thankful he did not, as she wished to finish as quickly as possible. When she was done, she looked up into his eyes, trying to read his thoughts, his conclusions.

"You have left something out," Geoffrey said, rubbing his chin in a thoughtful manner.

"What is that?" Elizabeth asked, frowning.

"Before, with the first telling, you said that one of the men wearing the hoods was injured . . . stabbed, I think you said."

"Yes, I did forget that," Elizabeth answered. "Margaret stabbed him. Why? Is that important?"

"Perhaps. Where did she stab him?" he asked, his voice casual, his eyes alert.

Elizabeth concentrated and pictured the scene again, trying to keep herself as detached as possible. In her mind she saw Margaret turn and raise her dagger and . . . "Just below the shoulder, the right shoulder. I saw the blood come through the cloth." She looked again at Geoffrey but found no answer in his gaze. "What are you thinking?" she asked.

"Not now," he hedged. "But when I return from my journey you will have your answers."

"Always you ask me to wait," Elizabeth said, unable to keep the anger out of her voice.

"You have given me your trust," Geoffrey reminded her. He almost added that she had pledged him her love too, but decided not to bring that subject up again. "You have made a pledge to me," he substituted instead.

But I have made a pledge to my parents and my sisters too, she argued to herself. Should they not come before her pledge to her husband? She sighed with weariness. If only he could understand her position, she thought.

"I made another pledge," she whispered. She turned before her husband could respond and hurried out of the room. There was much she had to consider, and she needed to be alone. She went back to the bedroom and sat down on the bed. Have I become obsessed with my vengeance? she asked herself. Is it so wrong to want justice so that their souls will reach heaven?

The sobs caught her by surprise. She couldn't hold them back any longer. She buried her face in the covers and cried until she was exhausted, weeping for the loss of her family. I will not fail you, she told her parents, her sisters. I will find a way to bring justice so that you may rest in peace. The vow was barely repeated in her mind when the idea took hold. Rupert! She would go to him, pull him from his grief with her knowledge of her uncle's treachery. Aye, she would give him cause to leave his room. She would give him her vengeance. The transfer of the vow would also, she admitted, leave her free.

Vengeance had kept her sane when she would have elsewise gone mad, it would do the same for him, Elizabeth decided. It would give him purpose. Rupert would vow revenge and was strong enough to challenge Belwain for the truth. He would not be so concerned with the law, Elizabeth thought.

She dried her eyes and bounded off the bed. There was much to do, and before the day was over. She must convince Hammond to accompany her and order him to find another willing to aid her. He would do it, she thought with determination, if she threatened to go alone. And he would not betray her to Geoffrey either. No, she thought, he is loyal to me first.

She would leave as soon as Geoffrey and his men were on their way, early tomorrow morning. And it wasn't such a great distance to Rupert's home, not if she could remember the way of the cut-through her father had chanced upon. With any luck she would be back before Geoffrey returned. She hadn't a hope that her absence would go unnoticed by the men he left behind, but by then it would be too late and the deed would have been done.

Chapter Ten

ELIZABETH SOAKED IN THE WOODEN TUB OF STEAMING, rose-scented water for a long while. Geoffrey had washed and changed and she sent him away to the dinner table with a wave of dismissal. "I will join you shortly," she promised with a wink.

"Perhaps I will join you now," Geoffrey teased, hesitating at the door. He wanted to stay and gave her a look that told her as much.

"You cannot," Elizabeth replied, laughing. "Your men and my grandfather wait for you. If you are late, they would know what we . . . my grandfather would guess . . ."

Geoffrey threw his head back and laughed at her discomfort.

The wet rag hit his forehead and he was forced to pull

Elizabeth from the tub and give her a long kiss. "Until later," he said in a husky voice full of promise.

"Yes," Elizabeth whispered, "until later. But now you will have to change, my lord, for I have shared my bath with you." She laughed again and sat back down in the water, casually splashing him with one hand while her other covered her breasts from his view.

Ah, he was a magnificent man, she thought as she seductively studied her husband's physique. He was dressed all in black, save for the golden crest proclaiming his worth, and the water was truly invisible against the dark fabric. She was pleased that he had worn the black, for it would go well with the surprise she had planned and had even gone to great lengths to see that he did. Both the black braies and the bliaut were spread out upon the bed, with the white chainse atop, and Geoffrey, though he had raised an inquiring eyebrow when he saw that his wife had selected his outfit, changed into it without a question.

What a contradiction she is, Geoffrey thought as he watched his wife. She hides her breasts from me with the shyness of a virgin, yet stares at me with a hunger that matches my own. "Your lust is showing, wife," Geoffrey said with extreme smugness. He shook his head with feigned despair and walked back to the door. "Ever you would delay me," he said in parting.

She heard his laughter through the door and smiled with anticipation. "Tonight, dear husband, you will delay me from my sleep. I will see to it."

She hurried with her task of drying herself and then pulled the black ankle-length chainse from her chest. It was one of the new gowns the seamstress had fashioned for her, under protest, for the chainse was usually of a lighter color to give added contrast to the bliaut worn, but Elizabeth had been insistent. She would match her husband tonight, in both dress and passion. Sighing, she pulled the gown over her head and let it fall against her bare skin. She had decided that she would not wear a chemise, and felt herself blush with her wanton behavior. Oh, the surprises I have in store for you, husband, she thought, smiling with anticipation. Even when she slipped the black, knee-length bliaut over the chainse, it still hugged her curves. She brushed her hair, deciding against plaiting it, and then hurried back to the chest once again to remove the wide piece of material she had hidden there. She had designed this herself, though the gifted seamstress had been the one to do the actual sewing, and Elizabeth was extremely pleased with the result. Embroidered upon the golden strip of material was her husband's crest, sewn in contrasting black threads, looking quite wonderful, she thought with pride.

She slipped the material over one shoulder and draped it across one breast, down to the opposite hip, where it tied into place. Then she pulled the black cloth shoes from under the bed and put them on. She was ready.

She reached the door and opened it wide, just as the squire Gerald was about to knock. His hand was poised in the air, but he stood frozen in the act as he looked at his mistress.

"You are beautiful," Gerald blurted out. "You wear his crest."

"It is fitting, is it not?" Elizabeth asked with a smile.

"It is, it is," Gerald stammered with embarrassment. "I did not mean that it was not, my lady."

"I know that you did not," Elizabeth soothed. "Did you wish something?" she asked, changing the subject.

"I did," Gerald admitted, though he did not continue his explanation. He just stood there, grinning from ear to ear, and Elizabeth wanted to laugh at his silly expression. She did not, of course, for she had no wish to hurt his feelings.

"And what is it you wished to see me about?" she

coaxed, folding her hands with a relaxed stance that suggested she would stand there for as long as it took for the squire to gather his thoughts.

"Your husband. He awaits you and grows impatient," Gerald remembered to say.

"Then I will go to him," Elizabeth answered.

She scooted around Gerald and started down the hall. "It is a warm evening," she said, trying to put the boy at ease, "and I can smell the scent of new flowers in the air. The warm weather will be welcomed by the men, don't you think?"

Elizabeth turned to hear his reply and found herself alone at the end of the hall. Gerald was still standing at her bedroom door, looking after her with what Elizabeth could only call a stupefied expression. With a laugh she could not contain, she called to the lad and waited for him to reach her side.

"Accompany me to the hall, Gerald. Your lord awaits your service."

Gerald nodded and clutched at Elizabeth's arm, awkwardly leading her down the steps. I only hope that my husband is as affected, as surprised and pleased, she thought, as the knight holding her arm with trembling fingers.

She was not disappointed. When she reached the entrance to the hall, she stood with her hands at her sides and waited for her husband's attention. The talk and the laughter receded as each of the men spotted her, and by the time Geoffrey glanced up from his position at the table, silence filled the hall.

Still she did not move. She merely stared at him with a becoming smile on her face and waited for him to come to her.

Geoffrey saw his wife and was stunned speechless, like the rest of his men. His breath got caught somewhere in his throat and his legs tried to trip him as he stood and slowly made his way to her.

The crest was visible from across the room, and

Geoffrey's chest swelled with pride that she wore it, proclaiming to all the world just who she belonged to.

He stopped when he stood directly in front of her. "You grow more beautiful with each passing second," he said in a whisper.

"Thank you, Geoffrey," Elizabeth answered. She placed her hand on his arm and walked with him to the table.

The talk between the soldiers gradually resumed, but Elizabeth continued to feel their stares and smiled with pleasure.

Her grandfather sat down across from Elizabeth and Geoffrey. "You look lovely, granddaughter," he said. "Don't you think so, Geoffrey?" he asked, turning his gaze to his grandson-in-law.

"I had not thought on it," Geoffrey replied in a mild tone, and then grinned when his wife nudged him with the tip of her shoe. "But now that you mention it, I think you might be right. She is not too displeasing."

Elslow laughed as hard as Geoffrey and Elizabeth looked toward the heavens with exasperation. When she had first met her husband, she had despaired at his lack of humor, and now found she had created a tease that surely rivaled her grandfather.

A fine red wine appeared and Elizabeth toasted her husband and her grandfather. She found herself giggling over the most absurd statements all through the meal and realized that she was drunk with anticipation of the time she would share alone with her husband. She kicked one shoe off and began to rub her toes against her husband's muscular legs and delighted in seeing his reaction, which he tried to mask as he talked with her grandfather. He would have me believe that he is unaffected, she thought with another chuckle.

"Stop that," Geoffrey whispered when she slid her bare toes higher, "else you will be made to pay the price."

"I will get the coin," Elizabeth replied in a saucy whisper, "you have only to name the amount."

"And who will give you the coin?" Geoffrey asked in a growl against her ear that sent shivers of warm need down her legs.

She pulled away and favored him with a long, sultry look and then answered, "My husband. There is much I could barter in exchange."

She gave him a slow, calculated wink then and puckered her lips.

Geoffrey laughed, causing everyone to look their way, and then leaned down toward her again. "I think you try to seduce me, wife," he told her.

"Nay," Elizabeth answered him with a hopefully innocent gaze. She casually slipped her hand to rest in his lap and added, "I do not think it, Geoffrey. I know it."

Geoffrey could not remember the rest of the meal. He knew that he ate his fill in record time and that he had removed his wife's hand from his lap countless times, only to find it nestled there again and again. Before Elizabeth could take more than two bites of her food, he had hauled her to her feet and into his arms. To the cheers of his men and a roar of approval from Elslow, he carried her out of the room. One bare foot peeked out from beneath her gown and Geoffrey smiled as he ignored her protests and strode out of the hall.

What a confusion this wife of his was, Geoffrey thought as he carried her to their bedroom. She defies me in the morning, ignores me the rest of the day, and now plays the enchantress. There had to be a reason for this change in her behavior, Geoffrey realized, but he would be most content to wait until later to find out what it was. Now he wanted only the satisfaction she could give him.

When the bedroom door was closed, Geoffrey leaned

against it, still holding her in his arms. Elizabeth turned his head toward her with the tip of her finger and smiled at him. It was a smile full of tenderness and love. She slowly wet her lips with her tongue and then did the same to his, knowing from the look in his eyes that he was pleased with her aggression. She kissed him then, opening her mouth as he opened his, welcoming his tongue inside as he explored the moist sweetness she offered. Only when the kiss threatened to overpower her did she draw back. She gave him another smile and began to unfasten the lacings at his neck, pausing often to kiss and stroke him while she worked.

Geoffrey did not say a word. He let her slide to the floor and stood as still as a statue while his wife undressed him. Her fingers were like the wings of a dove as she removed his garments. This game, this twist where she was the seducer, excited him. He would see how far she would go before bowing to his expertise, already noticing the blush covering her cheeks when he stood nude before her.

She stood back when the task was finished and carefully removed the sash she wore. She felt some embarrassment now, knowing that her husband watched her every motion, and she did not hesitate until the tunic had been removed and it was time to pull the gown from her body. She looked up at Geoffrey for a long moment, nervous now that she wore nothing beneath the gown, and hoped that he would not think her shameful. Ever so slowly she edged the gown up, over her hips, her breasts, and finally her head, before dropping it to the floor.

Geoffrey was so startled by her nudity that he could only stare at her. She was like the goddess he had imagined her to be when he first saw her in the forest, Geoffrey thought, proud and magnificent, and golden.

He reached out for her but stopped when she shook her head. She was not smiling now, even when she glanced down and saw she still wore one shoe. She flipped it off and then looked back at her husband. He could see the passion ignited in her eyes, her expression, and knew that it matched his own in intensity.

"You blush, Elizabeth," Geoffrey said in a voice that sounded hoarse to his ears, "yet I have touched and kissed you everywhere. Do you think you will soon overcome this shyness?"

"I will try, my lord," Elizabeth promised. She walked over to the bed and pulled the covers back. "Come, Geoffrey. It is my turn to learn your secrets as you have learned mine. It is my turn to kiss you everywhere and see if you will blush with the memory tomorrow."

Her absurd remark that he was capable of blushing made him grin. Her words excited and intrigued him, for he had taught her all that she knew about the art of loving. His eyes hooded, he walked over to her and lifted her chin. He kissed her softly on her lips and then stretched out on the bed, pulling her down on top of him. He would let her continue the game a while longer, he decided, until he felt his control slip or until she could go no further due to her inbred inhibitions, and then he would take over, pleasure her as she had yet to be pleasured. It was his last coherent thought.

Elizabeth began her gentle assault at his neck, using her mouth and her tongue to taste and explore, moving ever so slowly downward in her quest to touch every inch of her husband. She would worship him this night as he had worshiped her in their nights before. She would give him such excitement and satisfaction that he would forgive her for what she must do in the morning. Tonight, she promised as she moved her hips against his legs, tonight you will love me, Geoffrey, and that will balance your anger with my disobedience when you learn of it.

She felt his intake of breath when she reached his

hips and smiled with the knowledge that she held him captive. This role of aggressor was to her liking, she decided, for she was the one in full control now, not her husband.

Twice Geoffrey tried to pull her back to his chest, to kiss her until she was as affected as he, but both times Elizabeth resisted. Her hand found and closed over him and he groaned with reaction. And then he felt the touch of her tongue against his pulsating heat and her mouth take him inside and his mind left his body. He growled his pleasure and his hands found her legs. With a forceful jerk, he turned her and began to pleasure her as she pleasured him. Elizabeth moaned and began to move against him with both her mouth and her hips, and Geoffrey knew he could not hold back much longer. He stopped her with his hands and moved her on top of him, her knees braced on either side of his hips. And then he thrust inside her, with such force that Elizabeth cried out. He hesitated, concerned that he had hurt her, but her hips urged him on. "Do not stop," she moaned, "do not . . ."

Her words drove him wild with need. He pushed into her again and again, mindless of the world. Only he and Elizabeth existed now, riding toward the crest of fulfillment. And when Elizabeth arched above him and cried out his name, Geoffrey allowed himself release, holding her tightly against him as the explosion overtook them both.

"I love you, Geoffrey, more than my life, I love you." Elizabeth collapsed on top of her husband and snuggled against his chest but not before he saw the tears streaming down her cheeks. The silent crying did not last long, and though she tried, Elizabeth was unable to keep the sobs inside.

Geoffrey held her, whispering gentle words meant to soothe her, but she could not hear them over the echo of her own hiccups. "You tell me that you love me and then you cry?" he asked when she had calmed a bit. "You are unhappy over our lovemaking? You were not—"

"Nay," Elizabeth interrupted. "It was wonderful, you were wonderful, and gentle and . . ." Renewed sobs stopped her litany of his qualities and Geoffrey found himself shaking his head.

"Then why do you cry?" he persisted.

"I cry because I am happy," Elizabeth insisted between sniffles.

Geoffrey rolled over, taking Elizabeth with him, and pinned her to the bed. Holding her face in the cup of his huge hands, he looked into her eyes and said in a gentle voice, "You are a contradiction and I vow it will take me years to understand you fully, but I think there will be sweet joy in the confusion of it all. What think you on this?" He leaned down and kissed her on her lips and then pulled back to await her answer.

"I think I will have been suffocated long before then, husband, unless you release me and let me breathe," she replied, a hesitant smile curving her mouth.

Geoffrey immediately lifted his weight with his elbows but kept her firmly in place beneath him. His feet locked hers into submission when she tried to squirm away, and his expression remained serious. "I would know why you cry when we finish loving each other."

"I am confused," Elizabeth admitted.

"About loving me?" Geoffrey asked. The thought made him uneasy and his brow wrinkled with irritation.

"No, Geoffrey," Elizabeth answered. "I will not take back the words, for I meant them . . . for now and always."

"That is good," Geoffrey replied, grinning. He rolled to his back and let Elizabeth get settled against his side.

"Geoffrey?" Elizabeth asked, her tone hesitant.

"Yes?" Geoffrey answered as he reached out with his hand and squelched the light from the single candle on the table next to the bed. The room was thrown into darkness. "You wish to maul me again?"

Though she could not see his face, Elizabeth could hear the laughter in his voice. He had certainly taken to teasing, she thought, just as a duck takes to water, and she might have challenged him for more loving had she not been preoccupied with her other thoughts.

"If a vassal came to you and asked your help, or if you promised one vassal that you would give him something, and then another vassal came along and wanted your promise for the same, what would you do?" She had phrased her question badly and the confusion of it all registered in her mind. How could he help her know what to do if she couldn't even explain?

"You cannot give to the second what has been promised to the first," Geoffrey answered very matter-of-factly. "That is the law."

"Always the law," Elizabeth snapped.

"We would be animals without it," Geoffrey argued with a yawn. "Why do you concern yourself with the problems of vassals?" he asked.

"It is all so confusing, these promises and vows," she admitted in a whisper.

"That is because you are a woman," Geoffrey returned, trying to keep his voice neutral so that she would not know he baited her.

"And women are not capable of understanding?" Elizabeth asked. Her body tensed beside him as she waited for his reply.

"That is true," Geoffrey said, waiting for her fury. When she remained in her stiff position beside him, he grinned into the darkness and added, "Now a horse . . ."

She realized then that he was teasing and relaxed against him. "Always you bait me, husband," she sighed.

Geoffrey dislodged her with his hefty laugh. "*I* bait

you? It is the opposite, and well you know it!" He snorted again and then hauled her back against him. "Enough talk, wife. I'm tired. Close your eyes and sleep."

"So a man tires easily after making love? He is so weak that he must immediately sleep for hours upon hours? Now a woman . . ."

Geoffrey stopped her words and her thoughts with a determined kiss and then rested his head next to hers.

"Pleasant dreams," she whispered as she closed her eyes.

"I have just finished my dreams," Geoffrey whispered against the top of her head. And it was most pleasant indeed, he thought, smiling as he fell asleep.

Geoffrey rode out with the first light of day, careful not to disturb his sleeping wife. He kissed her on the forehead and had to be content with only that, as he did not want to chance waking her and having to deal with her questions as to his destination.

Roger and fifty of the soldiers were saddled and waiting. Geoffrey took a few minutes to go over his plans once again with Elslow and then led the procession through the gates. His expression turned grim; it was the face now of the warrior about to do battle.

Elizabeth watched her husband leave from her view at their bedroom window. As soon as he was out of sight, she turned and began to dress. Hammond and another, a strong peasant called Tobias, waited with the horses, already outside the walls, and Elizabeth knew that she would have to hurry to meet them, before the entire house was roused for the new day. She dressed in a dark blue gown and tied her hair in a knot at the base of her neck. Then she covered herself in her long cape, though the weather was warm enough to go without, and pulled the hood over her hair to hide its bright color. The dagger and the bow and arrows were her arsenal in case of danger along the way.

She took the same direction as the day of the massacre, down the hidden stairway and out the side door, and then across the vacant courtyard and through the stable, to another door that faced the wall. A ladder was braced against it, put there by Hammond the night before, and Elizabeth was up and over the top with little effort. Hammond stood at the bottom on the other side, bracing the second ladder to keep it steady as his mistress climbed down.

Together they walked to where the horses were hidden among the trees, and without a word, they mounted and rode into the forest.

Elizabeth led the way, concentrating on the cutoff path she would follow, all the while trying to block her feelings. But her subconscious would not let her rest, and by the end of the long day's ride, without stopping for food or water, Elizabeth was exhausted, both physically and mentally.

They made camp a good two hours before nightfall, in a thick, wooded area about an hour's ride from her brother-in-law's land, and while Tobias saw to the horses, Hammond opened his burlap sack and divided the food he had brought along.

Elizabeth ate little of the fare, save for a small chunk of hardened bread, and spoke not at all. They dared not risk a fire, and the chill sweeping in before the night forced her to huddle under her cloak while she rested against the bark of a tree. "My lady," Hammond said, "we are so close to our destination. Perhaps after you have rested, we could continue on and reach your brother-in-law's home before night is upon us."

Elizabeth did not answer her servant but shook her head. She let Hammond assume she was too tired to continue on. He did not question her again but announced that he would take the first watch. Elizabeth nodded that she had heard, and closed her eyes. She was in agony, mental torment, and she was losing the battle inside her soul and brain, for no matter how hard she tried, she could not blank her mind to the guilt and accusations camping there.

She tried to convince herself that what she was doing was not wrong. But it was, she finally admitted. Very wrong! Oh, she thought with acute despair, I have fooled myself long enough. Last night I knew, in my heart . . . that is why I was so forceful in seducing my husband, in pleasing him. I knew I would betray his faith in me soon. But I cannot do it! I cannot. Forgive me, Father, but you must wait as I must wait, for I cannot go against my husband. I have placed my faith in him and he will avenge your soul. I will have to be content that he will keep his promise, rather it take twenty years or not.

"Hammond!" Her whisper startled him and he hurried over to kneel at her side, a worried look on his face.

"You have heard something?" he asked in a nervous whisper. He glanced back over his shoulder, looking toward the thickness beyond, his sword at the ready. "I fear my hearing is not what it used to be," he admitted after a moment. "I am a sorry one to protect you, my lady."

"No, Hammond, rest your fears. I have heard nothing," Elizabeth replied, patting him on his shoulder. Hammond turned back to stare at her, a puzzled look covering his frown. Elizabeth smiled at him, her measure to try to reassure him. "Think we could make an hour's time back the way we have come before this bleak night descends on us?"

Hammond leaned back on his haunches, opened his mouth, and then closed it again. "I do not understand," he finally confessed. "You wish to return to Montwright?" There was a spark of hope in his voice, which made Elizabeth bow her head with renewed shame. She had placed both Hammond and Tobias in a less than tenacious position with their new master, Lord Geoffrey. She had not considered their possible fate as a result of their disobedience, thinking only of herself and her foolish need for vengeance.

"Hammond, what I was about to do, to go to Rupert, it is wrong and I have only just realized it. I would be disloyal to my husband by taking my concerns to my brother-in-law. I am sorry that I have placed both you and Tobias in such jeopardy with my foolishness and pray you will forgive me."

Before Hammond could reply, Elizabeth flung the cloak aside and stood up. "Come, now, and we will try to make distance while the light guides us."

Hammond closed his eyes with relief. His mistress had finally come to her senses. He was sure his prayers to the Almighty had helped her along, and he crossed himself in thanksgiving. And then he was in motion, saddling first Elizabeth's horse and then his own.

The threesome rode hard through the forest until the last fingers of light began to recede from the sky. They had pushed caution aside, in favor of haste, and stayed on the road. Elizabeth was the first to spot the lake in the distance. She slowed her pace and called to Hammond, "Think we should stop here for the night?"

Hammond was about to tell her yes, that there were several good hiding places that would serve their needs, but the thunder coming down the road toward them stopped his thoughts.

Elizabeth too heard the horses. Her face drained of color and she tensed, confusing her mare by nudging her with her knees while her hands held him back by the reins. The horse began to prance about in agitation and confusion, and Elizabeth took precious minutes trying to regain control.

"Go to the lake," she yelled to Hammond and Tobias. "I will follow." Tobias needed no further urging and took out in full gallop, but Hammond shook his head. He drew his sword and waited while Elizabeth struggled with her horse. It was too late now, and

Hammond was convinced that he was about to die with his mistress.

And then the thunder was upon them, and the leader almost collided with Elizabeth. Her mare reared in reaction to the army that had just rounded the curve in the road, and the hood Elizabeth wore fell to her shoulders. She fought with her horse and glanced at the men blocking her path. Geoffrey! Saints be praised, it was her husband. Elizabeth almost fell off her mare when she saw who it was, and found herself smiling with relief.

Geoffrey could not believe what he was seeing. Blinking did not remove the sight either, he found. His wife! Here, in the middle of the forest, with but one old man to offer her protection. Had he gone crazy? "Elizabeth?" he heard himself ask, and hardly recognized his own voice.

"Good eve, my lord," Elizabeth replied in a soft whisper.

"Elizabeth!" This time her name was fairly bellowed, and the roar caused her animal to become upset all over again. Roger came to her rescue and she was most appreciative, as her husband seemed unable to move a muscle, save for the one pulsating in his cheek.

Elizabeth was thankful that they were not alone. The look in his eyes was beyond frightening, and she found she was extremely nervous. She turned her gaze to his companion and tried to pretend that all was right with the world. "Good evening, Roger. It has been a fine day, has it not?"

Roger seemed dumbfounded by her question. He opened his mouth to say something but couldn't think what it was. And then he found himself grinning, but God's truth, he could not help it.

Elizabeth widened her smile and brushed her hair out of her face. She was careful to keep her gaze away from her husband and continued to smile—much like a simpleton, she thought—to his men lined up on the road behind him. "I apologize for interrupting your ride, husband," she said in his general direction, "and we will be on our way now. God speed you on your journey," she added.

She knew it wouldn't work, but then, there wasn't really any other plan, she thought. She grabbed the reins and spurred her horse, hoping only to get him away from his men so that he could kill her without an audience.

She did not get a single gallop in. Geoffrey held the reins to her horse before she had half-skirted him, and pulled her in just like a fish on a short string. And now he will kill me, Elizabeth thought a little hysterically. And all for nothing!

The shrill cry of her hawk high above the group forced Elizabeth to automatically glance up. "Roger," she heard her husband say, "I think you best protect her from the hawk."

Elizabeth looked back at Geoffrey and frowned. "My hawk would not harm me," she said before looking back to the sky. She frowned again as she watched her pet's frantic circles.

"He is very close to beating you," Geoffrey stated. He kept his voice soft, but the anger was most obvious.

Realization dawned. Elizabeth looked back at her husband, her eyes wide with fright. He was referring to himself, by the name his men had given him.

"Geoffrey, I *would* explain," Elizabeth stammered.

"Aye, you will," Geoffrey snapped, trying not to grab her by her neck and wring some sense into her. He dared not touch her at all until his temper cooled and he was in control.

Another screech from the sky drew her attention again. She watched her hawk circle again and again and said, almost to herself, "Geoffrey, something is wrong, else he would land."

"Ride!" Geoffrey's command broke the quiet. Like a flash of lightning, he pulled Elizabeth into his saddle and threw the reins of her mare to Roger. He goaded his stallion into motion and Elizabeth held on for dear life as they flew into the forest. She closed her eyes and buried her face against Geoffrey's chest so that the branches could not scrape her, though there was no need, for her husband guarded her well, using his shield to guard her against injury.

When they neared the edge of the lake, Geoffrey called a halt. "James, take two others and ride back toward the road. Keep well hidden and report who passes."

Geoffrey watched three of the soldiers disappear, swallowed by the trees and the dense foliage, and then turned his attention to his wife. She still clung to him and Geoffrey reached into her hair and gave a hard tug, pulling her head back and her face up, just inches from his own. He knew he caused her discomfort from the way she held her lower lip between her teeth, and could well feel her tremble in his arms, yet it was nothing compared to the agony she had just put him through. "When I get you to my home, I will lock you in my room and throw away the key," he vowed in a low voice, and from the look on his face, Elizabeth had no doubt that he would do just that.

"I will not complain," Elizabeth whispered in reply. "Whatever you decide to do to me I will deserve and not make complaint, though I wish you would let me explain," she ended.

Geoffrey was totally unimpressed with her humble acceptance of his threat. He was still too angry. "Why in God's name are you here?" he asked.

"I was on my way to see Rupert," Elizabeth admitted. Her reward for complete honesty was another hard tug on her hair and she almost cried out with the pain.

"It is fortunate for you that I was able to stop you, then," Geoffrey said in a harsh voice. He eased up on his hold when he saw the tears in her eyes but his fury knew no limits.

"But I was on my way home," Elizabeth said.

"You saw Rupert?" His voice sounded incredulous and he found himself pulling on her hair again.

"Nay," Elizabeth replied. "Geoffrey, you hurt me! Loose me and I will explain," she pleaded.

Geoffrey obeyed her request but promptly captured her shoulders in a tight grip. "I am waiting," he said. His face was a mask, but Elizabeth could still feel the anger in him.

"It is true, I was on my way to see Rupert, but I could not do it. I could not go to him. It would have been disloyal to you. And so I turned around and was headed home when you chanced upon me."

"Disobedient," Geoffrey corrected, "not disloyal." He let go of her shoulders and realized his hands were shaking. She would have ridden into hell had she ventured into Rupert's web, Geoffrey knew. And he would thank God each and every day for the rest of his life that she had not.

"No, Geoffrey, I was disloyal as well." Elizabeth's confession sounded like a tortured whisper.

"God give me patience with you," Geoffrey muttered. "Always you contradict me." He shook his head and waited for her response.

"I was not going to Rupert just to offer comfort in his time of need. No, my motives were selfish and sinful, Geoffrey. I grew impatient waiting for you to do something and decided that Rupert would champion my cause. I thought to tell him about Belwain, and in his grief he would not be so concerned about the law . . . and he would go to Belwain and make him confess."

Tears began to stream down her face and Elizabeth wiped them away with an impatient hand. She could tell from the look on her husband's face that he was furious with her confession. He acted like he had just received a blow to his midsection, and Elizabeth cried all the more, for she was the cause of his anger, his pain. "I am guilty of disobedience and disloyalty and lack of patience. I admit to each sin, and will cut my hair and wear a peasant's garb for a year if that be my penance. But, Geoffrey, last evening I knew I could not go through with my plan. I had given you my trust. By going to Rupert I would have been telling you that I had no faith in you. Geoffrey, I was so confused. I had made the vow to avenge my family's deaths . . . and then I made the vows to you . . . and I did not know which came first. Oh, Geoffrey, I cannot be vengeful any longer. Belwain's death will not bring my papa back to me. This constant thought of revenge truly goes against my nature." She wiped her cheeks with the edge of her cloak and wished her husband would say something. Oh, how she longed to hear him yell at her. Anything, to show her she had not destroyed any affection he might have felt for her. "If you decide never to look for proof of my uncle's treachery, then so be it."

It took Geoffrey a long while to calm down. He almost shuddered when he realized how close he had come to losing her. The danger! And she had no idea, none at all. That was probably his fault, he admitted. Aye, he too was to blame. If he had not been so stubborn, so bent on teaching her her place, none of this would have come to pass. Yet she had just admitted that she was on her way to another to champion her cause. How dare she? his mind demanded, when she had given her trust into his care. Aye, it was disloyalty, in thought and in action. He would have to address this problem, but not until he had time to think. It was unwise to make snap judgments and decisions, for they could well prove unchangeable. He needed time . . . time and distance away from his wife, to sort this confusion out.

"Elizabeth, it was Rupert behind the whole of it."

She did not understand what he was saying. Not at first. She shook her head, trying to deny what she just heard. No, he was Margaret's husband! He would not, could not . . .

"He hides until the wound from the knife heals," Geoffrey said, watching the play of emotions crossing his wife's face.

Elizabeth was too stunned to say anything. The enormity of the situation was too much to consider.

Geoffrey dismounted and lifted her to the ground. "It is true. You would have ridden into hell and not known it until it was too late."

"How did you find out?" Elizabeth finally managed to ask.

"From the moment you told me the story, I was suspicious of Rupert. The fact that he suddenly became too ill to accompany his wife to Montwright, that planted the seed of doubt in my mind. Then, when Elslow arrived, he told me that Rupert was one of the leaders of the rebels against William, though Rupert does not know that Elslow could name him traitor. The final proof came from the messenger, the *first* messenger. One of Rupert's ill-treated servants let slip the news that Rupert's injury was slow to heal. That bit of information, added to the fact that Rupert refused to answer my call . . . Aye, Elizabeth, he is the one behind the whole of it. I would stake my life on it."

"Dear God, he killed Margaret," she whispered. "And you were on your way to confront him, weren't you? You sought to put an end to this nightmare and end my torment. Geoffrey, I—"

"I was on my way to challenge him, yes," Geoffrey said, his voice hard again. "But not to put an end to your torment, wife. You place too much worth on yourself if you think you are my main concern. Rupert attacked what belonged to me, and your father was my loyal vassal. Montwright is but one of my holdings but I protect all I own. And *I* am loyal to all who place their trust in my hands. Your nightmare is your own, Elizabeth, your torment yours to keep. You are narrow of purpose, thinking only of yourself. Aye, you are selfish and foolish, and that is a most dangerous combination."

Geoffrey knew that he hurt her with his harsh words but he was too angry to take them back. She had just admitted that she had been disloyal. Added to that fact was her foolishness in placing herself in such jeopardy . . . and all to go to a madman who would have taken great pleasure in killing her. He let his anger run free, knowing full well that his wife was the only available vessel for his wrath, his hurt.

"What is my worth, Geoffrey?" Elizabeth's softly spoken question took him by surprise. He had thought that his words would have angered her and she would have responded in kind. He found he was disappointed and admitted that he wanted a good fight. He studied her for a long moment, noting that she held her head up and her shoulders straight. There was pride in her stance, but no arrogance or anger in her gaze. Geoffrey looked into her eyes and could only read defeat there . . . defeat and sorrow.

"Do not ask me that question now," Geoffrey snapped, "else I will say something I may regret. You have the ability to make me lose my temper like no other." Geoffrey clasped his hands behind his back, calming somewhat by her docile attitude, and said, "You do not fight with me and I cannot help but wonder at your motives. Perhaps you have realized that you have gone too far this time?"

Elizabeth refused the bait. She could not handle any more harsh words. "Why Rupert?" she asked, changing the subject. "Did he also want Montwright?"

"I think not," Geoffrey said. "No, it was havoc he was after," he concluded.

"Margaret was so gentle, so loving," Elizabeth said, shaking her head, "and he killed her."

Roger interrupted with a shout. "The men return, Hawk."

Geoffrey and Elizabeth both turned.

The soldier called James dismounted and hurried over to his lord. "They come this way and outnumber us three to one. They ride from the east."

"Rupert?" Elizabeth asked her husband. She started to tremble and could not seem to stop.

Geoffrey did not answer her. He lifted Elizabeth into his arms and carried her to her horse. Placing her in the saddle, he called to Roger. "See to her protection." Pulling his sword from its sheath, he turned from her and began ordering his men into position.

The sun was slowly slipping from the sky, casting a soft orange glow to the lake. Another half hour, and the woods would be in total darkness. Roger led Elizabeth's mare away from the water and between two tall trees. He motioned to James again and two others and Elizabeth was surrounded by men on horseback. "Do not leave her side," Roger ordered, and the men immediately nodded. "I know you would not," Roger corrected when he realized he had insulted them with his order. They would die before letting harm come to their lady, just as he would.

"God protect you," Elizabeth whispered to Roger. He nodded and started toward her husband. And you protect my husband, she added to herself.

The rebels could be heard in the distance, riding hard and fast through the denseness. They aimed for the water, to refill their pouches, Elizabeth thought. But she was wrong. One minute the only sound was that of hard-ridden mounts, and the next, the bedlam of battle. The enemy had ridden into the clearing with their weapons drawn; aye, they were ready for battle. Geoffrey and his men did not have the element of surprise on their side and they were outnumbered, as James had stated.

As soon as the war cry sounded, the shields were up, blocking Elizabeth's view. She listened to the screams and the clashes of iron against iron. She pictured

Geoffrey injured or dead, and covered her ears with her hands. And then she could stand it no longer. She prodded the soldier blocking her view and demanded that he lower his shield so that she could see that her husband was safe. The trees and the receding light hid them well, and the soldier agreed.

"They need your help," she said when she saw the numbers. "Go and lend your skill," she demanded of James. "I will be safe here with just one of you to protect me."

James needed no further urging. He was eager to do his part and agreed that the men could use his aid. He motioned to the others and all but one followed him, each giving the cry for battle as they rode down the slope with their weapons drawn.

Elizabeth watched her husband as he battled with another. She held her breath when a blow just missed his stomach by inches, and then released it when he felled his opponent.

Two others approached her husband, one with a lance and the other with a battle ax. Geoffrey made short work of killing them.

Her attention turned to Roger, fighting against two men at the water's edge. As she watched, another joined the twosome, and she saw that Roger was losing, and had no place to move. He was silhouetted against the setting sun, an easy target for the enemy, with the lake just inches behind him. Elizabeth frantically looked about to see if anyone was coming to Roger's aid and then remembered the bow and arrows she carried. "Move aside," she called to her one protector. She placed the arrow against the string and took aim, hesitating for the barest of seconds while she prayed that the rebel would stand still and that God would forgive her for taking a life, and then let go. The arrow whistled through the air and found its target, lodging in the back of the rebel's head. Another prayer for forgiveness and thanksgiving for her accuracy and the rebel's foolishness in not wearing a helmet, and she was ready to shoot another arrow. This time the weapon lodged in the back of the second rebel's neck, and he fell to his knees, screaming in agony. Elizabeth told herself she was not sorry for it, as he would have killed Roger if she had not interfered. Yet her stomach made a lie of her thoughts, twisting and churning at her deed.

Roger looked down at the rebel kneeling before him and saw the arrow protruding from his neck when he fell forward on his face. His curiosity almost caused his death. The third rebel took advantage of Roger's inattention and rushed forward.

Roger did not have time to do more than block the blow from the spear, sending it flying into the air. He was not injured, but lost his footing and fell backward into the lake. The rebel promptly turned and ran to fight another.

"He will drown," the soldier protecting Elizabeth yelled. "His armor will hold him under."

"He will not!" Elizabeth shouted the denial. Her gaze flew to Geoffrey. He would know what to do. But he can do nothing, Elizabeth realized as she watched him fight the rebels trying to surround him.

"Do you have rope?" Elizabeth shouted. The soldier nodded and she said, "Jump into the water and tie it around Roger's waist. Between the two of us, we will be able to pull him out."

"I too wear armor," the soldier told her. "It would do no good."

"Then I will do it," Elizabeth decided. "Hurry! Ride to the water's edge with me and hold one end of the rope. When you feel a pull on it, drag Roger to the surface. Do not argue," she screamed when she saw he was about to protest. "My husband would wish this."

She did not give the soldier time to consider what he should do, but urged her mount into action and raced to the water's edge. She slipped off her mare and grabbed the rope. "Hold tightly," she said, and then took a deep breath and made a clean dive into the water. The distance to the bottom was greater than she had anticipated, but she found Roger almost immediately. She pushed at his shoulder but he did not respond. Praying that she was not too late and that he still had air inside of him, she hurried to make a slip knot around his waist with the rope. It was difficult work as the mud was thick and resistant to her struggle to get the rope around the knight. Her lungs ached from the strain but she did not give up her task. As soon as she had the knot secured below the heavy chest mail, she tugged the rope and pulled on Roger's shoulders. When she could not stand the pressure a second longer, she kicked away from the knight and headed for the surface.

As soon as the soldier felt the pull on the rope, he began to back his steed, and within seconds the limp body of Geoffrey's faithful vassal was pulled from the water.

Roger was doubled over and the tightness of the rope acted as a squeezing vessel below his ribs. It forced great gushes of water from his lungs, and by the time he was dragged clear, he was coughing and sputtering.

Elizabeth did not hear him. She tried to climb out of the water but was crying so hard that she couldn't seem to keep a hold. She was too late! And now Roger was dead.

Geoffrey had gained victory over his opponents and was on his way to fight another when he glimpsed Elizabeth just seconds before she dived into the water. He reacted with almost superhuman power then, screaming like a wild animal as he raced to get to her. His men saw to his back, saving his life countless times as he passed the rebels without a glance. And then the fight was over, the remaining rebels running to safety.

Geoffrey was tearing at his armor, intent on diving into the water to find Elizabeth, when she surfaced just a few feet in front of him. Relief such as he had never known washed over him, and he found that his legs would no longer support him. He knelt down and bowed his head and gave thanks.

Her soft sobs renewed his strength, and his rage. He thanked God that she was alive so that he could kill her, and shot up to his feet with a bellow of fury. "I thought you drowned," he screamed as he hauled her out of the water. "I thought you drowned," he repeated. He was shaking her as he screamed, and then suddenly stopped and pulled her against his chest.

Elizabeth heard the agony in his voice and cried all the more. "Nay, Geoffrey. It is worse," she said, sobbing. "It is Roger. He is the one drowned."

Her husband did not seem to understand. He began to shake her again, yelling at the top of his lungs. He confused her with his tirade. And then Roger's coughs reached her and she began to cry louder. "He is not dead, Geoffrey. He is not! Do not be angry any longer."

"You are a stupid woman," Geoffrey ranted. He pulled her against his chest and said something she could not hear, and then jerked her back and was shaking her all over again. It was as if he could not make up his mind. She started to cry again, uncaring that an audience had formed as a half-circle behind her husband, and tried without success to get the mass of wet hair out of her face. "I would explain," she sobbed, wishing she could just find a place to sit and calm herself.

"You will not," Geoffrey bellowed, grabbing for her shoulders again. He pulled her to his chest once again and said in a softer voice, "Quit your weeping, Elizabeth. It is over."

He felt Elizabeth nod against him and found himself

taking deep breaths to stop his tremors. Lord, he was acting more like a woman each day he spent with Elizabeth, he thought, and a smile of disbelief crossed his face. He spotted Roger, drenched but very much alive, and motioned him to his side. "It was this stupid, disobedient wife of mine that saved your life, Roger. What think you of that?" he asked.

"I am most grateful," Roger answered. "Though I would disagree that she is stupid, my lord."

Geoffrey almost laughed.

Roger pointed to the men on the ground behind him and said, "Recognize the arrows, my lord?"

"They are mine," Elizabeth acknowledged, pulling free of her husband's hold. "And don't you dare yell at me again, Geoffrey! My ears are ringing from your shouts. You were outnumbered and I did what was needed."

"It was my duty to protect you, wife, not the other way around," Geoffrey replied, clearly exasperated. "You risked your life."

"It is *my* life to risk," Elizabeth argued. She placed her hands on her hips, flung her hair out of her face with a jerk of her head, and gifted him with a long, scorching look. "Think you own it?" she challenged. Her arrogant tone was lessened somewhat by the hefty sneeze she couldn't contain.

"I do," Geoffrey bellowed. His hands were now on his hips, his stance threatening. The muscles of his bronzed thighs and legs, braced apart for battle, intimidated her just as much as the frigid look in his eyes.

Elizabeth's stomach twisted; she suddenly felt very vulnerable arguing with her husband in front of his men, for though they appeared busy burying the dead and seeing to one another's injuries, it was obvious that they could well hear the shouts from their leader and his mistress. Why, Elizabeth realized, her mother would never have raised her voice to her father in such a fashion. It was unseemly, undignified. Of course, her mother would never have gotten herself into a situation such as this in the first place!

Elizabeth's hands dropped to her sides in confusion and defeat. "You are most unreasonable," she said. Turning away from his glare, she started to walk back toward the trees. "I've no doubt you would like to put me in chains and drag me behind you," she muttered over her shoulder.

She was jerked around and pulled back into her husband's arms before she could gather another breath. "Do not dare to walk away from me when I am speaking to you," Geoffrey stated in a harsh whisper.

When he saw that her eyes were once again filling with tears, he shook her and then eased up on his fierce hold. "Your idea of chains has merit," he said, dragging her toward the privacy of the woods, "perhaps then you would stay where I put you."

Elizabeth was wise enough to know that silence would have been the best course of action at the moment, but could not help defending herself once again. "Geoffrey, if I had stayed an observer, your loyal vassal and my good friend, Roger, would be dead. Can you find no merit in my action?" she asked, ringing her hands in frustration and wishing she could ring his neck as well. "I am sorry if it was unseemly for me to kill those men with my arrows. I have never killed anyone before and I know I will burn in purgatory for at least a hundred years, but like it or not, I would do the same again." She started to cry again and hated herself for her weakness. It was just that he made her so mad! And she was so very tired. Dark was full upon them among the trees, and Elizabeth, in her haste to turn from his angry stare, stumbled over a stone. Geoffrey caught her and lifted her into his arms. She buried her face in his neck and tried to quit crying.

"What am I to do with you?" Geoffrey addressed the question to the top of her head. "Look at me," he commanded. When she complied, he continued, "In the space of one meager day, you have disobeyed me God knows how many times and openly admitted your disloyalty." He placed her on the ground, facing him, and then added, "I have killed men who have ventured less."

"I am not a man, I am your wife," Elizabeth replied, shrugging his hands off her shoulders.

"It is you who forgets that fact more often than I," Geoffrey retaliated. He turned from her and called to his squire, "We camp here for the night. See to my tent." Turning back to Elizabeth, he noticed that she trembled, and assumed it was due to the chill of the night. "You look like a drowned pup and your gown clings to you in an inappropriate manner. Find your cloak and cover yourself." His voice was as cold as her clothes, and Elizabeth found she no longer felt like crying. God's truth, she wanted to scream again!

She watched her husband walk away from her, barking orders as he moved toward his men, and shook her head. And I thought I understood him, she thought with despair. "Ha," she muttered aloud before sneezing once more. "I swear he is the most unreasonable, hardheaded, stubborn mule of a man that ever walked this earth," she ranted while she paced between the trees. "And to think I thought he would find merit in my deed! No, he finds no merit, for he has no mercy, no understanding, no love in his heart." The squeak of her waterlogged shoes seemed to underline each negative remark she made.

"Mistress?" Roger's voice intruded on her rantings and she was glad for it. She turned and saw that he held her cloak in his hands. "I imagine after your swim you have need for this," he said, his voice gentle.

She accepted the garment and wrapped it around her shoulders, grateful for its warmth. "I thank you for your thoughtfulness, Roger. And are you feeling well after your swim?" she asked, trying to keep her tone light. No need for the vassal to know how miserable she was feeling, she decided.

"I am," Roger replied. "Come now. Gerald has the Hawk's tent set up. I will find you some food and see you settled. I would think you quite exhausted after the day's events."

"I do find I am rather tired," Elizabeth admitted in a soft voice. She walked beside the knight toward the camp. Roger seemed agitated as they neared the group of soldiers, stopping several times to turn to her before resuming his silent walk again. Elizabeth knew the cause for his anxiety and finally placed her hand on his arm to gain his full attention. "Roger, you are glad that I helped to pull you from the water?" she began in a hesitant voice. She did not wait for him to answer before continuing on, "But at the same time you wish I had not contradicted my husband's orders. Is that not the way of your thinking? The reason for your frowns?"

Roger nodded and then spoke. "I am thankful to be alive and it was you who saved me. I owe you my life," he added in a fervent voice.

Elizabeth didn't quite know how to respond to his statement. If she agreed that she had indeed saved his life and he should be thankful, then she did not practice the virtue of humility, she considered. On the other hand, if she denied her deed, she wasn't being honest with him . . . or herself. Worse still, if she belittled the act and acted quite blasé about the happening, then wouldn't she be telling the vassal that she placed little significance on his life? Humility be damned, she decided. "I would do it again, regardless of my husband's wrath. Please understand, Roger, your lord is not angry that you were saved; he is only displeased with my unseemly behavior. You must consider that he is unfamiliar with having a wife . . . and he is—"

"Do not trouble yourself explaining your husband to me," Roger replied, smiling. "He has already discussed the matter with me and he is most thankful that you were able to save me."

"He told you that?" The amazement was obvious in her voice. Then why has he carried on so? Elizabeth asked herself, though she dared not question the knight. It was not his place or his duty to instruct her in the ways and thoughts of her husband.

Roger took hold of Elizabeth's elbow and bent his head toward hers. "They light the fires now. Come and stand close to one and warm yourself. You tremble with the cold."

"They risk a fire?" she asked as she followed the vassal through a group of soldiers. "Won't Rupert's men—"

"Do not concern yourself," Roger admonished in a quiet voice. "Your husband knows what he is about. You have only to trust him."

"Aye," Elizabeth immediately responded, embarrassed that she had asked the question of the knight.

There were perhaps ten or twelve soldiers circled around the fire as she and Roger edged up to the center, and Elizabeth noticed that each time she made eye contact with any of the men, they smiled and then lowered their gazes, as if in deference . . . or embarrassment. Elizabeth wasn't sure and found herself feeling very awkward and somewhat hurt by their attitude. It was another puzzle after a long day of puzzles and confusions. "My presence seems to intimidate the men," she whispered to Roger with an embarrassed little sigh.

"They are in awe," Roger whispered back, giving her elbow a little squeeze.

"Awe?"

"Your courage has shaken them," he said, smiling at the surprise in her eyes. "They have never known one such as you, for you are not like other women."

"And that is praise?" Elizabeth asked, smiling in return.

"Aye, it is," Roger explained. "You are a fitting bride for their leader," he proclaimed.

Their leader does not agree with you, Elizabeth thought. She glanced around, looking for her husband, but Roger's gentle tug on her elbow turned her thoughts back to him. From the look in his eyes, it appeared that he was not quite finished with his gratitude. "I am sorry that you placed yourself in such danger for my benefit, yet now that it is over and done with, I am glad. I will thank God each and every morning that you had the courage to do what you did." He chuckled when he saw the flush on her cheeks his praise caused, and added as a jest, "Why, I will even pray to the souls of your parents for having the foresight to see that you learned how to swim, since I was the one who benefited from their schooling." He was grinning with his last remark, and Elizabeth smiled again.

Geoffrey had walked up behind Elizabeth, as quietly as a panther stalking in the night, and found himself losing some of his anger with Roger's remarks. He was about to pull his wife into his arms and lead her to his tent when her words stopped his actions.

"I am afraid your prayers to my parents would only confuse them, Roger, for God's truth, I do not know how to swim yet. Though I tell you it does not appear to be overly difficult if you remember to hold your breath and—"

Geoffrey's bellow of rage jarred Elizabeth a good foot off the ground. She clutched at her heart and whirled around only to bump into her husband.

"Geoffrey! What is the matter?" Elizabeth could barely get the question out, so shaken was she by his scream.

"Do not say another word," Geoffrey rasped, "do not . . ." His anger was fresh as a new flower just bursting into bloom, and he felt he was close to being totally out of control, and if he could just get her into his tent, away from his men, perhaps then he could calm himself enough to merely throttle her.

Elizabeth was half-dragged, half-pulled into the small tent and then dropped like a sack of barley onto a blanket.

"Now what have I done?" Elizabeth asked, rubbing her arms where her husband had clenched her. "I will be black and blue and it will be from your hands, not the enemy, Geoffrey. You do not know your own strength, I think," she ended.

Geoffrey did not immediately respond. He took his time lighting two candles and sat down crossed-legged in front of her. When Elizabeth got a glimpse of his face, she wished she had the nerve to blow the candles out. Oh, but he was furious, the tendon pulsating in his neck was testimony to that fact, and Elizabeth was good and sick of it. She backed up a space, until her shoulders were touching the side of the tent, and readied herself for his yells.

"You will answer my questions with a simple yes or no, Elizabeth," her husband began. She was surprised by his soft, almost gentle tone of voice, though she detected a small tremor in it and looked up at him. Now, what is his game? she asked herself; he was clearly near the brink of exploding, as far as she could discern.

"Geoffrey, I would—"

"A simple yes or no," Geoffrey insisted, snapping each word out.

Elizabeth nodded her agreement and waited. She watched her husband take several long shuddering breaths and then rest the palms of his huge hands on his knees. She thought she saw his hands tremble before he braced them against himself, but discounted that notion and forced her gaze back to his face.

"I could not help but overhear your conversation with Roger," Geoffrey began, his tone deceptively mild, "but I may be mistaken. And I am always a reasonable man. Yet I could have sworn on William's sword that I heard you tell Roger that you did *not* know how to swim." His voice had risen in intensity, and when Elizabeth, trying to ward off another screaming match, opened her mouth to answer, Geoffrey reached out and clamped one hand over it. "Now you will answer me. Do you know how to swim?"

Since he continued to hold his hand over her mouth, Elizabeth could only shake her head, and that small gesture of denial upset her husband yet again.

"You jumped into the water knowing you did not know how to swim?" he asked, his voice incredulous now.

"I held the rope and I—"

"A simple yes or no." Geoffrey roared the order in a voice that shook the tent.

There is nothing simple about my actions, Elizabeth longed to say. But there was no reasoning with him, she decided. Since he does not wish to hear the whole truth, then let him be upset. "Yes," she said as she folded her hands in her lap.

A loud cough from outside the tent turned Geoffrey's attention from Elizabeth. "Enter," he yelled, louder than he had intended.

Roger lifted the flap of the tent with one hand while he balanced a wooden tray with the other. Without a word, he placed the tray on the floor between Geoffrey and Elizabeth and withdrew to the outside.

Slices of freshly cooked meat, hard crusts of bread, and orange berries filled the tray to overflowing, but neither husband nor wife made a move to touch the fare. Roger reappeared with a single cup and a leather pouch filled with water or wine, Elizabeth surmised. She looked up at the vassal and smiled but Roger did not glance her way and did not see it.

"Thank you, Roger," Elizabeth said when he turned

to leave the tent. Though he did not respond with an answer, Elizabeth saw the slight nod.

"You do not thank a vassal for doing his duty," Geoffrey muttered. He took a large chunk of bread, tore it in half, and handed a portion to Elizabeth.

"Why is that?" Elizabeth asked as she accepted his offering. "He has done a kindness. It is only proper to thank him."

"It is not. He does his duty, wife. All of us have duties, obligations . . . it is the way of things," he stated emphatically. "By thanking him, you imply that perhaps there are times when he does not do his duty to your satisfaction. To counter that, you would have to say thank you each and every time an act is performed in your behalf."

"That is why I have never heard you say thank you or give any praise to your men . . . or to me!" Elizabeth frowned and could not resist adding, "You boast that you are a reasonable man and yet what you have just said makes no sense to me. To be grateful and to tell of your gratitude is not a weakness, Geoffrey," Elizabeth pointed out in a soft voice. "And the weak shall inherit the earth," she quoted from memory, giving support from the Church for her argument.

"Meek!" Geoffrey bellowed. "It is the meek who shall inherit the earth, woman. I am neither weak nor meek and I do not have any desire to inherit the earth."

"I did not mean to imply that you were," Elizabeth protested. "I merely stated that—"

"Enough! Do not lecture me on what you know nothing about. God's truth, I have run out of patience with you. You have run me in circles since the day I met you and I will not have it. My life is ruled by discipline. Discipline! I know that word is foreign to your nature but I vow it will not be for long. Erratic actions, unplanned responses . . . these things can be deadly. Had I not happened on you this day, you would most probably be in Rupert's hands now. Have you considered that?" he asked. Yet before Elizabeth could consider her answer, Geoffrey asked another question of her. "Where would you be now if the soldier holding the other end of your rope had been slain?"

"You wish me to tell you that I have acted most foolish?" Elizabeth asked, her voice low.

"I do not need to hear you voice what I already know," Geoffrey corrected. "I'll tell you this, wife. Your action with Roger . . . it was an act of courage on your part. Yet the other, your decision to be disloyal to me . . ." Geoffrey shook his head and then added, "It is unforgivable."

His voice was flat, and Elizabeth felt as if a sentence had just been pronounced on her future. Confusion clouded her thoughts. If her action was unforgivable, then what future did she have with Geoffrey?

"I have admitted to you that I was going to Rupert but that I changed my mind because it would have been disloyal to you," Elizabeth responded. "And you find that action unforgivable?"

"I do," Geoffrey argued. "You became disloyal the moment you left Montwright."

"Perhaps you are right," Elizabeth answered. "Though I would not admit it to myself until after the deed was done. Then I turned around and was headed home when you chanced upon me."

"It makes little difference to me when you acknowledged your disloyalty," Geoffrey answered, his voice harsh.

"And you cannot find forgiveness in your heart?" Elizabeth asked. She felt shame that she had hurt him, knew that she had, though he would never admit it, and at the same time, nurtured a deep anger that he was so unbending in his reasoning.

"I do not know," Geoffrey admitted. "This has never happened before. Few have been disloyal to me and those that have I have killed. I have never allowed a soldier to be in my surroundings after such a foul deed."

"Then how shall we go on?" she asked, trying to keep her voice as devoid of emotion as her husband.

"The past cannot be changed," Geoffrey said. "You will learn your duties as my wife but will not have my council," he decided. "Your first duty . . . aye, your only duty will be to give me sons."

"Has it not occurred to you that I could have lied to you about my reasons for going to Rupert?" Elizabeth challenged. "I could have told you that I was going to visit him and offer my comfort."

"I would have seen through your lies," Geoffrey answered, frowning.

"By being completely honest with you, I have doomed this marriage," Elizabeth replied. "Is that the way of it?"

"I do not know. I must think on this. I do not act in a rash manner like you."

"While you are thinking, consider this," Elizabeth said, letting the anger spill out in her voice. "You have said you cannot forgive me. Now I tell you that I cannot forgive you. I gave you all my love, knowing full well you did not return the affection. I gave you my understanding, when you have exhibited none. I have admitted that my vow of trust to you wavered, but only because of another vow—foolish and vengeful though it was—made before. I gave you my body and my future, my honesty and my heart, and you talk of duty and discipline. You reject all I have to offer and demand what I most lack. Well, from this moment on, you shall have your discipline and your duty. I shall keep my love in my heart and not share the joy of it with you. I do not know if I can keep from loving you, but God's truth, I will try. You are a most unlovable man, Geoffrey, and I will remind myself of that fact in my daily litany. *If* you decide to forgive me," Elizabeth said in a derisive voice, "then perhaps I will decide to forgive you for belittling all I have given to you."

"So be it," Geoffrey answered, as angry now as she. "Give me only what I ask, and we will do well with each other. Save the love and affection for our children. I do not need it."

The saints were in sympathy, Elizabeth decided, for they nudged Geoffrey from the tent before she began to cry. She did not want him to see how hurt she was, how broken in spirit and motive. Her tears would just show him another weakness, another lack in her character. Until she had met Geoffrey, she had had no idea how many flaws permeated her being. Always she had been taught to look for the good in people, accept the flaws. Geoffrey had obviously been taught just the reverse. Find the flaw and attack . . . was that his way of thinking? she asked herself. She was too tired to consider her position now, too drained physically and emotionally. She pulled the wet garments from her body and draped them over the rope across the top of the tent while she tried to clear her mind of her torment. Wrapping herself in her cape, she huddled against the pallet and cried herself to sleep.

Chapter Eleven

ALL WAS IN READINESS. THE ATTACK ON RUPERT'S HOLD-
ing would take place with the first light of dawn.
Elizabeth would be well protected, with twenty men to
see to her safety. There wasn't time to take her back to
Montwright before confronting her brother-in-law.

Somehow the rebel had heard of Geoffrey's intent,
the attack by the edge of the lake proved that theory to
Geoffrey, and time was now critical. Rupert was no
one's fool. Given enough time, he would muster a
sizable army of discontented men to meet the challenge.

By the light of the moon Geoffrey walked around the
lake, his hands clasped behind his back, while he
thought out his plan of attack. The thought that
perhaps Rupert's overlord, Geoffrey's equal in both
strength and holdings, warned his vassal of the impend-
ing danger briefly entered the warrior's thoughts. Geof-

frey considered the idea and then shook his head, denying that possibility. He knew Owen of Davies, admittedly not well, but enough to know that he would not betray Geoffrey's intent. Aye, Geoffrey had sent a messenger to him, explaining not only his intent in the matter, but more important, his reasons for his actions. Owen had responded immediately, stating by way of his messenger that he would not support his rebel vassal and offered to send men to lend Geoffrey a hand. No, Geoffrey thought again, Owen would go himself to confront Rupert had Geoffrey not decided to deal with the issue. Loyalty was as important to him as it was to Geoffrey.

Once Geoffrey had reviewed his plans for tomorrow's battle, his mind turned to his wife. He scowled into the darkness as he reflected on the harsh words he had exchanged with her. He knew he hurt her with his insults and accusations. The pain was there for him to see in her gaze. He had no wish to hurt her, he declared that much to himself, but thought that it was the only way to deal with her. Lord, she had taken chance upon chance without one pure thought to her safety. I would explain, she demanded impatiently. Ha! Geoffrey muttered, explain indeed! She jumped into the water with no inkling of how she would get out, placing all her faith in a single soldier holding the other end of the rope, never once considering that he might have been killed and unable to perform his duty to her, but had a quick speech all prepared if only he would listen. And explain too, she promised with her beguiling wide-eyed innocent gaze, just how she came to be in the middle of nowhere without benefit of his protection! Aye, Geoffrey concluded as he quickened his pace, that was the heart of the matter, the reason anger continued to grip him: she had ignored him, his position, his power, to go off on her own. She wasn't impressed with his might, his strength, his capabilities, so sure was she of her own ability to see her plans through. By all that was holy,

Geoffrey suddenly realized as he came to a stumbling halt, she didn't think she needed him.

The appalling realization gave his ego a stunning blow. Of course she needed him, he muttered to himself, she was puny in strength, innocent in deceit and treachery, and could not last a day by her own skills—except for the time she lived quite on her own, he reminded himself, before he had come to her aid. By God, she needed him now, he growled, she just hadn't realized that fact . . . yet. Oh, but her schooling was lacking! Would she never learn the way of things?

The frustrations of the day and the clutter filling his mind exhausted him. He resumed his journey around the lake while he tried to make reason out of his wife's attitude. Did she have no vision of her jeopardy? Did she not realize the hell she had put him through with her ill-thought-out actions? Did she not consider her importance to him? Geoffrey paused as the truth hit him. No, Elizabeth could have no idea of her worth to him. He had carefully, yes, foolishly kept that knowledge well hidden, even from himself. Damn! He loved her, with his whole heart, his soul. He did not think he was capable of such an emotion, and now found it filled his purpose. He was not immediately pleased with his new insight, considering first the ramifications of this turn of events. And then he grinned.

Geoffrey remembered that he had called his wife foolish and admitted now that he was the foolish one, not Elizabeth. He had accused her of embracing her vengeance, ignored her when she vowed she was done with it, and told her that she was narrow of intent, obsessed with her single vow to find justice for her family. Yet now he admitted that the very fault he found in his wife's nature lurked beneath his skin as well. Aye, he was forcing his flaws upon her. Hadn't William pointed out during Geoffrey's training period that the flaw one finds in the opponent is usually that which hides within oneself? He had ignored that lesson, for he did not think it applied off the battlefield, and now realized the error of his thinking. He was the one with the single purpose: to keep Elizabeth at arm's length, to shield his heart from caring. And he had called her a fool?

How had she done it? he asked himself. How had she captured him so completely? Was it her beauty? Yes, she was beautiful, grew more so with each passing day, but there were others he had known in the past more appealing to the eye. No, his love was not so shallow. It was her mind, her courage, her spirit and loyalty that had conquered his heart. She met him measure for measure in all things.

Geoffrey picked up a stone and threw it into the lake, watched as ripple upon ripple widened the smooth surface, and considered that Elizabeth was much like the pebble. Her actions affected a great many lives, just as the pebble affected the calmness of the water. She was the center of his life now, and to ignore that fact was foolish indeed.

The pain and desolation he had seen in Elizabeth's eyes haunted him as he made his way back to the campsite. The hurt stemmed from her admission that she had been disloyal. Hardened to her pleas to explain her behavior, he had readily concurred that she had been disloyal. Anger had ruled him in that moment. Aye, he admitted, he had agreed to her guilt and refused to give her forgiveness or understanding. Now he faced the truth. He had not dealt honestly with her, for, in reality, she had not been disloyal to him at all. Knowing however, the great significance she placed on that attribute called loyalty, he had decided to let her feel shame. His hope was that she would reflect on her behavior and become the docile wife he expected her to be. Docile and submissive. Geoffrey chuckled again, knowing in his heart that Elizabeth could grow ugly and hunchbacked before she could become either docile or submissive. And in his heart, he was glad for it!

There would undoubtedly be a lifetime of arguments between the two over the issue of submission, and Geoffrey found himself looking forward to the gentle squabbles. He laughed aloud, a great echoing sound that reached across the water, and admitted that Elizabeth had taught him that: how to laugh. Now she would teach me how to jump through a flaming hoop, just like the trained bear he had seen at a village fair, if only he would allow it. She tries to improve upon my nature just as I try to improve upon hers, he thought. And I try to swallow her up in my strength just as she tries to lock me in her gentleness, and we are both the winners for it, for there is strength and gentleness in loving. Aye, Geoffrey thought with a sigh, we have each other.

He again clasped his hands behind his back and with a purposeful stride hurried toward his wife.

And how would he proceed now? he found himself wondering. He would tell her of his love soon. When they were settled in his home, when she was safe within his walls, then he would undo the damage he had inflicted on her this eve. He would tell her then. For now he would continue with the mask of indifference, hopefully teaching her a well-deserved lesson. Perhaps his displeasure with her actions would make her more concerned in the future. A nagging doubt that this might not be the best course of action plagued him, but he could not think of another plan. Odd, but he had always thought that love was like a shackle, weakening the victim locked within its hold. Now he knew better. He felt a new strength and freedom with his admission. In such a short time, Elizabeth had replaced his shield and his sword. She had become his strength. God's truth, he felt invincible.

Geoffrey reached his tent and found Elizabeth fast asleep. He stared at her a long minute, appreciating the curve of her thigh and leg, and then quickly stripped out of his clothes. An occasional hiccup told him that she had cried after he left. Dealing with tears was difficult for him, and feeling guilty or not, he was thankful he was spared the ordeal. The fact that he was the cause of her distress held no import. He would end her torment soon, he vowed as he stretched out beside her.

No sooner had his head touched the pallet than his wife, sensing in her sleep that Geoffrey was near, rolled over into his ready embrace. She was tangled in her cape and Geoffrey pulled the garment clear, using his body as her blanket and warmth. He heard her sigh as she snuggled into his chest and smiled into the darkness. "In sleep you need me, wife," he whispered. And then he sighed, with contentment.

The battle was quickly done. Rupert was slain, by Roger's hand. Geoffrey was sorry for it, wishing it had been his blade that ended the traitor's life instead of his vassal's. He ordered the body stripped and saw the half-healed injury on Rupert's shoulder.

Elizabeth had slept through the commotion of the men leaving the camp. By the time she had awakened and dressed, Geoffrey and his men were already returning.

It was Roger who gave her the news of her brother-in-law's death. Elizabeth accepted the information without expression. She only nodded that she had heard and then prepared herself for her journey home. Never once did she glance about for her husband, though she knew that he was safe, listening to his booming voice, which was as huge as his body this morning as he ordered his men into haste.

Elizabeth continued to ignore him while she waited for her mare to be saddled. When Gerald had finished with the task, he helped her into the saddle and she told him thank you, the first words she had spoken all morning. No sooner had she reached for the reins than Geoffrey rode up beside her. He plucked her from her mount as effortlessly as he would a berry from a tree, and settled her in front of him on his stallion. "You ride with me," he stated in his arrogant tone. Then the shield was up, protecting her from the branches, and they were galloping through the woods.

Elizabeth tried to hold herself rigid so that she could touch him as little as possible, but after ten minutes her back protested. She gave up her discomfort and leaned back against her husband, ignoring the soft chuckle she heard. Not another word was spoken on the long ride back to Montwright. It was just as well, Elizabeth decided, as she used the time to sort her feelings out. There were decisions to be made, but as she went over and over the discussion of the previous evening, she found herself growing more and more confused.

She certainly had made a mess of things, she admitted, but her heart had been in the right place, hadn't it? Her motives, once she gave up her need for revenge, were innocent in gain.

You are a stubborn and unbending man, Elizabeth thought. Well, I will give you what you wish, she decided. I will become the kind of wife you seem to want.

It would take discipline on her part, but she was up to the challenge. No longer would she try to imitate her dear departed mother, no longer would she try to share a marriage such as her parents had. She would learn to be docile and unargumentative, for those two qualities seemed to be high on her husband's list of duties. God help her, she would even learn how to sew, though she had no patience for the task. She would give him all he asked, but not an ounce more. He does not need love or joy to make his life complete, so I will benefit him with neither. Elizabeth felt good and spiteful for a time and then realized how foolish she was behaving. How could she ever make her husband realize the happiness he was missing? By denying him what he has come to accept and enjoy, she countered. Do not show him the affection and joy of the past. He will soon miss the laughter shared, wouldn't he? Elizabeth frowned as she considered all the possibilities. What did she have to lose in her new quest? she asked herself. She never had his love to begin with, did she?

Discipline and duty! His favorite lecture, she thought with a grimace. He would have me as obedient as a lap dog, eagerly awaiting a word of kindness or approval when his mood deigned it, just like a bone thrown to an anxious and hungry dog. Well, you shall have both discipline and duty, husband, and rue the day you made those demands. I can be as unbending as you are. It is time you learned a lesson, I think. Time indeed!

Elizabeth felt better with her new resolutions. She refused to address the issue of her disloyalty, knowing in her heart that she would start to cry again if she did. What she treasured most in others she now found tarnished within herself. And if she cried, Geoffrey would start to yell again, she admitted, and she frankly was not up to the ordeal this day.

She was not foolish enough to think that Geoffrey would quickly forgive her, but in time perhaps he would soften in his attitude. Until then she would try to give him what he most wished, and pray each and every day that he would see the errors of his ways. Perhaps she could help him with his realizations. Too much discipline and too much concern for duty . . . surely he would tire of it.

Why do I bother? she asked herself. He is a most stubborn man. The answer was quick and honest. Whether she called him stubborn or unlovable, her heart belonged to him. Until death do us part, she thought, repeating the vow she had made to her husband. The question was, who would kill whom first?

Her thoughts returned to the present when the gates of Montwright opened wide for the troops. Elizabeth spotted Elslow standing with his hands on his hips, Thomas at his side. The look on her grandfather's face showed relief and expected anger. She should have left word for him, some sign of her intent, she thought, so that he would not have worried so. Of course, she argued with herself, had she left word, Elslow would have followed her.

Geoffrey slid off the stallion and lifted Elizabeth to the ground. "You have caused your grandfather needless concern. Go and make your apology," he said in a controlled voice.

Elizabeth nodded and turned to walk toward her grandfather. When she was a scant foot from him, she lifted her head and said, "I apologize for the worry I have caused you, Grandfather, and beg your forgiveness." She lowered her gaze then and waited for his response.

Elslow was so relieved when he sighted his granddaughter safe and sound in her husband's arms. But like a parent who has lost his child at the village fair and then found him again, the urge to both hug and smack tugged at him. "You have taken to bathing in the mud?" he asked instead, gaining time to calm his emotions.

Elizabeth quickly brushed the dirt from her bliaut before returning her gaze to her grandfather. Elslow was quick to see the sadness there, and he suddenly realized she hadn't returned safe after all. There was injury there, hidden inside, where it could do the most damage. And he would soon know who was the cause of such pain.

"Come and give this old man your embrace," Elslow requested in a soft, coaching voice. "There is time for explanations later." He decided against questioning her at the present.

Elizabeth lifted her skirt and ran into his arms. "Can you forgive me, Grandfather?" she asked, squeezing him to her.

"Of course I forgive you," Elslow replied, patting the top of her head. "Go inside now and find clean clothing. Then you must see to your stubborn dogs.

They have not touched food or water since you disappeared. Did I not know better, I would guess they were as worried about you as I was."

Elizabeth sighed and started toward the castle. Thomas grabbed hold of her hand and Elizabeth stopped to smile down at her little brother. It was all the encouragement he needed and he immediately launched into a gleeful interpretation of his grandfather's reaction to her disappearance. Elizabeth ignored him until he asked her if Geoffrey had beaten her. "He did not! Why would you think such a thing?" she asked, pulling him along with her.

"Grandfather said he should," the boy explained, clearly disappointed.

Elslow folded his arms across his chest and watched his granddaughter disappear behind the doors. He turned his anger loose and confronted Geoffrey, who had come up to stand beside him.

"What have you done to her?"

"*I?* What have *I* done to *her?*" Geoffrey's astonishment over Elslow's question undermined Elslow's thought that Geoffrey had been the one to cause Elizabeth such pain. "You should ask instead, what has *she* done to *me!* I tell you this, Elslow, at the rate she is going, I will be dead and buried before our first child is birthed."

"Tell me what has happened," Elslow demanded. "There is defeat in my granddaughter's eyes. I saw it and am concerned. Elizabeth is not one to give up easily. What has caused her this pain?"

"She causes her own pain," Geoffrey snapped, irritated by the interrogation. "She rushes off to see Rupert, having no idea of the danger—"

"She did not! Why, she would have—" Elslow interrupted.

Geoffrey began to walk toward the castle. "I know. I know. She had no idea he was behind the murders, and then she jumped into a lake to save my vassal and had the gall to admit after the deed that she cannot swim. Now tell me, Elslow, would you fault me for beating her?"

Elslow, pacing himself beside the warrior, answered with a swift denial. "I would not. Why, I think I would even help you."

Both men exchanged a look that admitted the truth, and they began to laugh. "Neither of us could lift a hand to harm her," Elslow said.

"You must know this also," Geoffrey said, growing serious. "I was most difficult with her, even accused her of disloyalty, and I plan to keep after her with my harsh manner until she learns a little restraint. Restraint and discipline. It is the only way I can think of to keep her alive, Elslow. I have no wish to train another wife," he ended.

"And did she do it?" Elslow suddenly asked.

"Do what?"

"Save the vassal."

"Aye, she did it."

"I did not doubt it for a second," Elslow said with a gleam in his eyes.

"You have missed the point, old man," Geoffrey snapped with irritation.

"Without restraint and discipline?"

"What say you?" Geoffrey asked suspiciously.

"She saved the vassal without restraint or discipline?"

"Elslow, do not bait me! I am thinking of your granddaughter's safety. She must learn caution."

"You must do what you think best," Elslow stated.

"Aye. Though I promise to use a gentle hand in guiding her," Geoffrey stated very matter-of factly. "It is not so easy to break a habit of long standing without running the risk of breaking the spirit as well. She has been given free rein and allowed to run wild. All that must change."

"Are we discussing my granddaughter or one of your horses?" Elslow inquired with an ironic tone.

"I will do as I think best," Geoffrey stated, ignoring his barb. "I do not wish to lose her."

It was as much as he would admit. Elslow was astute enough to realize that. He nodded and swiftly changed the subject, asking for the details concerning the battle with Rupert.

Geoffrey was much more responsive to that subject and told in great detail the strategy and the outcome.

"Now that Rupert is dead, how will you prove Belwain's involvement?" Elslow asked.

"I have not considered all the possibilities. Do not concern yourself on that topic. I will find a way to deal with him. My first priority is to get Elizabeth settled in her new home."

"When do you leave?" Elslow inquired.

"I had thought tomorrow, but have decided that Elizabeth will need to rest first. And I must go to Owen and give him an accounting. It would not be right to send a messenger. Ten, maybe twelve days hence and we will leave."

"You still wish to leave me in charge?" Elslow asked.

"I do. The boy would do better with you for his council. We will send for him soon enough. Now come and share a drink with me. We will toast to victory."

"I will join you and propose my own toast, Geoffrey. To your future. May it be all you wish."

Chapter Twelve

GEOFFREY WASTED LITTLE TIME BEFORE HE WAS ON HIS way to give Owen a personal accounting. It was an accounting to an equal and Geoffrey treated others of his worth as he would have them treat him. Sending a messenger with the news of the outcome of the battle with Rupert would not have been fitting, and Geoffrey would always do his duty.

There was very little conversation or interaction with Elizabeth in the two days he took to prepare for his leave. He rode from Montwright knowing that his wife thought he was still furious with her, and while it pained him to witness her distress and quiet disposition, he reminded himself that it was all for her own good. If this lesson could teach her caution, then the pain would have been well worth the agony. Yet, even though he cloaked his true feelings from her, he could not resist hauling her to him and giving her a sound, aye, passionate kiss before he left.

Elslow watched the farewell between husband and wife with quiet amusement. He had always considered Elizabeth to be most intelligent and found himself amazed that she could not see through her husband's facade. Could she not see the love radiating in her husband's eyes? Why, it was very obvious to anyone with an ounce of thinking ability that the man was clearly besotted with his wife!

In the past, Elizabeth had always mirrored his traits, his personality, but of late, she acted more like the whipped animal than the independent wildcat he had seen raised.

He had already decided to interfere, knowing it was not his place, and not caring in the least. He would see his daughter's child content, so that he too could find contentment. Aye, he decided, his motives were selfish in one sense.

Elslow let Elizabeth keep her own council for the long day and waited until they were seated in the silent hall for dinner. Geoffrey had taken half the contingent of men with him, including Elslow's new friend, Roger, and the quiet, after so much chaos with Geoffrey's presence, was unsettling.

"I challenge you to a game of chess, Elizabeth," Elslow stated when the meal was finished.

"I fear my heart will not be on the game," Elizabeth replied with a tired sigh. She was giving in to her melancholy, now that Geoffrey was not there to witness it, and was quite enjoying her despondency, Elslow decided.

"I do not want your heart in it," Elslow said as he set the pieces of the wooden chest on the table, "I wish you to use your head. In all things you should use your head, Granddaughter."

"You sound like my husband," Elizabeth replied. "What is your aim?" she asked with a suspicious look at her grandfather. She moved a pawn to start the game and tried to concentrate.

"You let your heart rule your actions, that is all," Elslow stated with a smug voice. He meant to rile her, and from the look on Elizabeth's face, he knew he had accomplished his deed.

"I do not!"

Elslow moved his pawn into position with a chuckle, ignoring her protest. "Elizabeth, do not try to fool this old man. You have gone into mourning since the moment your husband left you. It is most difficult to talk to you, for your head is hidden in your chest as you walk around in circles. Love need not be so pitiful."

"Pitiful! I am pitiful?"

"Do not parrot me, child. Truly, you act like your dogs on occasion," he said, grinning at the irate look on his granddaughter's face. He could understand how Geoffrey had enjoyed fencing with his wife, for Elizabeth was easy to bait.

"What is it you wish to say to me?" Elizabeth demanded. She made a rash move with one of her knights, drumming her fingertips on the table when Elslow quickly took possession of the piece. He would win this game in short order if she did not give her attention to his moves. "Tell me and be done with it, so that I may give attention to this game. I have beaten you in the past, Grandfather," she reminded him, "and I shall beat you tonight."

"Ha!" her grandfather snorted. "I fear you will not, lass. Your heart is not on the game."

"My heart has nothing to do with it," Elizabeth snapped as she watched Elslow take another of her pawns.

"Have you told your husband that you love him?" Elslow suddenly asked, barking his question out with the speed of a hawk attacking his innocent prey.

"I have no wish to discuss my husband," Elizabeth

replied with anger, staring at the board in an effort to dismiss the subject.

Elslow would have none of it. His fist landed on the tabletop, jarring both Elizabeth and the pieces of the chess set. "I would have your attention when I speak to you," he demanded. "I am your elder and you would do well to remember that. I have a wish to discuss the matter and you *will* comply," he added in a booming voice.

"Very well," Elizabeth replied, stung by his anger. "I do not know how you have come to the conclusion that I love my husband, but," she added when she saw her grandfather was about to interrupt, "it is true. I do love him."

"And did you share this information with your husband?"

"Aye, I told him that I love him." Elizabeth moved the pieces back into position on the board and said, "It is your move, Grandfather."

"When I am ready," Elslow replied. His voice was calmer now, and Elizabeth looked up to read his motive. "Was Geoffrey pleased to hear your declaration?"

The question opened the cap on Elizabeth's hurt and anger. "He was not!" She rushed out the denial, keeping nothing from him with her pained expression. "He cares nothing for love or affection. Those were his very words," she stated when Elslow showed his disbelief. "I am to save my love and affection for our children. Love weakens the spirit and the cause," she explained. "I tell you this, Grandfather, my husband is most unfeeling." As an afterthought, she muttered, "Except when he is angry."

"Ha!" Elslow fairly bellowed with glee. "There, methinks, is the key."

"I do not understand," Elizabeth answered, frowning. "You laugh at my misery and speak in riddles.

Geoffrey is always angry, and I am good and sick of it. He is unbending, unreasonable, and uncaring. I will tell you what I am thinking to do, Grandfather. I will try to abandon my love for him. Yes! I will, I tell you. It is a futile endeavor. I am like a knight, surrounded by an enemy army, and I know when I am defeated."

"Nonsense, child. Put your misery aside. I am about to share a secret with you. Your husband loves you." Elslow laughed at his granddaughter's reaction to his statement. Disbelief was there, and anger too. "Before this game is ended, I will prove my point to you," he promised. "But I must have your full cooperation in the matter." He waited for Elizabeth to nod, and when she finally did, he continued, his tone most factual. "Now, tell me what happened when you saved the vassal from drowning. I would hear all of it, so leave nothing out."

Elizabeth knew when her grandfather was in one of his stubborn moods. It was the set of his jaw and his tone of voice that now told her she had best do as he requested, else she would sit at the table long into the night. As quickly as possible she recited the happening, including the information about killing the enemy with her arrows—a fact that drew a wide smile from her grandfather, she noticed—and ending the tale with her husband's most unsatisfactory reaction to her deed. "I thought he would be pleased with my help, but he was not."

"Tell me what he did," Elslow persisted. Now he was the one drumming his fingers on the tabletop, his impatience with his granddaughter obvious.

"I do not know what you seek," Elizabeth protested. "He was angry and yelled, of course—he always yells at me—and he would not let me explain my motives."

"You miss my question, child," Elslow stated, his tone gentle. He could see that the conversation upset her, but he felt he must continue. Picking his words carefully, he said, "Did he pull you from the water by your hair? Did he throw you to the ground and kick you?"

Elizabeth gasped at his outrageous questions. "He would never hurt me. You know that, Grandfather, you know he is honorable and—"

Elslow's slow smile stopped her tirade. "Paint what happened in your mind again and tell me each detail, from the time you were in the water."

"You insist?" Elizabeth asked, not wishing to comply.

"I do!"

"Very well. He pulled me from the water, but not by my hair," she said, shaking her head, "at least I think he pulled me from the water, and then, in front of his men, he began to shake me, so hard I thought my teeth would come loose. It was so embarrassing in front of his men, the way he shook me," she said with renewed irritation.

"Continue," Elslow encouraged.

"And then he . . ." Elizabeth's eyes widened with astonishment as memory took over. Ever so slowly the frown left her face, and a sparkle of hope entered her gaze.

Elslow witnessed it and sighed. His granddaughter was coming to her senses. "He what?" Elslow asked, trying hard not to laugh.

"Why, he pulled me to him and embraced me. It is true. I was crying so that I could not hear what he was saying." Elizabeth grabbed Elslow's hand and began to smile. "God's truth, he treated me like a rag doll, Grandfather. First he would shake me, and then he would hug me, and then he would repeat the ordeal again and again. It was as if he could not make up his mind over the matter."

"Aye, that is how Roger recounted it," Elslow confirmed, grinning. "Now," he added, his voice firm, "I just heard you call him unbending, unreasonable, and uncaring."

"I have," Elizabeth admitted. "I *would* be honest," she explained.

"With everyone but yourself," Elslow amended. "I will not question you further, Elizabeth. You will begin to use your head now and find your own solutions."

"Tell me your thoughts," Elizabeth begged.

"My thoughts are insignificant," Elslow hedged. The look of disappointment softened his resolve. "Very well. To me, it is all quite simple. The man loves you, whether he wishes to or not."

"If what you say is true," Elizabeth answered, "then there is still one problem."

"Aye?"

"He does not know it . . . yet."

"Then it will be your duty to instruct him," Elslow stated with a sparkle in his eyes.

The game of chess continued, but Elizabeth could not concentrate on what she was doing. Her mind was busy trying to think of a plan of action in dealing with her husband, and it took her full effort.

"Grandfather?" she interrupted at one point. "Geoffrey thinks I have been disloyal to him, and I do not know how to change his way of thinking," she admitted.

"In time his attitude will soften. Your motives were pure, child, and he will surely realize that soon enough," her grandfather answered as he studied the board.

Elizabeth considered her grandfather's words and then interrupted his concentration again. "You have always taught me to form a plan before making a change. I have considered that I could—"

"Do not tell me your intentions," Elslow stated. "I would remain innocent of your deceptions."

"Deceptions! You shame me, Grandfather. I will deal with my husband with honor. Always," she stated with emphasis. "If Geoffrey truly loves me, then what I plan will be most honorable."

"Checkmate!"

"I beg your pardon?"

"The game, Elizabeth. I have won."

"Nay, Grandfather," Elizabeth denied with a smile. "It is I who has won."

"What say you? I have your queen, and your king cannot move. The game is mine."

"Aye, that is true," Elizabeth conceded with a nod. "The game is yours . . . but the knight is mine."

While Geoffrey was gone from Montwright, Elizabeth prepared her belongings for transfer to her husband's home. It was a most difficult task. Each morning, upon awakening, Elizabeth would fight waves of nausea. Bile would push for release, and more often than not, her contrary stomach would have its way. Elizabeth found herself eating less and less, thinking to purge the poison that had mysteriously found its way into her stomach, and rested several times during the day in an effort to gain new strength.

She dared not wear the ring of garlic around her neck as a safeguard, for she wanted to hide her sickness from her grandfather. She had no wish to cause him worry, but she could not help becoming concerned. The sickness was strange indeed, for after each morning's battle with her stomach, she would suddenly find herself feeling quite normal. Until nighttime, when the battle would be resumed.

She blamed her upset on the fact that Geoffrey was gone. Love was playing havoc with her body as well as her mind, she concluded. Yet, when Geoffrey returned to Montwright some seven days later, Elizabeth's condition did not improve. Her husband was too busy with his preparations for departure to give Elizabeth much notice. Elizabeth found herself both pleased and disgruntled by her husband's lack of attention. It was soon obvious that he was avoiding her, obvious even to the most dim-witted. He would come to bed long after

Elizabeth had fallen asleep, and be gone before Elizabeth opened her eyes in the morning.

Elizabeth maintained an outward calm while her stomach continued its war, gaining new strength each time her grandfather would gift her with a wink or a smile. Each nod, each smile was a reminder of their conversation . . . an acknowledgment that her husband did love her.

Lord but he was stubborn! Why, he was still so angry with her that he barely glanced her way whenever they were in the same room. And he did not touch her, not since his return. Her heart pained her as much as her stomach when she realized how much she longed for his kiss, his embrace, his love.

Elizabeth found herself struggling for control on the morning she and Geoffrey were to leave for his home. It was unusually hot for early summer and Elizabeth was feeling quite melancholy as she made her goodbyes. She knew her husband would not be pleased if she became overly emotional, and she kept reminding herself of that fact as she tickled and hugged her little brother and then turned to her grandfather. "I will miss you," she told him in a whisper.

"Did you remember to pack your banner?" her grandfather asked. "A small remembrance of your past will help you deal with the uncertainty of the future."

"I did remember," Elizabeth replied. "I love you, Grandfather. God protect you and Thomas."

Her grandfather embraced her in a powerful hug and then lifted her onto her mare. "You have been through much in these past months, child," Elslow stated in a soft voice. He took hold of her hand and squeezed it. "But you are made of strong stuff. It is God's will that you follow your destiny and your husband. The two are entwined, just like the vines that cling to the castle walls. Be not afraid, Elizabeth. And remember, trust your heart but use your head."

Elizabeth smiled at her grandfather's confusing order and replied, "I will do my best."

Geoffrey observed the farewell between grandfather and granddaughter from the steps of Montwright. He was proud of his wife, knowing how she held her emotions in check. She looked so dignified and serene; yes, he thought, she is as regal as a queen, yet he knew how difficult this parting was for her. She was leaving all that was familiar to her to follow her husband, a man she thought incapable of feeling any emotion other than anger.

Geoffrey admitted that he liked the tender show of affection between Elslow and Elizabeth and found himself irritated that he was the observer and not the participant. Yet he did not know how to enter into the farewell, and so continued to stand and watch, a brooding expression on his face.

Thomas demanded the warrior's attention. The child launched into Geoffrey's leg, barely nudging the lord with his puny strength. Geoffrey effortlessly lifted the child high into the air and then slowly lowered him until the two were eye to eye. "You will behave and listen to your grandfather!" His voice sounded harsh to his ears, but the child seemed unafraid. He grinned and nodded his answer.

Geoffrey pretended to drop Thomas, and the boy let out a squeal of delight. The lord placed the child on the ground and seemed undisturbed when the little one wrapped himself around Geoffrey's leg. Indeed, he was pleased that the boy was so open and honest with his affection, and patted him on his head as he watched Elslow stride over to him.

"I will watch Thomas well," Elslow said.

"And I will watch your Elizabeth," Geoffrey promised in a solemn voice.

"And we will both be led a merry chase," Elslow said with a chuckle.

Geoffrey found himself smiling, and then turned to

glance at Elizabeth. He saw the distress she tried to hide. "I must hurry, before my wife changes her mind and refuses to leave," he told Elslow. He started to walk toward his mount and then stopped and turned back to Elslow. "There is still danger as long as Belwain has his freedom. Walk with caution," he said. It was the closest Geoffrey could come to admitting his concern and affection.

Elslow, however, harbored no such inhibitions. He whacked Geoffrey on his back and threw his arm around his shoulder. "Son, you'll miss this old man," he advised the serious-faced knight.

Geoffrey chuckled and replied, shaking his head, "Never have I been surrounded by so many who are so unafraid. It is a mystery," he admitted.

"That is because we are family," Elslow stated.

"Aye," Geoffrey said, mounting his steed, "family." He gave Elizabeth a long look and then turned toward the gates. Roger was saddled beside Geoffrey, and the two, flanked by Elizabeth's wolfhounds, led the troops surrounding Elizabeth out of Montwright.

Geoffrey had left half his contingent of men with Elslow and felt no unease. He looked forward, eager for the ride.

Elizabeth preferred to look back, straining to memorize the walls of her home. The future frightened her, and she felt a devastating loneliness that tore at her heart.

Her physical discomfort soon took her mind off her loneliness. It seemed that every hour or so, both her bladder and her stomach demanded release. It was both awkward and embarrassing to have to stop so often. She should have found a female servant to bring along, she decided. Another woman would have eased her embarrassment, and perhaps share her worry.

By the time the sun had reached its zenith, Elizabeth was hot, miserable, and exhausted. She closed her eyes for a moment's rest and almost fell out of her saddle, but Geoffrey was suddenly there, beside her, and caught her just in time. He lifted her and settled her against him without breaking his stallion's stride. Elizabeth sighed her acceptance and quickly went to sleep, her head nestled against her husband's chest and her arms wrapped around his waist.

With one arm, Geoffrey held his wife close to him, savoring the feel of her softness against him. She smelled of wildflowers, Geoffrey thought, rubbing his chin against the top of her head as he inhaled her sweet scent, and apples too, from the meager lunch they had shared. He heard his wife sigh in her sleep, and silently echoed the sound.

Elizabeth slept the afternoon away. Geoffrey finally called a halt to the fast pace an hour before sundown. Elizabeth's legs would not support her when she finally touched the ground, and she found she had to hold on to Geoffrey's arm until the shaking subsided.

"You are ill?" Geoffrey made the question sound like an accusation, and Elizabeth straightened up at once.

"I am not!" she contradicted. "Just a little indisposed. It will pass."

She tried to look away, but Geoffrey placed his hands on her shoulders and pulled her toward him. It was the first show of affection in such a long time that Elizabeth felt herself becoming shy.

"It is your time of the month?" he asked in a gentle whisper.

Shyness evaporated with his intimate question. Elizabeth gasped and shook her head furiously. "We must not discuss such things," she said, blushing. "It is unseemly."

She tried to pull away but Geoffrey would not let go. "And if husband and wife do not discuss this . . . thing, then when am I to know when I cannot touch you?" he asked in a logical voice.

"Oh! I do not know," Elizabeth whispered her answer, looking down at the ground. A sudden thought turned her gaze back to her husband. "That is why you have not, that is the reason we have not . . ." she stammered, unable to put her thoughts into words. She waited with the hope that Geoffrey would finish her sentence but he remained silent and watchful. "That is the reason you have not touched me?" she finally asked.

Her voice was like the whisper of the wind, but Geoffrey heard. "Nay," he replied. His voice was gentle and most confusing to Elizabeth.

"Then you are still angry with me?" Elizabeth asked. "That is the reason." In her heart she prayed she was right, that it was Geoffrey's anger over her conduct that kept him from her bed. She didn't know how she would deal with any other reason. If he no longer found her desirable . . .

Geoffrey watched the play of emotions that swept across his wife's face, and longed to take her fully into his arms and kiss away all her doubts, her worries. He could barely conceal his hunger for her. His promise to wait until Elizabeth was settled into his home before telling her of his love, before showing her his love, now seemed highly unreasonable. And, Geoffrey reminded himself with a grin, he was always most reasonable, wasn't he?

Elizabeth witnessed the grin and became more confused. What was he thinking to bring such a smile? she wondered. Would she ever understand how Geoffrey's mind worked?

"Come, Elizabeth. We have camped near a clear stream. Refresh yourself while I see to my duties."

"I may have a bath?" Elizabeth asked, her voice eager. Her clothes felt hot and she knew she was covered with a layer of dust. She lifted the heavy hair from the back of her neck, letting the soft breeze cool her neck.

"After you have eaten," Geoffrey stated. "Then I will find a secluded place for you to bathe." The way his wife stood, holding her hair atop her head, caused her breasts to strain against the fabric of her gown, and Geoffrey found himself hard-pressed not to grab her.

"I will look forward to it," Elizabeth answered. She turned and walked toward the stream so that she would be out of the way of her husband's duties.

I also look forward to it, Geoffrey thought with growing anticipation. Tonight, my love, I will share my heart with you, tonight and forever.

"My lord?" Gerald's voice intruded on Geoffrey's thoughts and he turned with a grunt of displeasure to give his squire attention. "You wish your tent placed in the middle of the camp?" he inquired of the knight.

"Not tonight," Geoffrey answered. He glanced about and then motioned to an area among the trees. "With the trees to my back, away from the men," he decided. "And hurry with your task, Gerald. I would have dinner over and my bed made ready as soon as possible."

Gerald nodded his answer with his hand over his heart and quickly turned to see to his duty.

It seemed an eternity to Geoffrey before the dried meat, bread, and fruit were spread before him. He guided Elizabeth to the tent and saw her settled beside him and then all but force-fed her.

"You seem in such a hurry, my lord," Elizabeth stated. "Do you seek rest early this eve? I could have my bath another time if it is not convenient."

"No!" Geoffrey answered, his voice gruff. "Finish now and gather your cape and whatever else you will need. We must be done before the sun disappears."

Elizabeth hurried to find her soap and cape and then followed Geoffrey. He seemed irritated and impatient with her, but Elizabeth searched her mind and could find no cause for his behavior. She raced to keep up with Geoffrey but refused to question him on his hurry. If he wished her to know his thinking, then he would tell her. She had learned that much in their short marriage, she admitted. Her husband kept his own council and she would have to be patient until he was ready to tell her his thoughts.

Elizabeth and Geoffrey followed the bank of the stream a small distance, until it curved and deepened. The spot Geoffrey chose required ducking under several thick branches to reach the area, but the discomfort of the prickly thorns against Elizabeth's arms was forgotten when she straightened up and saw the beauty surrounding her. Giant trees, posted like sentries, circled the enclosure. Branches reached out, acting as a canopy that allowed only narrow streamers of sunlight to filter through. The red and gold tones of the fading sun cast an eerie, almost mystical spell upon the leaves and grass. "Geoffrey, it is beautiful here! It is magical," she whispered.

"Not magical, only private," Geoffrey corrected, smiling. "I followed the stream earlier, before dinner, with your dogs, and found this place."

Elizabeth nodded and sat down on the bank to take her shoes off. She finished the task and glanced up at Geoffrey. She stilled her action when she saw that he too was removing his boots. As she watched, Geoffrey continued to remove all of his garments.

She knew she blushed, and felt foolish for it. Yet she couldn't seem to take her eyes off her husband, mesmerized by the power and muscle he so casually displayed.

"The sun paints you as a god," she whispered. His skin was golden in the light, his raw beauty magnificent.

Geoffrey shook his head and his thick black hair fell against his forehead. "Your foolish talk will land you in purgatory," Geoffrey admonished.

"I did not mean it as blasphemy," Elizabeth stated.

Geoffrey smiled at Elizabeth. "Need I be your maid to see to your undress?" he questioned in a soft, husky voice. His words were meant to tease, but his look, so full of passion and hunger, erased the jest.

Elizabeth felt his warmth invade her. She could not return his smile but only stare at Geoffrey. Slowly she raised her hand, and Geoffrey took hold and pulled her to her feet. Without a word, he began to remove her clothes. First he released the leather belt surrounding her hips, and then lifted the bliaut over her head. Next he pulled the chainse from her and finally, the ivory-colored chemise. His hands were careful not to touch her breasts, though his fingers brushed the sides more than once.

Geoffrey and Elizabeth stood facing each other for a long, silent moment, letting desire flow between them like a rising wind. When Elizabeth could not stand the distance any longer, she took a tentative step toward her husband. "Geoffrey?" His name was a plea, and Geoffrey knew for what she asked.

"In time, Elizabeth," he whispered. He turned and walked into the water and did not stop until the clear liquid covered his chest.

Elizabeth took her soap in her hand and quickly followed Geoffrey. She let out a gasp when the water touched her. "It is too cold," she called to Geoffrey, retreating a step. The water covered her hips and Elizabeth gingerly cupped some of the water and slowly wet her arms. Trembling, she lathered the soap and hurried to get her bath done. She turned her back on Geoffrey out of shyness as she scrubbed the dust from her body.

"Come to your husband, Elizabeth."

Elizabeth turned, saw the distance, and frowned. "I am cold, Geoffrey," she repeated. She held her lower lip between her teeth and waited, hoping Geoffrey would come to her.

"I am waiting, wife." There was laughter in Geoffrey's voice and Elizabeth found herself smiling. "It is your duty to come to me," he advised with mock gruffness.

"I would always do my duty," Elizabeth called out.

She took a deep breath and began to walk toward Geoffrey, letting the water cover her breasts and shoulders. And then she stopped, bracing her legs against the current. "Now you must come to me, Geoffrey," she said. They were just a few feet away, the frigid water lapping against both of them. She was about to tell him that she would be completely under water if she ventured any farther, and to remind him also that she could not swim, lest he had forgotten that fact.

Geoffrey's gaze stopped her from forming the words, from thinking coherently. She could say nothing, only meet his stare as the smile left her face. She was becoming bewitched by his gaze, so hot and demanding. He was calling to her without speaking a word. She heard the command with all of her senses and did not hesitate to answer.

They both took a step toward each other at the same instant. And then Geoffrey's arms were around Elizabeth's waist. He pulled her toward him, locking her legs between his, letting her feel his desire.

"I had thought to bathe you with your soap, to savor each touch against your skin, and then to bathe you with the love words all gentle women yearn to hear." His voice was gruff and halting as he continued, "I have never wanted anyone as I want you, Elizabeth. My aim was to woo you this night, to play the tender pursuer."

Elizabeth's eyes widened with her husband's declarations.

"Now that the time has come, wife, I find I do not know the words of wooing, and admit that I am lacking in the discipline and patience for the task. Had I taken your soap and tried to bathe you, the bath would have been forgotten and I would have taken you then and there."

A smile tugged at the corners of Elizabeth's mouth. "You call wooing a task, my lord?" she asked in a soft voice.

Geoffrey looked so serious and purposeful, and Elizabeth was both amused and disgruntled by his words. "Geoffrey, I do not have much patience for wooing either. I would hear your feelings without the flowery words, and be most content."

Geoffrey looked surprised and then frowned. "What know you of wooing?" he demanded.

"Very little," Elizabeth admitted as she rubbed her fingers across his rib cage. "It just seems to me that saying words of love to each other should not be considered a task." She pulled at one of the soft hairs on his chest to underline her words.

Geoffrey stilled her hands by placing her arms around his waist and then began to stroke the length of her back. "It is much like learning to yield the blade," Geoffrey commented.

"I do not understand," Elizabeth replied, tilting her head back to see if he was jesting.

"This wooing. It requires practice," Geoffrey explained.

Elizabeth laughed, ignoring her husband's frown. "There is no need, my lord. Courting is for those who have not declared their love for each other. *I* have already told *you* what is in my heart."

"But I have not explained my feelings for you, Elizabeth." Geoffrey sounded exasperated. "I know what you wish to hear and I would get on with it," he muttered.

"You have my full attention," Elizabeth replied in a soft voice. Inside she was fairly screaming with joy. She felt like laughing and weeping at the same time. Geoffrey loved her, just as Elslow had predicted.

"You will be serious," Geoffrey demanded, pinching the curve of her bottom.

Elizabeth nodded, rubbing her face against his chest.

"I had considered that when I was older and had given up many of my duties, then I would find time to tell you that I cared for you," he began. He was distracted from his speech when Elizabeth began to place soft kisses on his chest.

Elizabeth used her tongue to circle and stroke Geoffrey's sensitive nipples and heard his sharp intake of breath.

"Elizabeth!"

"I love you, Geoffrey." A bare whisper, inhaled like an aphrodisiac, arousing Geoffrey's senses, releasing his heart.

"And I love you." So quietly spoken, so joyfully received.

Geoffrey chained his hands in her hair and tilted her head back. Slowly he lowered his head, intent on sealing his vow with a kiss. Elizabeth parted her lips and waited. Tears of love and pleasure filled her eyes. Geoffrey's lips touched hers, the tip of his tongue stopping to stroke the soft outline of her mouth. Elizabeth made a sound that sounded like a contented kitten's purr. Geoffrey took control of her mouth fully then, thrusting his tongue inside to caress and stroke the sweet warmth inside. His hands left her silken hair and slid sensuously down her back to knead and fondle the soft flesh of her bottom.

The kiss devoured and replenished, and neither was the victor or the conquered. Geoffrey finally tore his mouth away. Elizabeth opened her mouth to protest, and Geoffrey immediately silenced her with another kiss, letting her tongue invade his mouth, wanting her to know and feel the darkness and mystery also.

"So beautiful," he whispered when his mouth moved down to her neck. He lifted her up so that he could worship her breasts, forcing her to wrap her legs around his waist.

When his mouth covered one breast, Elizabeth clung to his shoulders with trembling hands and groaned her pleasure. The roughness of his cheek against her tender skin was an erotic stimulus. Geoffrey continued to suck the hard nipple until Elizabeth began to pull on his hair. "Do not make me wait," she pleaded in a half-whisper. "It has been so long, Geoffrey. Please."

Geoffrey lifted his head and looked at Elizabeth with eyes darkened by passion. Her breath left her with a low moan. The love and hunger radiating in Geoffrey's hot gaze burned and melted, caressed and scorched. He was the flame, she the fire.

"You are exquisite torture," Geoffrey groaned, burying his head in her silken hair.

Elizabeth's answer was to hug him as tightly as possible. Geoffrey held her hips with his hands and slowly walked toward the bank.

When he had reached his destination, he let Elizabeth slide down his length and held her against him. Then he gently pulled her arms away from him and turned to spread her cape upon the grass. He turned again, to beckon Elizabeth, but his wife was already there, throwing herself into his arms. He felt her shiver and immediately lowered her to the ground, intent on covering her with his body. "You are cold," he whispered against her ear, "but I will warm you."

"I am not cold," Elizabeth whispered. She nibbled on the soft lobe of his ear and then touched the inside with the tip of her tongue.

Geoffrey responded by rubbing his hardness against her in a slow, sensuous motion and then moved downward. His mouth circled her navel while his hand stroked the moist golden triangle guarding Elizabeth's heat. His fingers sought and found her, again and again, becoming more demanding with each touch, each change in pressure. Elizabeth began to move her hips against him, her eyes closed in splendor. She felt like she was about to shatter into a thousand pieces and moaned her need.

"I will taste your sweetness, drink your nectar," Geoffrey said huskily against her. His mouth and tongue replaced his hand and Elizabeth turned to liquid fire. Her hands dug into the grass and she could concentrate on nothing but the wild flame stroking her so intimately. And then the fire consumed her, released her. She trembled, almost violently. "Geoffrey!" His name was a cry of pleasure and fear.

Geoffrey heard the confusion, recognized the fright, and hushed Elizabeth with soothing words. He moved up to cup the sides of her face, willing her to look at him. Tears streamed down Elizabeth's face and he gently wiped them away before placing a tender kiss on each eyelid. "Do not be afraid of what happens to you when you are with me."

"I lose all control when you touch me," Elizabeth whispered. She saw the look of male satisfaction in Geoffrey's eyes and knew her words pleased him. "In that brief time, my body is no longer mine, and it is so easily done and so forceful that it frightens me." Her fingers traced the outline of her husband's mouth as she spoke, her honesty and vulnerability there in her eyes, unguarded.

"It is the same with me," Geoffrey told her. He moved restlessly against her, letting her feel his need. "Your softness beckons me. I will lose myself in your warmth but will not give up my strength. You have become my fountain of power, Elizabeth. Your love replenishes. When we are together, like this, I feel invincible. Let me come to you now, love. Give me your fire." His mouth covered hers, his tongue plunging inside in a tender invasion that excited her. His hands spoke of male hunger as they stroked and caressed. Embers ignited, and when he at last entered her fully, thrusting to the core of her soul, the fire of desire and love raged unchecked between them. They gave to each other the fire purified and renewed, and each felt the victory of release at the same instant. Elizabeth opened her eyes and saw the transformation overtake Geoffrey. There was profound joy between the two, shared and coveted. There was love.

Geoffrey buried his head in Elizabeth's shoulder and sighed with contentment. She echoed the sound, holding him close to her, embracing his weight.

Geoffrey shifted his weight, holding her in his arms. He kissed her cheeks, nuzzled against her ear, and whispered outrageous compliments and promises that brought a blush to his wife's face.

"When did you realize that you loved me?" Elizabeth asked, stroking the line of his jaw with one fingertip. "Was it when you thought me drowned?"

Geoffrey chuckled and shook his head. "I was too angry to think of love then," he admitted. He rolled onto his back, letting Elizabeth prop her head with elbows braced against his massive chest, and then continued, "Warriors do not record such facts in their heads. When I decided I loved you is not significant," he teased.

Elizabeth smiled. The golden chips in his dark gaze fascinated her. How had she ever thought him cold and unbending? she found herself asking.

"When did you realize that you loved me?" he countered. His hands began to gently knead the curves of her bottom as he waited for her answer.

"I do not remember," Elizabeth said. The sparkle was back in her eyes, and Geoffrey found himself grinning, knowing that she was about to tease him yet again. "Wives of warriors do not record such facts in their heads," she giggled. "Besides, when is not significant."

Geoffrey gave her a playful squeeze. "Ever you would tease, wife. I will put up with your silliness for the rest of our days together, for I love you with my heart."

"I thought I would never hear you say the words," Elizabeth whispered. The smile left her and she leaned down and kissed him.

"I had some foolish ideas of love," Geoffrey replied when the kiss ended. "I thought it would weaken me and now know how wrong I was. You give me new strength of purpose, Elizabeth. A part of me longs to lock you away in our bedroom and share you with no one else."

"I will always belong to you, Geoffrey," Elizabeth answered.

"I know that is true," Geoffrey said. "And I will have faith and confidence in your loyalty to me. Would you believe that I find it difficult to share you even with your grandfather and your brother? I used to scoff at men who let jealousy take control of their lives, and now find that if I am not careful, I too will be ruled by it."

Elizabeth's eyes showed her surprise and Geoffrey grinned again. "I have not had the closeness of family like you have," he explained, "and I would know that I come before all others."

"There are all kinds of love," Elizabeth answered, her voice soft. Her husband was letting her see his vulnerability, and she knew in her heart that she would cherish this moment for the rest of her life. "What I feel for my grandfather and for little Thomas is a different sort of love than what I feel for you. In time I think you will love them as much as I do, and in just the same way. What I feel for them does not take away what I feel for you."

Geoffrey pulled her down and kissed her for a long, breathless moment. Elizabeth clung to him, matching his passion and hunger.

With regret, Geoffrey finally pulled away. "It grows dark," he said. "Hurry and dress so that I can take you back to our tent and undress you once again." He gave her a sound slap on her backside and chuckled at her pretended outrage.

Neither spoke a word until they were headed back toward the camp. And then Elizabeth spoke, her voice as soft as the rustle of the leaves underfoot. "You are truly jealous of my family?" she asked.

"I will get over it," Geoffrey answered, squeezing her hand. "A knight is loyal and vows fealty to only one overlord, as I have, with William, my king," he began. "You have committed yourself to me," he continued, "and I do not expect you to stop loving your family because you love me. Yet I would know that I am first in your heart and that you would choose me above all others, as I would choose you."

Elizabeth covered her smile. She understood that falling in love was new to her husband and that he was trying to deal with it as he would everything else in his life. He was trying to give it order and a proper place. His mistake was in using logic as his tool to deal with his emotions.

"There would never be a time that I would have to choose between you or my. . . " Elizabeth was going to say *family*, but quickly substituted the word *relatives*. "You are my family now, Geoffrey, just as I am your family. And Elslow and Thomas . . . they are our relatives. We all belong to each other, but not as vassals and lords."

"You are right, Elizabeth. You will never have to make a choice," Geoffrey said. "I would not allow it. Nor would I ever demand such a test of your loyalty, for I begin to understand your reasoning. I love you, and that is all that matters."

"Were you still so unsure of my loyalty to you that you left Elslow with Thomas at Montwright?"

"I wanted to have you all to myself for a time," Geoffrey admitted.

Elizabeth leaned against her husband's side and thought about his words. He had shared his inner feelings with her this evening, and there was joy and love in her heart. He had come a long way, learning to show affection and voicing his thoughts to her, and Elizabeth was content. There was still a small distance to go, she realized, for Geoffrey remained unsure and (though she would never say the word) insecure. Soon this too would change, and talk of tests and making choices would cease. No one would ever ask such a terrible thing. No one.

Elizabeth dreamed that night, and it began in a most pleasant way. She was dressed all in white, in a gown that seemed to float around her ankles. She was walking through the bailey of a great palace and a fine mist covered the ground. She was smiling as she opened the doors and walked into a great hall. And then the dream changed to a nightmare. Someone was calling her, but she did not know who. Her pulse quickened with the horrible sound of agony and despair in the voice calling to her. She hurried, searching for the voice, pushing through a crowd of laughing men who seemed not to know that she was even there. When she reached the very center of the room, she stopped. A scream filled her lungs. Standing before her was her husband, his hands and feet chained with heavy steel links. He did not see her and was looking toward the other side of the room. Elizabeth turned and saw her grandfather, also chained.

The voice began again, but the sound had turned from agony to triumph. It was Belwain. The mist at her feet turned red, and in the nightmare Elizabeth knew it was a symbol of the blood that would soon be shed.

Belwain lifted his hand and pointed at her. "You will choose and one will die. And if you will not choose, then both will be killed." He laughed then, an evil devil's laughter that clawed at Elizabeth's soul.

She shook her head, denying what was asked, and Belwain pulled Geoffrey's sword and lifted it high into the air.

Her screams woke Geoffrey. He reached for his sword and then realized that Elizabeth was right beside him. His hands shook as he pulled his wife into his arms and gently rocked her against him. "Open your eyes,

Elizabeth. It is only a nightmare," he whispered, again and again. "I am here."

Elizabeth awoke with a start. She clutched at Geoffrey's shoulders and took great gulps of air, trying to calm her heart. "It was terrible," she whispered.

"Do not speak of it," Geoffrey soothed. He tenderly brushed the hair from her forehead and kissed her. "You have been dreaming, that is all. The pace was too fast for you today and you are overly tired. Rest your head against me and close your eyes. All is well."

"I am afraid," she told him. "If I sleep, I will have the nightmare again."

"No, you will not," Geoffrey whispered. He shifted positions, until Elizabeth was beneath him. His arms bore his weight, anchored on either side of his wife. "You will dream only of making love to me," he vowed. With those words spoken, Geoffrey leaned down and kissed Elizabeth.

He murmured words of love with a velvet voice and soothing hands that turned Elizabeth's thoughts only to him and what he was doing to her. The nightmare was forgotten.

Chapter Thirteen

ELIZABETH ADJUSTED TO HER NEW HOME WITH VERY little difficulty. When she first sighted Geoffrey's domain, she was overwhelmed by the massive structures and the giant wall surrounding them. The stone fortress was so large that it made Montwright seem puny in comparison.

Yet once inside the walls, a cold starkness prevailed and Elizabeth found it most unsettling. She quickly set about making her mark on both the inside of the castle and the inner bailey. Geoffrey let her have her way, though he did a fair amount of balking when he found her on her knees, transplanting wildflowers the colors of the rainbow, along the castle walls. Elizabeth ignored his mock anger with teasing replies that totally undermined her husband's thoughts.

The servants, at first suspicious and frigid toward

their new mistress, soon melted under her gentle smiles and softly spoken requests. They soon became her champions and eagerly awaited her next order of change. Fresh flowers adorned the tables, and bright colorful banners, carried from Montwright, graced the newly washed stone walls of the castle. Peace and contentment replaced the bleak starkness. The inhabitants of Berkley Castle were in awe. Their fortress had become a home.

By the end of July, Elizabeth was certain that she carried Geoffrey's child. She cherished the news and took several days rehearsing and planning in her mind just how she would tell Geoffrey. He would be pleased and probably act most arrogant, Elizabeth decided, and that would please her.

Elizabeth sat at the dinner table, awaiting Geoffrey. She had decided that she would share her news with him this evening, when they were alone in their bedroom. She could barely contain her excitement and found herself laughing out loud. The servants tending to the table gave her puzzled looks, and Elizabeth knew she was acting quite strange. Tomorrow, after Geoffrey had received the news, she would explain her odd behavior, and they would understand.

The soldiers began to file into the hall, and Elizabeth straightened her position, eagerly looking for Geoffrey. The squire Gerald drew her attention. He raced around two burly men and hurried over to his mistress. "Messengers have arrived from William," he all but shouted. "They would speak with my lord as soon as possible."

Elizabeth frowned over this information and then said, "Show them into the hall, Gerald. I will tell Roger and he will find Geoffrey."

Roger was already walking toward Elizabeth and she gave him a greeting before telling him about the messengers. "Why are they here?" she asked, unable to keep the worry out of her voice.

"It is not unusual," Roger answered. "Ah, here is your husband. He will tell you the reasons."

"You have no greeting for me?" Geoffrey said when he reached Elizabeth's side.

Elizabeth immediately smiled and reached up to place a chaste kiss on her husband's cheek. "I seem to remember a time when showing affection was not allowed," she said in a whisper.

Geoffrey laughed and pulled his wife into his arms. "That was before I realized how important it was for you to touch me," he teased.

"I am most undisciplined," Elizabeth responded with a grin.

"Geoffrey," Roger interrupted, "there are messengers from William. They await you in the corridor."

Geoffrey nodded, seemingly undisturbed by this information. "I thought that our king was still in Rouen," he replied.

"He must have only just returned," Roger commented.

Geoffrey turned back to his wife and said, "Begin the meal without me so that my men can eat. Roger and I will see what news the king sends us."

Elizabeth wished to listen to the messengers too, but realized that it was not her place to ask. She would have to wait and hear the news from her husband. Geoffrey had begun to confide in Elizabeth more and more, and she had no doubt that he would tell her what their king requested.

Father Hargrave, a visiting priest from nearby Northcastle, entered the room. He offered Elizabeth his arm just as Geoffrey was leaving. She assumed her role as hostess and gave the elderly priest her full attention.

Elizabeth sat beside him at the table and bowed her head while he gave the blessing, trying to concentrate on his prayer. Her mind kept returning to the messengers, speculating on various reasons why the king would send word to them, and finding none acceptable. Geoffrey had already given his required number of days' duty to his lord. William held court only three times during the year, and Geoffrey had attended those sessions also.

Perhaps it was the Domesday Book, she considered, referring to William's accounting of the number of subjects under his jurisdiction. Because the record included each person's worth, from the number of animals to the amount of coin each held, his loyal subjects grumbled among themselves and called the record the Domesday Book. Their logic was simple and, in Elizabeth's estimation, probably quite accurate. Once the king had a true accounting of each person's worth, the taxes would be raised. It was an age-old problem, this raising of taxes, Elizabeth knew, for she had heard her father balk about the unfairness of the system more than once.

Geoffrey and Roger returned to the hall just as the meal was served. From the looks on their faces, Elizabeth knew that they were not pleased with the news. "It is the Domesday Book?" she whispered to Geoffrey when he was seated at the head of the table.

Geoffrey took hold of Elizabeth's hand but did not answer her. She looked across the table and smiled at Roger. Elizabeth always sat on her husband's right and Roger always sat on Geoffrey's left.

One of Geoffrey's squires began to serve the meat and Geoffrey spoke a few words to the young boy. Elizabeth took advantage of his inattention and leaned toward Roger. "It is the Domesday Book?" she asked, hoping Roger would give her a quick reply.

Geoffrey gave Elizabeth's hand a quick squeeze. Roger looked like he was about to answer Elizabeth, but Geoffrey's small shake of his head stopped his action. Elizabeth saw Geoffrey's motion out of the corner of her eye.

She sighed with frustration. "I do not think the king would take kindly to hearing his accounting called Domesday," Geoffrey said.

The priest cleared his voice and began to repeat a favorite story they had all heard at least five times since his arrival, but out of courtesy, Geoffrey and Roger and Elizabeth gave him their attention. They laughed when the humorous story was ended, and the priest was pleased. So pleased, in fact, that he launched into yet another and another tale.

As soon as the meal was over, Geoffrey said to Roger, "Go and see to the preparations for tomorrow." He then turned to Elizabeth and suggested that they retire for the evening.

Elizabeth quickly agreed. "There is something I must speak to you about," she told Geoffrey with a soft smile.

"And I must also talk to you," Geoffrey replied. His voice held no emotion and Elizabeth frowned with concern. When her husband tried to mask his feelings, as he was now doing, there was usually grave cause. She held his hand and followed him without a word.

When the bedroom door was shut against the world and they were alone, she still did not speak. She was learning her husband well and knew that he was considering his words with caution before he spoke. His frown told her that much.

Each undressed the other in silence. It had become a ritual for Elizabeth to take Geoffrey's sword and place it near the head of the bed, on her husband's side. This completed, she slipped between the covers and waited.

Geoffrey did not blow out the candles this night but came to Elizabeth with the lights glowing around them. He took her into his arms and kissed her gently.

"I would tell you my news first?" Elizabeth asked.

"I would rather have mine over and done with," Geoffrey replied. There was an almost savage tone to his voice and Elizabeth immediately felt a knot of worry form in her stomach. Geoffrey anchored Elizabeth's legs with one of his and held her against his chest. He could not see her eyes, her face, and admitted that he did not want to. His words would cause her pain, and her pain would become his. "There is no easy way to tell you, Elizabeth," Geoffrey began as he stroked her hair.

Elizabeth pulled back, forcing Geoffrey to look at her. "Then tell me with speed," she suggested, becoming more frightened by the minute.

"The summons from William concerns Montwright," he stated. He watched Elizabeth as he spoke, saw her confusion, and hurried to conclude. "Your grandfather has been charged with treason."

"No!" Her denial sounded like the cry of a wounded animal.

"There is more," Geoffrey said. His voice was quiet and firm and Elizabeth forced herself to stay calm and listen. "Belwain has petitioned William for guardianship over Thomas. They are all in London by now and I have been called there. I leave tomorrow."

"I must go with you," Elizabeth stated. "We both must go. Please," she begged. "I would not be left behind, Geoffrey."

Geoffrey could not turn away from the agony in his wife's expression. "Yes, you will go with me. It is your family and it is only right," he concluded.

Elizabeth began to cry. "Our family," she corrected her husband. "What will happen?" she asked Geoffrey. "What will the king do?"

Geoffrey felt her trembling and held her tightly. "He will listen to all sides and then decide. Do not worry, Elizabeth. William is a fair king. Have faith in him."

"I cannot!" She buried her head in Geoffrey's shoulder and continued to weep.

Geoffrey held her until she was finished with her tears, soothing her with gentle words. "Do you have faith in me?" he asked when the weeping had subsided.

"You know that I do," Elizabeth answered.

"Then when I tell you all will be well, you believe me," Geoffrey argued.

"If you say it, then I will believe it," Elizabeth promised.

"I give you my word. I will not let your family be harmed."

"But what about you?" Elizabeth asked. "Can you promise me that you will not be harmed?"

Geoffrey was surprised by her question, for he was not in jeopardy. "I promise," he told her. "Now try to sleep. We ride hard tomorrow and again for two more days."

Elizabeth did not forget the news she wished to share with her husband. Her hand rested on her abdomen, in a protective gesture. She would not tell Geoffrey yet, she decided. He would not let her accompany him to face William if he knew she carried his child. And so she would wait until the problem with Belwain was solved. Then she would share her joy with Geoffrey. For now she would protect their babe, just as Geoffrey would protect her.

Elizabeth closed her eyes and tried to clear her mind. She would need her rest to meet the challenge ahead.

During the dark hours, she had the nightmare again. Geoffrey soothed her when she called out, telling her that she was distraught and overly tired and that was the reason for her terror. He asked her to share the dream with him, but Elizabeth could not. She clung to Geoffrey and prayed. Prayed that the nightmare was not an omen.

The trip to London took three long days. Elizabeth was exhausted and barely looked around when they entered William's domain. She wanted only to see Elslow and little Thomas, but Geoffrey would not allow it.

"You will have a bath and then rest. In the morning you will see them," he stated. "And meet your king."

She did not want to meet the king, and admitted only to herself that she was terrified of him. Although in her mind she knew that many of the stories about William were probably exaggerated, in her heart she believed them all.

They were given a spacious room overlooking the courtyard. The bed was twice the size of their bed at Berkley, and once Elizabeth was bathed and changed, she curled up in the middle of it, trying to keep her eyes open while she waited for Geoffrey's return. He had gone to give his greeting to William, and to find out what he could about Elslow and the charges.

She did not wake up until the following morning, vaguely remembering Geoffrey undressing her and warming her during the night. Her husband was again absent. A tray of food rested on the table near the bed but Elizabeth did not touch it. Her stomach was too upset to handle food. She dressed with care, knowing there was no way out of meeting William. She would look her best to make Geoffrey proud that she was his wife.

When she was done, she stood at the window and observed the people in the courtyard. She grew more tense with each passing second, praying that Geoffrey would hurry with his duties and come for her.

Roger came in Geoffrey's stead. "Where is Geoffrey?" she demanded with a tremor in her voice.

The loyal vassal took hold of Elizabeth's arm and guided her out the door. Elizabeth saw that two of Geoffrey's men guarded the door and was mildly surprised.

"Your husband is with the king," Roger answered. "And so is your grandfather." He glanced at his mistress and saw her distress, yet there was nothing he could offer as comfort. He was as concerned as Elizabeth, though far better schooled in hiding his emotions. Geoffrey had not had time to confide in Roger, and so the vassal had no idea of the plan of action his lord would take.

"Your attendance has been requested," Roger stated. "By the king himself."

They had begun walking, but with Roger's words Elizabeth stopped suddenly. "He is the voice," she whispered. "I cannot go, Roger! It is the dream. I cannot go!"

Roger had no idea what Elizabeth was talking about, and wasn't sure how to proceed. "Your husband wishes you by his side," he said finally, knowing instinctively that Elizabeth would never deny Geoffrey.

His reasoning worked. Elizabeth straightened her shoulders and forced the terror from her eyes. "Then I must go," she responded.

She walked at Roger's side, through a maze of damp, ill-lighted corridors. They entered a large room, filled to capacity with people. All were dressed in splendid cloth, proclaiming their worth, and Elizabeth assumed that they were all titled subjects, waiting their turn for an audience with their king.

A path was cleared for Roger and Elizabeth. She could see the huge double doors at the far end of the room. They were doors similar to the ones in her dream, and Elizabeth knew a terror unlike anything she had ever witnessed or felt in the past.

She kept her gaze directed on the doors, ignoring the whispered comments and appraising looks of the crowd as she continued forward.

A trio of soldiers guarded the door. One of the men acknowledged Roger with a curt nod and beckoned them forward. The doors opened with a squeak of protest and Roger motioned Elizabeth to enter. "You will stay behind me?" she asked in a soft voice.

Roger was surprised by her question. To the casual observer, Elizabeth looked the picture of serenity and sureness. He was sure he was the only one who could read the nervousness in her eyes, the only one who could hear the fear in her voice. "I would have you near," she explained, "should my husband require your assistance."

Roger could not help smiling. "I will stand right inside the door," he replied. He did not add that he would protect her back just as he would his lord's. It was his duty to see to their safety and need not be spoken.

Elizabeth turned and walked into the room. And the nightmare became reality. Straight ahead, seated on a gilded throne three steps above the floor, was King William. At the bottom of the steps, on the left, stood Geoffrey. Facing him, though several feet apart, stood Elslow. They were not in chains.

There were several other people in the room, but Elizabeth did not take the time to see if she recognized any of them. She smiled at Geoffrey and then at Elslow as she continued toward the king. When she reached the first step, she knelt down and bowed her head.

"My lord, I would present my wife, Elizabeth." Geoffrey's voice was clear and firm and Elizabeth could hear a faint tinge of pride in his voice.

"Stand and let me look at you," William barked. His voice was as huge as his body, and Elizabeth hurried to do his bidding. She finally looked at his face and was most surprised to find him smiling at her.

He was a giant of a man, though his middle was as large as his height, and his eyes were cunning as he looked at Elizabeth. She did not flinch from his appraisal and met his stare without undue effort.

"It appears you have done well, son." William addressed his compliment to Geoffrey, though he continued to study Elizabeth.

"I am content, my lord," Geoffrey replied.

"And now to the matter at hand," William stated. "Send the accuser in," he demanded in a loud voice.

He looked from Geoffrey to Elslow and then to Elizabeth again. "Child, stand with your family while I attend to this matter."

Elizabeth nodded, quickly genuflected, glanced over at her grandfather and smiled, and then walked to Geoffrey's side. She stood as close to him as she could, letting her arm touch his, and looked back at the king.

For some untold reason, the king laughed, nodding his pleasure several times.

"You have secured her loyalty, Geoffrey," the king praised.

"Always," Geoffrey responded. He looked down at Elizabeth and smiled, letting her know his pleasure. Elizabeth felt like she had missed some vital part of the dialogue but dared not question Geoffrey now. Later he would explain why the king seemed so pleased. He certainly seemed to understand what William was thinking.

The squeak of the door caught Elizabeth's attention and she turned and watched Belwain enter the room. The expression on his face was smug and victorious, and Elizabeth found herself clutching Geoffrey's arm while she held her breath. She realized what she was doing and immediately let go of him.

Geoffrey felt her distress. He casually placed his hand on her shoulder and pulled her against him, willing her to accept some of his strength and courage.

Belwain awkwardly knelt before the king but did not bow his head. William grunted his displeasure and then said, "Your case against this Elslow is serious. You accuse him of treason but offer no proof of his guilt. I would know your reasons now."

Belwain stood and pointed his finger at Elslow. "He is Saxon, and all Saxons are traitors. He has always wanted to regain Montwright, and has tricked your vassal, Geoffrey, into believing he is loyal to you. His motives are false. I know that he has joined the group of rebels against you."

"You have proof of this accusation?" William demanded, leaning forward.

"I cannot give you proof, for the one who could validate my charge has been killed."

"Who is this man you speak of?" William asked.

"His name was Rupert, and he was brother-in-law to Geoffrey's wife, Elizabeth. He was Norman."

"Ah!" William looked at Geoffrey and nodded. "I have heard the tale of Rupert. Norman or not, he was disloyal to me. You, Belwain, are a fool to use him as your proof." The king turned to Elslow and said, "Do you belong to this rebel group?" he demanded.

Elslow shook his head and replied in a clear voice, "I do not, my lord."

William grunted again and turned to Geoffrey. "You believe him?" he asked, his voice softer.

Geoffrey nodded. "I do."

"Since there is no proof, I will be content with my vassal's judgment. The case of treason is dismissed. I will not allow a fight to determine the truth but will listen to my loyal knight."

"But what of Montwright?" Belwain whined. "It belongs to me. It is my right to have guardianship over the boy until he is of age. Yet he"—Belwain jerked his head toward Geoffrey—"has placed a Saxon in my position. The law is on my side."

William leaned back in his chair, a frown on his face. Silence reigned as the king considered the problem. Elizabeth directed her gaze toward her grandfather. His anger and disgust over Belwain was apparent, and Elizabeth could tell that he longed to reach out and grab him. His stance was rigid and his hands were held in tight fists. She realized then that she imitated her grandfather, and forced herself to relax.

"It is a difficult decision," William finally said. "Geoffrey, you have told me that you do not trust Belwain and have decided to keep the boy with you until he is of age. That is your right," he added with a nod. "Yet the question of a Saxon as master of Montwright remains a problem. I am a fair man, and have given a few estates to Saxons, as you well know. Yet now I am having difficulty deciding," he admitted. "I do not know this Saxon. You could argue for your side of this question, Geoffrey, but you are like my son and would argue with a Norman heart. And you," he said, turning to Elslow, "could argue as the boy's grandfather, but you would speak with a Saxon heart. Pity there is not one who is neither Norman nor Saxon to council me."

"There is one." Elizabeth's voice was clear and forceful. She stepped away from her husband and faced the king. William looked at Elizabeth and nodded for her to continue. "I am neither Saxon nor Norman," she said. "I am both. My father was Norman, full-blooded, and my mother was Saxon. And so I am half of each." Elizabeth smiled then and added, "Though my father would often call me Saxon when I disobeyed him, and my mother vowed I was full Norman when I displeased her."

The puzzled look left the king's face and he smiled. "Then you will state each side of this case for me and I will decide," he said. "First tell me of the Saxon."

"I will tell you what my mother told me," Elizabeth replied. She folded her hands together and began, "By your order, and my father's request, my mother was married to my father and Montwright given over to him. My grandfather left Montwright and moved to London. Shortly after my parents married, my mother ran away. She ran to my grandfather for protection. My grandfather listened to her tales of misery and then promptly took her back to my father. He told my mother that she belonged to my father now and that she was to be loyal to him. A truce was formed between my grandfather and my father, and friendship blossomed. The Saxon branch of my family places great store on loyalty, King William. Elslow knelt before you the day of your coronation and pledged you loyalty, and I know that he would die before he broke that pledge."

"And now state the case for the Normans," William suggested. He seemed amused by Elizabeth's storytelling and gifted her with a smile of encouragement.

"My father was loyal to his lord, Geoffrey, and when he was killed, Geoffrey took control. He married me and righted the damage done. My brother-in-law was behind the deed, and Geoffrey killed him. My husband is most methodical in his thinking, much like my father, and he made sure that he knew the guilty one before acting. I have inherited my impatient nature from my Saxon mother," Elizabeth admitted, "but my husband convinced me to be patient. In the end, he promised that justice would be done, and he was right. If you ask me who I am loyal to," Elizabeth continued, "I would tell you that I am loyal to my husband and to you, my king."

"And if I asked you to decide between the Saxon and the Norman?" the king asked.

Elizabeth did not hear the teasing lilt in his voice and frowned. "I would choose my husband above all others," she replied immediately. "Knowing in my heart that my husband would protect Elslow as he protects me. My grandfather, my brother, and I all belong to Geoffrey now, just as we all belong to you. My husband would not harm his family."

William nodded. "I think that if all my subjects were as loyal as you, I would have an easy time of it," he complimented. He looked at Belwain then and said, "I do not go against my vassal's wishes, Belwain. Your claim is denied."

Belwain could not contain the gasp of outrage. His face turned a blotchy red and he stared at Elizabeth with eyes full of hatred.

The king ignored Belwain's reaction. His attention turned to Elslow. "I do not recall your pledge of loyalty but the day of my coronation was full of disorder."

Elslow grinned. "I was there and saw the riot," he admitted.

"Kneel before me now, Saxon, and give me your pledge anew."

Elslow did as he was requested, placing his hand over his heart. He repeated his vow of loyalty with Geoffrey and Elizabeth as witnesses.

The king seemed content. "Leave me now," he commanded. "Geoffrey, I will speak with you at the dinner hour," he commanded. "I would have you at my side."

"As you wish," Geoffrey replied. He bowed before his lord and took hold of Elizabeth's arm.

Husband and wife did not exchange a word until they were almost back to their room. Elslow and Roger had left them, in search of a cool drink and a game of chess.

"Have you a single doubt of my pride in you?" Geoffrey asked when they reached their room. "You showed great courage, Elizabeth."

"I have learned it from you," Elizabeth replied. She entered the room and turned to face her husband. The realization that the torment was over and done with made the room begin to spin.

"See how fair and kind our king is?" Geoffrey remarked. "There was never anything to fear, was there?"

"Fear? I was never afraid!"

Geoffrey laughed at Elizabeth's obvious lie and reached for her. He wasn't a second too soon and caught her just in time. His strong and courageous wife fainted in his arms.

"You are sure?"

"I am most sure."

Elizabeth was snuggled against Geoffrey late that night. They had just made love, and Geoffrey was about to fall asleep when Elizabeth decided to tell him about the baby. "You are pleased?"

"I am," Geoffrey stated. He placed his hand on Elizabeth's stomach and kissed her again. "I am the luckiest man in the world," he said. "Soon I will have a warrior to train. He will be healthy and strong and the image of his father."

"You are most humble," Elizabeth teased, smiling.

"We will take our time going home," Geoffrey remarked. "You must take every care, wife. Do not concern yourself with Belwain," he added.

"I will not," Elizabeth agreed. "I know that you will deal with him when the time is right. He already suffers, losing what he most wanted," she said. "Montwright and Thomas are both safe from him."

"I will worry while you carry this child. If anything should happen to you . . ."

"Do not concern yourself," Elizabeth soothed. "All will be well. When the time comes, I will be just like you, Geoffrey. I will be strong and courageous and will do my duty. I will give birth with honor and will not make a sound of protest."

She screamed like a banshee. Geoffrey held her hand during the long hours of labor, echoing her distress with greater shouts of his own, until he was forced from their bedroom by a disgusted midwife.

Elslow observed it all and remarked to Roger that it was without a doubt the loudest birth ever recorded in history.

Elizabeth finally produced the child and gave Geoffrey his warrior. Geoffrey was overwhelmed with pleasure and gratitude.

The warrior was perfect. They named her Mary, in memory of Elizabeth's mother.